Praise for
The Breakaway

"*The Breakaway* is sexy and suspenseful and so much fun, even as it asks us to imagine lives unconstrained by convention or the Supreme Court. It's the lobster roll you get with mayo and melted butter—because why choose? To quote Mary Oliver grossly out of context, 'Let the soft animal of your body love what it loves,' whether it's noodles or romance or even the uncertainty that comes with getting to decide who we want to be."

—*The New York Times*

"Weiner is the undisputed queen of the fun yet thoughtful poolside read."

—*Vogue*

"A zippy rom-com with genuine heart and soul."

—*People*

"A fun, smart, and powerful reminder to follow your own path."

—*theSkimm*

"Incredibly fun . . . A lovely, compulsively readable story about finding your path and believing in your own worth."

—*Kirkus Reviews* (starred review)

"This is a winning combination of a light read with serious emotional depth, the very mix Weiner's many fans have come to expect from her. Weiner's annual summer release is a welcome (and highly anticipated) treat for readers of relatable relationship fiction."

—*Booklist* (starred review)

"Charming . . . Lively banter reels the reader in. . . . This breezy outing goes down easy."

—*Publishers Weekly*

BOOKS BY JENNIFER WEINER

FICTION

Good in Bed

In Her Shoes

Little Earthquakes

Goodnight Nobody

The Guy Not Taken

Certain Girls

Best Friends Forever

Fly Away Home

Then Came You

The Next Best Thing

All Fall Down

Who Do You Love

Mrs. Everything

Big Summer

That Summer

The Summer Place

NONFICTION

Hungry Heart

FOR YOUNG READERS

The Littlest Bigfoot

Little Bigfoot, Big City

Jennifer Weiner

The Breakaway

A NOVEL

ATRIA PAPERBACK

New York   London   Toronto   Sydney   New Delhi

ATRIA
PAPERBACK

An Imprint of Simon & Schuster, LLC
1230 Avenue of the Americas
New York, NY 10020

First Atria Paperback edition May 2024

ATRIA PAPERBACK and colophon are trademarks of Simon & Schuster, LLC

Simon & Schuster: Celebrating 100 Years of Publishing in 2024

For information about special discounts for bulk purchases, please contact Simon & Schuster Special Sales at 1-866-506-1949 or business@simonandschuster.com.

The Simon & Schuster Speakers Bureau can bring authors to your live event. For more information or to book an event, contact the Simon & Schuster Speakers Bureau at 1-866-248-3049 or visit our website at www.simonspeakers.com.

Map by Jeffrey L. Ward

Manufactured in the United States of America

1 3 5 7 9 10 8 6 4 2

Library of Congress Cataloging-in-Publication Data has been applied for.

ISBN 978-1-6680-3342-5
ISBN 978-1-6680-3343-2 (pbk)
ISBN 978-1-6680-3344-9 (ebook)

For Tim Carey, and all the riders and leaders
of the Bicycle Club of Philadelphia

I do not wish [women] to have power over men;
but over themselves.
　　　　　—Mary Wollstonecraft,
　　　　　　A Vindication of the Rights of Woman

Life is like riding a bicycle. To keep your balance,
you must keep moving.
　　　　　—Albert Einstein

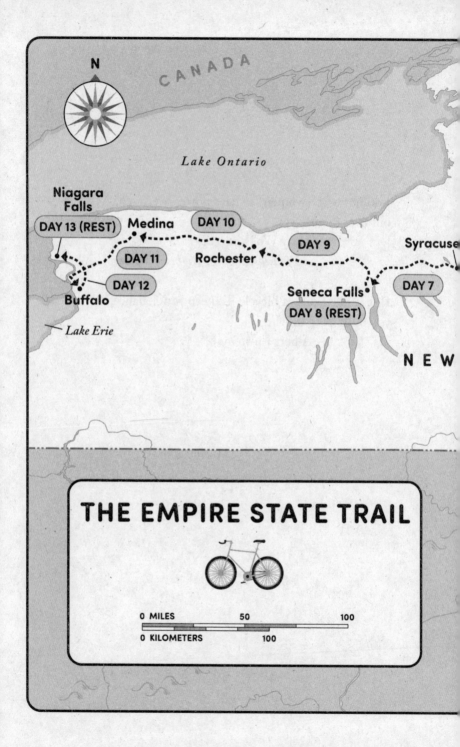

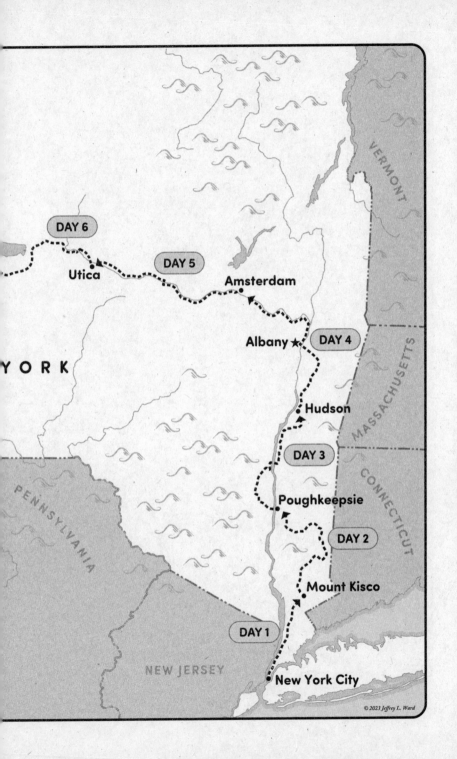

Abby

1996

"Are you ready?"

She wasn't. But her sister and her brother had both learned how to ride their bikes before they turned six, and Abby was a few weeks away from her seventh birthday, and her dad had already spent twenty minutes taking the training wheels off her bike. She knew she had to try.

"Okay, I'm going to hold the seat until you get your balance, and then I'm going to let go."

She nodded without turning from her perch on her bike's seat. If she took her feet off the pedals she'd be able to touch the ground with her tiptoes. Still, she felt like she was in outer space, that the ground was a million miles away; that if she lost her balance she'd go plummeting to her doom.

"Okay. Here we go."

She felt her daddy's hand on the back of her seat, steadying the bike. She made herself push with her right foot. The pedals turned. The wheels spun.

"Here you go! Pedal, pedal, pedal! You've got it!" her daddy shouted.

And then he wasn't there. It was just Abby, alone on her bike . . . and she wasn't falling. She clutched the handlebars, not paying any attention to where the bike was headed, and she pedaled, pedaled, keeping her balance, and the wind was cool on her cheeks, brushing back her hair, and she was picking up speed, only wobbling a little, and *she wasn't falling*. She was riding.

It felt like floating. It felt like flying. It felt like she was far away from everything that hurt her. The icy silences that stretched between her parents. The way her mom would always put a plate of cut-up carrots or bell peppers by her plate, and no one else's, at dinnertime. How Dylan McVay at school had started calling her Flabby Abby, and now all the boys called her that.

"Abby! Stop! Turn around! Don't go on the busy street!" Her daddy was yelling, chasing after her, his voice getting farther away with every rotation of the pedals. And Abby wasn't falling. She was riding, on a bike that could take her anywhere. She was free.

Abby

'm getting *married*!" Kara hollered into Abby's ear. The words came borne on a gust of tequila-scented breath as Kara grabbed Abby's hand and squeezed. "I'm so *happy*! Are you happy for me?"

"Of course I am," Abby said, guiding her friend over a crack in the sidewalk. "If you're happy, I'm happy."

"I AM!" Kara shouted into the Brooklyn night. "I AM happy!"

"Maybe let's be happy a little more quietly," Abby suggested as Marissa, another member of the bridal party, came teetering toward them and slung her arm around Abby's neck. At the beginning of the night, Marissa had given each of the women a pink feather boa, and they had started to shed. Abby saw pink feathers floating in the air, drifting gently down onto the pavement.

"You're next," Marissa said, poking her finger against Abby's chest. "You and Mark."

"Mark and I have been on exactly two dates," Abby said, bemused.

"Doesn't matter," Marissa said, and looked Abby in the eye. "He loves you. He's been in love with you since he was thirteen!

That's . . ." Marissa wobbled to a halt, her cute nose wrinkled, incapable of walking drunk in high heels and doing math at the same time.

"Eighteen years," said Abby, who was not precisely sober but who was also not anywhere near as tipsy as her friends. "But we've only been back in each other's lives for fifteen minutes."

"Doesn't matter." Marissa gave a dismissive wave of her hand. "He loooves you."

Abby surveyed the rest of the party. There were Kara's college friends: a trust and estates lawyer, a crisis communication expert, a banker who lived in San Francisco. There were a few other summer camp friends—Marissa, who lived in a suburb of Chicago with her husband and two little girls; Hannah, a physician's assistant; and Chelsea, who worked as a public radio producer in Portland, Oregon. Then there was Abby, an employee of a doggie daycare called Pup Jawn, a freelance dog-walker and sometime Uber driver, who'd started and dropped out of two different master's degree programs, one in early childhood education, the other in library sciences. Abby had gotten used to being the biggest girl in a group, but now she'd arrived at a point where she was both the biggest and the least accomplished. This development did not fill her heart with joy.

As Kara wobbled and Marissa giggled, Abby realized that she had two choices: either she was going to have to stop drinking until she felt less maudlin, or keep drinking until her brain turned off. She adjusted her own boa, arranging it to lie against the V-neck of her tee shirt, which was black, with the word BRIDESMAID spelled out in crystals on the chest, and followed the group into a bodega, past the cash register and the indifferent clerk behind it, down an aisle stocked with ramen and crackers and candy bars, boxes of steel wool scrubbing pads, and bottles of Fabuloso, then out its back door. Their night had started six hours ago with dinner and cocktails at Nobu. There'd been more cocktails at a dueling piano bar, a club in Manhattan, and a dive bar in Park Slope. Abby prayed this would be their final stop of the night. *I'm too old for this,* she thought as Marissa led them down a trash can–lined alley, pausing once or twice to peer at her phone.

"Are you sure this is right?" someone asked as Marissa stopped in front of a dingy metal door and knocked three times. When a slot in the door's center opened, Marissa gave a password and collected everyone's IDs and vaccination cards. When the documents had been inspected, the door swung open, and Abby followed her friends into the thumping, crowded darkness. The music was deafening, the bass so loud that Abby could feel it vibrating through her fillings. Girls in bodysuits and booty shorts with trays of shots around their necks threaded their way through the crowd, twisting like contortionists to serve customers lounging on the couches. The dance floor was packed with people, dancing and hollering along to the music.

Abby was throwing her arms in the air with the rest of the bridesmaids, gyrating happily and singing along to a remix of Cher's "Believe," when she noticed a guy standing in the corner, staring at her. He wore dark jeans and a short-sleeved tee shirt. His thick brown hair fell over his forehead just so, and his pale skin looked almost luminous in the club lights.

Abby turned away. She kept dancing, but her gaze kept landing on him, taking in a new detail each time—his full lips, his thick, straight eyebrows. She knew she was staring, but she gave herself permission. Looking at this guy was like looking at a two-thousand-dollar gown on the Nieman-Marcus website: a gorgeous thing she could appreciate, while knowing she would never take it home. And home was a hundred miles away, which made the likelihood of bumping into this handsome stranger at a dog park or a coffee shop unlikely. Abby could stare to her heart's content.

Except, strange but true, it seemed like the guy was looking right back at her. Looking at her and smiling.

Abby watched as he detached himself from the wall and moved through the mass of dancers, until he'd arrived to stand right in front of her.

Bridesmaid? he mouthed, pointing at her chest. Abby nodded, and he leaned in close, saying something she assumed was his name. She felt the warmth of his breath on her neck, and he smelled delicious, musky and spicy and sweet.

Abby shouted her name at him, which was all the conversation the music would allow—a good thing, because his next question would have probably been *Where are you from,* and at some point he'd follow up with *What do you do,* and Abby would have to choose between lying or stumbling through an explanation about the gig jobs she took to pay her bills. It was embarrassing to be her age, to have made so many false starts and still not be any closer to figuring out what she planned on doing with her one wild and precious life. She reminded herself that her indecision, while unseemly, wasn't actively harming anything or anyone.

Somehow, she and the guy had drifted away from the rest of the bridesmaids until they were dancing as a couple (Marissa, the only member of the bridal party who'd noticed this development, gave an enthusiastic thumbs-up, which Abby hoped the guy hadn't noticed). He was close enough for her to feel the heat of his body. His scent made her mouth water; made her want to press her lips against him and taste the skin of his throat. After two songs, he started to touch her—reaching for her hand, letting his hand rest on her hip, always looking at her, eyebrows raised, waiting for her nod. Abby could feel herself flushing with each brush of his fingers, her skepticism—*Me? This guy's into me? Really?*—warring with her desire.

After another three songs, he took her hand and inclined his head toward the corner. Abby let him lead her into the shadows, thinking *Do with me what you will.* She knew this was borderline scandalous behavior. She also knew that the guy might think she was acceptable, kissable, sleep-with-able, at two in the morning in a dark bar, with loud music and limited options and God only knew how many drinks inside of him, but that he might find her less impressive when he was sober. And there was Mark, back in Philadelphia. They'd been on only two dates since they'd found each other again, but maybe Marissa was right. Maybe there was potential for something serious.

Abby knew all that. But this guy smelled so good, and his hands were so warm, and Philadelphia had never felt farther away. As soon as they'd made it to the corner, Abby stood on her tiptoes, and the guy bent his head and reached down to cup the back of her neck and bring his mouth down against hers. The first brush of his lips was gentle, respectful, a careful taste. Abby was the one to deepen the kiss, the one to slip just the tip of her tongue into his mouth, shivering as she'd felt, more than heard, his groan.

He brought his mouth down to her ear. "Come home with me." Abby felt her body flush as the words vibrated through her. Immediately, she nodded. It had been years since she'd kissed a stranger in a bar, and she had almost never gone home with a guy she'd just met. But, somehow, this felt inevitable, like it was the only choice she could possibly make.

When they were outside, the silence rang in her ears. Without the crush of the crowd or the DJ providing a distraction, now that the guy could really see her, Abby felt awkward and unsure.

"It's Abby, right?" he asked, after he'd used his phone to summon a car. "I'm Sebastian," he said, which saved her from asking, and let her appreciate his exceptionally resonant and deep voice. He had a birthmark, like a single dark freckle, right in the center of his throat, and she couldn't stop thinking about kissing him right there.

She gathered enough sense to text Marissa that she was leaving. She used her phone to take a snapshot of his driver's license, which she sent to Lizzie, her best friend back in Philadelphia. "So if you kill me and cut me into pieces they'll know where to start the search," Abby said.

Sebastian rolled his eyes a little. "If I kill you and cut you into pieces I'm not going to keep the evidence in my apartment."

"You might," Abby said, shrugging. "Some serial killers take souvenirs."

He stared at her for a moment. Abby waited to see if she'd freaked him out, but all he did was grin and shake his head.

"I can tell you're a romantic."

"Safety first," said Abby. She put her hands on his shoulders, pulling him close, standing on her tiptoes to kiss him.

They kissed on the street while they waited, then they continued kissing in the backseat of the Uber, and they barely stopped kissing after the car pulled up to the address he'd given and he took her hand again and led her down three steps and into his apartment. Abby had a blurred impression of a small kitchen, a short hallway with a high-end-looking bicycle hanging on the wall. At the end of the hallway, there was a bedroom so small that the queen-size bed filled every inch of the space. There was a thin-looking comforter on the bed—black on one side, gray on the other—and four pillows in white pillowcases, piled at its head.

Abby flung herself onto the bed, giggling, still barely believing that this was happening, that she was doing this. Sebastian lit a few candles on the ledge of his windowsill and lay down on his side, facing her. He slipped his hands up the back of her tee shirt, and Abby's brain went quiet. He pressed her back against the pillows and kissed her for long, dizzying moments, licking her lips and sucking her tongue and nibbling at her neck as he stroked his thumbs against her cheeks and ran his fingers through her hair. He smelled incredible. His hair was so soft as Abby touched it, then tugged it. His deep voice sounded as lovely as she'd thought it would as he groaned and murmured compliments against her skin, and his body felt so good, so unbelievably, outrageously good, pressed against her.

When she couldn't wait any longer, she helped him pull off his shirt. She rubbed her hands over his shoulders, his chest, admiring him in the candlelight. She asked, "Can I?" and waited for his nod before unbuttoning his pants and helping him work them off, until he was just in a pair of stretchy gray boxer briefs, and Abby was just in her panties. She thought he'd take off his underpants, or maybe hers. Instead, he pressed the length of his body against hers, and took both of her wrists in his hand, pinning them over her head, making a noise that was almost a growl against her neck.

"Oh, God," Abby breathed, flushed and trembling all over, so aroused that the throbbing between her legs was almost an ache. She lifted her hips, trying to press herself into him, but every time she tried to move things along, to reach down and touch him, to try to take off her underpants, or his, he would hold her wrists down again. Gently but firmly, leaving no doubt as to who was in charge. "Please," Abby moaned, thrusting her hips, pressing herself against him shamelessly. "Oh, God, please, please, please . . ."

She hadn't been to bed with too many guys, and usually, during sex, it was hard to get out of her own head. Abby was curvy. *Rubenesque* if you liked your euphemisms, *obese* if you were a doctor, *fat*, which was what Abby called herself; a word she'd forced herself to use, over and over and over, until all the sting had been leached away and it no longer felt like a slap. She was soft and warm and yielding. She was strong and she was healthy, no matter what the bullshit BMI charts said. And, the world being what it was, she knew that there were more important things to change than her body. But even so.

In college, there'd been a guy named Chris, who had definitely not been her boyfriend, nor even a friend with benefits. He'd been no kind of friend at all—just a guy who'd been willing to sleep with her. Chris would call her after midnight and invite her over, or show up at her room at two in the morning and creep out of her dorm before the sun came up, so that no one would ever see them together. It had left a mark. In the post-Chris era, when Abby went to bed with someone new she would keep her clothes on for as long as she could. She'd keep blankets or, better, if there was one handy, a pillow over her midsection, and she preferred to make love in the dark. She worried about how she smelled, how she sounded, how her body felt, how it looked. It was almost impossible for her to stop thinking about all of that, to be, as her yoga teacher said, present in the moment.

But that night was different. Maybe it was the booze, and maybe it was being in a different city, with a stranger she'd never see again, but Abby felt half out of her mind with desire, her brain a humming white blank. She wasn't thinking about the curve of her belly or the cellulite on her thighs or how her breasts looked different without the benefit of industrial-strength underwire. All she could think was how badly she needed Sebastian to touch her, and when he'd finally, finally, slipped his thumb under the leg band of her panties and brought it up, unerringly, exactly where she needed to feel it, she'd let out a yelp that was loud enough to be shocking.

"Shh," he said against her neck, his thumb flicking, teasing, rubbing firmly, then lightly, circling her clitoris, then descending down again to trace her lips. "Pretty thing."

Abby felt her eyes fill with tears, even as her hips arched off the bed. *Pretty thing.* She felt like she could count the times a man had made her feel pretty, or dainty, or cared for and small on one hand, and still have fingers left over.

Sebastian pulled off her panties and put one warm hand on each of her legs, easing them apart, and then he rested his head on the inside of her right thigh and breathed on her, warm and steady, one long exhalation. When she felt the first brush of his tongue, Abby forgot that she knew words, and when he slipped his fingers inside of her, she forgot to breathe. "How are you so good at this," she gasped at one point, and felt, as much as heard, Sebastian's amused hum in response. Abby forgot to worry about how she tasted or how long she was taking or anything, because he seemed delighted to be right where he was, doing just what he was doing. He made her come that way, and then he produced a condom from somewhere and rolled it on, kneeling in front of her, looking unreal in the candlelight, like he'd been carved instead of born.

Abby held her arms out, and he slid inside of her on a single stroke that took her breath away. Sebastian set a slow, almost decadent pace, and for long moments they rocked together, panting, and kissing. Abby tried to get him to go harder, or faster, but Sebastian refused to be hurried, no matter what she did, or how she begged. When she swiveled her hips against him, he'd pull out until he was barely inside of her at all, waiting until she went still, then started again.

Abby could feel sweat gathering at her temples. Her legs were locked around his waist, her arms wrapped around his back, and finally, finally, she could feel his control start to waver. His hips pumped, hard, and her own hips rose up to meet him. Their bodies slapped together, and he was groaning, and she was crying out, thinking she'd never known it could be like this, that she'd never even imagined. She had her second orgasm on her back, which hardly ever happened during intercourse, and then, he'd rolled them, so that he was on his back and Abby was on top of him, with his hands cupping her breasts, his eyes wide open, both of them breathing hard. She remembered how his face and lips and hands had all tasted of her when he pulled her down for a kiss. They finished in that position and fell back, sweat-slicked and breathless, against the pillows. Sebastian looped one of his arms around Abby's shoulders, pulling her close. She let her head rest on his chest.

"Jesus," he said.

"Mmm," Abby agreed. She felt confident she'd remember words at some point, but, at the moment, sounds were all she had. Sebastian disposed of the condom, then pulled her close, spreading the comforter out and letting it settle against them, soft as a sigh. Abby gave a contented hum, and they both fell asleep.

It was still dark when Abby woke up. She was lying on her back with Sebastian curled around her. They turned toward each other wordlessly, mouths meeting, hands roaming. The second time was slower, sweeter, full of pleased murmurs and gentle caresses and something that felt like tenderness. When Sebastian brushed her hair back from her face, when he braced his body up and leaned close to drop kisses on her cheeks and forehead, or gasped "Sweetheart," with his mouth against her neck, she felt closer to him than to any of the four other guys she'd been with.

When it was over, they flopped back against the pillows again. And then, just when Abby thought things couldn't get any better, that she'd hit the absolute peak of her sexual experiences, maybe even the peak of her entire life, Sebastian asked, "Are you hungry?"

Trick question, Abby thought. Just as she'd struggled with sex, she'd also struggled with eating in front of guys, with what she'd allow herself, and how much of it, but in Sebastian's bed, the combination of the liquor and the postorgasmic endorphins buzzing through her bloodstream erased any self-consciousness.

"I'm *starving*," she said emphatically before she could overthink it.

Sebastian looked pleased. He got up and padded, naked, into the kitchen. "Stay there," he said. "Be right back." Abby snuggled under his comforter, which was not too heavy and not too light, and smelled like fabric softener and Sebastian's subtly spiced cologne.

He didn't have a headboard, but he did have a top sheet and a fitted sheet, plus the four pillows pushed against the wall. *Points for that,* Abby thought and began arranging pillows in her customary fashion, one behind her head, two more parallel to the edge of the bed, a bulwark between her body and the floor. She'd slept that way since she'd been a little girl and had developed an irrational fear of rolling out of her bed in her sleep. *Building your burrow,* her father had called it. He'd called Abby his little badger. It had been a much better nickname than Flabby Abby.

When Sebastian came back to the room, holding two steaming bowls of pasta that smelled deliciously of garlic and cheese, he looked at the pillows, then at her. "It's my burrow," Abby said without thinking.

"Got it," he said. Abby sat up, and he handed her a bowl. "Pasta *alla mamma*," he said. Abby twirled a forkful of noodles. The pasta had a perfect bite, and the sauce was creamy and salty and meltingly rich.

"You just made this?" she asked. "Just, like, went into the kitchen and whipped it up?"

Sebastian looked pleased. "It's just leftover pasta. You crack an egg into it, and grate in a bunch of cheese," he said modestly. "Oh, and garlic and fresh cracked black pepper." He cleared his throat. "It's actually the only thing I know how to make, besides ramen with an egg. But it's good, right?"

Abby took another bite and groaned. "Why don't you have a girlfriend?" she asked, with her mouth mostly full, because she didn't want to stop eating. "Or a wife?" She took another bite. "Or a harem?" She swallowed and licked her lips. "Why has no one chained you to her stove and made you cook this every night?"

He smiled, and said, "Do you want to chain me to your stove?" He'd put on pajama bottoms and a white undershirt, and he was almost unbearably appealing like that, so handsome and endearing that Abby couldn't look at him directly for too long. She contented herself with taking peeks as he climbed onto the bed and sat cross-legged beside her, balancing his own bowl on his knee.

"I don't know," Abby said. "Are you available?"

Instead of answering, Sebastian twirled her a forkful of pasta from his bowl and offered it to her. Abby opened her mouth and sucked the fork clean. She told herself it didn't matter if the guy thought she was a disgusting pig. She'd never see him again. She could even ask for seconds! She smiled at the thought, and Sebastian smiled back, reaching out for one of her curls, pulling the light-brown strands straight and letting the curl re-form and bounce against her temple.

"So, what do you do when you're not cooking pasta?" she asked.

"I'm a writer," he said. "For a website, right now. I do investigative reporting."

"Impressive," said Abby.

"And what do you do when you're not at bachelorette parties?"

She paused, reminding herself that she'd never see this guy again, that she could tell him anything she liked. She thought about making up a story, saying she was in medical school, or in law school, or learning to be a teacher, or that she was a grad student, which had been the truth at one point, years ago. Instead, she said, "Right now, it's a little bit of this, a little bit of that. I'm still figuring it out."

"It's a lot," he said. He'd been rubbing her back, long, slow strokes, with the perfect amount of pressure, not too hard and not too light. "Come here," he said, setting the bowls on his window-sill and more or less scooping her into his arms, until the top of her head was tucked under his chin, her cheek and right arm on his chest. "Your skin is so soft," he said, his voice a low rumble that she felt in her bones. "Like velvet. Or satin. Whichever's the soft one."

Abby wanted to say the most ridiculous things. She wanted to call him *honey* and *darling*. She wanted to tell him that she'd never felt this way about anyone, and hold his hand, and cuddle him as he fell asleep. And the strange thing was, she thought it was possible that he wouldn't freak out if she said those things; that maybe he was feeling the same way. Which, of course, was ridiculous. It could not possibly be true.

He started kissing her neck again, his hands still on her back, moving insistently, sliding down to cup her bottom, fingers spread wide, like he wanted to touch as much of her as possible. Like he couldn't get enough. Like he would never let her go. Abby thought she had never felt so lovely, so desired, so treasured. "Sweetheart," he said again, and that, even more than the pasta, even more than the orgasms, that had been the best part, the memory she'd tuck away to cherish.

He was holding her when she woke up for the second time. The sun was rising. Abby could see the faint light filtering through the slit of his window. She could feel a hangover pulsing in her temples, settling into her belly, and a wave of guilt, like scummy gray dishwater, rolling in with it. She imagined Mark sleeping blamelessly in his bed in Philadelphia, with his phone plugged into the charger beside him, the alarm set to wake him up in plenty of time for his shift at the hospital. She was sure that if she looked at her own phone, she'd find texts from last night: *Say hi to everyone* and *Have a great time*.

Sebastian muttered something and rolled onto his back. Abby looked down at him. She touched her fingertips to her lips, then pressed them quickly against his bare shoulder, a kiss by proxy. Quietly, she gathered her clothes and carried them to the bathroom—tiny but clean—where she dressed and splashed water on her face. She thought about leaving a note—*Thank you for a lovely evening?*—or her number. In the end, she decided not to do either. The night had been perfect. Abby didn't want to taint it, and it seemed greedy to hope for more. She didn't want to wait for a call that wouldn't come. Nor did she want to meet up with him somewhere and watch him try to hide his disappointment when he saw her, without beer goggles, sober and in the light. Better to leave before anything could go wrong, to go back to her real life.

She stepped outside, wishing she could lock the door behind her, hoping that Sebastian would be safe. On the sidewalk, she called for an Uber, and watched the sun rise as the car drove her over the Brooklyn Bridge. Back in her hotel room, she chugged a bottle of water, swallowed two Advils she'd had the foresight to pack, and tucked herself into her bed. She fell asleep immediately and didn't wake up until Marissa pounded on her door at ten o'clock to tell her they were meeting in the lobby in half an hour for dim sum, and that Abby needed to get up, because Marissa wanted details of her night.

Abby kept it vague with Marissa, feeling, somehow, like if she shared too much about what had happened it would lose its luster, and sound tawdry or porn-y instead of the way it had felt, which had been romantic and magical. She managed the brunch, nibbling at pork buns and shrimp dumplings, honey-basted spareribs and congee, listening to the group moan about their hangovers or talk about the wedding, or their own husbands, and their kids.

She and Mark had plans for Saturday night. It was going to be their third date, which meant, she guessed, he'd be asking her to come home with him, unless she asked him to come to her place first. Mark had changed a lot since they were teenagers at summer camp, but he was still appealing, with the same sense of humor, the same sweet smile. Mark was plausible. Mark made sense. They had a shared history, similar backgrounds, and they lived in the same city. He'd been the first boy she'd ever kissed, the first boy who'd said he loved her. Maybe Mark didn't light the same fires that Sebastian had; maybe she didn't feel as desperately drawn to him. In spite of that—maybe because of that—Abby had no trouble imagining herself and Mark starting up where they'd left off, falling instantly in sync, moving forward smoothly and in tandem.

But God, last night had been so good. For the entire bus ride back to Philadelphia, Abby kept her eyes closed, and thought about how Sebastian had touched her; the sound of his voice, the way he'd looked at her. How it had felt to be so desired by someone who was, himself, so desirable. How perfectly in tune they'd been. It felt like, for a handful of hours, she'd stepped into someone else's skin, even someone else's life, and it had been wonderful.

Abby replayed every minute, from their first kiss to the last touch of her fingers to his shoulder, determined to inscribe every detail on her mind. When the ride was over, she deleted the photo of the guy's license from her phone, pulled her backpack down from the overhead rack, stepped out into the diesel-scented sunshine, and headed south, toward her apartment, toward the dogs who'd be waiting for her on Monday morning, and the guy who'd be waiting on Saturday night.

Abby

Give it to me," Abby said in her sultriest voice.

Mark shook his head, feigning reluctance. "I don't know. Are you sure you're ready?"

"Oh, I'm ready," Abby purred.

Mark hesitated, then pulled his phone out of his bag. "Okay, standard disclaimer. This is not my patient, or a patient at any institution with which I am affiliated. No one's HIPAA rights were violated."

"Just hand it over." Abby reached across the table, palm extended. She was in a wonderful mood. She and Mark were at Estia, one of their favorite restaurants. He'd come with pictures, and they had the entire weekend ahead of them.

Mark shook his head, giving her a rueful look before handing Abby his phone. She turned it around and looked at the picture of a foot with a big toe's nail that had gotten so long it had curved down, completely covering the tip of the toe, curving toward the sole. She squealed. "Ew!"

"Yeah, that's one for the gallery," Mark said modestly.

"How did that happen?"

"How does anything happen?" Mark replied. "You just decide to let it go for a few days. And then a few days turn into a week, and a week turns into a month, and the next thing you know . . ."

". . . you're wearing toenail slippers." Abby texted the picture to herself, picked up her own phone, and added the image to her "Nasty Feet" album. "Have you ever seen anything like this?" Mark was a podiatrist, which meant it was at least possible that he had.

"No comment." He patted his lips with his napkin, then sighed. "You know, sometimes I think you just love me for my photographs of medical oddities."

Abby made a show of thinking it over. "Nah," she finally said. "I also love you because you talk to my mother so I don't have to."

"I do," said Mark.

"And you're handy for getting things off high shelves." Mark was only a few inches taller than she was, but it made a difference.

"I got that jar of pickles open that one time," he said. "Don't forget that."

"As if I could." Abby reached across the table and, tenderly, touched Mark's cheek. "If it wasn't for you, I might still be there, standing in my kitchen, trying to get that jar open."

"You'd have had to resign yourself to a gherkin-less life."

"And that," Abby said, "would have been a tragedy. So you see? You have many fine qualities. And you're paying for dinner." Their eyes met. "You are paying for dinner, right?"

"I am indeed." The truth was, Mark paid for most things. He made much more money than Abby did—how much more, she didn't want to think about. They'd talked about it, early on, with Mark arguing that it made sense for him to be the one who picked up all the checks when they went out to dinner and paid for things like theater tickets and vacations. *It's my pleasure,* he'd told her, so sweetly and sincerely that she'd immediately believed him. *Whenever he's around you, Mark looks like the heart-eyes emoji,* Abby's best friend Lizzie had said once. Like he can't believe he got so lucky. And Abby felt lucky, too.

A waiter set down a bowl of baba ghanoush and a basket of pita triangles fresh from the oven. Abby picked up a wedge of warm bread. Mark picked up a spoon.

"So listen," he said.

"I'm listening," Abby replied, feeling warmth and affection, and the slightest twinge of anxiety. Mark was smart and handsome, hardworking and successful. He was funny, and he appreciated Abby's sense of humor. And he loved her. Over the past two years, they'd built a life of shared routines, of puzzles and Netflix and Sunday morning walks through South Philadelphia that ended at the French bakery in the Bok Building (Abby would get a croissant or a pain au chocolat; Mark would get a glass of water). Their relationship had progressed without a single hitch or misstep. They'd slept together after their third date and had agreed to be exclusive the next morning. In the months that followed, they'd attended weddings and brises and baby namings as a couple. They agreed on most of the big things, and rarely fought over the small ones. At some point, they'd move in together, and at some point after that, Abby assumed, Mark would propose.

As Mark ate a spoonful of eggplant dip, she swallowed hard and wondered if *at some point* was now. Wondering, too, why she felt anything besides joy and exultation and triumph, with, perhaps, a hint of gloating: *You see, Mom? Someone loves me, even though I'm fat!*

"What's up?" she asked. Mark put down his spoon and picked up his phone.

"I got my schedule for the next six weeks, and I want to talk through the calendar."

"Sexy," Abby murmured, and opened up their shared calendar on her phone, watching as Mark entered the weekends he'd be on call, as large chunks of the next month went from blissfully empty to shaded red.

"We've got Elizabeth's wedding the first weekend in September," she reminded him.

"I know, I know. I asked to be off. And your mom's doing break-the-fast this year?"

"As always. Yom Kippur is her Super Bowl." The Day of Atonement, which observant Jews spent fasting, was, of course, the holiday Eileen Stern Fenske would choose to host. Eileen would have plenty of company as she starved herself all day, and, when the sun went down, she would set out the traditional bagels and platters of smoked fish, help herself to half of a poppy seed bagel, ostentatiously scoop out its inside, and consume it in tiny bites, frowning if Abby dared to even glance in the direction of the full-fat cream cheese.

"And then it's October." Mark paused and gave her a meaningful look. Abby raised her eyebrows.

"You want to figure out our Halloween costume? I was thinking Machine Gun Kelly and . . . Kourtney Kardashian? Is that who he's with?"

Mark refused to be distracted.

"Always happy to discuss Halloween," he said pleasantly. "But I wanted to remind you that your lease is up in October."

"Oh, right. Yes. Of course. Right, right right." Abby's mouth felt unpleasantly dry, and her heart was beating painfully hard. When she noticed that she was tapping her fingernails on the table, she made herself stop.

"I know you love your place," Mark was saying.

"I do."

"And I know you think my place is . . . ." Mark paused.

"Terrifyingly neat?" Abby offered. "Slightly sterile? A Marie Kondo fantasy? Basically an operating room with a couch and a TV?"

Mark looked at her fondly. "You can redecorate."

"We can redecorate."

"We'll merge."

"And you'll be okay with it if I leave dishes in the sink?"

"I'm not making any promises," Mark said. "But I'll do my best."

Mark smiled at Abby. Abby smiled back, even though the truth was she couldn't picture a dish reposing in Mark's sink . . . or, really, anything she owned in Mark's place. Mark lived on the nineteenth floor of a high-rise on Rittenhouse Square, a one-bedroom apartment with views of the Walt Whitman Bridge. Her comfortably worn blue velvet couch wouldn't look right in Mark's living room, with its glass coffee table and glass-and-metal shelves. Her brightly colored kilim rugs would look weird layered over his beige wall-to-wall carpet. Nor did Mark have any interest in the vintage Weight Watchers cookbooks that Abby had collected over the years and displayed in her kitchen.

Meals, Abby suspected, might also become an issue. Mark ate the same five dinners, in rotation: baked salmon, turkey burgers, tofu stir-fry, chicken breasts, and halibut. *Food is fuel,* he liked to say, and just as a car didn't complain when you filled its tank with the same gasoline every single time, Mark didn't mind eating the same meals over and over and over again. At least, that's what he'd always told her, and why was Abby thinking about food right now? Why was she thinking about sofas, or rugs, or meal planning? This was big. A big step. Moving in together meant an engagement was coming, and an engagement meant marriage. A life with Mark Medoff. She should have felt happy. Ecstatic. Overjoyed. And she was! Only . . .

Mark was looking at her strangely. She must have missed

something; a question, a statement. She opened her mouth to ask when the waitress replaced their basket of pita with another basket of fresh bread, still steaming from the oven.

"Careful, they're hot," she said.

Abby lifted a triangle of bread, blistered light brown on the outside, pillowy-soft on the inside, and swiped it through the hummus, popping it in her mouth and chewing blissfully.

Mark's smile looked a little tense as he scooted the basket across the table, so it was closer to Abby. He'd told her, over and over, that it didn't bother him to watch her eat the foods that he couldn't. She still wondered if he could smell the warm bread, if the scent bothered him, if he ever dreamed about a feast of carbs, pita and bagels and soft cinnamon rolls slathered in icing.

She watched as he picked up a slice of red pepper. Holding his knife in one graceful hand—surgeon's hands, Abby always thought—he spread the thinnest layer of hummus on the pepper, popped it into his mouth, and chewed . . . and chewed . . . and chewed some more, twenty times total (Abby had counted once, early on, and realized that Mark chewed every bite twenty times).

That night, they'd each ordered their usual selections, apportioning the food in their usual manner. Abby got all of the buttery phyllo dough from the spanakopita. Mark got the spinach-and-cheese innards, plus the hummus and baba ghanoush, sans pita. His main course was a Greek salad with grilled chicken, dressed with just red vinegar. Abby got a lamb tagine, rich chunks of braised lamb shoulder in a pyramid of couscous studded with plump sultanas, slivered almonds, and dates. It was one of her absolute favorite dishes in the world. That night it tasted like wet cardboard, and she had so little appetite that, halfway through, she'd pushed her plate away.

"So what do you think?" Mark was asking. "You should probably let your landlord know if you're not going to be renewing your lease."

"Oh, Kate's not going to have any trouble finding a new tenant." Abby lived in Bella Vista, a neighborhood that wasn't as fancy as Mark's. The rowhouse whose top floor she rented had been built in the 1870s, while Mark's twenty-eight-story building had been constructed more than a hundred years later, but Abby loved her place. Even though the hardwood floors were a little tilt-y, and the closets were shallow. Even though her bathroom floor and walls were covered in salmon pink tiles, and she was pretty sure the fixtures hadn't been updated since the invention of flush toilets.

"Still, you should let her know."

Abby nodded. She imagined herself carrying all her belongings back down the stairs, giving Kate the keys, moving into Mark's place. Instead of picturing the two of them in prewedded bliss, she found herself thinking about the moment when they'd walked into the restaurant. The hostess had given Mark a slow, approving up-and-down. Then her gaze flickered over to Abby, and her face had cramped, briefly, with what looked, to Abby, like a combination of confusion and disgust. Abby had felt herself stiffen, then relax as Mark had pulled her closer, keeping his hand on the small of Abby's back, pulling her chair out for her, kissing her cheek before he sat down.

Abby knew that, by now, she should be used to it. She and Mark didn't match. Mark was as good-looking as a movie star (albeit a slightly miniature one, like he'd been left a little too long in the dryer). He was dark-haired and dark-eyed, with a sharp jawline and skin that glowed gold even in the winter, and a lean, muscled body kept trim with the six-mile runs he did seven days a week. Mark ran in the rain, in the snow, and, once, in a polar vortex.

"You know, you can take a day off," Abby had told him that

morning, watching as he'd swathed himself in layer after layer of technical, water-repelling fabric, while her phone buzzed with warnings, telling people to stay indoors. "Or run on a treadmill. They're saying it's actually dangerous to be outside today. And it's not like you're going to end up on *My 600-Lb. Life* if you miss one run."

"No," said Mark. "That won't happen unless I miss two." He'd kissed the tip of her nose and headed out the door.

Abby was not a runner. Nor would anyone think she looked like a movie star, shrunken or otherwise. Abby was short and pale and round, with curly light-brown hair and skin that burned and freckled. Even though she'd been an ardent cyclist for years, she was not what people saw when they pictured an athlete. When she was with Mark she'd see people staring at the two of them, trying visibly to make it make sense. She'd think about what she'd say to them, if she were brave enough: *I have a great personality,* or *I'm incredible in bed,* or maybe just the truth: *he used to be fat once, too.*

"I saw my mom today," Abby said, desperate, for reasons she didn't completely understand and did not want to dwell on, to move the conversation away from the topic of her lease.

"Am I still Eileen's favorite?" Mark asked.

"I think you'd have to actually kill someone to not be her favorite. And, even then, she'd probably think it was the victim's fault."

"Any news?" Mark asked.

Abby rolled her eyes. "Where to begin. My cousin Rebecca is engaged, my brother got a promotion, and my sister and brother-in-law are redoing their bathroom. Heated floors, and a shower that converts to a sauna. Eileen told me all about it." Abby did not bother sharing the subtext of Eileen's report, which was that Abby, who hadn't been promoted and who did not own a house, was a disappointment. Unlike her sister, Marni, who'd earned an MBA from Wharton, and her brother, Simon, who did something finance-related in New York, unlike her father, who was a rabbi, and her mother, who'd say she was a homemaker but whose real job was full-time dieter, Abby had still not identified anything resembling a career path, had failed to provide her mother with even a minimum allotment of *nachas*. She was still working at Pup Jawn; still picking up the occasional odd job or dog-sitting gig. She knew she wanted to do something bigger, something that made a difference in the world, but, so far, she hadn't managed to figure out what that something might be.

And that was one of the many reasons Mark was so appealing. Marrying Mark, having a family with Mark, would fill in the blanks. It would give her a life to step into, with all the milestones preordained. She'd have his babies. Manage their house and their schedule and, eventually, their family's schedule. She would book their vacations, buy their clothes and groceries, do their laundry, prepare their meals—or hire someone who would. It was a world at the ready; a carriage with luxurious fittings and a destination selected. All Abby had to do was climb aboard.

And it wasn't like she doubted Mark, who'd been her summer camp sweetheart; who'd met her when she was thirteen and had loved her when Abby had been in desperate need of love and affirmation. Mark wasn't looking for a skinny girl, nor was he convinced that there was one residing inside Abby, just waiting for the right set of circumstances, or some combination of surgical interventions and weight-loss drugs, to emerge. He understood that Abby had made a different set of choices from his own about weight and food and her body, and he respected those choices. At least, he did his best, although she'd caught him relocating her ice cream to the very back of the freezer (where it would, inevitably, get freezer burn), and, once or twice, he'd thrown out her leftover samosas or pork buns. Accidentally, he'd said. Abby wasn't sure.

Mark didn't eat carbs. Mark didn't eat desserts. He'd once told her that, if he wanted something sweet, he'd brush his teeth, or floss with cinnamon dental floss. When Abby told him that was the saddest thing she'd ever heard, he'd stiffened, looking chagrined.

"It has to be this way for me," he'd said. "The surgery was a tool. I'm the one who has to keep on top of the food, and the exercise. It's just easier for me to not eat sugar than to try to eat just a little bit, or just once in a while."

"I understand," said Abby, who didn't. She couldn't imagine a life without any sugar, ever, and was not sure such a life would be worth living. Eventually, she got to the point where she rarely ate desserts around Mark, keeping ice cream and brioche and chocolate croissants at her apartment instead of at his, limiting herself to the occasional pain au chocolat or warm pita when they were out.

Mark was worth it. He'd never seemed ashamed of her. He'd been happy to take Abby out on dates, proud to introduce her to his friends. Eight weeks into their relationship, he'd brought her home to remeet his parents, who lived out on Long Island, and with whom he had a warm and functional relationship, the kind that Abby admired. She and Mark both liked reading and doing puzzles, strolling along Forbidden Drive or exploring the city's neighborhoods. And if Abby had more of an appetite for dancing and live music and karaoke nights than Mark did, if the sex was consistently satisfying without ever making her feel like the world had rearranged itself, those were quibbles, minor complaints, barely worth a mention.

Abby didn't understand her own hesitation. All she knew was that the thought of actually giving up her apartment, emptying its rooms, taking her posters off the wall, her dishes out of the cabinets, carrying her furniture down the stairs, commingling her belongings with Mark's, made her knees feel trembly, and her belly feel like she'd swallowed frozen rocks.

Mark was talking about heated bathroom floors when Abby's phone buzzed in her pocket. She felt an unseemly rush of relief as she pushed her chair back. "It's Lizzie," she said.

Mark nodded, gesturing for her to take the call. That was Mark. He was not threatened by Abby's friendships. He didn't resent the other people in her life or begrudge the time she spent away from him. He was wonderful. Practically perfect in every way. So why wasn't she jumping at the chance to move in with him? Why wasn't he enough?

Abby pressed her phone to her ear and hurried away from the table, threading her way through the high-ceilinged, tiled rooms, hearing laughter and conversations, passing the hostess's stand, and stepping out onto the sidewalk.

"Abby?" Lizzie said.

"Sorry, yes. Hi. I'm here." Abby realized she'd forgotten even to say hello. "Are you okay?"

Lizzie, who was in her sixties, had gone through a bout of breast cancer eighteen months ago. Abby had driven her friend to appointments and, on the day of Lizzie's lumpectomy, sat in the waiting room until the surgeon came out and said, "Good news!" She'd taken Lizzie to her subsequent radiation sessions and to follow-up mammograms and MRIs. Lizzie had healed, and had tolerated the treatments well, and so far, everything looked fine, but they were still in the five-year window, and Abby still worried.

"I'm fine. But I'm having a bit of an emergency," Lizzie said. "Work related, not health related," she quickly added. "It's a Breakaway thing."

It took Abby a few seconds to remember that Breakaway

was one of Lizzie's employers, a bicycle touring company that hired Lizzie to lead trips in the summer. Or, at least, they had hired Lizzie to lead summer trips in the pre-COVID years.

"So listen." Lizzie was speaking quickly. Possibly she was imagining that if she delivered her request fast enough, Abby wouldn't say no. "Marj just called me. They're running a trip from New York City to Niagara Falls, and the guy who was supposed to lead it flaked at the last minute. The trip leaves Sunday, and they're desperate."

"Sunday as in this Sunday? As in, four days from now Sunday?"

"Yup. Is there any chance—any chance at all—that you'd lead it?" Lizzie sounded a little breathless after blurting out her pitch. "You'd be saving Marj's life."

This wasn't the first time Lizzie had asked her to lead a Breakaway trip. Abby had always turned her down. But that night, out on the sidewalk, with Mark waiting for her at their table, Abby found her heart was beating quickly. Part of her—most of her— was thinking *No way,* while another part—the dark, frightened part that had been pulsing, quietly but emphatically in her brain as soon as Mark had started talking about Abby's lease—was thinking, *Yes, you can.*

Instead of the no Lizzie was surely expecting, Abby said, "I haven't ever led a bike trip."

"You lead rides all the time!" Lizzie countered.

This was true. At least once a month, on a weekday morning, Abby would lead a group of eight or ten fellow members of the Bicycle Club of Philadelphia on a twenty-five- or thirty-mile jaunt that always included a stop at a farmers market or a restaurant or a coffee shop. "Okay, but those are just rides, not an entire trip."

"And what is a trip, but consecutive days of rides?" Lizzie asked rhetorically. "Listen. You know how to manage a group of riders. You know how to change a flat. And it's a supported trip, so you don't have to help set up tents, or cook over a campfire. The guy driving the sag wagon is great—I've worked with him before. It's two weeks. Fourteen people. Very reasonable mileage. And Marj said she'd pay two thousand dollars."

Abby licked her lips. Two thousand dollars wasn't much less than she earned for an entire month at Pup Jawn.

"And you're not doing anything pressing at the moment, right?"

Abby slumped against the restaurant's brick wall. "No. Not now, and not ever."

"Stop that," Lizzie said sharply. "You can have your existential crisis later. Right now, just tell me if you can do this or not."

"How many people have you and Marj already tried?"

"Not important," said Lizzie. Translation: *lots*.

Abby considered. Riding her bike was her favorite thing in the world. It had been, ever since she was a girl . . . and she loved bike trips. She was rarely happier than when she got to load her gear and her clothes into panniers and head out for an all-day, sixty- or seventy-mile ride, on paved rail-to-trail pathways, or packed dirt towpaths or back roads or on the wide shoulders of busy city streets, alone or with a friend or with a group. She loved how it felt when she was starting out, when the sun was just coming up and the streets were quiet and it felt like she had the whole world to herself. She loved how it felt when the ride was over, and she'd climb off her bike, take a long, hot shower, rinse the road grit and sunscreen off her arms and legs and scrub away the grease that her chain left on the inside of her right calf as the aches in her legs and in the small of her back faded. She loved the first sip of beer, the first bite of pizza, after a long day in the saddle, and the feeling of climbing into her sleeping bag in her tent or tucking herself under the covers in a hotel room and falling into sound, dreamless sleep.

Even though she'd never led a trip, Abby knew that she was at least somewhat qualified. She'd been through her club's ride-leader training, and she'd taken a class at her local bike shop, where she'd learned basic safety and repairs and first aid.

Abby looked through the restaurant's windows. She could see Mark, at their table, looking at his phone, smiling at the server as she refilled Abby's water. "How many people did you say?" she heard herself asking.

"If you want to swing by tomorrow, I can give you all the details. This would be, like, an all-time good deed. You'll have a star in your crown in heaven, as my sainted mother would say."

Abby looked at her boyfriend. She considered that prickle of unease, the dark, doubting thoughts slithering through her head. She thought about how leading a ride through upstate New York for two weeks would keep her from having to make a choice; how the trip would buy her a little time. She'd be able to think, figure out what was wrong—or, better yet, convince herself that nothing was wrong. Nobody got the total package, and if Mark was 99 percent of what she wanted, how foolish and selfish would she have to be to hold out for more?

"Tell you what," Abby said to Lizzie. "How about I swing by your place after dinner?"

Abby had lived next to Mr. and Mrs. Mathers for her entire life, but it wasn't until she was eight years old that she finally met their grown-up daughter, Lizzie, who lived on a houseboat in Portland, Oregon. After Mr. Mathers died, Lizzie had come back east to clear out their house and put it on the market and move her mother into assisted living. Once the house had sold, Lizzie had returned to Portland. Fifteen years later, after Sally Mathers had succumbed to a combination of dementia and heart disease, Lizzie had come back east. She'd used the inheritance her mother had left her to augment her savings and purchase a tiny three-story trinity-style rowhouse in Queen Village, a neighborhood adjacent to Bella Vista, where Abby lived. That had been her home base for the last ten years.

Abby loved Lizzie's house. Trinities, as the name suggests, are three stories—Father, Son, and Holy Ghost—and classic trinities had just one room per story, with the kitchen traditionally in the basement. Lizzie's trinity had been constructed in the early 1800s but had been enlarged and renovated since then. Her basement level now held an office-slash-guest room, with floor-to-ceiling bookshelves on three of its four walls. Each shelf was filled with books and framed photographs and souvenirs from Lizzie's travels. There was a bedroom, a dressing room, and a full bath on the trinity's top floor. The living room and kitchen, as well as a tiny powder room tucked underneath the staircase, were on the ground floor. Lizzie's sleek road bike, with aero tubes and disc brakes and glossy red paint on its carbon-fiber frame, hung on the wall by the door. The bike was a work of art, gorgeous and aerodynamic, light enough to lift with a single finger. Lizzie had bought it as a reward for herself, after her last round of radiation.

"So it's twelve days of riding with two days off," Lizzie said. She and Abby were sitting on her couch, with Lizzie's dog, Grover, an irascible and elderly gray schnauzer, curled between them. Lizzie had her laptop open in her lap, and was reading the itinerary off the screen. "'Welcome to Breakaway Bicycle Tours, where adventure awaits; possibilities unfold with every turn of the wheel, and there's something new to see around every bend in the road!'"

Abby rolled her eyes. Lizzie smirked and kept reading.

"'Your journey through the small towns and wide-open spaces of Upstate New York follows the recently opened Empire State Trail, which, at seven hundred and fifty miles, is the longest multiuse trail in the country. The trail combines existing rail-trails and runs from New York City north to the Canadian border, and west from Albany to Buffalo. You'll ride on paved trail, crushed cinders, and you'll occasionally share roads with cars, as you travel from Battery Park in Lower Manhattan to Buffalo, then west to Niagara Falls. On average, mileage will range between fifty to seventy miles a day. A sag wagon will transport your luggage—and you, if you've had enough! A ride leader will keep you on course, and a mechanic will be on hand to keep you rolling. Breakfasts and lunches are included, as are lodgings in hotels or bed-and-breakfasts. We'll eat dinner as a group, but riders are always free to make their own arrangements or explore on their own. This is the perfect trip for couples, families, or first-time cycling tourists.'" Abby listened as Lizzie read through the two-week-long itinerary: "'New York City to Mount Kisco, Mount Kisco to Poughkeepsie, Poughkeepsie to Hudson, Hudson to Amsterdam, Amsterdam to Utica, Utica to Syracuse, Syracuse to Seneca Falls—you get a rest day there—and then Seneca Falls to Rochester, Rochester to Medina, Medina to Buffalo, and another day off in Niagara Falls.'"

"You realize I don't know where any of those places are." Years ago Abby had done a weeklong trip through the Finger Lakes region but didn't remember any of the towns' names. She knew that Albany was north of New York City, and she'd read about the Hudson Valley in the *New York Times* Sunday real estate section, which had written about the Brooklyn residents who'd fled the city during the worst of the lockdowns and bought places in the country. Beyond that, she was lost.

Lizzie looked up from her screen. "The good news is, because you're riding mostly on a trail, there's no map reading. You don't have to worry about people getting lost. And I know you can handle the mileage."

Abby had to admit that, as far as first rides to lead went, this sounded close to ideal. But she was still nervous. "And just to confirm, I'm the only leader?"

Lizzie nodded. "Jasper will be on the road, you'll be on the trail." Lizzie leaned over her laptop again. "Here's who's signed up. A family of four—mom, dad, two teenage boys. Then there's a mother and a teenage daughter, four senior citizens, a husband and wife and two single guys."

Abby ran through the roster in her mind. Moms and senior citizens were encouraging. Single guys, less so. "Do you really think I can do this?"

Lizzie closed her computer and gave Abby a look that combined fondness and exasperation. Her iron-gray hair was cut short on the sides, left long enough to brush at her earlobes on top. She wore oversize horn-rimmed glasses, a black tee shirt advertising WXPN, Philadelphia's alternative radio station, cropped linen pants, and her usual assortment of silver rings on all five fingers plus her thumb, along with bracelets and ear cuffs. "Yes. You really, one hundred percent, can do this." She leaned across the couch and put her hand on Abby's shoulder, looking deeply into Abby's eyes. "I believe in you."

"What if someone's bike falls apart?"

"You call Jasper and wait on the side of the road until he comes and makes it all better."

"What if someone dies in their tent?" Once, Lizzie led a bike-packing trip where that very thing had happened.

"No tents, remember? But if someone expires in their hotel room, you call the authorities, get the rest of the group on the road, and tell Marj. You don't even have to notify the next of kin." Lizzie patted Abby's knee. "See? Easy!"

Abby licked her lips. "What if nobody listens to me?" She let the quiet part stay quiet: *What if they don't listen to me because they don't think I know what I'm doing? What if they assume that I'm out of shape and can't actually help them because I'll spend the whole time huffing and puffing?* Which, of course, was followed by an even worse thought—*What if I do spend the whole time huffing and puffing?*—even though Abby knew it was unlikely. Fifty or sixty or even seventy miles a day wasn't nothing, but it was doable. By her, at her current size and level of fitness.

"They'll listen. Abby, you can do this. You're ready. I know you're nervous, but I think you're going to surprise yourself." Lizzie said it firmly, with conviction. Like she believed it. Abby was still dubious about the idea of leading a trip but, somehow, she was even more unsettled when she thought about giving up her apartment, of taking such a large and permanent step toward a future with Mark. Which made no sense—she loved Mark! She did!—but, somehow, there it was.

"Fine. I'll do it."

"You will? Oh my God, you're the best." Lizzie looked at Abby, who hoped her face hadn't betrayed what she was thinking. Except it must have betrayed something, because Lizzie asked, gently, "What's going on?"

"What is wrong with me?" Abby asked. She dropped her head into her hands. Her voice came out slightly muffled by her palms. "Mark was talking about moving in together when my lease is up. And I panicked."

"Okay," Lizzie said.

"And I don't understand why. Mark is the guy that every heroine in a Hallmark movie wants to meet when she comes home for Christmas."

"Except he's Jewish," Lizzie pointed out.

Abby waved her hand, dismissing Lizzie's complaint (remembering, too, that Hallmark had recently debuted a Chanukah movie). "He's smart, he's kind, he's employed, he's generous. He makes me laugh. He loves me." She paused. "And it's not like there's hundreds of other guys waiting in the wings."

"Mark is a sweetheart," Lizzie concurred. She pushed herself off the couch and padded toward the kitchen. "But that doesn't mean there aren't other men out there who would like you. I like you," Lizzie said, filling the kettle, taking a box of shortbread cookies out of the cupboard and shaking a handful of them onto a plate.

"I'm not your type," Abby said.

"For which we both should be grateful." Lizzie carried the plate to the living room, pausing to light a pair of candles. "You know, straight girls used to totally be my thing."

Abby nodded. She'd heard all about Lizzie's wild days at Wellesley.

Lizzie passed Abby the cookies and took a seat on the couch. Her eyes held Abby's gaze; her face, usually quick to grin or grimace, was very still. "If it's not right with Mark, you shouldn't try to force it."

"But there's nothing wrong!" Abby said. "I love him! We're happy!" She slapped her hands down on a pillow in a colorful kilim pillowcase. Grover growled. "Except . . ."

"Except?" Lizzie prompted.

Abby bit into a cookie. In a low voice, she said, "It sounds silly. But I do kind of wish he rode a bike." She'd been shocked, back at camp, when Mark had told her that he'd never learned how. "Chubby kid plus neurotic parents, and a mom who was around to drive me places," he'd explained. His parents hadn't been cyclists, and the neighborhood kids who did ride bikes rode in a pack that wouldn't have welcomed him. Abby had understood, even as she'd wondered whether Mark might have become a different person, or made different choices, if he'd had some of the independence and confidence cycling had given her when she'd been young and chubby.

"If riding a bike matters to you—and I totally understand why it does—then maybe you shouldn't compromise." Lizzie took a cookie, and said, "Life is short."

Abby nodded again, feeling petty for complaining about her boyfriend's shortcomings to her friend, who'd survived cancer. She nibbled her cookie and turned toward the windows. They were just a few blocks away from South Street, with its bars and restaurants and packs of rowdy teenagers and twentysomethings who overflowed the sidewalks and made the streets impossible to drive down on the weekends, but here, in Lizzie's trinity, it was quiet, the only sound the rustling of the trees outside the windows. Half of her brain was insisting, in a voice that sounded a lot like her mother's voice, *Mark is perfect, Mark is great, and you'd be an idiot to break up with him, because, let's be real, there's probably not another Jewish doctor out there, or Jewish man out there, or man, full stop, out there, who'd want to be with you.* The other half was thinking about Lizzie. Specifically, Lizzie's house, and how it felt like an extension of its owner, a place that embraced visitors and made them feel as welcome as Lizzie herself did. Could she ever have a home like that with Mark? With any man? Or were places like the one Lizzie had made for herself, lives like the one Lizzie had built, big, free lives, only available to women like Lizzie; single women without children?

"I think I need some time," Abby finally said. She said it quietly, like a confession.

Lizzie smiled. "Well, then, aren't you lucky to be spending the end of the summer on your bike?"

Abby

Day One: New York City to Mount Kisco
Fifty miles

H ello, everyone!" Abby locked her knees so they wouldn't tremble and injected as much confidence as she could into her voice as she stood on the edge of a planter in Battery Park. The riders she'd be leading were standing below her in pairs or groups. When the chatter didn't abate, Abby clapped her hands, calling, "Excuse me! Everyone! Can I have just a few minutes of your attention, please?"

It took a little while for the group to settle down, time that allowed all of Abby's fears and insecurities to come surging to the forefront of her brain. Even though she was wearing bicycling shorts and a purple and silver Breakaway jersey that said LEADER on the back, she was considerably younger and significantly larger than many of the guests. *What if they don't listen?* she thought. What if they never shut up? Eventually, though, the talking stopped, and Abby could begin.

"All right," she said, doing her best to sound confident and competent, like she'd led a hundred tours, instead of none. She was so nervous she could only look at her fellow travelers in quick glances—a pair of legs in spandex shorts here, a torso there. "Hello, everyone, and welcome to Breakaway Bicycle Tours. My name is Abby Stern, and I'm one of your leaders. I'll be riding with you every day. We'll be following the Empire State Trail, riding from New York City north toward Albany, which is about two hundred and ten miles, then turning west and following the Erie Canal three hundred and fifty miles to Buffalo, then on to Niagara Falls in Canada, at which point we'll loop back to Buffalo and head home. If this is not the trip you signed up for, please come find me after the introduction and we'll get you safely on your way to your chosen destination." That remark earned a few chuckles, along with one of the aged parties asking loudly, "What'd she say?" and the low murmur of one of the other seniors standing on her tiptoes and presumably repeating Abby's words directly into the hairy cup of his ear.

Breakaway specialized in midrange, supported trips. Their tours weren't as luxe as what some of the high-end outfitters offered. The riders wouldn't find four-star hotels, Michelin-starred restaurants, or wine pairings with their meals when the day's riding was done on this trip. They'd be staying in midrange hotels and bed-and-breakfasts, which were comfortable and clean but would not be mistaken for the Four Seasons. The food would be tasty and plentiful, but not gourmet: more pizza and fried chicken than foie gras and sweetbreads. Breakaway attracted lots of families, younger riders on budgets, and seniors on fixed incomes, who wanted to see the world but who did not have ten thousand dollars to drop on an eight-day jaunt around Lake Como.

"By now, you all should have met Jasper," Abby said, and pointed him out. Jasper gave an amiable wave from his spot toward the rear of the group. "Jasper is our chef and our mechanic. He'll be preparing breakfasts and lunches. He also drives the sag wagon. He transports our baggage, and cyclists, as needed.

He'll give you a ride if you want one. He'll fix your bike if it's broken. You will want to make Jasper your friend."

"Hi, everyone," Jasper said. "Welcome."

"Hi!" chorused the group, except for the same aged gentleman, who asked, loudly, "What?" Jasper was in his early thirties, lean and fit in a Breakaway tee shirt and cargo shorts. With his slender hips, the steely-looking tendons in his forearms, and calves that could have been used as an illustration in an anatomy lesson, he looked much more like most people's idea of an athlete than Abby did . . . but, because Jasper was Black, with locs that hung halfway down his back, he, like Abby, was not necessarily what people pictured when they imagined a bike-trip leader. There'd been efforts, in recent years, to make the sport more inclusive, but in general, Abby knew, cycling was still a pastime of the white and the wealthy.

"I know you're all eager to hit the road," Abby continued. She gave her sweaty palms a quick wipe on her bike shorts. "I'm going to go over the route and the rules of the road. Today we're covering the most urban portion of the ride as we make our way out of New York City. We'll be riding along the Hudson River Greenway out of Manhattan and into the Bronx, over the Broadway Bridge and into Van Cortlandt Park. In case anyone was worrying, we are riding under, not over, the George Washington Bridge." Abby thought she saw one of the ladies looking extremely relieved at the news. "We'll stop for lunch in Yonkers, about twenty miles in. Then we've got another thirty miles or so until we're done for the day. Some of the signage leaving the city gets confusing, especially around Manhattan College, so I am going to ask that we all stick together for the first thirteen miles. I'm also going to ask each rider to wear a reflective vest. They help with visibility, which you'll want, especially on days when we'll be riding in traffic."

Jasper was making his way through the group, handing each

rider an orange mesh vest with a triangle outlined in reflective tape on the front and back. The enthusiasm with which the riders accepted these items decreased along with their age. The older folks took them with good grace and, sometimes, enthusiastic thanks. Meanwhile, both of the young guys had their backs turned, but Abby was pretty sure she heard one of them mutter *What's the point* under his breath, before folding up the pinny and shoving it into one of the pockets in the back of his jersey. *My first troublemaker*, Abby thought, and narrowed her eyes, thinking, *I hope your bicycle seat chafes you somewhere really uncomfortable.*

While she waited, Abby's thoughts wandered to Mark, who hadn't been happy to see her go. He'd told her it was fine, that she should go for it, that he was happy for her, but Abby had seen his expression—puzzled, disappointed, maybe even a tiny bit angry—after she'd given him the news.

"It's good money," Abby said. "And two weeks isn't forever."

"I know. I just wish—well."

"What?" Abby made herself ask.

"I wish I'd had a little more notice. I could have signed up for more shifts. But I understand this just came up," he said, before Abby could interrupt to remind him of that very thing.

"It's just two weeks," Abby said again. "And when I get back, we can figure out the apartment situation."

Mark nodded, but his expression made him look off-balance, confused, and very young. It made her heart ache. "If we're going to find a new place, we really should start looking soon."

"When I get back," Abby repeated. Then she'd put her hands on his shoulders, pressed herself against him, and started kissing his neck and the underside of his chin. Mark looked surprised. Probably this was because they'd gotten in the habit of having sex only twice a week, on Wednesday and Saturday nights. It made Abby sad, when she let herself think about it. When they'd started dating, after meeting again in Philadelphia, they'd tumble into bed—or the shower, or Abby's couch—at all hours of the day. Sometimes it would be an intense quickie that wouldn't involve actual undressing, and sometimes it would be slow and languorous. It wasn't like that anymore . . . but wasn't that what happened in every relationship? Things slowed down. The sex got a little less frequent, a little more routine. Wasn't that just growing up?

"You know, I've got to get up at five o'clock tomorrow morning," Mark said, his breath coming a little faster as Abby slipped her hand along his admirably flat belly and into his boxer-briefs.

"I won't keep you up all night," she'd said, before she'd dropped—gracefully, she hoped—to her knees. She'd wanted to please him, because Mark deserved pleasure. She also wanted to keep him from asking any more questions she wasn't ready to answer.

The next morning, Mark left for work after his run and a quick breakfast of smoothies made with Greek yogurt, protein powder, and frozen spinach. Abby had spent the day doing laundry, packing, taking her bike to Queen Village Bicycles for a pre-ride tune-up.

Mark had been at work when Abby had strapped her panniers onto her bike, rode to Thirtieth Street Station, and taken a train to New York City. Just before the train pulled into Trenton, her phone buzzed with a text. *Just because I love you,* Mark had written. Attached was a picture of two feet with six-inch toenails on each toe, each one painted bright red.

Abby sent him a blushing face and a heart. *Have fun,* Mark had texted back. Which meant, she hoped, that she'd been forgiven . . . or that at least she'd gotten a reprieve.

Back in the park, Abby realized there were a dozen people looking at her expectantly, including Jasper, who'd finished handing out the vests. She swallowed hard.

"Let's quickly do some introductions. Tell everyone your name and where you're from." Abby pointed toward the quartet of senior citizens. The hard-of-hearing fellow—tall, a little stooped, with pale, freckled white skin, skinny arms and knobby knees—gave a wave. He had a fanny pack looped over his shoulder and tucked under his arm, purse-style; hearing aids in both ears, and a turtle-ish aspect, with a round, sunburned face jutting forward from the wattled stalk of his neck.

"Good morning," he began, in a slightly louder-than-polite volume. "I'm Ted, and this is Sue." He indicated the gray-haired woman beside him, who waved at the group. "We live in Rye, New York, and we do a trip every summer with our dear friends, Ed and Lou, who live in Ridgefield, Connecticut." Ed was as short as Ted was tall, with a bald head as tanned and round as an acorn, and a belly that stretched his Lycra jersey in a taut curve. Lou was even shorter than her husband, with a cap of white curls and rosy cheeks.

"So it's Ted and Sue and Ed and Lou. But if that's confusing, we also answer to . . ." He turned around to display the words THE SPOKE'N FOUR emblazoned over a line drawing of four bikes with riders, all in a row. Mild laughter rippled through the group. "Good one," Jasper called.

"The four of us have our own sag wagon." Ted pointed toward the street, where a monstrous RV was parked—probably illegally—by the curb. "We take turns driving it. So, every day, three of us will be on the road, and the fourth will be behind the wheel. And, of course, you're all welcome to come aboard, if anyone needs a bathroom break, or if it's hot and you want to cool off, or it's raining and you want to stay dry."

The woman beside him—Sue, Abby reminded herself—grabbed his wrist and tugged him toward her so she could speak directly into his hearing aid.

"Oh!" Ted said. "Sue has reminded me to tell you that I'm a little hard of hearing. Please try to look at me while you're talking and speak slowly and clearly."

"Thank you, Ted," Abby said, slowly and clearly. Lizzie had filled Abby in on the RV situation, explaining that the Spoke'n Four used it as a safety net on their self-supported trips, in case one or a few of them ended up being unable to complete the day's mileage. "Can't they just use our sag wagon?" Abby had asked, and Lizzie had said, "I think they like knowing they can take care of themselves." She'd shrugged. "Or, who knows? Maybe one of them just really hates using Porta Potties."

"Everyone hates Porta Potties," Abby said.

"No lies detected," said Lizzie.

Abby nodded at the woman who'd looked relieved about the bridge news. She introduced herself as Lily Mackenzie, and said she was riding with her daughter, Morgan. Lily was petite, with bright blond hair, big, blue eyes, and long manicured fingernails. She wore black Lycra cycling shorts, but instead of a stretchy cycling jersey with pockets above the hips, she had on a long-sleeved tee shirt top. Abby also spotted a cross on a fine gold chain around her neck. Her daughter, Morgan, was taller than her mom, with shiny light-brown hair that, Abby guessed, uncharitably, had probably been her mother's original color. Morgan wore biking shorts, with a baggy tee shirt that hung almost to their hem, and a necklace that matched her mother's. A gold ring on her left ring finger caught Abby's eye. Could the girl be married already? It didn't seem possible. She was just a kid.

"There were supposed to be three of us, but now Morgan and I are doing a little mother-daughter bonding, while my husband's leading a men's retreat in Arizona." Lily smiled at the group, and Morgan gave a little nod, licking her lips as her gaze slid toward the ground. The girl's posture was almost furtive, shoulders hunched, with her left hand cupping her right elbow and her body leaning away from her mother. It was a pose Abby remembered well from her own teenage years.

"Welcome." Abby hoped that the Spoke'n Four, with the KEEP YOUR LAWS OFF OUR BODIES bumper sticker visible on its RV, right beneath the Bernie Sanders sticker, would be able to play nicely with the Mackenzies, and resolved to keep the conversational topics confined to biking, the weather, and what everyone was watching on TV.

"I'm not really an experienced cyclist," Lily was saying, "but I'll do my best to keep up." She looked at Morgan fondly. "I'm just happy to be spending time with my daughter."

"No worries," said Abby. Morgan, who appeared decidedly less thrilled, managed a wan smile as she shuffled farther away. "And that reminds me to remind all of you that this is a vacation, not a race. You're not here to win a spot on the Olympic team or qualify for the Tour de France. Don't worry about going as fast as you can. We want you to enjoy all the things being on a bike lets you see and hear . . ." (*and smell,* Abby thought, but didn't say, as she recalled certain sewage plants she'd ridden by, during her cycling club's annual New Hope–to–New York ride, which passed through some especially redolent sections of Elizabeth, New Jersey).

Abby already knew that, in some cases—mostly male cases— her little speech would be ignored. Between the apps you could download to your phone and the devices you could clip to your handlebars, bikers had real-time access to reams of data: how long they'd ridden and how far they'd gone, average speed and cadence count and feet of elevation, how many miles they'd gone on a trip and how many miles were left and how fast they were going compared to previous rides on the same route, or compared to other riders that day, that month, or that year.

It was a challenge. No matter how much the ride leaders urged folks to unplug from their devices and enjoy the scenery, there'd inevitably be some data-drunk riders staring at their screens for the entire trip, focused solely on going as fast as they could . . . or, at least, faster than the guy riding beside them, or faster than they'd gone the day or week before. Abby knew that Breakaway's founder, Marj, had played with the idea of flat-out forbidding the apps and computers, but that she'd eventually decided to let it be the riders' choice. Probably she'd known how many cyclists wouldn't even consider a trip from which they couldn't return with souvenirs, memories, photographs, bragging rights, and lots of data, including the knowledge, down to the merest fraction of a mile, of how far they'd gone.

"So please—take your time, look around, enjoy the ride," Abby continued. "There's some beautiful things to see. And if you've had enough"—Abby made eye contact with Lily, then with each of the Spoke'n Four—"don't feel like you need to push yourself. This is not a no-pain, no-gain kind of trip. You're not getting any points for riding if it hurts. Just pull over and let me know, and if you don't see me, call Jasper, and he'll come and get you."

Abby nodded at the middle-aged man who'd been expressionless as he listened to the introductions, with his shoulders hunched toward his ears, and arms crossed over his chest. He had close-cropped brown hair, white skin with a faint olive tinge and a thin-lipped frown that Abby guessed was his usual expression. The road bikes he and his wife were holding were good quality, but they had some nicks and scratches and were clearly not brand-new. Their two teenage boys had gravel bikes with knobby tires, the kind of sturdy, all-purpose, relatively inexpensive bikes you'd buy when your kids were still growing, and you didn't want to drop thousands of dollars on new bicycles each year.

"I'm Dale Presser." He indicated the woman standing beside

him, who was in her late thirties or early forties, Abby guessed, tanned and cheerful-looking, with the glow of someone who'd spent much of her summer outside. She had a round face, and her brown hair was pulled back in a ponytail that probably fit neatly under her helmet. "My wife, Kayla."

"The old ball and chain!" Kayla Presser's smile was cheerful, more open and less guarded than the one her husband had produced. She wore a short-sleeved purple cycling jersey, cycling shorts, and low-cut purple socks, and looked fit, but not intimidatingly so. The boys also wore black Lycra cycling shorts—Abby imagined there'd been a fight to get them into the close-fitting, padded garments—and tee shirts. "And these are our sons," Kayla said, pointing at the two boys, who towered beside her. "Ezra's fourteen, and Andy's sixteen. They are both delighted to be here, and not back home playing video games with their friends. They can't wait to put their phones away and get out in the fresh air."

That got some smiles and an *I-feel-your-pain* nod of commiseration from Lily. Abby would have expected grumbles and rolled eyes from the boys themselves, but Andy, the older one, smiled at his mom, while Ezra made a show of handing over his phone. Andy was taller than both of his parents, skinny and freckly, with bright blue eyes, with a nose that dominated his face, hands that seemed too big for his arms, and enormous feet. He reminded Abby of her brother at that age. Simon would eat and eat and eat and still be hungry—Abby remembered enormous bowls full of pasta or cold cereal, entire half-gallons of milk and sleeves of Oreos disappearing in an afternoon. Ezra was built more along his father's lines, a little shorter and broader.

"First bike trip?" Abby asked and wasn't surprised when Kayla answered for the family.

"Dale and I used to bike together before we had kids," she said. "This is our first trip with the boys. We're glad to be here."

"We're glad to have you." Abby watched as Andy sidled toward Morgan and said something that made her smile. *Good for you, kiddo,* Abby thought.

"Next!" Abby knew she could postpone it no longer. She braced herself, remembered every encouraging thing Lizzie had said to her, and pointed at the two men she'd avoided looking at, the ones she was already thinking of as the Inevitable Bros. She'd been on rides with guys like them before: fit-looking men with expensive equipment and haughty attitudes. Frequently, these men were former high school or college athletes looking to relive the youthful triumphs they'd notched before time and knee replacements slowed them down. These were the riders who'd inevitably dismiss her tips about ignoring their devices and noticing their surroundings; the guys who would always choose the extra mileage options when they were offered and then spend meals comparing splits and climb times, cadence counts, and resting heart rates. They'd make travel plans with the goal of checking big climbs and centuries off some kind of imaginary list—although, for all Abby knew, the list might be real, and every young-to-middle-aged male cyclist in the country might have been issued a copy. For all the enjoyment they seemed to be getting, these riders might as well have stayed in their basements, grinding out the miles on the Pelotons they always had (and which they'd always let you know had been acquired before they got trendy and, subsequently, untrendy). Guys like these, in Abby's experience, were the demographic least likely to believe that women in general, young women in particular, and young, fat women most of all, had any pertinent experience, skills, or expertise. They did not, as a rule, join in group rides that went at Abby's pace, and when they did, they would ignore her, argue with her, talk over her, or treat her with a polite condescension that was somehow worse than scorn.

She was unsurprised to see that today's Bros both had top-of-the-line road bikes fitted with high-end components and skinny leather saddles that made her tender bits ache just to look at. But maybe this was a good thing. Maybe, Abby thought, she wouldn't need to hear them comparing their heart rates over lunch. Maybe they wouldn't even stop for a lunch break, and they'd just throw down some salmon jerky and a Gu at a red light, before racing away at eighteen miles an hour. Their loss.

And their choice, Abby reminded herself as she tried to consider the young men objectively. One Bro was Black, in his early thirties, a little stocky, a few inches under six feet. His brown skin had reddish undertones; his hair was clipped short. He had dimpled cheeks and a cleft in his chin and wore a gray-and-white jersey, a gold wedding band, and steel-rimmed glasses that he'd pulled off and was polishing with a cloth he'd taken from his back pocket. He gave Abby a friendly smile. *Maybe not so bad,* Abby thought.

She turned her attention to the other guy, who was tall, with pale skin and brown hair, and . . .

No.

Abby felt her heart stop and the breath *whoosh* from her lungs. Everything in the park froze; the conversations silenced and the traffic halted; like time itself had stopped as Abby stared, her brain gasping out single words and fragments of sentences like, *No,* and *Can't,* and *What are the chances?*

Because the guy with the brown hair and the light eyes, the guy with the beautifully molded lips and the birthmark in the exact center of his throat, was Sebastian. Mr. Bachelorette Party. The guy she'd gone home with one night, two years ago.

In more evidence of life's unfairness, Sebastian seemed to have gotten even more handsome since Abby had seen him. His biceps bulged against the sleeves of his dark-blue jersey, his thighs strained the seams of his shorts. Abby allowed herself a single peek at his face, his wavy brown hair and full lips, looking just long enough to gather an impression of a haughty expression, and a lock of hair that flopped charmingly over his forehead. Abby bet that wasn't an accident. She further bet that a parade of ladies had used their fingers to smooth back that unruly curl.

Abby forced herself to smile and reminded her heart and her lungs to do their jobs. When she was reasonably certain her voice would be steady, she asked, "Do you gentlemen want to introduce yourselves to the group?"

"I'm Lincoln Devries," said the guy who wasn't Sebastian.

"Sebastian Piersall," said the guy with whom she'd had, hands-down, the best sex of her life. *Maybe he doesn't remember me,* Abby thought, a little wildly, as Sebastian looked at her. His eyes widened briefly. Then he gave her a slow, undeniably intimate smile; a smile that let her know that he remembered everything, including exactly how many times Abby had conjured his face behind her eyelids and his voice in her ears when she'd touched herself, or—oh, the shame—when Mark had been touching her.

"Abby," he said, his voice warm, his smile slow and sweet as warmed honey. "Nice to see you again."

Sebastian

Sebastian Piersall was a lucky man. He knew it was true. He would have known it even if Lincoln, his best friend, his parents, and sister and brother-in-law weren't constantly pointing it out. *That's Sebastian*, they would say, shaking their heads in good-natured resignation. *Falls into a pile of shit, comes out smelling like roses.*

Sebastian had grown up white, male, and comfortably middle-class, the second-born child and only son of a college professor father and an elementary-school art teacher mom. Sure, his mom had her struggles—specifically, white wine and vodka. And yes, her struggles had become his dad's struggles, as Sebastian's father had tried (and tried, and tried) to get her into rehab, or to stick with a program of recovery. But none of that really touched Sebastian. He'd been a teenager by the time things had gotten really bad, out of the house and in college before his mother's first stint in rehab. His childhood had been, in his mind, idyllic. He had fond memories of a fun mom, who'd let him stay home from school to watch cartoons, then take him bowling, a mom who'd laugh, shooing him out the door as they ran to go pick up pizzas before his father came home, after she'd fallen asleep on the couch and dinner had burned.

Sebastian, you know she let you stay home from school because she was too hungover to get you up and dressed, his sister had said, in the family therapy session at his mom's first rehab. *And she wasn't asleep on the couch, she was passed out!* Sebastian hadn't responded. He hadn't known. And if Fun Mom had been, in reality, Drunk Mom, he refused to let it change his memories of what his childhood had been like. *You've got your take on it. I've got mine,* he'd said. Greta had rolled her eyes, and the therapist had said something about denial, and how addiction was a disease of the family. Sebastian had tuned them out, thinking of his plans for the night ahead, and the woman he'd already arranged to meet.

He'd always been sociable and good-looking, academically successful, a standout athlete. He'd tried football and ice hockey and water polo, but his best sport was soccer. His high school team had made it all the way to the state finals; Sebastian had been named to the all-state team. Soccer wasn't a sport in which you could go pro and earn fame and fortune in the United States. It was, however, a sport where your skills were of interest to college recruiters. Sebastian had been accepted early decision at Wesleyan, his first choice, and the only school to which he'd applied—just one more example of the way the Universe showed its favor to him.

On the first day of college, he'd walked into his dorm room in a brick building called the Butterfields, dressed in the nylon shorts, tee shirt, and baseball cap he'd pulled on that morning. He'd found Lincoln, standing in front of an ironing board, dressed in khakis and a blue-and-white-checked short-sleeved button-down, pressing his shirts. Sebastian had stared, wondering, *Gay or just affected?* Lincoln had stared back at him, probably thinking, *Dumb jock.*

Sebastian had given Lincoln his most disarming smile. "Hey," he said, "I'm Sebastian." The closet's folding doors were open, and Sebastian could see ranks of neatly pressed pants and shirts on wooden hangers, arranged from lightest to darkest.

"Hello," said Lincoln. He introduced himself and told Sebastian that he played the violin, that he'd be auditioning for the orchestra, that he was not planning on bringing romantic partners back to the room and hoped that Sebastian would extend him the same courtesy.

Still smiling, Sebastian told him that was fine, even as he was thinking, *This is not going to work* . . . But ten minutes later, Lincoln was shaking his head over the piles of wrinkled clothes Sebastian had pulled out of his duffel, and five minutes after that he'd been ironing Sebastian's shirts, and then Sebastian had taken Lincoln out to the quad to teach him the basics of Ultimate Frisbee.

Proper, starchy, crisply creased Lincoln became Sebastian's best friend. They'd roomed together all four years of college. When they were sophomores, they'd launched a website called Scoop, which collected pieces of campus gossip, gave roundups of the Week in Wesleyan, and published a few in-depth, reported pieces on topics like the food services workers' efforts to unionize, or the controversy after a popular professor failed to get tenure. The website had been started as a lark but had gained readers every month. After graduation, Sebastian and Lincoln had moved to New York, where they ran Scoop as a weekly newsletter, a grown-up version of the college site, a mixture of gossip and news stories, delivered in an offhand, conversational style. "We'll see if we can make a go of it," Lincoln had said, after Sebastian had talked him out of going directly to business school. "We'll give it a year."

Sebastian and Lincoln had started off sharing an apartment, a tiny one-bedroom in Queens, which was also Scoop's headquarters, although they did most of their work at nearby coffee shops . . . and Scoop had thrived. When Lincoln had gotten engaged to Lana, a fellow orchestra member from Wesleyan, his parents had given them the down payment on a brownstone in Williamsburg as a wedding gift. The place was beautiful, three stories of high ceilings and crown moldings, plus a separate garden-level apartment with its own entrance. The plan was for Lincoln and his bride to live on the upper floors while renting the apartment, using the income to offset the mortgage, but Lincoln had convinced his parents to let Sebastian have the unit for less-than-market value.

So there he was, thirty-three years old, in the best city in the world, with a job he loved, with excellent, affordable living arrangements, his best friend right upstairs, and, thanks to the dating apps, a never-ending parade of available ladies. Sebastian could—and often did—meet one woman Friday night for drinks (translation: sex) and another woman Saturday afternoon for coffee, which, if he liked her, became drinks, or dinner, or both (followed by sex). If he wasn't feeling his afternoon date, he'd bid her a polite farewell, then jump on the apps and find someone else for drinks. Sometimes he'd meet yet another woman on Sunday for brunch (and more sex) . . . and if he wasn't tired, or busy, or if he was in the thick of reporting and needed a distraction, sometimes he'd even arrange for a Sunday-night hookup (which was no drinks or coffee; just sex).

Big girls and small girls, short girls and tall girls; Black, white, brown, Asian; Christian, Jewish, Muslim, every nationality and ethnicity and religion . . . Sebastian did not discriminate. His love life was a bottomless buffet, and Sebastian saw no reason to toss a napkin on his plate and say, "Thanks, but I'm stuffed."

True, Lincoln sometimes called him a man-whore with commitment issues, while Lana just looked sad. And yes, his sister muttered darkly about how this was compulsive behavior, that Sebastian was compensating for his dysfunctional childhood or something; that he'd never, quote-unquote, "faced his demons," or "dealt with his trauma," how he might even be a sex addict. Sebastian had just laughed.

"Sex isn't a substance," he'd told her. "And, if I'm an addict, I hope they never cut me off."

He wasn't lonely. He wasn't compensating. He absolutely wasn't traumatized. He just wasn't ready for anything more than the most casual of relationships. He'd had a front-row seat to the terrifyingly wholesome life Lincoln and Lana built together: their dinner parties and trips to the farmers market, the Christmas cookie swap they hosted where guests would gather around the piano to sing carols.

Sebastian did not throw parties. He preferred to entertain individual guests, as Lincoln put it, between the hours of Closing Time and Walk of Shame O'clock. But even though he wasn't looking for anything permanent, Sebastian did not treat women badly. He didn't objectify women. Indeed, if anything, women objectified him. He never hooked up with a woman who hadn't explicitly said that was what she wanted. He always asked and never did anything without his partner's full and enthusiastic consent. He'd never broken anyone's heart. At least not on purpose.

He wasn't some callous jerk with only one thing on his mind. But he liked sex, and variety, and situations that didn't allow for misunderstandings or confusion. With a few exceptions, the women he met on the apps were in perfect agreement. And thus had the first decade of Sebastian's postcollege life zipped by in a happy, horny blur.

There had been one girl, once: one girl he actually had wanted to see again. She hadn't come from the apps, which would have made it easier for him to find her again. He'd picked her up at a bar just before closing time. They'd had a memorable night together, and, when he'd woken up, she'd been gone. She hadn't left a note, and he'd never even gotten her last name. It had felt like a message from the Universe, that there was no such thing as love . . . or, at least, that Sebastian's time to find it had not yet arrived.

Except now, here was the girl, standing right in front of him! And they'd be together for the next two weeks. Sebastian beamed, pleased at yet another example of the world raining its blessings down on him; another instance of how things usually worked out the way he'd hoped they would.

"Nice to see you again," he said to Abby, in what he'd been told was his Barry White voice. Instead of looking pleased, Abby just looked . . . irritated? Frazzled? Scared?

"Wear your pinny, please," she said, and hurried away, leaving his friend staring at him.

"I take it you two know each other?" Lincoln's voice was extremely dry.

Sebastian knew that if he confirmed it, he'd be spending the entire trip listening to Lincoln complaining about Sebastian's wanton ways, and how there were fewer women in the world he hadn't slept with than women he had. Sebastian didn't need the hassle.

"Is there a reason she didn't seem entirely pleased to see you?" Lincoln inquired.

"No worries," said Sebastian. "It's all good." He smiled to himself, thinking that this trip, which he was already looking forward to, had just gotten exponentially more interesting.

Abby

The introductions had wrapped up with the Landons, Richard and Carol, an affluent-looking married, middle-aged white couple from Connecticut. Abby greeted them while she did her best to calm her racing heart and to not stare at Sebastian, or even look in his direction.

"Okay," she said. "Was everyone able to download the route, or grab a printed cue sheet?"

The moms and dads consulted their phones. The teenagers consulted their parents. The men of the Spoke'n Four fiddled with their cycling computers, while the woman who was either Lou or Sue (Abby had already forgotten which couple was tall and which was short) unfolded one of the cue sheets that Abby had printed. Morgan Mackenzie stood behind her mom, an icy oasis of teenage silence. Ezra Presser was being lectured by his mother—"No, you can't just follow me. You need to learn to read a map. It's an important life skill!" Abby heard Kayla say. Andy Presser, meanwhile, had sidled even closer to Morgan.

Abby walked to her own bike, the Trek touring bike that she'd bought secondhand for three hundred dollars of babysitting money and bat mitzvah gift cash when she was sixteen. She'd purchased it in advance of the first trip she'd ever taken, a five-day ride on Cape Cod with Lizzie. They'd packed tents and sleeping bags and ground cloths, and they'd spent two nights in Nickerson State Park in Brewster, one night in a hostel by the ocean in a town called Truro. For their final night, they'd slept on Race Point Beach in Provincetown. The sunset had been spectacular, and when they'd woken up in the morning they'd seen minke whales, mothers and calves, frolicking close to the shore.

Abby loved her bike. More than that, she identified with it. Trek had been making the 520 model since 1983, longer than any other bike it manufactured. The bikes were legendary: steel framed, practically indestructible, stable and sturdy, with brazed-on attachments that let riders mount racks for panniers alongside the back and front wheels. Touring bikes had what was known as relaxed geometry, a longer frame that prioritized comfort and stability over speed. When they were parked next to road bikes, they looked massive; like hippos that had wandered into a pack of gazelles. They were not fast or flashy, but they were hard to damage, they could carry almost any load and manage almost every surface. They weren't pretty, but they got the job done.

Abby's 520, which was almost twenty years old ("practically vintage," as Lizzie liked to say), had navy-blue paint with gold accents. Over the years, Abby had added a kickstand, three cages for water bottles, a handlebar mount for her iPhone, a floodlight for riding at night, and a bell in a case that looked like a rolling eyeball and made a pleasant but appropriately loud *ding* when she thumbed its lever. She had cushy handlebar tape, a back rack and front racks for panniers. Up front, her capacious Ortlieb handlebar bag was loaded with everything she might possibly need: a multitool, a flat-tire repair kit, her own extra tube, an extra battery for her phone, a first aid kit, a hand towel, emergency snacks.

"I'll be riding sweep, which means I'll be bringing up the rear," she told the group. *Don't look don't look don't look,* Abby thought, but she couldn't help her gaze from slipping to the Bros. She looked away before Sebastian could make eye contact, trying not to wonder what he was thinking. She still couldn't quite believe he'd remembered her name. "You should all have Jasper's number in your phone. Any kind of trouble—wrong turn, flat tire, existential malaise—pull off to the side and wait for me. If you don't see me, call him. Any questions?"

There were none.

"Okay!" Abby said. "Real quick, before we go. Does everyone have a spare tube, in case of flats? How about tire irons? You should have at least three." Abby made her way from rider to rider. Everyone was good, except the Bros, who had two tire irons and a single tube between them.

"Let me grab you another tube," Abby said.

"We'll be fine," said Sebastian. Abby allowed herself another look at his broad, high cheekbones, a widow's peak, and coppery highlights in that on-purpose-swoopy brown hair.

"Do you know how to change a flat?" Abby asked him.

Sebastian looked amused. "Yes, Abby, I know how to change a flat."

Abby opened her mouth. To say what, she wasn't sure—*Good for you,* or *Glad to hear it,* or, *I remember you were good with your hands,* or even, *Please don't say my name like that, I can't stand it*—when someone called, "Abby!"

She turned and saw a petite middle-aged woman with a let-me-speak-to-the-manager haircut wheeling a brand-new bike toward the group. "Hi, honey. Sorry I'm late."

And Abby Stern, who'd just been thinking that things were already awkward, stared at Eileen Stern Fenske, her mother, and realized that the Universe could always find a way to make them worse.

. . .

After she'd gotten the riders onto the path and heading in the right direction; after she'd checked in on every single one of them as they pedaled the first miles, when she couldn't avoid it any longer, Abby slowed down and waited for her mom to catch up.

"Mother," Abby said, matching pedal strokes with Eileen until their bikes were side by side, waiting to see if her mother would explain herself. After a few minutes, it was clear that Eileen would not, so Abby made herself ask. "What are you doing here?"

"I'm spending time with my daughter," Eileen said, her voice calm, her face serene. Although maybe that was the fillers, Abby thought. Maybe it was no longer physically possible for her mother to look irritated, or tired, or pissed, or anything other than pleasant. "I'm a delightful surprise," Eileen said airily.

"Well, you're definitely a surprise," Abby muttered.

"I heard that," said Eileen, still unruffled. "It's fine. We're going to have fun! I'll get to see you in your element!"

Abby examined the remark from all angles, looking for implied criticism, then shook her head. *Be the bigger person,* she told herself. No pun intended. Maybe Eileen was being sincere; making a real (although belated) effort to get to know her daughter on Abby's turf and Abby's terms. She'd purchased a nonstationary bike, and the right clothes: terry cycling shorts, a hot-pink sleeveless jersey with three stretchy pockets in the back, padded gloves, and clip-in cycling shoes.

"Lizzie took me shopping," she said, to Abby's unasked question. So Lizzie was in on this, too? Abby made a mental note to have a full and frank conversation with her best friend at the earliest opportunity. "Don't be mad at her. I swore her to secrecy," Eileen continued. "I wanted to surprise you."

"And you certainly have." Eileen was trying, she thought

again. True, Eileen's hair was probably freshly blown out beneath the helmet, and yes, she was wearing a full face of makeup, and she'd clearly found time to have her legs waxed and her nails done, but she was here. On a bike. On the road. With Abby.

Which didn't mean that Eileen was prepared for what was coming.

"Have you done any training, at all?" Abby asked her mother. "When was the last time you were on a bike?" Eileen opened her mouth. "An actual bike. Not a Peloton," Abby said. Eileen shut her mouth and sniffed, looking affronted.

"I do the hour-long rides three days a week," said Eileen. "The advanced ones. It's not nothing."

"No, but it's not the same as riding a bike outside," Abby said. "Where your bike's actually moving, and you have to balance, and there's bumps, and potholes, and dirt paths, and other people—"

"I'll be fine," Eileen said, nimbly steering around a bike messenger with a giant padded backpack to prove it. "You know what they say. It's just like riding a bike." She pointed her chin toward Lily Mackenzie, who was wobbling along ten yards in front of them. "I'm already doing better than she is."

"Mom—" *At least I came by my propensity for judgment honestly,* Abby thought.

"I'm not here to cause you any trouble," Eileen said. "I just thought it would be nice for us to be together."

"Why?" Abby blurted.

"Because I'm sixty-three," said Eileen. Abby waited, wondering if that was supposed to mean something. Eileen looked at her and shook her head. "You probably don't remember. But my mother was sixty-three when she died."

"Ah." Abby could barely remember her grandmother Rina. Her mother's mother had died when Abby had been six.

"And I really do want to spend some time with you, doing

something that you love," Eileen continued. She had her eyes on the path, not on Abby, when she said, "I understand I didn't always make the right choices about your summers."

Was that an apology? Abby wondered. She and her mother hadn't talked about Camp Golden Hills in years. When Eileen didn't say anything else, Abby decided that maybe even a vaguely worded acknowledgment was better than nothing. And, quite possibly, the best she could expect.

"You'll thank me for this later," Eileen Stern announced from the passenger's seat as their car rolled through the Camp Golden Hills gates. Abby didn't answer. She was in the backseat, behind her father, looking out the window. There was an oversize wooden knife and fork, neatly crossed and nailed to the arch at the camp's entrance, like the heraldry on a knight's shield. Underneath the wooden silverware was Camp Golden Hills' motto: A HEALTHY TODAY . . . A HAPPY TOMORROW!

"I know it doesn't feel that way now," Eileen continued as they drove underneath the arch. "But, someday, you'll be grateful."

Abby had her arms crossed over her chest. Her thighs were sticking to the seat. She didn't bother answering. *I will never thank you for this,* she thought. *I will hate you for this, for as long as I live.*

Her father drove slowly along the bumpy dirt road, following signs that directed campers to the Welcome Center. At their first stop, a skinny, smiling young woman in a pink camp tee shirt and khaki shorts stuck her head through the open window. "Abby Stern," Abby's father said.

"Great!" said the young woman, like this was the best news she'd heard all day. "I'm Kelsey. I'm one of the senior counselors. And a Golden Hills alum!" Abby didn't miss the approval on her mother's face as Eileen looked at Kelsey's flat belly, skinny hips, and long, cellulite-free legs.

"Mom and Dad, you can park over there." Kelsey waved toward a parking lot, where ranks of cars were already lined up. "Abby, grab your swimsuit, and come with me."

Abby pulled the swimsuit she'd been told to have ready out of her backpack, and plodded after the counselor, up a hill and into a wooden cabin. Inside was what looked like a doctor's office, complete with a paper-draped examination table, a wheeled stool, and in the corner, the dreaded Medco scale.

"Hop on up and we'll get your weight," Kelsey said.

Abby held up her swimsuit. "Should I change first, or . . ."

"Nah, just take your shoes off." Kelsey gave her a confiding wink. "For weekly weigh-ins, you'll want to take off as much as you can, but not for this one."

Abby toed off her sneakers and got on the scale. She closed her eyes as Kelsey slid the weights to the right, but she couldn't close her ears when Kelsey said the number.

"Okay, now you can change." Kelsey bounced out of the room. Abby shucked off her shorts and tee shirt and pulled on her plain one-piece navy-blue swimsuit. A different counselor (also skinny, with a dark-brown ponytail) ushered her into a room with a plain brown paper backdrop against the wall, and a Polaroid camera on a tripod in front of it. Abby was directed to stand in front of the backdrop while the counselor snapped pictures: front, back, left profile, right profile. After the camera spat out the images, the counselor used a thick black marker to write Abby's name, and the word BEFORE, on the bottom of each shot. She handed Abby the Polaroids, along with a folder containing a sheaf of pages. One turned out to be her daily schedule. Another detailed the 1,200 calories a day she'd be eating for her stay. "Good luck!" the counselor chirped. Abby didn't even try to smile back.

On its website and brochures, in the ads that it ran in the back pages of the *New Yorker* and the *New York Times Magazine*, Camp Golden Hills mentioned "health" and "wellness" dozens of times. The words *weight* or *diet* were used sparingly. That did not prevent anyone from knowing that Camp Golden Hills was fat camp. Abby had been exiled there in advance of her bat mitzvah in October.

"You want to look good in the pictures, don't you?" Eileen had pleaded, after a morning spent dress shopping at the Cherry Hill Mall, where they'd discovered that Abby had already outgrown the juniors' department and was wearing a women's size twelve. This fact hadn't troubled Abby too much. At least, it hadn't surprised her. She saw her body every day and how the world reacted to it. But Eileen was almost in tears by the time she said, "Let's take a break" and ushered Abby to the Nordstrom café.

At the counter, Eileen had a chicken Caesar salad, dressing on the side, and coffee, which she took black. She'd ordered the same salad for Abby before Abby could ask for her usual turkey club and fries.

"What I want," Abby replied, "is to go to theater camp, like we talked about." She'd looked at her mother, whose expression was stony. "Why is this such a big deal? Aren't you supposed to be worried about my d'var Torah, or whether I know the prayers?"

"You don't understand now," Eileen said, her voice low. "But, I promise, when you're my age, and you're looking back at those pictures . . ."

"I'm not going to care!" Abby said, stabbing a crouton with the tines of her fork.

"You will," Abby's mother said, leaning forward, her eyes intent. "You will care. You'll thank me for this."

Abby shook her head. She speared a chunk of chicken breast and doused it in the little cup of dressing. She wouldn't look at her mother or eat a single leaf of lettuce from her salad, and, when lunch was over, she refused to try on any more dresses, until Eileen threw up her hands and took her home. Abby had gone for a bike ride. Her mother, she guessed, had found Camp Golden Hills, and put her plot into motion.

When Abby emerged from the camp office with her Polaroids and her schedule, her parents were in the parking lot, arguing.

"You deal with her, I swear to God, I can't take any more of her sulking," Eileen said, drumming her manicured fingernails on the roof of the sedan.

Her dad had been the one to extract Abby's monogrammed pink duffel bag from the trunk, to ask a counselor for directions and escort Abby up the gentle slope to Bunk Five.

Abby dragged her feet up the hill, giving one-word answers to her father's questions. She opened the creaking cabin door and peered into the dimness. Six sets of bunk beds were lined up against the walls. Half of them had been claimed, and a few girls were unpacking, putting clothes away in one of the dressers, or using sticky blue Fun-Tak to affix photographs and posters to the walls. Her father picked a bottom bunk, seemingly at random, and put Abby's bag on top of the skimpy, plastic-topped mattress. His expression was glum as he turned and faced her.

"I know this isn't what you wanted."

Abby didn't bother to reply. Both of her parents knew she'd been planning all year to go to theater camp in Maine. Abby had taped her own application, singing "Matchmaker, Matchmaker," which she'd learned playing Tzeitel in her middle school's production of *Fiddler on the Roof*. She'd loved the camaraderie of rehearsals, how all the kids, the actors and the crew, had become friends, and on the night of the first show, she hadn't been nervous at all. She loved performing. Even though she'd been, at the time, a head taller than both the girl playing Golde, her mother, the boy playing Tevye, her father, and bigger than almost every other kid in the cast, she hadn't felt ashamed, and everyone told her what a good job she'd done. Her father had had tears in his eyes as he'd handed her a bouquet. Even her mother had looked impressed.

Abby had been so happy when she'd gotten accepted to theater camp in March. She'd been corresponding with her fellow campers online, all of them trying to guess what the summer's musical would be. Then Eileen had sprung the fat-camp trap.

Abby had gone to her father, begging him to intervene, but all he'd done was say things about *shalom ha'bayit*, which was Hebrew for *peace in the house*. Which, Abby knew, really meant peace between her parents, at Abby's expense. And now here she was, in the middle of Nowheresville, New York, stuck in a cabin that smelled faintly of mold at a camp that didn't even have a theater, preparing for six weeks of starvation when she should have been getting ready to sing her audition piece, which was going to be "Adelaide's Lament," from *Guys and Dolls*.

"Dad," Abby said quietly. "Do I really have to do this?"

Her father pushed his hands into his pockets. The dusty shafts of sunlight coming through the cabin's windows highlighted his potbelly, the weary slump of his shoulders, and the new strands of silver in his hair. Abby found herself startled by how old he looked.

"Your mother wants you to be healthy," he said, a little woodenly, like an actor who'd memorized his lines but hadn't yet figured out how to deliver them with any conviction.

"I am healthy," said Abby. "Nobody's saying I'm unhealthy. Dr. Raskin has never said I'm unhealthy. I'm just not thin. And neither are you! And neither is Grandma! And—"

"More active, then. Your mom wants you to be more active and make movement more of a habit. She didn't think there was going to be enough physical activity at that theater camp." This, too, sounded like something he'd been told instead of something he believed.

"There was swimming! And volleyball!" Abby's throat was tight, her eyes felt hot. She still couldn't quite believe that she was here, not in Maine; that her father wasn't going to rescue her. That this was really going to happen.

"Abby." Her father took her hands and gazed into her eyes. "Please. I am begging you. For the sake of everyone's sanity, please just get through this summer, and next year you can go anywhere you want."

"You promise?" she asked, thinking that the summer before eighth grade wasn't too late. "You swear?"

"I promise," said her dad, and he kissed her goodbye. "I'll get your mother," he said, once he'd reached the cabin's door. "I know she'll want to say goodbye."

"We said goodbye already."

"Well, then, she'll want to make your bed."

Abby shook her head again. "I can do it myself," she said, and waited, in stony silence, until her dad hugged her again and walked out the door.

Abby unpacked her sheets and pillow and smoothed her comforter out over the thin plastic-covered mattress. When she saw that most of her bunkmates had stuck their "before" Polaroids to the wall beside or above their beds, she did the same. She put her clothes in the two drawers she'd been assigned, shorts and tee shirts in one; bras and underwear and swimsuits and socks in the other. Then she went outside to sit on the cabin's steps to watch two girls play a desultory game of tetherball and take in her surroundings. The cabin looked like the pictures from the website, with pine wood walls, screened windows, and picnic tables out front, but the website hadn't communicated the smell, a blend of must, mildew, and old bug spray—the essence of buildings that had been shut up tight since September. Abby slapped at a mosquito and opened her folder, scanning the sample meal plan—*four ounces grilled chicken breast, one-half baked sweet potato with one teaspoon butter, unlimited steamed broccoli, one serving ice milk.* She wondered if she was expected to measure things like a teaspoon of butter or four ounces of chicken breast, or if the camp would do that for her.

When all eleven of her fellow campers had arrived, it hadn't taken Abby long to realize, with a feeling of shameful pleasure, that she was actually one of the smaller girls in the bunk. After a lifetime of always being the biggest, in her class or on her team, in a play or at the pool, this was a refreshing change. Not only was she relatively small compared to her bunkmates, but she also had the most desirable of the three silhouettes described on one of the handouts she found in her folder.

"Lucky you," murmured Leah, who'd taken the bunk above Abby's. "You're an Hourglass." Abby could hear the capital *H* when Leah pronounced the word.

"What are you?" Abby asked.

"Oh, she's an Apple," said Marissa Schuyler, who had the lower bunk opposite Abby's. "I am, too." Marissa's hands were pale and graceful. Her nails, Abby saw, were manicured and polished pale pink. She wore delicate gold rings, a pair of patent leather slides, and a rose gold bangle that fit tightly on her wrist.

"What are the other options?" Abby asked.

"Pyramids," said Leah, reading from her handout. "Apples are round all over. Pyramids are smaller on the top, bigger on the bottom."

"Hourglass, Apple, and Pyramid," Abby repeated. "What about the boys?"

Marissa and Leah looked at each other. "I don't know," Leah finally said. "I think they're just boys."

Kelsey from the parking lot, with her shiny ponytail and permanent smile, was their counselor. She bounded in, made them do a round of introductions—"Tell us where you're from, and give us an adjective that starts with the first letter of your name that describes you!" Abby had picked Amazing, even though Angry would have been more true. As soon as Kelsey had bounded out again, Marissa reached into her pillowcase and produced a bag of sour gummy bears.

"Enjoy them," said Marissa, when Abby hesitated. "It's probably going to be the last sugar you have for a while." Marissa and Leah were both Camp Golden Hills veterans. Marissa had started the previous summer, and Leah's first summer had been the year before that. As Abby watched, Marissa walked around the cabin, going from girl to girl, laying a single gummy bear on each of their tongues like a Communion wafer. Then she'd linked her left arm through Leah's and her right arm through Abby's. "Come on," she'd said. "Let's go look at the boys!"

Abby had planned on hating everything about Camp Golden Hills, but in spite of herself, she'd ended up having a surprisingly good time. She'd made friends. She'd had her first boyfriend, her first real kiss. And, of course, she'd also gotten her first taste of the dieting life, not to mention previews of how the world would treat girls like her.

The last weigh-in of the summer was the day before everyone's parents came to take them home. Abby listened as her bunkmates emerged from the cabin with the scale to either exult or mourn over the news. Marissa had been celebrating because her parents had promised her a Tiffany heart necklace if she lost twenty pounds, which she had. Kara was fretting because she'd lost only nine and a half pounds—"But I'm going to round up and say it's ten. Ten is good, right? Ten pounds isn't nothing!" And Vicki had lost thirty-eight pounds, which

Abby thought was tragic, because the truth was, you couldn't really tell.

On pickup day, her parents arrived late, so she'd gotten to see everyone else's parents and how they had reacted to their daughters. She saw how Kara's mother scowled and snapped, "If they hadn't told me you'd lost weight, I wouldn't have guessed."

Abby had watched how Kara had flinched. She'd listened, shocked and saddened, as her brash, funny, outspoken friend said, "I tried my hardest," in a tiny voice. She'd cringed as Kara's mom had muttered, "It doesn't look like your hardest was very hard."

Marissa's mother, meanwhile, made a show of walking right past her daughter, then turning around in pretend shock, saying, "Who is this gorgeous supermodel, and what has she done with our child?" Marissa glowed, her smile enormous, her eyes bright, happier than Abby had ever seen her as she picked up her bags and practically skipped out of the cabin.

Abby remembered how, one night, Kara had cried as she'd talked about her mother, how she'd said, "It's like it hurts her to even have to look at me." Other girls had told their own stories. Everyone had an anecdote about a parent's shame, a sibling they'd overheard claiming they weren't related, or a grandmother who, instead of pinching a granddaughter's cheeks, would grab her love handles, and give them a painful twist, and say something about how you couldn't get a man without a cute figure.

Eileen Stern had gasped when she saw Abby for the first time. She'd pressed her hands to her heart, beaming, saying, "Abby, you look beautiful!" She had smiled for the entirety of the three-hour drive back to Philadelphia, asking Abby once every ten minutes how she felt, and if she was proud, and didn't she agree that Camp Golden Hills was the best thing she could have done with her summer. At home, Abby found a party dress—pink lace with a tulle skirt, its bodice covered with glittering silver paillettes—

hanging on the back of her bedroom door. "Come on, let's see how it looks," Eileen instructed. Abby had complied, and Eileen threw her arms around her daughter, laughing triumphantly after she'd pulled up the zipper. "Look at yourself," she said, her hands on Abby's shoulders, turning her daughter toward the mirror. "You're gorgeous." Abby hadn't wanted to smile, to give Eileen that satisfaction, but she'd been pleased with what she'd seen, in spite of herself.

Eileen's delight had felt bittersweet, and Abby's memory of the moment had only soured as time had gone by. The less of Abby there was, the more Eileen liked it. The more Eileen liked her. And, the older Abby got, the more she read and learned and saw how the world worked, the more disappointed she felt. Eileen wanted her daughter to shrink herself to fit into the space the world allotted, instead of fighting to change the systems and institutions that wanted women to keep themselves small. She treated Abby like a problem in need of solving instead of asking, even once, whether it was the world, not her daughter, that might have been wrong.

"I know you don't think that I made the best decisions," Eileen was saying, breaking the silence as she and her daughter pedaled along the paved path, with the Hudson River on their left and the West Side Highway on their right. "I know that now."

Please stop talking, Abby mentally begged, feeling desperate to prevent her mother from stumbling around the minefield of Abby's teenage years. If Eileen shut up, she'd be able to tell herself that her mother had apologized, or tried to apologize. They could end this horrible conversation and move on.

Of course, though, Eileen kept going. "But you should know that everything I did was because I wanted the best for you."

"Sure," Abby said, in what she hoped was a neutral tone.

"It's true," said Eileen, and lifted her chin.

This was an old argument, well rehearsed, but Abby couldn't refrain from making her case again. "I understand you believe it. But, just for the record, you did not want what was best for me. You wanted me to be thinner. Those things are not the same." Abby could feel herself flushing, her heart beating faster, the anger that lived inside her waking up, uncoiling and stretching, sharpening its claws. "You wouldn't have cared if I'd come home from that place with an eating disorder. You know, a lot of girls did."

Eileen sounded horrified. "That's not true!"

"Yes, it is. Remember my bunkmate Kara? She ended up needing in-patient treatment for anorexia when she was in high school."

"No," said Eileen. "I'm not saying that girls didn't come home with"—she paused—"with problems. I'm saying I would have cared if you'd come home with one."

Abby didn't answer. She was wondering, not for the first time, if Eileen would have actually preferred an anorexic daughter to a fat one.

"And I meant what I said," Eileen said, her voice fractionally softer. "I'm here because I want to spend time with you while I can."

"What do you mean, 'while you can'?" Abby asked. She turned her head, taking her eyes off the path to look at her mother. "Are you dying?" A cold finger pressed itself against Abby's heart.

Eileen sounded impatient when she said, "No, Abby. I'm not dying. I'm not sick. Nothing is wrong. It's just that people's lives change. And you and I might not get this kind of time together anytime soon."

The cold finger was back, pressing harder, because, surely,

something other than whim, or memories of Grandma Rina, the passage of time, was responsible for Eileen showing up on a two-week bike ride through unglamorous Upstate New York. Abby wondered if Mark had talked to her parents; if Mark had—God forbid—asked her father for Abby's hand. Did people still do that? Would Mark have done that?

"So you just . . . decided to come?"

"I've been thinking about asking if you wanted to do something for a while. Go to a spa for a few days, or take a trip somewhere. When this came up, I thought, 'Why not?'"

"Why not," Abby repeated.

"And there's only so many summers, you know? If you have children, you'll be busy."

"I am not planning on having children anytime soon," Abby said.

"Well, if you want kids, you can't wait forever," Eileen said.

"I don't even know if I want children," Abby said.

That closed her mother's mouth. At least for a minute or two. Eileen seemed to be considering a few different responses before settling on, "Who can say what the future will bring?"

"Um, me," said Abby. "I can say. Me, and Dr. Kravitz, who put my IUD in last year."

Eileen looked at Abby, eyebrows arching toward the smooth expanse of her forehead. "An IUD's a smart choice. And you can get it taken out and start trying the next month, right?"

Abby didn't answer. *I'm not getting it taken out, and I'm not going to start trying.*

"And it doesn't have the side effects, right? I know the Pill can cause weight gain."

And there they were, back at Eileen Stern Fenske's favorite topic. It was amazing, Abby thought. Just like pop culture buffs could link any actor to Kevin Bacon in fewer than six steps, her mother could swing any conversation around to weight in just two or three.

"I'm going to go see how the rest of the group is going," Abby said.

"Okay! Have fun!" her mother called, and Abby sped off, pumping her legs faster and faster, wondering why on earth her mother was really here—on the same trip as her hookup!—and what on earth she was going to do about it.

Lily

Lily Mackenzie could hear Abby, the ride leader, and Abby's mother, Eileen, just behind her, talking companionably. She couldn't make out words, but she could hear the low hum of their voices as they rode together, side by side. It made her heart ache. *Will it ever be like that with us?* she wondered. She tensed her muscles and lifted her head long enough to peer along the trail, trying to find Morgan, but her daughter was nowhere in sight.

Lily's bike wobbled, and she struggled to straighten it out. She was gripping her handlebars so hard that her wrists and fingers ached. A droplet of sweat crept down her forehead and into her right eye. She tried to rub her stinging eye against her sleeve, but that made her bike wobble even more violently. *You can do this,* she told herself, keeping her eyes on the back of the elderly man just ahead, who was pedaling along confidently, smooth and steady and stable, not a care in the world, sometimes not even bothering to hold on to the handlebars as he glided nonchalantly along, past one of the stainless steel bollards that narrowed the path, like a belt cinching a lady's dress. Lily panicked whenever she had to navigate past them. The other riders barely seemed to notice them at all. *You can do this. You'll be fine. People say it's just like riding a bike when they mean it's something you can pick right up again, no problem, so this is going to be okay. You won't get hurt. Everything will be fine.*

Lily tried to look past the man, still hoping to catch a glimpse of her daughter, wishing that Morgan had stayed back with her, that she hadn't gotten so far ahead. *She's a teenager,* Lily reminded herself. And Morgan was a good girl; sweet-natured, and kind, a diligent student, a talented artist. Oh, there'd been a few rough patches of back talk and boundary pushing when Morgan was thirteen and fourteen and she'd argued with Lily and Don at every opportunity. She'd broken her curfew. She'd made friends Lily and Don didn't approve of. She'd purchased a push-up bra and a thong from Victoria's Secret. Lily knew because she'd found these items tucked away at the back of Morgan's underwear drawer.

She and Don had talked it over. They'd waited . . . and the curfew-cutting had ended, and the back talk had mostly abated. There was, still, the matter of Olivia. Morgan had met Olivia in her after-school art class and now claimed that she was her best friend. Olivia went to public school. She had two mothers, and she did not belong to their church, or any church at all. Olivia's hair was brown, but sometimes dyed pink or blue. She wore overalls, with striped shirts underneath, and what looked like construction-workers' boots with platform soles that added at least four inches to her height. When Morgan had brought Olivia home for dinner, Olivia had cheerfully told Don that she was an agnostic, that her family was "culturally Jewish"—whatever that meant—and that, if she got married—"to a man," she'd blithely added—she wasn't planning on submitting to her husband as head of the household.

"We'll pray for you," Don had said, his voice a little strangled, and Morgan had looked away, with a little smile—a very adult smile—playing at the corners of her lips.

Lily never thought she'd miss the arguments, the fights, the deliberate provocations . . . except, in the last few months and weeks, Morgan had gotten quiet and withdrawn. Maybe it was because she was growing up, Lily told herself. That, or missing her boyfriend. Brody had been Morgan's first love. They'd dated last spring, when Morgan had been a sophomore and Brody was a senior. He was a polite young man who'd come to the house and asked Don's permission before he'd taken Morgan out. Brody had enlisted in the army and left for basic training two weeks after high school graduation. Lily had expected Morgan to mope for a while, before her daughter's usual sunny nature reasserted itself. She hadn't expected weeks of her daughter retreating to her bedroom, with sad, dreary-sounding music filtering out underneath the door.

Morgan had kept up with her chores. She would do her laundry and take out the trash; she'd set the table before dinner and help with the dishes after. She'd gone to church with Lily, every Sunday. Her grades had been fine. But, at the table, she'd pick at her food and barely speak to her parents. For the past three Sunday nights she hadn't come downstairs for their usual game of Uno or charades or Monopoly. "I'm tired," she'd say, before drifting back to her bedroom. "I just want to lie down."

"She's a teenager," Don had said, when Lily had told him she was worried. He'd had his back to her as he stood in their walk-in closet, standing barefoot in his suit trousers, pulling off his shirt. "Teenage girls have moods." He sniffed at the shirt's armpits before returning it to its hanger.

"I think this is more than a mood," Lily said.

Don nodded absently, then went back to examining his ties. "Have you seen the blue and silver one? I was going to take it to Arizona."

Wordlessly, Lily handed him his tie. The plan—at least, the

original plan—had been for Don and Lily and Morgan to do the bike trip as a family. Every summer, they did some kind of trip—camping in Vermont or New Hampshire; hiking in Montana. The Breakaway trip was to be that summer's adventure. But then the senior pastor of the church hosting a big men's conference had gotten COVID, and Don had been asked to preach on Sunday morning. It was a big honor, one that came with a generous honorarium and lots of visibility. Don and Lily talked it over and decided he'd be foolish to pass it up.

At that point, the trip was nonrefundable. And so they'd discussed it and decided that Lily and Morgan would do the trip as a duo. Lily had agreed, thinking, privately, that the trip would be a chance for her to talk to Morgan, to find out what was really going on. She hadn't wanted to explain to Don how hard being a teenage girl was; how a dozen different things could go wrong between the end of breakfast and the start of homeroom, and how many of those things had to do with boys and men. Morgan went to a private Christian school, a school affiliated with Don's church . . . but bad things could happen, even there. This Lily knew from personal experience.

She'd been praying that the bike trip would help, even though cycling was something Morgan and Don did together. Lily could ride a bike, but her plan had been to pedal a few leisurely hours each day before hopping aboard the sag wagon and meeting her husband and daughter at the lunch stop or the hotel.

The morning after Don had gotten his phone call and they'd settled on the new plan, she'd gone to the garage to check out her bike, which she hadn't ridden in . . . weeks? Maybe months, she decided. Her bike was slumped on two flat tires, with cobwebs ornamenting the brake levers. For a minute, Lily just stared, feeling like the bike was a version of what she'd become. Old. Forgotten. Sagging. Obsolete.

Lily knew that she looked fine for her age. She'd gained only a few pounds since she'd gotten married, but that weight had settled in her hips and thighs and belly, and not even the most stringent diet could budge it. Her hair had gotten thinner, her feet had gotten wider. The only glow her skin could boast, these days, came from cosmetics, and her breasts could only achieve their prematernity perkiness with the help of an underwire bra. Lily did her best to look nice for Don. She colored her gray hair, she exercised and watched what she ate, she wore clothes that were flattering and age appropriate without being matronly. Lily knew she looked good . . . but she also knew that she looked good for thirty-seven, while Morgan looked fifteen, like a rosebud still unfurling, its petals creamy and pristine. A flower, opening itself to the sunshine, certain that nothing in the world would hurt it.

Lily had wiped off the cobwebs, wrestled the bike into the trunk of her car, and driven it to the bike shop. There, the repair guy had inspected it, and her, without even bothering to hide his skepticism.

"So you'll be riding, what? Twenty, thirty miles a day?" His scraggly, light-brown beard meandered from his chin toward the center of his chest. There were tattoos all over his arms, and rubber discs stretching his earlobes.

"Closer to forty," Lily lied, trying not to stare. It was actually more like fifty miles most days, and even longer on a few, but the guy was already giving her a *there's-no-way-lady* kind of look, and Lily didn't want to risk him becoming even more skeptical or telling her that what she'd planned would be impossible.

"And the trip leaves when?"

"Next week." The trip actually left in five days, but *next week* made her situation sound slightly less dire.

"Have you been riding a different bike?" the guy asked, with a dubious note in his voice. "Because that's a lot of miles to start with if you haven't been riding for a while."

"I'm sure I'll be fine." She smiled brightly, feigning confidence. "I do Zumba, so I'm in pretty good shape."

"Zumba," the guy repeated.

"It's like a dance thing," Lily said.

"No, no, I know. My nana does Zumba. Hang on." He lifted the bike up (effortlessly, Lily saw) onto a frame, where he clamped it in place and gave its rear wheel a spin. Even Lily could see it wobbling as it turned.

"Your wheels need to be trued," he said.

"Of course," Lily said, and nodded like she knew what he meant.

"Chain needs to be lubed," the guy said. "I'll want to take a look at the brake pads, and the derailleur. And the gel in your saddle looks pretty shot." He stopped talking to himself and looked at her. "Any idea when your tires were last replaced?"

Lily shook her head. At the guy's direction, she climbed aboard a stationary bike and let the guy take measurements and adjust her bike's seat and handlebars. She sat on a cushion that took an imprint of her bottom (her sitz bones, the guy said, but it looked like her bottom when she got up, which was the last thing Lily wanted to see). She picked out a new saddle, a pair of padded, fingerless gloves, and three pairs of cycling shorts with pads that looked like Depends sewn into the crotch and made her waddle when she walked, shorts the guy promised were essential for rides longer than a few hours. "You'll want this, too," he'd said, handing her a tub of chamois cream. Lily was too ashamed to ask him where the cream was meant to go.

When she got back home, it was early afternoon. Morgan was still at school. Don was still at the church. Lily dabbed sunscreen on her face and cream on the bike short's padding, per the Internet's instructions, before putting them on, along with a tee shirt and the gloves. She wheeled her bike to the end of the driveway. *You can do this,* she told herself, swinging one leg over the top tube. *It's just like riding a bike.* That first trip around the block had left her dismayingly exhausted, and the next morning she'd been so sore that she'd almost screamed when she sat down on the toilet. But she'd kept going, riding every morning and every afternoon, first five miles, then ten, then twelve. She had persisted. She was not going to let her daughter down.

On Friday night, Don had helped them load their luggage into the trunk and their bikes onto the rack and hugged them both goodbye. Lily and Morgan had driven eight hours from Ohio to New York City. The city's traffic had terrified Lily, but she'd made it to the hotel, happy to hand the keys off to a valet, who'd helped her and Morgan get the bikes off the rack, and up to their room.

That first night, Morgan had been fine, her cheerful, sunny self. She'd kept up a stream of bright chatter, reading Olivia's texts from the Jewish, kosher, vegan summer camp on a working farm where her two moms had sent her (*HELP ME* Olivia had written, in all capital letters, beneath a picture of the meatless shepherd's pie, which, even Lily had to admit, did not look very appetizing). They'd taken the subway to Chinatown for dinner the night before, and had gone back to their hotel near Battery Park, where they'd watched a movie and gone to bed early, their bikes parked at the foot of their beds, waiting.

And now, here they were. Or, rather, here she was, pedaling unsteadily along the bike path with her thighs and calves aching and sweat stinging her eyes and her daughter somewhere up ahead, off in the distance, not seeing, or caring, how Lily was struggling.

Abby had told them that the first thirteen miles would be

the most challenging, and Abby hadn't lied. The terrain was easy enough, flat and paved and smooth, but those very things meant that the bike path was completely jammed. There were people on sleek racing bikes and bulky rented bikes and little kids on one-wheeled bikes with seats attached to the backs of real bikes, pedaled by their parents. Signs at regular intervals read NO MOTOR VEHICLES/E-BIKES/E-SCOOTERS, but Lily had seen examples of the latter two, plus people on Rollerblades, which were allowed, and motorized unicycles with light-up neon wheels, which probably were not. Messengers wearing bulky insulated DoorDash backpacks zipped past, weaving through the slower riders, calling, "On your left!" as they rocketed by, so close that Lily could feel the wind rush against her in their wake. Little kids went caroming from one side of the path to the other on push bikes or bikes with training wheels, their helmeted heads looking too big for their bodies, usually with a parent or two in their wake calling out instructions, telling Colton or Hazel to *get out of the way,* to *be careful,* to *ride on the right, no, not that right, the other one!* The only good news was that pedestrians had their own paths. Whenever Lily managed a glance sideways, she could see them: runners and walkers and people with dogs on leashes, all of them moving briskly along.

Where was Morgan? How far had they gone? Were they close to getting out of the city yet? Lily knew she could check her odometer, but she was scared to look down. It felt like they'd been riding for hours. Except they still hadn't gone under the George Washington Bridge, which meant that, as unbelievable as it seemed, they were still in Manhattan, and they hadn't even covered the first thirteen miles.

Lily felt like she could barely force air into her lungs. Her hands, inside her riding gloves, were slick with sweat, and her padded bike shorts had gotten bunched up, with the padding slid off to one side. Her nose itched, but she was too afraid to let go of the handlebars to scratch it.

You're fine, she thought, repeating the words like a mantra. *You got this. You're fine. You can do this.*

One of the older ladies, the short one with bright blue eyes, rode up alongside of her. "You're Lily, right? Are you doing okay?" she asked, sounding sympathetic. Lily wondered how lost she must look, if she was getting sympathy from the seventy-five-plus set. She managed a nod and a clenched-toothed smile.

"It'll get easier. I promise," the woman said. "And it's wonderful that you're doing this with your daughter."

Lily nodded again.

"Enjoy it," said the woman. She smiled, and, still pedaling, took her hands off the handlebars (*How?* wondered Lily. *How?*) and stretched them up over her head, leaning first left, then right. "When my kids were young, people would tell me that the days are long but the years are short, and I'd think they were crazy. It all felt so endless. I thought I'd be changing diapers for the rest of my life!"

Lily nodded. She could remember being a new mother, so tied to the rhythm of Morgan's waking and sleeping and eating that she'd lost all sense of herself as an independent person, and felt like she'd turned into a servant-slash-feeding station that existed solely for her daughter's nourishment and care. But she'd loved those years, when Morgan had been small, when Morgan had needed her, when Lily knew how to solve all of her daughter's problems, when any pain or heartache could be banished with a bottle or a cookie or a Band-Aid and a kiss. She remembered how Morgan used to wake up early, at four or five in the morning. She'd fuss a little, and Lily would go to collect her. Morgan would be lying in her crib, looking around, blinking like a wise little owl in stretchy pink footie pajamas. Lily would change her and carry her back to bed. She'd sit with her back against the headboard and Morgan warm in her arms, nursing contentedly, then staring up at her with her fathomless dark eyes while Don slept beside them, on his belly with his arms flung wide and one leg kicked free of the covers. *This is all I ever wanted*, Lily would think. She would reflect on the dark times she'd endured, the bad things that had happened: her father, who'd had a temper, her mother, who'd been so worn down by marriage and work and Lily's three brothers that she had no time or energy left by the time Lily came along. She'd think, too, about the handful of desperate weeks right before she'd started college, and tell herself that those things had served to bring her to this place. *I'm so blessed*, Lily would think, with her daughter in her arms. *I'm so lucky. I hope things never change.*

Of course, things had. That was the nature of life. Kids get older. Marriages evolve. In the last ten years, Don had gotten busier as the congregation expanded. There was the men's Bible group to run, the annual couples' retreat to organize, the youth pastors to mentor. When the pandemic happened, Don had started streaming Sunday services, which had become surprisingly popular. The church had gotten more members, and Don had gotten more attention, which had eventually meant more money. There was enough to pay for Morgan's college now; enough to take more vacations, enough to say that their struggling days were over . . . and if Don was barely home, if he was distant and distracted when he was around, that seemed a reasonable trade-off for the chance to bring the Gospel to so many more new believers.

A time for every purpose under heaven, Lily told herself. Sweet little babies became beautiful young women. Handsome young husbands became still-handsome middle-aged men. They get distinguished silver hair and lines around their eyes and new veneers on their teeth, an expense Don justified because of all the people watching him in high definition. *Do you really think they'll decide to give their hearts to Jesus because your teeth are extra shiny?* Lily had thought, before chiding herself for being uncharitable.

Daughters grow up. Husbands buy shiny new teeth. And young brides become middle-aged moms, and end up on crowded bike paths, half a mile behind their daughters, trying not to fall.

"Oh, there's the bridge!" said the old lady, and pointed. Lily jerked her head up, long enough to glimpse the George Washington Bridge stretching over the Hudson.

"Beautiful," she said, without turning her head, feeling the other rider's scrutiny.

"Are you sure you're all right?" the older woman asked.

"Fine," Lily said, trying to sound like she meant it as the path curved, angling into a short, steep uphill.

"Downshift!" the other woman called merrily . . . too late for Lily, who almost fell off her bike because she was in too high a gear to keep pedaling. She bit her lip and pushed her bike up the hill, half-walking, half-jogging, trying not to fall too far behind as the group pedaled under the bridge and into the Bronx.

"And watch out for the switchbacks!" she heard the other woman call.

The what? Lily had time to think before she saw the section of path she was on end in a hairpin turn. She almost fell . . . but she didn't. She swung her bike around the turn, and then around the next one, again and again until she'd ridden off the path and onto the street, where the rest of the group was waiting.

"I did it," Lily whispered to herself, pedaling along the pavement. Then she said it again, out loud. "I did it!"

"On your left!" someone shouted, the instant before he or she went whipping past her in a blur of pumping legs and spinning wheels.

"Oh, sugar!" Lily squeaked, and jerked the handlebars. Her front tire hit the curb, and suddenly the bike was sliding out from underneath her and the ground was rushing up to meet her. Lily fell onto the street with a bone-jarring thud, her left hip and shoulder taking most of the impact, the bike landing on top of her. She could feel herself bleeding where the pedal's serrated teeth had scraped the meat of her calf.

Lily closed her eyes. *This was a mistake,* she thought. She wasn't ready for this kind of trip, for riding this kind of distance, day after day after day. They should have rescheduled, waited until next summer, so that Don and Morgan could ride, like they'd planned, and Lily could do her handful of miles, and meet them for lunch. But Morgan had been so insistent, so determined that it had to be this trip, this summer. *Please, Mom, it looks like so much fun,* and *I really want to see Niagara Falls, Olivia said it was so beautiful* and *We'll just be rattling around the house with Daddy gone.* Morgan had seemed frantic, almost desperate to get Lily to agree, and when Lily had, her daughter had hugged her, unprompted. She'd seemed so happy. So where was Morgan now that Lily was on the ground, bleeding, with her bicycle on top of her? Somewhere in the distance, oblivious, and getting farther and farther away.

"Are you okay?" asked the sag wagon driver—Jasper, Lily remembered—who'd appeared out of nowhere and was bending over Lily, picking up the bike, then offering her his hand.

Lily made herself nod, and Jasper helped her to her feet.

"I'm sorry," Lily said.

"Why are you sorry?" Jasper asked. "You didn't fall on purpose, did you?" He lifted her bike over the curb, leaned it against a tree, and guided Lily toward a bench. "Just sit for a minute. Take a breath, okay?"

Lily swallowed hard. Her knee was scraped. Her calf was bleeding. Her shoulder throbbed where she'd landed. She felt clumsy, and old, and weak. She felt, in a word, pathetic. She struggled not to cry as Jasper unzipped a first aid kit, knelt down, and gently dabbed the blood and grit off her leg.

"Just a little road rash," he announced, wiping off her calf. "I don't think we'll have to amputate."

"Road rash?"

He gestured toward her leg. "Cyclist plus pavement equals road rash. Happens to all of us. Have you been drinking?" At first Lily thought Jasper was asking about liquor. She'd started shaking her head, preparing to explain that she wasn't drunk, just desperately inexperienced, before realizing that he was talking about water, not alcohol.

"A little," she said. It was a hot day, and she'd been thirsty for at least the last hour, but she wasn't coordinated enough to pull her water bottles free and drink while she was riding. Maybe she'd get one of those hydrating backpacks that some of the riders had, with a tube that hung over your shoulder so you could just pop it in your mouth. The guy at the bike shop had tried to sell her one, but she'd refused. She hadn't wanted to look like she was trying to impersonate a real cyclist, and have the other riders think she knew what she was doing, when she didn't.

She drank half of the water in the bottle in a few swallows, and tried to apologize, to explain that her husband was supposed to be the one doing the riding. "I'm not very good at this. As you probably noticed."

Jasper didn't answer. He was probably too polite to say *You're terrible and it's obvious.*

Lily took another pull from the water bottle. Her knee had stopped bleeding, the scrapes gleaming under a sheen of Neosporin. "I thought it would be nice for Morgan and I to have some time together, but she's barely spoken to me since we got in the car."

Jasper gave a sage nod. His braids rustled as he moved. "I've got two sisters. I know how that goes. Teenage girls and their mothers." He pushed his hands together and made a noise like an explosion before pulling them apart. "How about I put your bike in the van and we motor on to the lunch stop?"

"That sounds . . ." Lily swallowed hard against the lump in her throat. "Yes. Please. Let's do that." Jasper got to his feet, extending his arm, waiting for Lily to put her hand in his so he could pull her to her feet.

"What did your mother do?" Lily asked as he walked beside her, wheeling her bike to where the van was waiting. "When your sisters were awful?"

"She hung in there," he said. "She waited until they got older. I think that's all you can do. And call on Jesus, if that's your thing."

Lily started to say that it was absolutely her thing, that her husband was a pastor, that maybe Jasper had seen him on You-Tube. Then she pressed her lips together. Sometimes Morgan got funny about having strangers know she was a preacher's kid. "I'll call on anyone who can help me," she said, and Jasper held the door open, giving her a boost up into the van. Lily pulled her seat belt across her chest and stared at the cars and buildings rushing past the window. She thought that maybe Jasper's mother had the right idea. The way things were going, it actually would require a divine intervention to get Morgan to open up.

Sebastian

Lunch the first day was a picnic in a park. They'd ridden another easy twenty miles, parallel to the Saw Mill Parkway, with cars humming past, just on the other side of the trees. Sebastian knew there were towns they were passing through, but it felt almost like riding through a tunnel, just greenery overhead and on either side, without a house or a street or a car in sight.

A few miles' ride off the trail, on twisty two-lane roads, brought them to their hotel in Mount Kisco at just after five p.m. Sebastian and Lincoln were sharing a room with two twin beds. They did rock, paper, scissors to see who'd get the first shower, and after they both picked paper, then both picked rock, Sebastian won the third round. The hot water made him groan happily. He tilted his head back and let the water rain down on his sweaty face, feeling his muscles unwinding after the day's sustained effort, his entire body glowing and relaxed. As far as Sebastian was concerned, that feeling was one of the best parts of working out, running, or riding your bike—not how you felt while you were doing it, but, instead, how you felt when it was done.

He stayed under the spray until Lincoln started politely

knocking and inquiring whether Sebastian intended to use up all the hot water. Then he dried off, pulled on his off-the-bike outfit of khaki shorts, short-sleeved navy-blue linen shirt and suede sneakers, patted aftershave on his cheeks, smoothed product through his hair, and sat on the bed to wait for Lincoln.

"Good day?" he asked his friend.

"Good day," Lincoln replied. "Let me see the pictures?"

Sebastian got his phone, and they compared shots from the day's ride: the wooden birdhouses nailed to tree trunks amid the verdant woods in Westchester; a sugar maple tree with leaves that had just begun to change, falling to the ground when the wind blew in a shower of green and gold coins. A squirrel, perched on its hind legs on the side of the path, watching the bikes blur by; the bridge over the Harlem River; the bits of milkweed fluff that filled the air, the brown water, far below. Sebastian's stomach grumbled, and Lincoln checked the time. "Let's go," he said. Five minutes later, the group was gathered in the parking lot. At Abby's direction, they piled into the sag wagon and the Spoke'n Four's RV for the ten-minute ride to the night's restaurant, which served, per their schedule, "traditional American cuisine."

The hostess led them to a long table and handed out the menus. Sebastian's stomach growled as he smelled fresh bread, garlic, and roasting meats. The old folks had claimed one end of the long rectangular table. The family of four was seated at the other side, with the rest of the group filling in the seats between them.

Sebastian saw that the chair across from Abby was conveniently vacant. He paused, eyebrows lifted. "Anyone sitting here?" he asked.

Abby smiled tightly. "Help yourself."

Sebastian grinned, sat, and perused the menu: steaks and burgers and a spicy fried chicken sandwich, various pastas and local cheeses. He thought he'd be able to eat one of everything and, after a quick consult with Lincoln, narrowed it down to shrimp linguine as an appetizer, a pan-roasted pork chop with spiced Hudson Valley apples for his main course, and a side of buttermilk Vidalia onion rings. He set his menu down to look at Abby, who had her head bent over her menu. There were the curls he remembered, still damp from the shower, the pale skin that had flushed so enchantingly, the full pink lips. The humorless expression, however, was new.

"Good ride today?" he said. She wore small sparkly earrings, which made him remember nibbling at the tender spot just beneath her earlobes.

"Yes," Abby said tightly, before turning away from him and toward the woman sitting beside her. Sebastian looked her over: middle-aged, petite, and well-maintained, with short brown hair, long eyelashes, lots of jewelry and a suspicious gaze. Abby said, "Sebastian, this is my mother, Eileen Fenske. Mom, this is Sebastian . . . Pierson?"

"Piersall," said Sebastian, extending his hand to the woman who, now that he was looking, bore a slight resemblance to Abby. Eileen's hair was darker; her body was almost boyish, but she had the same wide forehead and firm chin as her daughter. "Pleasure to meet you." He smiled more broadly. "You're Abby's mom? I would have guessed you were her big sister."

Eileen waved away the flattery with a smile that didn't touch her eyes, and studied Sebastian, tilting her head, lipsticked lips pursed. "Did you two know each other before the trip?"

"We've met," Sebastian said, at the same time that Abby said, "No."

Eileen's eyes flicked from her daughter to Sebastian and back again.

"We met very briefly. In New York. Years ago," Abby said.

"Hmm." Eileen's eyes were bright, her gaze even sharper. "Where in New York?"

Sebastian and Abby looked at each other. Abby said, "Convention," at the same instant that Sebastian said, "Bar."

Eileen tilted her head, looking like an inquisitive bird contemplating a worm.

"We met at the bar, at a convention," Sebastian said. He shot Abby a look that he hoped said, *Help me out.* Abby shook her head slightly and stared down at the table.

"What kind of convention was this?" Eileen inquired. "And why were you at a convention in New York?"

"It was more of a job fair," Abby said.

Eileen's brow furrowed. "So not a convention," she said.

"Convention, job fair. Six of one, half dozen of the other," Abby said, sounding a little desperate. She kicked Sebastian's shin under the table. Not gently. Sebastian winced.

"You were job hunting in New York?" Eileen's manicured fingertips tapped at the table as she stared at Abby.

Abby squirmed. "Just, you know. Keeping my options open," she said, her voice faint. "You know, I should probably go check on"—she gestured toward the end of the table—"everyone else."

Eileen wasn't letting her off the hook. "Would Mark be willing to move to New York?" she asked.

"We haven't discussed it," said Abby.

"Who's Mark?" asked Sebastian.

This time, it was Abby and her mother who spoke at the same time. Abby said, "My boyfriend," while Eileen said, "Her boyfriend."

Ah, Sebastian thought, and felt a twinge of disappointment.

"They've been together for two years," Eileen said.

Hmm, thought Sebastian, doing the math. Did that mean that Abby had been with Mark when she'd hooked up with him?

"Mark is a physician," Eileen said, her voice a little smug.

"Podiatrist," Abby said quietly.

Eileen ignored her daughter. "He's Abby's summer-camp sweetheart. They met when Abby was thirteen."

"Wow." Sebastian turned to Abby. "Have you been together all that time?"

"No."

"Oh, it's a lovely story," Eileen said, hurrying to fill the silence that even she had to notice wasn't quite comfortable. "Mark moved to Philadelphia to do his internship. They ran into each other when Abby was working as a camp counselor and Mark was volunteering. And they picked up right where they left off!" She lifted her eyebrows, looking toward her daughter. "Right, Abby?"

"That's right." Abby's voice was flat, and Sebastian was relieved to see the waitress approach.

Sebastian ordered his dinner. "And the cheese plate for the table." He smiled at Abby. "You'll have some, right?"

Abby bit her lip and didn't answer.

"And for you, ma'am?" the waitress asked Eileen.

Eileen asked for the lentil soup, then spent several moments negotiating the preparation of her Caesar salad—"dressing on the side, with grilled chicken, and if you can ask them to hold the croutons and go light on the cheese, that would be great." Abby's voice was barely audible as she asked for the salmon. Sebastian wondered if Abby was remembering the pasta he'd made for her. He tried, and failed, to catch her eye. Eileen's lips had thinned as she looked at her daughter. Abby had raised her chin, and her shoulders were hunched up around her ears. Neither woman spoke, but the tension hung over the table like a fog.

"So!" Sebastian began, determined to lighten the mood. "Eileen, have you done a lot of cycling?" He reached into his back pocket and pulled out his reporter's notebook. "This trip's actually business and pleasure. I'm writing a story about the Empire State Trail for Scoop.com."

"Oh, is this on the record?" Eileen said, looking flattered.

"If you don't mind."

"Well, it's actually my first trip." Eileen spread her napkin in her lap. "But I'm very happy to be doing it with Abby. I did a lot of indoor cycling during the pandemic, and it's a pleasure to be back in the world, with people."

"Abby, how about you?" Sebastian asked, writing down Eileen's quote. "Have you ridden the trail before?"

"No."

Sebastian chided himself for asking a question that could be answered with a single negative or affirmative. Rookie mistake. "What's your favorite part about trips like these?"

"The quiet," said Abby, giving him a hard look, before turning to Lincoln. "How'd you two find out about Breakaway?"

"We're doing a package about local getaways. I read about the Empire State Trail when it opened, and I was researching the different companies that lead trips along the trail."

Sebastian listened to them chat. He ate his pasta, politely offering some to Eileen, who declined, and to Abby, who looked a little regretful as she shook her head. By the time Sebastian set the fork down, Abby was talking to Lincoln, leaving Sebastian to stare at her profile. He watched as she gathered her curls and deftly twisted them into a bun at the base of her neck while saying something that made Lincoln laugh.

Okay, then. He turned back to Eileen. "So you're from Philadelphia?"

"The suburbs. But Abby lives in Center City. She and Mark like being right in the thick of things." She patted her lips a little smugly.

"Do they live near the Liberty Bell?" Sebastian riffled through his memories of a long-ago field trip for Philadelphia landmarks. "Or the Rocky statue?"

Eileen gave him a thin-lipped smile. "Mark lives in Rittenhouse Square, which is one of the nicest neighborhoods in the city. Abby's got an apartment in South Philadelphia, but I think they're planning on moving in together."

Sebastian felt something strange in the vicinity of his chest—a sensation it took him a moment to recognize as disappointment. Which was surprising. Maybe he assumed that Abby had been waiting for him, like a piece of luggage he'd never claimed, going around and around on the conveyor belt until he finally came back to fetch it. Of course, she hadn't put her life on hold for the past two years. And, he thought, a boyfriend was not a husband. Especially a boyfriend who wasn't around and wouldn't be for the next thirteen nights.

"Have you been to Philadelphia?" Eileen asked him.

"Not in a while. But I hear good things." He looked to see if Abby was listening, but she still had her eyes on Lincoln. *Patience,* he told himself. "Does Abby have brothers or sisters?"

"One of each," said Eileen. "Her brother's married with two kids. And her sister lives in New Jersey with her husband, right on the other side of the Delaware."

When the entrées arrived, Sebastian spent a few minutes tucking into his pork, which was, all things considered, delicious, flavorful, and tender. Eileen meticulously scoured her salad for errant croutons and removed each sliver of cheese while Abby nibbled at her salmon, talked to Lincoln, and continued to ignore Sebastian.

"So you're a reporter?" Eileen asked him. "Do you mostly do travel writing?"

"Mostly investigative stuff," Sebastian said. He told her

about the restaurant roundup they'd done recently, and the story they'd written called "Don't Go Drinking Without Me," where they'd gotten a bunch of sommeliers to talk about their techniques for upselling expense-account diners, and how civilians could enlist them to get the best bottles. He learned that Abby's parents were divorced, that Abby's father was a rabbi (Eileen took pains to point out that he'd been in finance while they'd been married), and that Abby worked in early-childhood education.

"'Worked in early-childhood education' means I taught nursery school for a few years," said Abby, who must have tuned in to their conversation at some point.

"You were studying for your master's degree," said Eileen, looking like she'd taken a brief break to suck on a lemon.

"Until I dropped out," said Abby.

Eileen asked, "Sebastian, did you always know you wanted to be a reporter?"

"Hmm. Not exactly. I kind of fell into it, I guess. I started writing for the school paper, then Lincoln and I started doing our own thing, and it turned out I was good at it . . ."

"Adequate," Lincoln said dryly.

"And I liked it. I got lucky."

"Lucky," Abby repeated. She sounded wistful. And, Sebastian saw, her mother was looking at her, with an expression that blended frustration and sympathy.

"Abby, what's the weirdest thing that's ever happened on a ride?" Sebastian asked.

"Well, I actually haven't led a trip like this," Abby said. "But my friend Lizzie leads a bunch. And she's told me some horror stories." She set down her fork, smiling faintly. "I remember she told me about an eighteen-day trip in Italy with a couple on their honeymoon. On the second day, the husband found out that his wife had been cheating on him with her maid of honor. The rest of that trip must have been delightful," Abby said.

"What about you, though?" Sebastian asked. "Anything funny happen on the rides you've led?"

Abby closed her eyes to think. "Well, let's see. The one trip I did, there was a couple on a tandem. The husband was the captain, of course, and the wife was the stoker. Except he was a really experienced rider who did a few centuries every summer—hundred-mile rides," she said to Eileen, who nodded. "And she'd mostly done spinning classes." Abby gave her mother a significant look, which Eileen ostentatiously ignored. "Maybe the guy thought it would average out. Like, if he could do a hundred miles a day and she could only do twenty, between the two of them, they could manage sixty."

"Ha," said Lincoln. "Not how it works, right?"

"Especially not on a tandem. The wife was so pissed that, by the end of the first day, she'd just stopped pedaling. Like, she literally unclipped her feet from the pedals and just sat there like a sack of potatoes." Abby shook her head, smiling a little at the memory. "It was beautiful."

The waitress reappeared, making her way down the table to take dessert and coffee orders. Sebastian requested tiramisu and a cappuccino. Abby got a cannoli and a coffee. Eileen asked for tea with lemon, no cream, no sugar, then excused herself and headed toward the restrooms.

Sebastian saw his chance. He looked across the table and cleared his throat, making sure Lincoln wasn't listening. "Hey," he said to Abby.

Abby looked at him, her face expressionless. "Yes?"

"Should we, ah, get our stories straight?"

She widened her eyes, smirking a little. "I guess we met at a bar at a convention."

"Job fair," Sebastian reminded her. "Except you're not supposed to be job hunting in New York, because of Doctor Mark, the doctor." He saw Abby smile, even though she was trying not to.

She leaned toward him, close enough for him to catch a whiff of her perfume and shampoo. "Look. I don't want my mother knowing we hooked up at a bar," she said, her voice low. "Is that so terrible?"

"No." Sebastian thought that Lincoln was listening to them. He dropped his voice. "But I wish you'd left me your number before you took off."

"Why?"

Lincoln was definitely listening. Sebastian plowed ahead. "Because I wanted to call you." The words had popped out before he could consider them. Abby looked surprised, then dubious. Sebastian gulped from his water glass, wondering what he was doing. "And it's good to see you again. You look good." *Good*, he thought, groaning inwardly. Such an eloquent compliment, from someone who used words for a living. It was true, though. In the sunshine, he'd been able to appreciate the healthy sheen of her skin, the shades of cinnamon and caramel in her hair, and her faintly freckled cheeks. And in the candlelit restaurant, she was as pretty as she'd been in his bed.

Abby gave him a stiff nod, but he thought he could see her softening, her shoulders descending and her posture becoming less guarded.

"I don't want to cause any trouble," Sebastian said.

She nodded again . . . but, in his head, he imagined a different scenario. Abby looking up at him, asking what he did want. Not the Abby currently sitting across the table, in a black short-sleeved tee shirt and cropped pants, but the Abby he remembered from their night together, wearing nothing but a pair of turquoise silk panties; flushed and fragrant and eager. The Abby who'd been just as into everything they'd done as he'd been. He remembered how he'd pulled her onto his lap, how her lips had closed around his fork when he'd fed her a bite of pasta. The softness of her skin; the sweetness of her mouth. He shifted on his seat, looking at her intently. And she was looking right back at him, lips slightly parted, her eyes gone dark.

"Hey—" he said. Abby straightened up as Eileen approached the table, and whatever had been swelling between Sebastian and Abby vanished like it had never been.

Abby leaned forward. "I have a boyfriend," she said, her voice quiet, her gaze intent.

Sebastian nodded. He'd heard what she said . . . but he thought he heard something else, too. A note of hesitation. A hint of doubt. He saw the way her teeth were digging into the soft flesh of her lip, and the crinkles at the corners of her eyes. Reluctance? Regret? Second thoughts? A burning desire to renounce Doctor Mark and join him in his bed that very night?

Sebastian couldn't remember the last time he'd been interested in a second round with a woman he'd already taken to bed. There were always new delights to sample, new lands to discover, and he was always eager to move on. Was it just the challenge of going after a girl who had her mother as a traveling companion and a boyfriend back home? Was it Abby herself?

Sebastian remembered thinking about Abby for days after they'd hooked up. Days. Weeks. Possibly months, he realized, remembering how he'd catch a glimpse of curly hair on the street, or smell familiar perfume in the subway, and he'd feel his heart swell and his pulse start racing; his feet moving faster as they tried to catch up, and the inevitable disappointment when the woman turned out to be a stranger. It wasn't just the challenge, or the novelty. It was her.

"Get a good night's sleep. Lots of miles tomorrow," Abby said, patting her lips, with a smile at everyone around the table.

Sebastian scooped up one last spoonful of tiramisu, and stuck close to Abby as they left the restaurant, plotting how he could sit next to her on the van for the ride back to the hotel, and convince her to ride with him in the morning.

Abby

H i, honey," Mark said. "How goes the ride?"

"So far so good." Abby had come back from dinner, gotten immediately into her pajamas, and curled up on her hotel bed. She knew it was likely that the bedspread upon which she was currently reposing had absorbed all manner of bodily excretions but was too exhausted to care. She'd lit the scented candle she'd packed to combat any strange hotel room smells, which could range from must and mildew to cigarette smoke or aggressive cleaning chemicals. She brought a candle with her on every trip, to make every new room at least smell a little bit like home.

"It's going well. Except . . ." Abby paused to yawn enormously, stretching her arms over her head, feeling how glad her body was to be prone and not upright, leaning over the handlebars. "My mother's here. She showed up at the bike shop this morning. I almost had a heart attack."

"Ah," said Mark. Abby knew that "ah." Her heart sank.

"You wouldn't have had anything to do with that, right?" she asked, keeping her tone light.

Mark paused. Abby felt her anger gathering. "She really wants to spend time with you. That's what she told me, and I believed her. She seemed very sincere."

"So you . . ." Abby's brain was fizzing. "You told her about the trip? You got her a bike?"

"Lizzie helped with that part." Mark paused. "Your mother told me that she'd taken a trip with Marni, right before she got married, and that she went somewhere with Simon after he finished college, and that she never took a trip with you."

"She never took a trip with me because every place she wanted to take me was some version of a fat farm." Over the years, Eileen had pitched these trips with words like "wellness retreat" or "mindful reset," "detox" or "cleanse." Five days doing yoga in Tulum! A spa week at Canyon Ranch in Arizona! A hiking trip in Ireland! All of Eileen's proposals had two things in common: lots of physical activity and healthy (translation: low-fat, low-carb, low-calorie) meals. Her last offer, Abby recalled, had involved a spa in California that was famous for its coffee colonics.

"Is she being awful?" Mark asked.

Abby took a deep breath, preparing to list Eileen's depredations. She called up the picture of her mother, riding alongside her. That had been . . . not awful. Not good, but at least, not awful. When they'd stopped for lunch and, then, at dinner, Eileen hadn't said a single word about anything on Abby's plate. Abby could feel her mother's scrutiny and judgment, but maybe that was her own interpretation, seeing what she expected to see, after all those bad years. *She's trying*, Abby realized. *I should be grateful*.

"No," she finally said. "She isn't being awful. I was just surprised." She adjusted the pillows. "And it's stressful enough, leading my first ride, without having my mom watching everything I do. And having to watch out for her. There's a big difference between riding a stationary bike and riding in the real world."

"I know." Mark's voice was gentle. "I'm sorry if this is causing you trouble. That was the last thing I'd ever want. But, like I said, she seemed sincere. And she was very persistent."

"I can only imagine."

"Please don't be mad at me," Mark said. "Or Lizzie." He lowered his voice. "I sent you a little treat. It should be waiting at your next hotel."

"Oh, that was nice of you."

"Am I forgiven?" he asked.

"Depends on how good of a treat you sent," Abby said.

"So tell me who else is on the ride, besides Eileen?"

Abby took him through the roster: Lily and Morgan; the Presser family, the fancy Landons, the four old folks, all of whom had ridden their bikes across the country—twice, in Ted's case. At dinner, Ted had showed pictures of himself dipping his bike's rear wheel in the Pacific Ocean in Oregon and his front wheel in the Atlantic in Virginia. "And there's a couple of guys about our age, but I've barely seen them. They're just grinding out the miles, going as fast as they can." Abby found herself hurrying through Sebastian and Lincoln. She didn't want to think too hard about why.

"Well, that's no fun." When Abby yawned again, Mark said, "Get some rest, I'll call you tomorrow." He paused. "I miss you."

"I miss you, too," Abby said, and tried not to dwell on what she wasn't saying.

Sebastian

Day Two: Mount Kisco to Poughkeepsie
Sixty-one miles

The alarm went off at six thirty the next morning. Sebastian groaned as he worked his way upright. His legs ached and his back felt stiff. Nothing that wouldn't disappear once he started moving around, he thought, and rubbed his face, checking to make sure Lincoln was still in bed before heading toward the shower. "Be a dear and make me a cup of coffee?" he called. Lincoln's hand emerged from underneath the covers to give him the finger.

When Sebastian stepped out of the bathroom, freshly shaved, with a towel around his waist, a cup of coffee was waiting for him, just as he knew one would be. The Universe loved him, and Lincoln did, too. Lincoln was sitting up in bed with his back against the headboard, peering at his phone. When he looked at Sebastian, his eyes, behind his glasses, were wide enough to show whites all the way around the iris.

An uneasy feeling wrapped greasy fingers around Sebastian's midsection. "What?" he asked.

"Did you, by any chance, look at TikTok last night?" Lincoln said. Sebastian shook his head. "You might want to sit down."

Lincoln cued up the app and handed Sebastian his phone. Sebastian sank onto the side of the bed as he looked at the screen, which displayed a young woman's face—her handle, he saw, was MissAlyssy.

Lincoln leaned over his shoulder to hit play, and Sebastian recoiled as he saw his own face, in the center of a Wild West–style WANTED poster. *Have You Dated This Man?* read the text. As he watched, a girl's head and shoulders popped up in front of the poster. "Hey, my BK ladies and they-dies," she said, in a high, breathy voice. A high, breathy, *familiar* voice, that Sebastian could recall, all too well, only the last time he'd heard it—two weeks ago? Three?—it had been squeaking his name in ecstasy. "Storytime! This morning I got together with my besties for brunch. We were comparing dating app horror stories—as one does—and it turns out that seven out of eight of us—I REPEAT, SEVEN OUT OF EIGHT—had all, um, spent time with this gentleman." The picture behind her switched to a screenshot of Sebastian's dating profile. His face was clearly visible, as were the words "free tonight?" circled in red. "Now, he's clear about just looking for a hookup, and you know ya girl is down for that. I'm not saying I was ghosted, or gaslit, or love-bombed, or in any way traumatized. No single ladies were harmed in the making of this video. But when you find out that the same guy has had"—she paused delicately—"encounters . . . with literally seven-eighths of your friend group?" Here, the camera panned briefly toward a clutch of young women seated around a table. Sebastian saw mimosas, French toast, and more than one familiar face as the women waved at the camera. "It kind of made me wonder how many more of us there are out there." The narrator smiled, a smug, cat-that-got-the-cream kind of smirk. "So I thought I'd ask. If you've met this fella, drop your name or your story in the comments. And let me know if you want part two."

Sebastian felt his eyes getting wide and his cheeks getting hot as he read the hashtags—#kissingbandit #datinghorrorstories #singleinbrooklyn #manbehavingbadly #manwhorealert #redflag #mensuck #ladiesbeware.

"Kissing Bandit?" he said, mostly to himself. Even though he knew he hadn't done anything wrong—even though the girl who'd made the video had clearly said so—he still felt guilty, like he'd been called down to the principal's office for cheating on a math test, or he'd been caught lying to his parents. *Sebastian, we're very disappointed in you,* he heard his mom saying—for once, she was the hook; for once, she wasn't the problem—while his dad stood behind her, shaking his head.

"I guess that's what they're calling you," Lincoln said. While Sebastian had been staring at his phone, Lincoln had gotten into the shower, and out of it, and was dressed in his cycling shorts and jersey, brushing his teeth with the electric toothbrush he'd insisted on packing.

"They?" Sebastian stared at his friend. "What do you mean *they*? Is there more than one post about this?"

"There are several," Lincoln said stiffly.

"It's not that bad," Sebastian said, half to himself, half for Lincoln's benefit. He started to scroll, then stopped. Was it better to know exactly what was out there? Or would he just be torturing himself?

"Well, that post isn't," said Lincoln. "It's the, uh, other posts. And there are a number of replies that are . . ." He sat down in the chair in front of the hotel room's desk, wheeling it forward, then back, then forward again. ". . . somewhat problematic."

Sebastian steeled himself before looking at the number of responses, which was in the low four figures. He clicked. "OMG I KNOW THIS GUY TOO!" said the first reply, with a screenshot of a text exchange. "So do I," read the reply after that. "Me three," said the one below that.

"Is this trending?" Sebastian asked sharply.

"No," Lincoln said, and Sebastian did not have to stretch very far to imagine he could hear *not yet*. "But there's a counter." Lincoln sounded apologetic. "It's already in the triple digits." He shook his head, muttering, "I don't know whether I should be impressed or horrified."

Sebastian drew himself up indignantly. "I didn't do anything wrong."

"Of course not," Lincoln said.

Sebastian couldn't keep still. He began gathering his dirty clothes and toiletries in jerky movements and cramming them into his duffel bag. "None of these women are saying I did anything wrong. Are they?"

"They are not," Lincoln said.

"There's nothing wrong with hookups." Sebastian yanked his bag's zipper.

"Not a thing in the world," said Lincoln. "But, just the same . . ." Lincoln ran his hands over his head. "It does call to mind West Elm Caleb."

Sebastian exhaled noisily. Ever since he'd read the post, he'd felt the specter of West End Caleb, a serial dater who'd been TikTok-infamous a few years back, floating in the hotel room's air, waiting to be invoked.

"West End Caleb told girls he was in love with them," Sebastian said, his voice clipped. "He told them all that they were beautiful and special and perfect. He sent them playlists. Then he never called them again. That's why he was a bad guy. I never did any of that! Nobody's saying I've done anything wrong!"

"No-o-o," Lincoln said, stretching out the word in a manner suggesting that he really meant "yes."

"Like, on Tinder. I only matched with girls in the 'free tonight' category."

" 'Free tonight?' That's a thing?"

Sebastian nodded. Lincoln looked slightly horrified, before saying, "I guess it's better than 'booty call.' Or 'DTF.' Or 'U up?'" He shook his head, then looked down as his phone chimed.

"What?" Sebastian demanded as Lincoln started laughing.

"Okay. I'm sorry. It's—well. This one girl compared your bedroom to a clown car."

Sebastian growled.

"It was funny!" Lincoln said.

"I didn't do anything wrong," Sebastian said again.

"Yes. I agree. I agree completely. I'm on your side. Come on." Lincoln pulled up the blankets and smoothed the pillowcases until his bed looked just as pristine as it had when they'd walked into the room.

"You know there are people who do that," Sebastian said.

Lincoln just grabbed his bike from where it was leaning against the wall. "This will blow over." He paused as Sebastian wheeled his own bike toward the door. "Except, here's an idea."

"What's that?"

"Abby," said Lincoln.

Sebastian tensed. Did Lincoln know he'd slept with Abby, too? And did Abby know about the video?

This was bad. Very bad. "What about Abby?"

"How about, just as a thought exercise, instead of trying to hook up with her, you try to be her friend?"

Sebastian stared at Lincoln. Lincoln met Sebastian's gaze with his eyes wide open.

"I wasn't trying to hook up with her," Sebastian finally said, praying that Lincoln didn't know he already had.

"I'm just saying, you have an M.O.," said Lincoln. "And not a lot of female friends."

"Lana is my friend," Sebastian protested.

"Lana is my wife," Lincoln said. "And, thus, the only woman

who's completely and indubitably off-limits to you." He looked sternly at Sebastian. "It's just an idea. But maybe, just this once, you try to do things differently."

Sebastian nodded. He wasn't holding crossed fingers behind his back, but he also wasn't verbally agreeing to anything . . . which, he thought, would give him plausible deniability in case anything did end up happening with Abby. Although that wasn't looking likely, he thought, glumly wheeling his bike out into the parking lot, preparing to start the day's ride.

Abby

Lizzie had done a seven-day trip from Buffalo to Albany, along the length of the Erie Canal, and had warned Abby about the scenery—or, more accurately, the lack of scenery—that upstate New York would feature. "It's pretty, but it's not superinteresting," Lizzie had said. Most days, they'd be covering similar terrain—a relatively flat path, sometimes paved, sometimes lined with dirt and crushed cinders, with a body of water—the Hudson River or the Erie Canal—off to one side, winding through forests, meadows, historic sites, and the scrubby backyards of small towns. Sometimes, they'd see the remnants of the railroad lines that had run before the trails had been converted—rusting trestles and decaying wooden ties. They'd ride through cemeteries, and pass monuments, old battlegrounds, reservoirs, and public parks. *Pretty,* Abby thought, as she led the group back onto the trail, *but not very exciting*.

They stopped for breakfast at a diner in Yorktown Heights and had lunch at a park in Brewster. Abby saw ducks and geese shepherding their goslings across the path, sometimes hissing at cyclists as they went by. There was also the occasional turtle sunning itself on a rock. Once, Abby saw a deer, standing in the forest maybe ten yards from the trail. It stared, wide-eyed, watching as Abby rode closer, before turning and bounding away.

It was another hot day, eighty-three degrees by noon, and humid. But fall was on the way, even if it still felt like summer. The leaves were beginning to change; the days were getting incrementally shorter, and the drugstore in Yorktown Heights, where they'd stopped to buy Lily some Bengay, had back-to-school supplies and Halloween candy on display.

Abby was riding sweep again. All the riders were up ahead, Sebastian and Lincoln in the lead, the teenagers behind them, the adults and senior citizens spread out in their wake, and Abby bringing up the rear, lost in thought.

Andy and Morgan, she saw, were riding side by side. Abby smiled to herself, remembering what it was like to be sixteen. She would pull out her phone after every class to see if Mark had emailed her on her AOL account, and she'd check the mailboxes at her parents' houses every day after school, because he'd send her little gifts—a bag of Fritos once; a small box of Godiva chocolates for Valentine's Day. He had wooed her at summer camp, and he'd never stopped, still never quite believing that she wanted him, always trying to win her heart.

Abby hadn't been excited about the prospect of Camp Golden Hills' boys. Back then, her heart belonged to Josh Hartnett and Adam Sandler. But Marissa had insisted that fat boys were better than no boys at all. "And you never know," she'd said. "Maybe some of them will be hot by the end of the summer. Come on!" she'd said, leading Abby and Leah down the path. "They're probably almost all here, and you've got to have someone picked out by Friday night."

Marissa and Leah had explained to the other camp newbies

the importance of staking a claim on a boy to go out with (what "going out with" as tweens at a summer camp meant, Abby would eventually learn, was treading water together during afternoon Free Swim and, eventually, attending the end-of-camp dance as a couple).

"What's Friday night?" asked Abby as Marissa towed her up a hill that overlooked the track and the athletic fields.

"Movie night," said Leah, with a doleful sigh. "They give us popcorn. Unsalted popcorn," she added.

Marissa tossed her hair and turned to Abby. "You just go to the nurse on Thursday and tell her you've got a sore throat. They'll give you salt for salt water to gargle with, and you save the salt for the popcorn." She rolled her eyes at her bunkmate. "Have I taught you nothing?" Turning back to Abby, she said, "I know all the tricks. Movie night is makeout night. They hand out blankets to sit on . . ." Another eyeroll, this one for the counselors' stupidity. "But kids just get under the blankets. And the counselors are supposed to, like, patrol, and break things up." She lowered her voice. "Only they're usually too busy sucking face with each other."

Leah said something in reply, but Abby didn't hear. She'd stopped listening, because that was the moment she saw Mark Medoff.

On an eighty-five-degree day, where the air was thick and hazy with humidity, Mark was wearing a Yankees sweatshirt, made of heavyweight cotton (to disguise his man-boobs, he'd later confess). His Air Jordans came up high on his shins, his board shorts hung almost to his knees, and his baseball cap was creased to keep as much of his face as possible in its shade. But he had the sweetest smile as he looked at her from beneath the brim of his cap. The sweetest smile and the kindest eyes.

"Ugh. No," Marissa hissed, when she saw where Abby's gaze

had gone. It was cruel, and ironic, but at Camp Golden Hills, as in the outside world, the heavier you were, the less status you had . . . and Mark was one of the heaviest boys at camp.

But by then Abby had seen Mark's smile. She'd also noted the goofy, slightly dumbstruck look on his face, a look suggesting that he'd seen her and had fallen instantly in love, just the way Eileen's Harlequins and the spicier novels her mother kept in a drawer in her bedside table had taught Abby that, someday, a man would.

She had also realized that, beside him, or in his arms, she would feel as dainty as Princess Buttercup when André the Giant carried her. Abby couldn't remember ever feeling dainty in her life. This boy could be her chance.

Boldly, she walked up to Mark, hearing admiring comments and even a wolf whistle, which was new. Back at home, nobody ever whistled at her, and the only comments she'd ever gotten from men on the streets were either "nice tits," "you should smile," or "you'd be pretty if you lost some weight."

"Hi," she said. "I'm Abby."

The boy ducked his head and said, "I'm Mark."

She asked where he was from (Long Island), how old he was (thirteen, same as she was), if this was his first summer at Camp Golden Hills (yes), and if he'd come because he wanted to, or because he'd been forced.

At that question, Mark finally stopped looking at his shoes and looked at Abby. "Little bit of both," he said. "Sometimes, I want to lose weight, and sometimes, I think I'd like to be four hundred pounds by the time I'm forty years old."

Abby blinked. "Really? Why?"

"Because," Mark said, "who'd be able to tell a four-hundred-pound man no?" He gave her a big goofy smile. "I'd be unstoppable. I'd do anything I wanted."

Abby laughed. Mark turned his smile toward her. His face was round, his cheeks full, his chins wobbly . . . but his smile was adorable. And he was funny. That counted for a lot.

"Do you want to sit with me at movie night?" she asked.

"Really?" he asked, once more managing to meet her eyes. Almost immediately he looked down again, his gaze sliding toward Marissa and Leah. "It's a joke, right?"

"No. No, it's not a joke."

"Promise?" he asked.

"Yes," Abby said. "I promise."

That night, when she came back to the bunk after the counselors led a sing-along around the bonfire (combined with lots of vigorous arm motions and marching in place, the better to burn calories), Abby found a note under her pillow, with the drawing of a heart, and her initials, and a small bag of M&Ms. *See you at movie night,* he'd written. *From your four-hundred-pound friend Mark.*

"Oh," she said, so enraptured that she forgot, for a few minutes, how hungry she was. She tucked the note away, after folding it carefully. She didn't see Mark the next day, but the next night brought even more treasures.

"OMG," Marissa breathed, as Abby reached under her pillow. There was another note—*I think you're beautiful,* it read—but, better than that, there was a snack-size bag of Fritos, the kind that kids (not Abby, but some of her classmates) got in their school lunches.

"Do you know how much he must've paid for these?" Marissa asked, cradling the Fritos as reverently as the Virgin Mary had ever held the baby Jesus.

Abby shook her head. She then heard about the vibrant black market at Golden Hills. A few of the counselors could be induced to look the other way when parents sent care packages or when older kids raided the hotel vending machines on field trips to Gettysburg and Washington. There were maintenance workers who could be bribed to bring candy bars or even fast food into camp. And Kara's sister, a Golden Hills survivor who was currently in college, would mail Kara sanitary supplies with Rolos and Twix bars and Laffy Taffy tucked into the maxipads.

"Ooh, he's got it bad," said Marissa. When Kelsey came bouncing into the cabin, Abby shoved the Fritos under her pillow. After lights-out, she ripped the bag open, as quietly as she could, and handed it around the bunk. Each girl got maybe three Fritos total. Abby tried to make hers last, setting them on her tongue to dissolve. She felt the burn of the salt and tasted the grit of the dissolving corn—or lab-made corn-like substance—and she smiled, remembering the feeling of Mark's hand in hers, how he looked at her like she was a goddess, or Paris Hilton, thin and pretty and perfect.

Mark lost a startling fifty pounds during his first summer at Golden Hills. By the last night of camp, he'd become something of a hunk, and the girls who'd once scorned him, including Marissa, were trying to flirt with him right in front of Abby. To no avail. Mark ignored them completely. He only had eyes for her.

"You'll come to my bat mitzvah," Abby said, at the end of the dance on the last night of camp. She and Mark had swayed together under the pavilion lights, leaning into each other with her hands on his shoulders and his hands on her waist.

"And I'll call you every Friday night," Mark promised. They kissed—that was as far as things had gotten that summer—and they'd both cried as they'd said their goodbyes. It was as satisfying and as sweet a first love as Abby could have hoped for.

Abby didn't expect to ever go back to Camp Golden Hills. Her father had promised her theater camp, and Abby still dreamed of going. But, later that fall, her parents' divorce became final, and

Abby's dad told her that there wasn't money for theater camp or for any camp—"not with Marni in college and Simon going next year." That spring, after her mother got engaged to Gary the Businessman, and started planning their autumn wedding, it turned out that there was enough money for camp. But not for theater camp. Just for Camp Golden Hills. "Don't you want to look good in the wedding pictures?" Eileen pleaded.

Abby told her, tersely, that she cared about how she looked in Eileen's wedding photos even less than she'd cared about how she'd looked in her bat mitzvah album. Once again, her begging and complaints got her nowhere.

In truth, Abby didn't resist that much. She didn't care about losing weight—if the second summer worked like the first, she'd only gain it back again. She wasn't thrilled about spending another six weeks starving, but she did want to see her friends again. And Mark.

That year, when she arrived, Mark was waiting for her on the steps of her cabin, with a bouquet of wildflowers in his hands, and a snack-size bag of Cheetos in the pouch of the hoodie he'd started wearing again.

"My goodness, will you look at that," Abby heard her mother murmur. Either Eileen didn't remember Mark from Abby's bat mitzvah, or she didn't recognize him, now that he'd gained back the weight. "How could that boy's parents let him get that big?"

Abby barely heard her mother. All she saw were Mark's eyes, his smile, the way he was looking at her, like she was his fondest dream come true. She got out of the car and ran to him. Mark got to his feet and opened his arms. When he hugged her, lifting her off her feet and swinging her around, it was like being embraced by a protective mountain, or like having an entire continent between her and her mother's disapproval and judgment. She pressed her face into his fabric-softener-scented sweatshirt, feeling small and protected. Whatever hurtful things her mother had to say would bounce right off Mark, and never make their way near her. "Hi," she whispered, and Mark had squeezed her even more tightly.

Abby and her sweetheart had a total of three summers at Camp Golden Hills. They ate their meals together: fresh fruit and a single serving of whole-grain cereal with skim milk for breakfast; salads with four ounces of salmon or chicken breast and low-calorie dressing for lunch; baked fish and sweet potatoes for dinner, with ice-milk sandwiches for dessert on Friday nights. In the afternoons, they walked laps around the track or they'd take advantage of the camp's hiking trails and of the counselors who preferred sitting by the lakeside, listening to music on their iPods, to keeping close watch over the campers. During Free Swim, Abby tried to coax Mark into the water. She'd tell him that nobody was looking, that no one cared, but most days he stayed on the shore, and, even when he joined her in the water, he never took off his tee shirt, and he always waited until at least some of the campers were distracted by a game of water volleyball or Marco Polo or keep-away before shucking his shoes and his sweatshirt and making a quick, jouncing dash into the shallows.

Mark taught Abby how to play Sudoku and Yahtzee and Chinese checkers. His generous allowance gave him access to a steady supply of contraband chips and Cheez-Its and candy bars. On Abby's birthday, he managed to get her a bucket of KFC, still mostly warm, and a chocolate malted milkshake, still mostly cold. He gave her his favorite Yankees sweatshirt, and Abby wore it everywhere, enjoying the feeling of being swallowed up by a garment that smelled like Mark, with sleeves that hung over her fingertips and a hem that draped past her knees.

Then there were the weekly movie nights, when Abby and Mark would cuddle on top of and, eventually, underneath a blanket, as the hour got later and the counselors less attentive. They'd kiss until their lips were chapped, until Abby's cheeks and chin were abraded by the stubble Mark had started to grow by their last summer. By July of that final year, when they'd both been sixteen, Abby let Mark work his hands up her shirt. By August, Mark let Abby touch his erection, but only outside of his satiny basketball shorts.

Finally, on the last movie night, while *Grease* played on the big screen, Abby slipped her fingers beneath the taut waistband of Mark's boxer shorts and, finally, felt her fingertips make contact with the silky skin of his unclothed penis.

In the humid August air, with the smell of the lake water clinging to their skin and their hair, she brushed his skin with her fingertips. Mark groaned, shuddering, pressing his body against hers, trapping her arm between their chests.

"Oh," she murmured, with her open mouth against his neck, as his body jerked, and warm, sticky liquid splashed out over her wrist and arm. Abby wanted to examine the slippery, bleach-smelling stuff. She thought that maybe she would even taste it, a desire prompted primarily by curiosity and only slightly by hunger (they'd served salmon for dinner, which was not Abby's favorite). She wondered what would happen if she rearranged herself, lying on her back on the blanket, and took Mark's hand and slid it under *her* waistband, down to where she could feel herself throbbing. Before she could try it, she heard Marissa hissing, "Incoming!" Mark hastily pulled a wad of paper napkins out of his hoodie's pouch. Gently, he wiped Abby's hand clean as one of the counselors came down the row of blankets, brandishing a flashlight, aiming its beam at each of the couples and saying things like "Hands above the equator, you two" and "Come on, guys, you know the rules."

When the counselor was gone, Mark pressed warm kisses on

Abby's forehead, her cheeks, her neck, her lips, whispering, "I love you," and Abby kissed him back, and said, "I love you, too."

The next morning, after the final weigh-ins, the parents arrived. Abby went back to Pennsylvania, and Mark returned to Long Island. They each took their newly reduced selves back to their respective high schools. Abby found herself the object of a great deal of male attention, and a senior on the football team asked her to go to the Homecoming dance with him.

She broke up with Mark over the phone. He took the news well, sounding sad, but not surprised. Abby told him that she wouldn't forget him; that she'd always remember kissing him under the blanket at movie night, how he'd gotten her fried chicken for her birthday, and how it felt when he held her, like no bad thing could hurt her.

After their last summer, they'd friended each other on social media. Abby had never unfriended or unfollowed. She had, however, muted Mark (probably around the time he'd posted his first picture of himself with a girl). She knew, through Marissa, who kept in touch with everyone from camp, that Mark had gone to Duke for college, then to California for podiatry school, but, beyond that, she'd heard nothing. She'd never looked. She'd let him slip from her mind, turning him into a sweet memory, a part of her past. Except Mark had set the standard for every subsequent relationship. It hadn't taken Abby long to learn just how hard it would be for subsequent boyfriends to compare.

She'd lost her virginity the summer before college, in her bedroom in her dad's house, when her father was busy teaching an adult bar mitzvah class. Then, six weeks into her freshman year at Penn State, she'd met a rugby player named Chris at a fraternity party. They'd both been a few beers past tipsy when they'd gone back to her dorm room, climbed into her single bed, and fooled around until Chris had passed out, snoring, beside her. When

Abby woke up she'd found Chris looking at her in the predawn dimness. Instead of the awed pleasure she remembered from Mark's face on movie night, Chris wore a look she recognized from her mother. Chris had looked displeased and disappointed. Possibly disgusted. Maybe even revolted. Like he couldn't get away from her fast enough.

Beer goggles, Abby had thought, hating him. Hating herself. Remembering every joke she'd heard about how even a 2 becomes a 10 at closing time, and thinking that, in the black skirt and black top she'd worn to the party, in the dim light, she'd probably looked better. Thinner.

Chris, meanwhile, had lurched to his feet so fast it was as if the sheets had caught fire. Abby watched as he bent over, groping for his shoes and socks, which he'd abandoned on the floor. She noticed that the hair on his chest and shoulders kept going, covering his back and legs in what was more or less a pelt. "I gotta get going," he'd muttered.

At five o'clock in the morning on a Saturday? "Do you have a paper route?" she'd asked.

Chris had blinked. "Huh?"

"Nothing. Never mind."

Chris had nodded uncertainly. "Well. See ya." He hadn't even bothered to put his shoes on before he'd opened her door, looked left, then right, then left again, to make sure the hallway was empty, before making his escape with his sneakers in his hand.

Abby had flopped onto her back, dispirited and disgusted with herself. At least she would never see or hear from Chris again. Penn State was a big school, with thousands of students and a huge, sprawling campus, and Abby didn't remember ever telling him her name or giving him her number, but she must have done one or the other at some point, because, two nights later, she'd been in bed at eleven thirty, doing the reading for the Intro to

Bioethics class that she'd taken on a whim, when her phone had chimed with a classic *U up* text. *It's Chris,* he'd added, and had attached a blurry picture of his face. Abby had toyed with writing back *New phone who dis,* but she'd been surprised, and curious enough to invite him back, thinking that maybe that unpleasant morning scene had been an aberration and that he'd reached out to make it up to her.

Ten minutes later, when he'd shown up at her dorm room, smelling of beer, he hadn't apologized. He'd just started kissing her, sliding his hands up her shirt and pushing his beer-flavored tongue into her mouth.

Chris had been six feet tall, a hulking, round-shouldered red-faced guy with shaggy brown hair and a beard that extended down the sides of his neck. His size had made him somewhat appealing—the way Mark Medoff had been appealing—except Chris had lacked Mark's sweetness and wit. He was almost a parody of a gross, grunting fraternity brother-slash-jock; crude, frequently drunk, perpetually horny. At least he'd been willing to take direction, to figure out what Abby liked in bed and try to execute some of it before passing out. And beggars, Abby had told herself, couldn't be choosers.

For three months, Abby had hooked up with Chris, in her dorm room or, infrequently, in his fraternity house, always between the hours of eleven at night and five in the morning. She'd gotten to the point where the taste of beer made her horny, where she liked the feel of his wiry chest hair brushing against her breasts. Or maybe she just liked the idea that some guy wanted her, and had convinced herself that being with Chris was better than being alone. The nights were at least somewhat enjoyable. The mornings, however, were awful. If they were at her dorm, Chris would wake up and slink out before the sun came up. If they were at his frat house, he'd set his alarm for 5:00 a.m., escort her down the stairs, and send her out into the early morning, when it was still mostly dark outside, never once offering to walk her to her dorm. Chris, clearly, didn't want to be seen with her; didn't want his teammates or the brothers of Beta Theta Pi to know that he was dating (or just sleeping with) a big girl.

Abby only told a handful of friends about Chris, and they were not impressed. They told Abby that she deserved better. She knew that they were right, but even so, it had taken her a shamefully long time to end it. *Half a loaf is better than none,* she would think when her phone had buzzed at midnight, or one in the morning. She would shove condoms and a change of clothes into her backpack and go to him. *A guy who only wants to sleep with me is better than no guy wanting me at all.*

Finally, Abby had been out at a bar on College Avenue one night when Chris and his rugby teammates, still in their jerseys, had piled in through the door. Chris had seen her. Their eyes had met, and he'd turned away, pretending not to know her, laughing when one of the brothers had glanced at her, then looked away, muttering something in a low voice—something that Abby was pretty sure was a joke, at her expense. *How do you get a fat girl into bed? Piece of cake.*

Abby had started college feeling okay about herself or, at least, with no more than the average allotment of insecurities. She'd had friends. She'd had boyfriends. Maybe Camp Golden Hills, and Mark, had let her live in a bit of a bubble, insulated from the world's judgment and scorn, believing that she was pretty and desirable. Staying with a guy like Chris would grind her down. It would leave her worse than she'd been at sixteen.

"Sure, cool, whatever," Chris had mumbled after the night he'd ignored her in the bar, when, instead of running to his fraternity house after he'd texted, she'd told him not to call her again and then had blocked his number, in case he decided to try. For the rest of her college years, there'd been no one steady. Occasional hookups, crushes that went nowhere. The guys she wanted to call her didn't; the guys she never wanted to see again did.

Her longest relationship after college and before Mark had lasted just six months. She'd met David at Pup Jawn, where he worked walking dogs during the day while making the rounds of comedy club open mics at night, trying to make it as a stand-up comedian. This meant, Abby had learned, lots of unpaid gigs—gigs she was expected to attend, and even more time spent online, helping David make memes and Vines and YouTube videos, hoping one of them would go viral. Then, much to Abby's surprise, one of them had. David had been a dead ringer for the then-president's eldest adult son. He had amassed almost a million views of a video he'd done lip-syncing along to one of the son's unhinged rants with talcum powder all over his upper lip and chin. Not the most sophisticated humor, Abby thought, but effective. In short order, David had acquired an agent, a manager, and a plane ticket to Los Angeles. "You understand, right?" he'd asked her, once his studio apartment—even less furnished than Abby's—was packed up, and his worldly goods piled into a backpack and a pair of trash bags.

"Of course," Abby had told him. The last time she'd checked, David had gotten a job writing for an online comedy show starring a former professional wrestler. She was happy for him. He'd had a dream, and he'd made it come true. She only hoped she'd be able to do the same, someday, she thought, as she pedaled on, catching up with Lily, the second-to-last rider, keeping her company as they finished out the morning's miles.

Sebastian

Hey, man! Slow down!"

Sebastian could hear Lincoln behind him, panting, practically gasping his way up the hill Sebastian had just finished climbing.

"Sorry," he said. He made himself ease his grip on the handlebars and forced his legs to slow down, letting his bike coast to a stop before pulling off to the side of the trail.

"You okay?" asked Lincoln, once he'd caught his breath.

"Yeah," Sebastian lied. It was a beautiful day, and he'd enjoyed the riding—or at least he supposed his body had enjoyed it. His mind, meanwhile, had been churning endlessly over the TikTok mess, composing screeds he'd never send to girls he'd never planned to see again. Not even screeds, really. Mostly just variations on the theme of *I didn't do anything wrong!*

"It's beautiful, isn't it?" Lincoln gestured at the grass and trees in varied shades of green and gold, the slow-moving brown water, the blue sky, dotted with cotton-puff clouds.

Sebastian nodded, even though he'd barely noticed the scenery, or the weather, or even how long they'd been riding. "Very peaceful."

Lincoln drank from his water bottle, wiped his mouth, recapped it, and put it back in its cage. He patted Sebastian's shoulder. "Just don't think about it," he said.

Sebastian glared at him. "How am I not supposed to be thinking about it? I'm the Internet's main character! The thing you're never, ever supposed to be!"

"Okay," Lincoln said. "I'm not saying this is ideal. But you know tomorrow it'll be somebody else's turn."

Sebastian shook his head and stared glumly off toward the water, where a bird—a duck? a goose?—was paddling, with a trio of smaller birds swimming behind it. He pulled out his phone and snapped a picture, to show Lincoln that he was still paying some attention to his job.

"Do you remember the girl?" Lincoln asked. "The one who made the video?"

Sebastian nodded reluctantly as a breeze stirred the leaves in the trees overhead. Her name had been Alyssa, and she'd come courtesy of Hinge. She'd been about his height, fine-boned and willowy, with big, blue-green eyes and long dark hair. They'd met on a Saturday night at Dos Hombres, a bar two blocks from Sebastian's place, one of the three or four spots he kept in rotation. When he'd arrived, Alyssa had been waiting at the bar, looking just like her pictures, smiling when she saw him, her long legs crossed and body angled just so.

They'd ordered drinks—beer for him, and the inevitable Aperol spritz for her. He remembered that she'd touched him a lot, putting her hand on his forearm for emphasis every third or fourth sentence when they were on their second drink, touching his cheek when they'd move on to their third, holding his hand when they'd progressed from drinks to shots. At some point, she'd ended up more or less in his lap. She'd also said his name a lot, so much that he'd wondered if it was a technique she'd picked up from a book or a dating podcast. *Tell me about yourself, Sebastian. How long have you lived in Brooklyn, Sebastian?*

Maybe it was just hindsight, but Sebastian could remember thinking that there was something off about her, an impression of subtle wrongness that had only intensified after they'd gone back to his place. At first, he'd ascribed his unease to her high-pitched voice, which he couldn't be mad about. It was not the kind of thing you could convey in photographs, and she hadn't lied, except, he supposed, by omission And what was she supposed to do? Write "By the way, I sound like Kristin Chenoweth after a hit of helium?"

He'd done his best to ignore it as Alyssa shrilled her way to ecstasy, calling out his name, eventually moving from a squeak to a teakettle whistle and, eventually, into pitches that he hoped not even the neighborhood dogs could hear. When it was over, he'd given his usual speech about having early-morning plans, but Alyssa had said, "My apartment's not in a great neighborhood. I'd rather go home when it's light out." She'd smiled, shyly apologetic, promising to be out of his hair, first thing . . . and what kind of cad would he have had to be to force her out into the night?

"Of course," he'd said, and made himself give her a smile. "No problem." She'd fallen asleep, and he'd lain awake beside her, barely daring to move or to breathe, worried that he'd wake her up and she'd want Round Two. He must have drifted off at some point, because in the morning he'd woken to the sound of female humming, and the smell of frying bacon and toasting bread.

Oh, no, he'd thought. *Not good.* He'd faked sleep until he'd heard Alyssa cooing his name from her perch on the side of his bed. She had put on one of his tee shirts, which hung loosely over her torso, almost down to her knees, and she'd put on makeup and done something to her hair. There was a tray with plates of eggs and toast and steaming mugs of coffee, along with a glass carafe of orange juice and a pair of paper napkins, waiting at the foot of the bed. Sebastian had squinted at the tray and the carafe, puzzled. Since when did he own such items? Was it possible this girl had shown up at the bar with them in her purse?

"Hey," Sebastian had said. His voice had been gravelly. He'd cleared his throat and started again. "Hey. Wow. This looks great. I wish I could hang out, but, like I said, I've really got to get going. I've got somewhere to be this morning. A reporting assignment."

"But it's Sunday," Alyssa had said, pouting prettily.

"I'm sorry," he had said. "I had a great time hanging out with you. But I've got a lot of work to get to."

Alyssa looked down at the tray. "You could at least eat your eggs," she'd said in a very small voice. *Fuck.* Sebastian hated feeling like the bad guy. He'd grabbed a fork, pushed a mouthful of eggs between his lips, chewed and swallowed and chased the eggs with a gulp of coffee hot enough to scald his tongue.

Great, he had thought. "Delicious," he had said. "I'm sorry. Look. I've got to get going, but you can stay if you want to. I really feel bad about this . . ."

Alyssa's smile had wavered a bit. "No. I'll go. I understand. Just give me a minute." She'd vanished into the bathroom. He had carried his plate back into the kitchen, scraped the food into the trash can, and gulped down the rest of his coffee. Then he'd waited, fidgeting, making himself sip ice water until, finally, Alyssa had reappeared, wearing the dress she'd worn the night before, which was navy blue and had skinny straps that left most of her shoulders and lots of her chest bare. "I guess it's walk-of-shame time." Her voice was light, but her smile had looked strained. "Well," she had said, with a brittle smile. "See you around."

"See ya," he'd mumbled, reminding himself, again, that he hadn't done anything wrong.

She had slung her purse over her shoulder and turned away. She'd had her hand on the doorknob, and he'd thought he was finally in the clear. Then she'd turned around.

"You know," she had begun. Her voice had been pleasant, but Sebastian had spent enough time around women to sense a storm on the way. "You could at least say thank you. I got up early. I made you breakfast."

I didn't ask for that, Sebastian had thought, but he knew not to say it. He might be an idiot, but he wasn't a complete idiot.

"Thank you," he said. "If I didn't say it already—"

Alyssa just kept talking, rolling right over him. "I came to that disgusting bar to meet you." Her voice had gotten louder. "I ate hot wings with you. I gave you a blow job . . ."

If Sebastian recalled, she'd been the one to unbutton his jeans and begin, unprompted, the trip down south. And the blow job hadn't even been that great. There'd been lots of ticklish licking, slow swirls of her tongue, like his erection was a cone of soft-serve custard that was melting fast, along with an unsettling amount of eye contact. The whole thing had felt like a performance and as if all she cared about were her reviews. And he'd reciprocated! He always reciprocated! He might not have wanted a girlfriend, but that didn't mean he was a lout.

"I didn't make you do that," he'd said.

"That's the point! You didn't have to ask!" Her voice had cracked as she had waved her hands at the ceiling. "I gave you head, and I made you eggs. I did everything right," she had said, and started to cry.

Sebastian felt his body sag. Women's tears were the one thing he couldn't handle; the one thing he couldn't stand. He approached Alyssa the same way he would have sidled up to a tiger in a zoo that had somehow gotten out of its cage, and he tried, ever so gently, to pat her back.

She had jerked away, glaring at him. "You're not ever going to call me again, are you?" she asked, nose red, eyes watering. She no longer sounded angry . . . just tired. Very, very tired. That, somehow, was worse.

Numbly, Sebastian had shaken his head. "I thought you were just interested in, you know. Hooking up."

She'd glared at him. "Nobody just wants hookups forever," she'd said. Before he could ask why she'd indicated on her profile that hookups were exactly what she did want, she'd spun around again. Sebastian had clenched his hands into fists, digging his nails into his palms, thinking that this was never going to end, not ever. He was in hell, with a girl he'd slept with who never left, who started to leave, who acted like she had every intention of going, but just stood in the doorway *almost* leaving, before turning around and hurling accusations at him, each one worse than the previous, forever and ever, world without end.

But, finally, Alyssa had gone. She hadn't even slammed the door. She had let it close, gently, behind her. And now, she'd discovered that he'd also spent time with some of her friends, and she'd reappeared in his life, in a TikTok video that declared him a man slut. Finally, his lifetime of luck had run out.

"It'll pass," said Lincoln. "I promise." Sebastian knew he was right. Still, it was so colossally unfair. And that it had to happen now, when he'd finally found the one woman he did want to see again, the one woman he'd actually hoped would make a reappearance in his life, and he'd been forced to declare her off-limits, to preemptively friend-zone her. *Karma*, he thought miserably, and wondered if, in some previous life, he'd been a person who'd kicked dogs, or handed out raisins at Halloween.

Of course, maybe the off-limits thing wouldn't be forever. *Be her friend*, Lincoln had said. It would have been easier if he'd just told Sebastian to avoid Abby completely, he realized, because spending time with her while knowing it could only be platonic would be torture. It might not be what she wanted, either. True, there was Doctor Mark, but he was pretty sure he'd sensed some hesitation when Abby had talked about him. A certain lack of enthusiasm, an absence of all-in-ness. Plus, Mark was a podiatrist. Did she really want to spend the rest of her life tethered to someone whose profession was feet?

Maybe she didn't really want to be with Mark. And maybe she didn't know about his disgrace. What were the chances that she was on TikTok? Lots of people weren't.

Sebastian started pedaling again. He pressed his lips together, grinding his teeth as he rode, faster and faster, until his wheels were barely skimming the path, until it felt like he was flying; like he could ride away from Lincoln, away from the other riders, away from his problems, away from—

"Hey!"

A car's horn blared. Sebastian jerked his head up to see that the trail had come to an intersection with the road; an intersection marked by STOP signs and a sign that read CYCLISTS WALK YOUR BIKE. A pickup truck with a State of New York logo on its side was on the road, directly in his path.

He squeezed his front and rear brakes as hard as he could, feeling the bike's frame shudder. For one awful moment he was convinced he was going to go flying right over the handlebars and into the side of the truck. The bike's rear wheel slued sideways, skidding, spinning 180 degrees before finally coming to a stop mere millimeters from the side of the truck. Sebastian tried to put his feet down, forgetting that his shoes were still clipped into his pedals. He bounced off the truck and fell onto the pavement, landing on his right side, with his bike on top of him. He lay there, like a bug, trapped under his bike, as the truck driver rolled down his window to deliver a lengthy and profane soliloquy, casting aspersions on Sebastian's eyesight ("Are you fuckin' blind?"), the legitimacy of his parentage ("Stupid god-damn bastard!"), and the obliviousness and arrogance of cyclists in general ("You assholes dressed up like Lance Armstrong think you own the road, like it's everyone else's job to get out of your way!").

Sebastian waved at the guy in what he hoped was an apologetic fashion and tried to work at least one of his feet free from his shoe, which was still clipped into the pedal. And then Abby was there, her eyebrows drawn down, lips pressed together, freckles prominent on her pale face as she got off her own bike and hurried toward him.

"Are you all right? What happened?"

Sebastian gestured at himself, and the bike that was still on top of him, and said the obvious. "I fell."

"He almost rode right at me!" yelled the driver. "Wasn't even looking! Didn't even slow down!"

Abby ignored the driver as she crouched down next to Sebastian. One hand rested lightly on his shoulder as she looked into his eyes, then at his helmet. "Are you hurt?"

"I'm fine." Sebastian finally managed to wrench one of his feet out of its shoe, wriggle out from underneath his bike, and get to his feet. "Sorry, man," he called to the truck driver. "Totally my fault. I should have been looking. I'm sorry." The driver grumbled a few more uncomplimentary observations before rolling up his window and departing. Sebastian could feel adrenaline spiking his bloodstream, could hear his pulse thudding in his ears. He knew that he'd been distracted; that he'd been the one at fault. Just one more asshole cyclist, clad in entitlement and spandex, giving everyone who rode a bike a bad name. The realization only made him angry at himself all over again.

"Did you hit your head?" Abby asked.

"I'm fine," he snapped. Abby's eyes widened. She stepped backward, away from him. That made him feel even worse.

"Let me see your helmet," she said, holding out her hand.

Sebastian unclipped his helmet and handed it over, watching as she ran her fingers along its panels, inspecting it for cracks.

"Are you sure you're okay?"

"What happened?" asked Lincoln, who'd finally arrived.

"Nothing," said Sebastian, aware that his entire right side was scraped and dirty, that his jersey was torn, and that he was still only wearing one shoe.

"I want Jasper to take a look at your bike before you ride it," said Abby.

"It's fine," Sebastian said. He actually had no idea whether the bike was okay or not, but in his current frame of mind, he didn't want Abby fussing over him. Or noticing him at all. Meanwhile, the rest of the group had arrived, and all of them were staring, some more obviously than others.

"What happened?" bawled the tall, hard-of-hearing guy.

"He fell," his wife shouted into his ear.

"I know, but why?" the man yelled back.

Because he's an idiot, Sebastian thought.

Abby clapped her hands. "Okay, everyone. Show's over. Time for lunch!" She led them to a playground a few hundred yards up the trail. Sebastian wheeled his bike behind her, and Lincoln walked beside him.

"What happened?" Lincoln asked him.

"Ah, I was just distracted."

Lincoln looked concerned. "And you're sure you're okay?"

"I'm fine." He could hear how pissed he still sounded, and knew that he wasn't angry at Abby, who'd only been doing her job, or even at the truck driver, who hadn't been at fault. He was angry at Alyssa. At TikTok. At social media in general. At every woman who'd posted about him, or liked Alyssa's video, or stitched it or dueted it or shared it. It seemed so unfair, because, really, what were the odds of so many women he'd slept with being friends? (*If you sleep with five different women a week, they're not too slim,* a voice that sounded a lot like Lincoln informed him.) He was angry at fate, at Karma, at God, who, if She existed, was undoubtedly having Herself a good chuckle. He was angry at himself, most of all because, if he'd just been a little more temperate in his habits, he'd be a lot more appealing to Abby. Who had a boyfriend, he reminded himself, again. Whose friend he was trying to be.

No cure for it, he thought, wheeling his bike over to Jasper, who was leaning against the side of the sag wagon with a scrupulously blank expression on his face. He'd just have to keep going. Let some time pass, let some miles go by, and the sting would fade, the Internet would move on, and, at some point in the future, Abby would forgive him . . . if, he thought, she ever found out about his disgrace at all. He'd been so lucky, for so long. Maybe there was still a chance that she'd never find out; that they'd become friends on the trip, and more than friends when it was over; and that all of this could work out the way he wanted.

Morgan

*C*an *you keep a secret?*

Morgan had said the words a thousand times in her head since the trip began. She'd imagined saying them to Abby, the leader. Or Andy Presser, who she'd seen looking at her when he didn't think she'd notice. She'd pictured herself saying it to one of the old ladies, or even Andy's mom, with her ponytail and her friendly smile. She imagined asking everyone but her own mother. *Can you keep a secret? Can I tell you why I'm really here? Will you help me?*

In addition to every other woman, and some of the men, Morgan had imagined telling her mother. *I had sex with Brody. We used a condom but maybe it broke or maybe he put it on wrong but I'm pregnant. And I can't have a baby. I can't.*

She could imagine saying all of that. The problem was, Morgan could also imagine exactly what her mother would say. *It's a baby, Morgan. From the moment of conception, it's a whole new life. And I can't let you kill a baby!*

That was what her parents had taught her. That was what they believed. Morgan knew that she was on her own with this. You could get an abortion in Ohio, as long as you did it before your twenty-first week, but you needed a parent or guardian's permission if you were under eighteen, and Morgan knew there was no way—no way at all—that either of her parents would consent. She guessed she was lucky that they had the bike trip planned. She'd gone over the itinerary, using the school's computer to look things up, and she'd found a Planned Parenthood in Syracuse, one of the cities where they'd spend the night.

Olivia had been with her when Morgan had bought the pregnancy test. She'd taken it in Olivia's bathroom, and she'd called the clinic from Olivia's bedroom, when both of her friend's mothers were at work. The lady on the other end had asked questions: *What's your date of birth? When was your last period? Is your cycle regular? Were you using birth control?*

The lady had explained that a doctor would examine Morgan and determine how far along she was. Once they knew, they'd decide whether she'd have to have a surgical abortion, or a medical one.

"What does that mean?" Morgan asked. Her voice was barely a whisper.

"For a medical abortion, the doctor would give you two different kinds of medication to take, and usually within a few hours, the contents of your uterus would empty."

The contents of my uterus. Morgan could imagine her father repeating those words, scornfully, from his pulpit. *Oh, they've got all kinds of pretty words to hide it, but what they're really talking about is a baby,* he would say. *A baby they'd be happy to murder, to tear, limb from limb, right up to the moment the mother gives birth.*

"Will it hurt?" she whispered.

"It depends. The cramping can be intense for some women, and the bleeding can be very heavy. For some women, it's not much worse than a regular period."

"Will I be able to ride my bike, after it's over?"

The woman chuckled a little. "No. You're going to want to spend the next day in bed, resting," the lady told her. But Morgan knew that wasn't an option. She'd just have to push through it, to keep her secret. She could handle pain, blood, cramps. She could handle whatever she had to handle, as long as her mom and dad didn't find out what she'd done.

All day long, with every rotation of her bike's wheels, Morgan thought about her secret. She reviewed the plans she'd made—how she'd hang toward the back of the group and then ride her bike to the clinic. She still didn't know what would happen there, and all the woman could tell her was *We'll examine you and see how far along you are. Then we can discuss your options.* It had been Olivia's idea to buy a cheap burner phone at the drugstore two suburbs away. Morgan thought it was unnecessary until Olivia had shown her a story about a seventeen-year-old girl in Nebraska and her mother who'd been charged with a felony after the police had gotten access to Facebook messages where the mom was instructing her daughter on how to take the pills that had ended her pregnancy. *If they got her messages, they can get your phone, and they can see who you've been calling,* Olivia had said. So they'd bought the phone at the drugstore, and had sat on Olivia's bed to make the call, once the bedroom door was locked.

"Can you just send me the pills?" Morgan had asked, her voice barely a whisper.

"There are places you can find online that will do that, and they'll send you instructions about how to use them," the woman said, carefully. "That isn't a service we offer." She paused. "You're how old?"

"Fifteen," Morgan said.

The woman paused again. "I won't tell you what to do, or that you shouldn't just go ahead and order the pills. That's an option, and it's your choice. But I will say that, because of your age, for your own safety, I'd feel better if a doctor could examine you, if you can get here quickly. If that's feasible." The woman paused, and what she said next made Morgan sure about her choice. "If you were my daughter, that's what I'd want."

"Okay," Morgan had said as Olivia, who'd been listening, nodded her assent. Morgan made the appointment for the day the trip would be in Syracuse. That, she realized, would be the easy part.

Olivia had offered to come on the bike trip with her, or to meet her in New York. But Morgan knew that Olivia bailing on the summer camp in Maine where her moms had sent her and joining the trip at the last minute, or showing up in Syracuse, would raise Morgan's parents' suspicions. She'd made Olivia promise not to tell her mothers, not wanting to run the risk of them telling Morgan's mom and dad what was going on, even though Olivia promised that they wouldn't; that they were on Morgan's side, that they'd help her.

"If it can't be me, you have to find someone to go with you," Olivia had instructed, her face still and serious, without even a trace of her usual smile as she'd leaned against her headboard with her knees pulled up to her chest. "You've got money?"

Morgan nodded, feeling glad that she'd saved everything she'd earned from babysitting over the last year.

"And you're sure you don't want to tell Brody?"

Morgan had nodded again, immediately and vigorously. She and Brody had only had sex twice, and she hadn't even liked it that much. Two times, for a total of maybe ten minutes, and it hadn't even felt good! *It'll get better,* he'd promised her, except now Brody was off at Fort Benning, with no idea about what was going on. Morgan knew, if she told him what had happened, he'd come rushing home. Maybe he'd go along with her plan, but maybe he'd want to marry her. Her parents would probably want that. And if she didn't marry Brody, they'd make her have the baby and give it up for adoption. She'd have to go through an entire pregnancy, walking around for months with a big belly and everyone knowing what she'd done. Giving birth. Her mom and dad would be so disappointed. Her dad might even lose his job, because who'd listen to a pastor whose own daughter had disobeyed him?

School would be a nightmare. The girls would all laugh, and some of the boys would think she was a slut; that if she'd slept with one guy she'd be up for doing anything with anyone. That would be bad. Spending the rest of her life knowing that there was a baby, out there in the world—a baby, then a toddler, then a child, a teenager, a person—that would be unendurable. It would be like burning up from the inside, every day, for the rest of her life. It would be more than she could take.

"I can't tell Brody," she said to Olivia.

"What about your mom?"

Morgan shook her head even more vehemently. "I can't."

Olivia smoothed her polka-dotted bedspread and nodded like she understood, even though Morgan was pretty sure she didn't. Olivia did not go to Morgan's church or any church. She talked to her mothers about everything—not just sex, but feelings. Relationships. Even masturbation.

But for Morgan, telling her mother something like this was unthinkable. Lily would be beyond disappointed. It would break her heart.

"You should find someone, then," Olivia told her. "You can't just go all by yourself. You need someone to take care of you and make sure you're safe."

Morgan had nodded. She'd promised. And she'd consoled herself by thinking that at least she had the big part figured out.

When her dad had gotten the call about the men's retreat

in Arizona, when it had looked, for one heart-stoppingly awful instant like they wouldn't go on the trip at all, Morgan had been terrified. *No, no, we have to go,* Morgan had told her mother, begging and pleading and telling her how excited she was about riding the trail and seeing Niagara Falls and spending time with her, until, finally, Lily had agreed. *I know it's a lot of riding, but I'll help you!* Morgan had said. She knew Lily was confused, and maybe angry, that Morgan had barely spent any time with her at all, but the truth was, she was terrified to be around her mom. Scared that she'd give herself away; that her mother would look at her and, somehow, just know; the way she'd known when Morgan was lying about sneaking cookies, or coloring on her dresser with crayons when she'd been little.

Can you keep a secret?

In the park, in New York, Morgan plopped a scoop of macaroni salad on her plate and swallowed hard as her stomach lurched. The noodles looked slimy and disgusting, and even the smell of tuna was making her queasy. Her mother was at a picnic table, with Mrs. Presser and Mrs. Fenske. Abby was over by the sag wagon, talking to Jasper, who was looking at Sebastian's bike. Andy Presser was sitting under a tree with his brother, devouring the third of four sandwiches he'd piled on his plate.

"Come sit with us!" he called.

She nodded, and walked over to him, trying to look normal, happy, and relaxed. Andy was her best bet. Morgan wondered what he'd think if she told him her secret; if he'd still look at her like she was a fairy-tale princess, Rapunzel in the tower, and he was the prince who would save her. Probably he wouldn't. And if she told him about her appointment, he'd probably tell his mother, who'd feel obligated to tell Morgan's mom. Morgan would have to keep her secret. In this fairy tale, the princess would have to save herself.

Abby

Abby had been proud of herself for the way she'd handled Sebastian's run-in with the angry driver. Calm. Collected. Appropriate. An experienced ride leader, Lizzie herself, couldn't have done any better. She thought that he'd thank her; take the opportunity to talk with her, or sit with her at lunch. She hadn't been oblivious to his smiles, his flirty looks. But that morning, he'd seemed tense and distant, and at lunchtime, he'd just filled his plate and gone off with Lincoln.

Abby ended up sitting with her mom and Lily Mackenzie, who cast mournful sideways glances at her daughter and Andy Presser, who'd gone off by themselves. Abby got Lily talking about her book club back home, and how she'd met her husband, and anything she could think of to keep her from looking so sad.

Afterward, there were thirty more miles to pedal before day's end. Abby rode sweep and then, with a mile left to go, she pedaled hard to get to the front of the group, then waited in the hotel parking lot, watching as the riders arrived, in various states of exhaustion. When Abby had gone to check in, the clerk had handed her a package along with her key card. Mark had sent her a box of John & Kira's chocolates. Her favorites. She smiled, and popped a truffle in her mouth.

In her room, she lit the crushed-mint scented candle she'd packed and savored her long, hot shower, twisting her torso from side to side, raising her arms over her head, rolling her neck. She'd just gotten out of the shower when her phone dinged with an incoming text. Probably Mark, she thought, who'd been keeping her entertained with pictures of feet and a link to a story about a college classmate who'd started doing low-cost vasectomies out of a van he'd nicknamed the Neuter Scooter. Abby was looking forward to telling him about the day's ride and how, as she predicted, the men had been the ones almost getting into accidents, or drifting toward the center of the path, or the road, completely oblivious to other bikes and cars. Lizzie's theory was that men rode their bikes the way they moved through the world—heedless, confident, making it everyone else's job to get out of their way. Women were more cautious. They followed the rules and were careful about staying to the side of the road, about observing stop signs and traffic lights and calling "On your left!" when they passed. Many men—maybe most men—couldn't be bothered.

She wrapped her hair in the special microfiber towel she'd packed—the one guaranteed to keep her curls from frizzing—picked up the phone from where it was charging on the bathroom counter. Mark hadn't texted. Lizzie had.

Is this guy on the trip? she'd written. Below the text was a link to TikTok.

Abby knew the text was a peace offering. She and Lizzie hadn't spoken since Eileen's surprise appearance at the park. Yesterday, Abby had fired off a *WTF!?!?* text, with a picture of Eileen on the trail. *Call me. I'll explain,* Lizzie had written. So far, though, Abby hadn't called.

She sat on the edge of the bed with her phone in her hand. Lizzie joked that she was the oldest woman on TikTok, and would tell anyone who listened that she'd only joined to keep up with her teenage nieces, but the truth was, she was just as addicted to the app as any Gen Z-er. Rarely a day went by when Lizzie didn't send Abby a video she'd seen: a viral dance, workout tips, recipes, makeup reviews, a video of a cat in a tie, or one featuring a mom who'd single-handedly remodeled her laundry room during her newborn's nap time. Smiling, Abby clicked the link. She felt her smile fade as she saw Sebastian's face in the center of a WANTED poster, and felt it vanish completely once she'd skimmed a few of the 3,467 comments underneath the video, which revealed that Sebastian had worked his way through seven of the original poster's eight-woman friend squad.

"Oh my God." Abby tossed the phone aside, feeling as breathless as if she'd been punched. Then she made herself pick up the phone and watch the video again, shaking her head in dismay. Of course Sebastian had turned out to be too good to be true. Unicorns weren't real, and neither were handsome, nonproblematic single guys who were both sexual savants and into her. She shouldn't have been surprised. Sebastian had to have acquired his superlative bedroom skills somewhere, and now Abby knew precisely where, and had a rough idea with how many whoms.

She ate another one of Mark's chocolates, swallowed hard, and looked down at her phone's screen. "I KNOW THIS GUY," AnnaCabana had written. So had IllieBeilish, Liminalia, Cass247, BellaLuna, and FondaWand15, who wrote, "His name is Sebastian Piersall and he works for Scoop.com." There went the last, lingering shred of doubt she'd held on to, Abby thought. She forced herself to keep reading.

"Ladies, best get yourselves tested for STIs," PhantaRay6 had written. Abby shuddered. "He's a 10, but his body count is higher than your town's population," User27847 had said. "IS HE TRYING TO FILL A BINGO CARD?" asked NikkiMenage.

One comment that read "This is slut shaming. We get mad when guys do this to us. Let's be better" had gotten 365 likes, while one that read "He could at least branch out and try some different zip codes" had gotten 1,454. And on and on it went. Commenters of both genders hailed his commitment to diversity or joked about his endurance. Some guys were trashing him. Others were defending him or just offering him virtual high fives.

Abby shook her head. Then she called Lizzie.

"It's the same guy, right?" Lizzie said. "I remembered the name from the trip roster, and I figured there can't be that many Sebastian Piersalls in the world."

"Yes," Abby said. Her voice sounded leaden. "Same guy."

"I knew it!" Lizzie crowed. "Hashtag Kissing Bandit!" She lowered her voice. "Lucky you. Your very first time as ride leader, and you've got a celebrity!"

Abby closed her eyes. "Lizzie," she said. "Do you remember the guy I met when I went to New York for Kara's bachelorette party?"

The ensuing pause felt like it lasted for a very long time. "Oh, Abby," Lizzie finally said. "Oh, no."

Abby didn't answer. Lizzie said, "Well, that was, what, two years ago? Maybe he wasn't, you know, um . . ."

"Sleeping with everything that has a pulse back then?" Abby said. She pressed her fisted hand between her eyebrows. "I feel so stupid."

"Why?" Lizzie asked. "How does this make you stupid?"

"Oh, I don't know. Maybe not stupid." Abby bit her lip. "Basic. Gross. Not special," she said. "And the thing was . . ." Abby squeezed her eyes more tightly closed and made herself say it. "I liked him."

"Oh, Abby."

"I did. I liked him a lot. He made me feel . . ." She swallowed hard. The detail her mind had snagged on wasn't the sex, or the feel of his mouth on her breasts or his hands on her hips, the things he'd murmured in her ear or how he'd looked at her, but how he'd made pasta, and carried two bowls back to bed. How he'd twirled a forkful of noodles and brought them to her mouth. How sweet he'd been. "He made me feel special. Like I was special to him," she finally said. "And, clearly, I was not."

"You are special." Lizzie's voice was calm, low, and soothing.

"It doesn't matter," Abby said. "It's not like I'm single." She squared her shoulders and straightened her neck, her mouth a firm line, her posture resolute.

"So give me an update. How's the ride?"

"Well." Abby told her friend about the Spoke'n Four, how Andy had a crush on Morgan and how Morgan was barely speaking to her mom.

"And how are things with Eileen?" Lizzie asked delicately. Abby didn't answer. "Before you get mad at me, let me just say this—she told me she wanted to spend time with you, and I believed her."

"Spend time with me. By which you mean monitor every bite of food I put in my mouth and ask me seventeen different times how much weight I think I'll lose, after all this biking. Or if Mark and I have made any plans yet." Abby's voice sounded like she was joking, even though she wasn't.

"She's trying," Lizzie said.

"I know," Abby said, and realized it was true. In her own belated, clumsy way, Eileen was making an effort. Which meant, Abby knew, that she'd have to be the bigger person—ha, ha, ha—and meet her mother's attempt as generously, as kindly as she could.

She said goodbye to her friend and got dressed for dinner in her off-the-bike outfit, wishing she'd packed something prettier, less utilitarian than her linen pants and tee shirt. Shoes on, hair combed, she stepped out of her hotel room at the precise instant that Sebastian emerged from the room next door—because of course he'd be in the room next door. He wore jeans and a dark blue tee shirt, and even with his shamefaced expression, he looked handsome and appealing.

Shit, Abby thought, trying to ignore the attraction that rolled over her like a wave, making her especially aware of her lips and her fingertips and every inch of her skin. Trying to remember the videos she'd seen, the comments she'd read.

"Abby," Sebastian said. He cleared his throat. "I'm sorry I was such a jerk this afternoon. It was completely my fault. I was preoccupied, and I wasn't paying attention."

"It's fine," Abby told him.

"It won't happen again," said Sebastian.

"It's fine," Abby repeated. "Totally okay. Really." She took a few steps into the parking lot, looking around for Jasper and the sag wagon.

Sebastian followed her. "You know, last year I went on a hiking trip. Part of it was a media detox. You'd hike and eat all your meals in silence, and you weren't allowed to look at your phones . . ."

Abby decided to put him out of his misery. "I saw the Tik-Tok."

Sebastian's mouth opened, then closed. "Ah."

"It's fine." Jesus. She needed to get away from him. Where was Jasper? Or Morgan and Lily? She'd even welcome her mother at this point. She could see the Pressers standing under a tree near the lobby, and the Landons coming down the breezeway, carrying a bucket of ice. "It's none of my business, anyhow." She took a quick glance at Sebastian, who looked miserable, with his hands in his pockets and his face scrunched up, like something hurt. "I'm going to go find my mother."

"Abby—" He looked like he wanted to say more. But he didn't. She could feel his eyes on her as she hurried away.

Dinner that night started off with baskets of warm, pillowy Parker House rolls, served with whipped honey butter. Abby tore a roll into chunks and buttered one lavishly (after angling her body so Eileen couldn't see). She popped it in her mouth and hummed with happiness. "Oh my God is that good," she said. When she opened her eyes she saw Sebastian looking at her, his gaze intense and heated.

Abby felt herself flushing. She turned to her left. "Lily," she asked, "how was the riding today?"

"Great!" said Lily, in her typically chipper tone. Abby suspected Lily would have given the same response, in precisely the same tone, if one of her legs had fallen off at lunchtime.

"You're not sore? Nothing hurts?"

"Oh, everything hurts," Lily said. She sipped her diet soda and smiled serenely. "But I'm managing."

"Morgan, how about you?"

Morgan was sitting next to her mother. She ducked behind her curtain of shiny hair and murmured something Abby couldn't hear and hoped was positive. She turned her attention to Andy Presser.

"Andy, how was your ride?"

His Adam's apple jerked as he swallowed. "It was good. Fine."

"How about you, Ezra?"

Ezra gave Abby a thumbs-up with his left hand while continuing to ferry chunks of buttered roll into his mouth with his right.

"Never get between a teenage boy and carbs," said Dale Presser, who appeared to have mellowed after two days outdoors. He'd gotten a little color in his cheeks, and his shoulders and neck had lost some of the tension Abby had observed back in Manhattan. His wife squeezed his hand, and he smiled at her. And Abby felt content, proud of herself for leading this trip; happy that she was doing some good in the world.

She finished her roll, then stood and walked to the end of the table, where the Spoke'n Four were sitting. There was an empty chair at the foot of the table. Abby sat down, and asked the group, "How was your day?"

"Perfect," said Lou. "A lovely day. Exactly what we were hoping for."

"We've been planning on doing this ride ever since they opened the trail," said Sue. "But then . . ." She sighed, and the four of them said, together, "COVID."

"How was the pandemic for you guys?" Abby asked.

"I went to four Zoom funerals," Ted boomed.

"My niece and her partner got Zoom married," said Lou. "Well, the actual wedding was in person—just the two of them, in their backyard, with the officiant six feet away."

"It's been hard to know what to do about celebrations," said Eileen, who'd appeared out of nowhere and had taken the empty seat next to Abby. Abby wondered if her mother was going to talk about how lucky it was that Abby hadn't gotten engaged during the pandemic, or how great it was now that the restrictions had been lifted. She wasn't sure, but she thought she noticed Sebastian's head swiveling toward them.

She bit her lip. The waitress came to take drink orders and tell them about the specials. By the time she was gone, the Spoke'n Four had gone quiet, their heads bent over Ted's phone. "Is that him?" she heard Ted rumble as Lou and Sue both shushed him, and Ed pulled his reading glasses out of his breast pocket.

"What?" Eileen asked, leaning toward them. "What's going on?"

Sue beckoned to Abby. "Is this our Sebastian?" she whispered, and showed Abby her phone. Abby braced for the same TikTok Lizzie had sent her. She saw the by-now-familiar picture of Sebastian's face in a WANTED poster . . . but this time it was attached to an article, not a video. Which meant that the story had jumped from social media to legacy media. She felt embarrassed on Sebastian's behalf. And on her own.

"'The Internet is abuzz over the story of a Brooklyn Lothario who, social media sleuths determined, has slept his way through an entire sorority of women, many of whom are friends,'" Ted declaimed in a voice loud enough to be audible to not just the Breakaway table but also all the diners nearby.

"Shh!" said Sue.

"Sorry," said Ted, and continued at a slightly reduced volume. "'The saga began at a brunch in Williamsburg, when a group of eight friends realized that seven of them had gone on first—and last—dates with a freelance writer named Sebastian, a man they'd all met on dating apps within the same six weeks.'"

Eileen frowned at her daughter. "Wait, Sebastian? That Sebastian?" She pointed, not even trying to be discreet. "Our Sebastian?"

Our Sebastian, Abby saw, was currently being glared at by his friend.

"Freelancer? Why did they say you're a freelancer?" Lincoln was demanding. "Are you writing for other websites?" He pressed his hand against his shirt, right against his heart. "Are you cheating on me professionally?"

Abby was glad that Lincoln was attempting to lighten the mood. But it didn't seem to be working. Sebastian pressed his lips together and ducked his head as Ted continued.

"'The eighth woman had matched with Sebastian, but hadn't set up an in-person encounter. By the time the brunch was over, one of the women, Alyssa Frankel, had uploaded a video about the amatory overlap.'"

"'Amatory overlap,'" Sue repeated. "I like that."

"'Within twenty-four hours, almost forty other women had chimed in to claim that they, too, had hooked up with Sebastian. "He was very clear that he wasn't looking for a relationship," Frankel told Page Six. "I wasn't expecting to see him again. I also wasn't expecting to find out he'd dated most of my friends, plus three of my sorority sisters. And my actual sister."'"

Dale Presser whistled softly. Lily Mackenzie was staring at Sebastian, wide-eyed and horrified. Abby watched as Sebastian got up from the table and stalked off. Lincoln followed after him.

"Well," Eileen said, and looked at her daughter, her expression sly and teasing. "Is there anything in the leader's instruction manual about this kind of situation?"

Abby felt very tired, like all the miles she'd pedaled so far had decided to hit her thighs and calves at the same time.

"Let's not give him a hard time," Abby said, looking meaningfully at her mother, then at Ted and Sue, then Kayla and Dale. She lowered her voice. "It's really none of our business. And he's on vacation. He deserves to enjoy himself, as best he can."

"Got it." Sue nodded.

"That's fair," said Lou, who nudged Ted, speaking directly in his ear until he nodded, too. Then the waitress was there, and everyone opened their menus, preparing to order.

"It's a shame," Sue said to Abby. "He seemed like such a nice young man. And it looked like you two were really hitting it off."

Abby felt her cheeks flushing . . . and what was she supposed to say to that? *I have a boyfriend*? Or, *Sebastian and I hooked up once, and he isn't the boyfriend kind of guy*? She ended up closing her mouth, smiling weakly, and saying nothing; telling herself that if her mom was quietly making plans to see if Sebastian would be mentioned on the late-night talk shows, if the Presser parents were horrified, if Lily Mackenzie was especially disgusted and confirmed in every prejudice about the Godless East Coast liberals, and if she herself was feeling more than a little broken-hearted, Abby knew she could ignore it.

Back at the hotel, Abby was unsurprised when she heard raised voices from the room beside hers, followed by the sound of the door opening and closing. She was also not entirely unsurprised when she heard a knock at her own door. She wasn't sure what Sebastian would want from her, but as she crossed the room, she made herself a promise that, whatever transpired, it wouldn't end up with the two of them in bed.

She gave her ponytail a tweak and opened the door to find Sebastian standing there, still in his clothes from dinner. His formerly glossy and perfectly arranged hair looked like he'd been tugging at it, and his expression was miserable.

"Can I talk to you?" he asked.

Abby opened her mouth to tell him that they had nothing to say to one another, then remembered that she had an official role to play. She was the ride leader and not just a fellow cyclist-slash-lady with hurt feelings. Maybe Sebastian was here on Breakaway business. Maybe he'd done something to his bike when he'd fallen, or hurt himself. "Sure. What's going on?"

Sebastian raked his hand through his curls. "I just . . . the thing on TikTok." He made an unamused scoffing sound. "Only it's not just on TikTok anymore. Page Six . . . TMZ . . ." He shook his head. "I want to talk to you about it."

"Like I said, you don't owe me an explanation."

He yanked at his hair, then looked at her. "If I'd been able to find you . . ."

She stared at him, puzzled, disbelieving, feeling her heart beating hard. "So you've been, what, exactly? Pining for me for the last two years? Trying to bury your sorrows in . . ." She paused, realizing, belatedly, that *bury* was not, perhaps, the best choice of words. It conjured some very specific memories; ones she wished weren't quite so vivid.

"It wouldn't have worked," she said. "We're in very different places."

He squinted at her, head cocked. "Are we, though?"

"Well, let's see. You're in Brooklyn, I'm in Philadelphia. You have a job, I have a boyfriend." Abby stopped, realizing that hadn't come out the way she'd thought it would. It sounded like she was saying that he did journalism for a living, and she did Mark. Which wasn't what she'd meant. Mark wasn't her job, and he wasn't a sugar daddy, either. "You're clearly interested in playing the field." And then, because she couldn't help herself, she added, "Playing all the fields."

She saw hurt flash across his face and felt a stab in her own heart.

"That's not fair," he said.

She pulled in a breath and nodded, admitting it. "I'm sorry," she said. "You're right. That was unnecessary. I— Look, I think it's just better for both of us if we . . ." She flapped her hands in a vague motion, one that she hoped he'd be able to interpret as *forget we ever met before the trip started, and speak to each other as little as possible until it's over.*

Sebastian stepped forward until he was standing right in front of her, so close that their noses practically touched. She could see the way his eyelashes curled up at the tip; his faintly stubbled cheeks and full lips. She could hear him breathing, and she could smell him: cinnamon and mint; shampoo and soap, the warm, clean scent she remembered from his sheets and his skin, something a little woodsy and also a little like toast. He put his hand on her upper arm, fingers curling around her biceps. Abby's inhalation sounded almost like a gasp, and suddenly, in spite of everything she'd read and everything she'd learned, Abby wanted to feel his hands on her again, holding her hips, or brushing her cheek, or cupping the back of her head.

"I asked you to come home with me because I liked you," he said.

Abby rolled her eyes a little. Sebastian's gaze didn't waver. His eyes were still on her face. Her mouth, specifically. Abby decided she needed to make explicit what she'd hoped her arm-waving gesture had implied.

"I had a nice time with you," she said. Her voice was a little too loud, slightly stiff. "But I have a boyfriend."

"Was he your boyfriend the night we met?"

Abby felt her face get hot and was glad she was being honest when she shook her head. "He wasn't my boyfriend yet."

"If I'd been able to find you . . . if I'd asked you to have dinner with me . . . do you think you'd still want to be with him?"

"How am I supposed to know?" Abby asked indignantly. "That's completely theoretical. And it doesn't matter. Because that's not what happened."

He smiled a little. Abby saw the faint crinkling at the corner of his eyes, and hated how appealing she found him, how every gesture, every expression, made him more endearing. "No. But it's interesting to think about. Maybe there's an alternate timeline where you and I are together, and we're riding our bikes through Tuscany."

Abby was tempted to ask if she had a job in this scenario, a job that let her pay for lavish Italian vacations. Instead she said, pleasantly, "Is this a timeline where you didn't sleep with half of Brooklyn?"

She saw her words register on his face, watching as his sweet, almost yearning look changed to surprise and disappointment, feeling the strangest mixture of triumph and relief and shame. Sebastian let go of her arm, and Abby stepped backward.

"I think we should just keep our distance," she said.

He held up his hands. "No worries. Whatever you want. I just want to be your friend."

"I have plenty of friends."

His gave her a tight-lipped smile. "So I'll be a new one."

"Good night, Sebastian." She hadn't meant to say his name, but there it was, the syllables rolling around in her mouth. "Get some sleep." She stepped back into her room and carefully closed the door behind her . . . then leaned against it, her breath coming quickly, her eyes squeezed shut and her heart thudding in her chest, part of her telling her to run from him, as far and as fast as she could, and the rest of her telling her to run after him, to grab his hand and pull him through the door and kiss him until nothing hurt him anymore.

Abby

Day Three: Poughkeepsie to Hudson
Forty-three miles

Abby had a hard time falling asleep, and she was awake an hour before her alarm trilled. She packed up her stuff, got dressed, found an urn of coffee in the hotel lobby, along with packets of oatmeal, prepackaged muffins, and a few wan-looking bagels next to a toaster. She sipped her coffee and waited as the rest of the riders arrived. Lily was walking stiffly, like every part of her body hurt. Ted boomed a greeting, his clip-in shoes click-clacking on the tiled floor. Sebastian gave her a fast look, then quickly looked away.

They got their bikes out of a locked storage room and assembled in the parking lot, where Abby went over the route for the day. "We'll be riding on some actual roads, with cars, so please be aware."

She took the lead as they rode over the Walkway over the Hudson, where there were signs about the area's history and coin-operated binoculars, and the river, far below. They pedaled past a mostly empty office park, off the trail and onto streets, through an actual neighborhood for a few miles before they were back on the bike path. Abby had to pay attention, guiding the group past playgrounds and historical markers and around little kids on training wheels and scooters. A detour caused by a fallen tree took them onto a street with a steep uphill and a hairpin turn. Abby was getting ready to tell Lily to put her bike in as easy a gear as possible, or even just walk it, instead of losing momentum halfway through the climb and falling, but she saw that the other woman had taken one look at the hill and preemptively, and wisely, had gotten out of the saddle.

"Slow and steady!" Abby called as Lily plodded past her. Abby thought the other woman's smile was looking a little strained. Maybe since Morgan had already made it to the top, with Andy Presser riding beside her, and without sparing her mom a backward glance.

Ted got a flat, which Abby helped him fix, feeling proud at how well she could manage that part of ride leadership. A dog behind a chain-link fence growled and chased them as far as his enclosure would allow. Sue told a story about how a friend of hers had been knocked off her bike by a loose dog and had broken her arm in two places, and Lou described breaking her ankle on the GAP trail between Pittsburgh and Cumberland, Maryland, and how the ride leaders had portaged her off the trail and onto the road.

Finally, the route became a trail again, mile after mile of straight, flat riding, where you could pedal mindlessly and your thoughts would wander, whether you wanted them to or not.

The weather that day was not being their friend. The sky was cloudy, a scummy pale blue that looked like a piece of paper that had been scribbled on, then erased. The air felt hot and sticky, with a headwind that sent eddies of dust swirling over the road and into open mouths and unprotected eyes. The forecast had called for a chance of thunderstorms, but the rain never came, just humidity and gusts of gritty wind and the occasional far-off boom of thunder. The group's average pace dropped below ten miles an hour, then below nine.

All of it fit Abby's mood as she pedaled along, each mile passing more slowly than the one before. She was ashamed of herself for how short she'd been with Sebastian; how unprofessional. And then, after she'd sent him away, Mark had called. Instead of answering, Abby had let the call go to voicemail. Her thoughts were an angry churn, and even though she knew she hadn't done anything wrong, she felt ashamed.

Eileen rode beside her for a while, shooting curious looks in her direction when she thought Abby didn't notice. "Windy," she observed.

"Not like Peloton, right?" Abby asked. She prepared for her mother to take offense, but Eileen just nodded.

"No wind, no flats, no kids on hoverboards. Just Britney Spears songs, and instructors telling you to pedal harder."

"Are you doing all right?" Abby asked.

"I'm fine!" Eileen said, her tone excessively bright and cheerful. Abby wondered how much she'd picked up on what was going on with Sebastian, or whether she'd start reminding Abby about her as-yet-unsettled future, or casually asking if she'd made any decisions about renewing her lease. But Eileen, blessedly, kept quiet.

As she rode Abby was remembering how it had felt when she'd reunited with Mark, and how she'd thought that relationship would spell an end to all the questions that had plagued her since she'd left college . . . and that it had. Until it hadn't.

She'd been working that week as a counselor for a camp run by her friend Gabriella, who was a librarian in Kensington, right in the middle of Philadelphia's most notorious open-air drug market. Gabi spent her days planning programming, helping patrons with their tax forms or their job hunts or their Internet searches. She'd check out books, read stories to little kids, monitor the public computer terminals, and, occasionally, barge into the bathrooms or race to the park across the street to revive someone who'd overdosed on heroin or fentanyl. The *Philadelphia Inquirer* had done a story about the heroic librarians of Kensington, who'd become as proficient with Narcan as they were with the Dewey decimal system. Inevitably, a GoFundMe had been set up and donations had arrived, along with volunteers who came to the park each morning to remove needles from the dirt and the grass, and to direct drug users to local soup kitchens, counseling centers, and needle exchanges.

Gabi had used some of the money to launch Camp Kensington, so that kids who lived in the neighborhood would have something to do during vacations when school wasn't in session. She'd recruited friends, including Abby, to work as counselors, and put out the call to a local hospital asking for doctors and dentists and nurses to volunteer.

Over spring break, at the end of March, Abby had been assigned to the littlest kids. That afternoon, it had been warm enough to be outside. Abby had set up a table in the park and been helping her campers twist colorful yarn around Popsicle sticks to make pendants, when she'd noticed the fourth-grade counselor shepherding a trio of girls across the street.

"We're going to see the doctor," the counselor said, giving Abby a wink. Twenty minutes later, Abby had seen the sixth-grade counselor making the same trek. "Troy is having an asthma attack," the counselor said. This appeared to be news to Troy, whose inhaler was still in his back pocket, but they were across the street and gone before Abby could ask any questions. Then, less than an hour later, she'd seen the fourth-grade counselor going back with a new group of kids.

At lunchtime, Abby cornered her friend to ask what was happening.

"Go take a look at the doctor," Gabi had said, smirking. "Then you'll understand."

Abby waited until the day was over before drifting over to the library, where she found herself stuck by the checkout desk, at the end of a line. She'd almost gone home. But the library was cozy, and she'd ridden her bike to work, which meant she didn't need to worry about catching the subway or a bus. So she'd refilled her water bottle and waited, bemused, outside of Gabi's office, until she was close enough to see a young man crouched down in front of a girl while the girl's mother stood by.

From her spot by the door, Abby couldn't see more than dark hair, a white coat, a masked face, and a trim body, neatly dressed. She appreciated both the consideration of the doctor getting himself to a six-year-old's eye level, and the quad strength required to maintain the position.

"Does it hurt when I do this?" the man asked, cupping the girl's elbow in his hand as he turned her arm to the left. His voice was a pleasant tenor, and something about him felt familiar, although Abby was sure she'd never seen him before.

The girl shook her head.

"Does it hurt when I do this?" He turned her arm to the right. Again, she shook her head.

"Okay. Does it hurt when I do this?" He tapped the tip of her nose. The girl giggled, shaking her head.

"Excellent! Well, your nose is in fine condition, and I think your arm is going to stop hurting very soon. You banged what's called your funny bone, which is why it feels kind of tingly."

"My funny bone?" the girl repeated.

"Yup. It's not actually the bone that's making it feel the way it feels, it's a nerve that goes right by it." He traced the nerve's path with his fingertip, before straightening up and reaching for a glass jar of lollipops. He pulled off the lid with a flourish. "I've got cherry, lime, and grape, my personal favorite." The girl said something quiet, and the doctor said, "Of course you can take one for your brother! You're very thoughtful to ask."

He'd sent the girl on her way, then turned toward the door, calling, "Who's next?"

And then he'd stared at her, looking as shocked as she felt. "Abby?" he'd said. A smile was spreading across his face, crinkling his dark-brown eyes. "Abby Stern?"

"Mark," she'd said, her voice high and squeaky as she finally recognized her summer-camp boyfriend, who appeared to have lost half of his body weight.

His haircut was different. No more bangs combed low over his forehead and hair raked toward his cheeks to disguise as much of his face as he could. Now Mark's hair was cut short and combed back from his face. He'd traded his baggy sweatshirts and billowing basketball shorts for trim-fitting khakis, a crisp button-down with the cuffs rolled up to display lean, sinewy forearms, and a pair of leather dress shoes that she knew were stylish and assumed were expensive. But Mark Medoff's kind eyes, and the awed way he looked at her, were both exactly as they'd been when they'd both been teenagers.

"Abby Stern. I can't believe it!" He'd taken her by the shoulders to look at her. Then he'd hugged her, giving Abby a chance to feel the newly firm terrain of his chest, before holding her out at arm's length again. "Look at you." Abby felt her heart melting, an actual softening sensation beneath her ribs, because she knew that he wasn't lying, or flattering her in an attempt to get her in bed. This was Mark, her first love. Once, he had known her better than almost anyone else in her life . . . and Mark had always thought she was beautiful. Best of all, he was, at that very moment, looking at her with the delighted regard she remembered from Camp Golden Hills; an expression that says *How did I get lucky enough to get to be with you?*

"Oh my God, what are you doing here?" said Abby. Her voice was embarrassingly loud, practically a squeal. *What happened?* she thought, and *Where is the rest of you?* She hoped those questions weren't showing on her face, but Mark must have expected them, because he'd looked at himself and given kind of a rueful chuckle.

"I'll tell you all about it if you're free."

"I can be free," she said, her voice still a little breathy. "Want to get coffee?"

"Anything you like," he'd said. "I'm all yours."

When he'd seen the last of his patients, Mark got in his car, and Abby got on her bike, congratulating herself for the foresight and excellent taste she'd had as a thirteen-year-old. Thirty minutes later, she and Mark were at a table for two at La Colombe in Fishtown, drinking iced coffees (Mark's black, Abby's, with cream, plus a blueberry muffin on the side) at a table in the corner of the high-ceilinged room.

Abby discovered that Mark had almost gone to podiatry school at Temple—"You would have been so close!"—before deciding on California. He told her he had taken a job in a practice in Center City just three months before and had been looking for volunteer opportunities when he'd googled Gabi's camp. She learned that he was single, that he and his graduate-school girlfriend had broken up ("amicably, for the most part") after she'd taken a postdoc fellowship in Cleveland, and that Mark now lived in a two-bedroom apartment in a high-rise on Rittenhouse Square.

"Why Philadelphia?" she asked him.

"Why not?" he replied.

"I mean, I love it here, but I know it's not for everyone." Philadelphia was, currently, the poorest big city in America. Crime had been on the rise for the last few years, and it seemed like there were more homeless people than ever, huddled over grates in the winter, or panhandling at busy intersections or highway entrances. The opioid epidemic—as Mark had surely observed—was decimating users, and the previous summer, there'd been a shooting on South Street less than a mile from Abby's house. More than once, Eileen had asked if Abby felt safe, if it wasn't time to give up the apartment and come home. More than once, Abby had told her that the city was home.

Mark appeared to be considering the question. "I knew I didn't want to live in New York—too big, too expensive, too close to home. But I did want a city. You know. Music. Museums. Culture." He pretended to preen. "I have always seen myself as a patron of the arts."

"There's great restaurants, too," said Abby. "Unless you've stopped eating completely." She regretted her words as soon as she'd said them, and saw, on Mark's face, some strange combination of pride and regret.

"I should probably tell you what happened," he said.

"You don't have to," said Abby, low-voiced, even though by then she'd guessed.

Mark inhaled audibly, then lowered his voice.

"Roux-en-Y," he'd said, gesturing at his midsection. "Gastric bypass surgery. I got it done when I was nineteen." His handsome face got a little sad. "By then, I'd gained and lost hundreds of pounds. I could lose the weight but not keep it off."

You and almost every other person who goes on a diet, Abby thought.

"I knew nothing else was ever going to work, long-term."

Abby had murmured something sympathetic as her mind whirred and clicked. Did Mark hate fat people now that he wasn't one? Did he have any interest in her now that he could probably have any woman he wanted?

While she was thinking, Mark was watching her face, looking at her in a way that made her skin feel flushed and her bones feel pleasantly liquid. "Look at you," he'd said, his voice getting a little lower, a little rougher. "You look just the same. Prettiest girl at Camp Golden Hills."

Abby had laughed, because she knew it wasn't true. She was, more or less, the same size she'd been at sixteen, the last time Mark had seen her, but she had faint wrinkles at the corners of her eyes. Her hair wasn't as shiny as it had once been, or as thick, and she had age spots along with her freckles. But Mark's expression was serious, and his eyes never wavered as he'd reached across the table to take her hand.

"Are you doing anything Saturday?" he'd asked. "Maybe you could show me around."

"I would love that," she said. He'd squeezed her fingers, and she'd smiled at him. Later, Abby would think that their reunion had felt as frictionless as a door swinging open on freshly oiled hinges; like something preordained.

If it had been any other old acquaintance, Abby would have anchored Saturday's tour with her favorite places to eat. There would have been brunch at Sabrina's, then some walking, and people-watching. There might have been a trip to the Barnes or the Philadelphia Museum of Art, followed by hummus and fresh pita at Dizengoff or tahini milkshakes at Goldie, then a stroll east to Spruce Street Harbor Park for fried chicken sandwiches at Federal Donuts, ice cream from Franklin Fountain, and drinks at Oasis . . . but could Mark eat any of that? Would Mark even want to?

"Do you want to walk?" Abby asked on Saturday morning. She'd met him at his apartment on Rittenhouse Square, where the carpet was immaculately vacuumed, the white couch was pristine, and the black-and-white beachscapes in their silver frames were precisely aligned on the wall. "Or we could rent bikes." There was an Indego kiosk a few blocks from Mark's apartment. Abby had passed it on her way there. They'd gotten lucky with the weather. After a stretch of bitterly cold days, the sun was shining, the wind had died down, and the temperature was in the fifties.

Mark's gaze had drifted toward the ground. "I don't know if you remember," he'd said, his voice low. "I don't actually know how to ride a bike."

"Oh, God," Abby said. "I totally forgot."

"I know," Mark said, a little shamefaced. "It's weird."

"It's fine. Really. Lots of people don't know how to ride bikes." *Just not many our age,* Abby thought, even as she was chiding herself for not remembering. "We can walk."

She'd ended up taking him through Rittenhouse Square Park, past the Liberty Bell and Independence Hall. They'd sat on a bench in Washington Square, where Mark complained that she wasn't showing him any of the city's real history. "Where was the first Wawa built?" he asked plaintively. "When are we going to the birthplace of the Eagles fans who threw the battery at Santa?"

Abby glared at him severely. "Okay, first of all, the batteries were at a Phillies game. The Eagles fans threw snowballs. And Santa deserved it," she said. "If you're going to live here, you need to get on board with that."

"Fine, fine," he said. "Let's continue with the Dead White Men tour." He shook his head sadly. "I have to say, though, I expected better of you."

Just for that, Abby walked him back to City Hall, and the statue of Octavius Catto, a Black athlete and activist who'd desegregated the city's trolleys and who was assassinated on Election Day in 1871 while he tried to bring Black voters to the polls.

They walked east, to the mural of a young Black woman's face on Eleventh and Sansom, which had been done by Amy Sherald, whose painting of Michelle Obama hung in the National Portrait Gallery, and Abby told Mark there was a tour he could take of the city's many murals.

"Are you hungry?" she asked. "Or shall we continue on to the Betsy Ross House?"

"I could eat," Mark said.

Can you? Abby wondered. She'd never known anyone who'd had the surgery and didn't know what Mark's limitations were.

"I can," he said when she asked. "Most foods. As long as I don't eat too much, and I chew everything really carefully."

Awesome, Abby thought, and hoped she'd kept her face expressionless. They walked east, toward the Delaware River, trading stories of the last decade and a half.

"This was my favorite place to take the kids when I was a nanny," Abby told him. "There's a skating rink at the end of the pier. You can ice-skate in the winter and roller-skate in the summer. And there's a dog park past that. And you can ride the ferry over to Camden and back again. Which little kids are surprisingly into."

Mark nodded. They'd gotten fried chicken sandwiches at Federal Donuts after all, and they sat on the ledge by the water to eat them. Abby had devoured half of her sandwich before Mark had even tasted his. She watched, trying not to be obvious about it, as he pulled off the bun and the pickles and painstakingly removed every bit of breading from his chicken breast.

"Are you sure this is okay for you?" she finally asked. "We can go someplace else. There's great sushi. And there's an amazing place where they make fresh hummus . . ."

"No, no," he'd said firmly. "This is fine." He'd taken a big bite of bare chicken to prove it. Abby had watched his jaw work as he chewed. She remembered how he'd looked when he'd told her about his surgery. "Nothing was working," he'd said, his head bent and his voice so quiet it was almost inaudible, as if what he was confessing—being fat and unable to become otherwise—was worse than being a criminal, or a sex offender. "And nothing was going to work."

"Yeah, most diets don't work, in the long term," Abby said. "And Camp Golden Hills probably did us more harm than good." By then, she'd done plenty of reading about shows like *The Biggest Loser* and places like Camp Golden Hills, and how the science showed that radically restrictive diets and hours of vigorous exercise yielded short-term loss that was almost inevitably followed by the dieter regaining every pound they'd shed and then some. She'd learned that losing the weight a second, or third, or fourth time was complicated by the way the dieter's metabolism slowed down, the dieter's body determined to hang on to the pounds the next time it was threatened with starvation. She knew about the weight-loss drugs, and the surgical options—mostly because Eileen insisted on mailing her links every few weeks, usually with a note attached that said something like *Gary and I would be more than happy to help with this!* She had done a lot of reading, and listened to a lot of podcasts about body positivity and health at every size, and how diet culture and Western beauty standards contributed to, and were fed by, capitalism and racism and misogyny in an endless loop that left women hungry and unhappy with empty bellies and depleted bank accounts, starving and tractable, too weak to change the world, or the way they had to move through it.

Hating yourself took a toll: on your finances, your self-esteem, your time. That afternoon, Abby told Mark that she'd decided to stop dieting and to focus on her health; that she did her best to practice intuitive eating honoring her body's appetites.

"My doctor doesn't even have a scale in her office. Which is refreshing. I can remember going to see my pediatrician for ear infections, and getting a lecture about being more active and eating more fruits and vegetables," Abby said. She told Mark that she exercised, only she did it for strength and endurance and flexibility and maintaining her sanity, not weight loss. She told him that her doctor thought that the BMI was garbage, that yo-yo dieting was worse than being quote-unquote overweight or obese, and that any body could be a healthy body, whether or not it fit current definitions of what was beautiful. She said that she was mostly okay—or that she was trying, every day, to be okay—at her current size and had no intention of trying to make herself smaller.

As she talked she looked at his face, wondering what he was thinking, trying to predict his response. Mark had nodded in all the right places. He'd said things like "That makes sense," and "You know, you're right" and "I completely understand." Still, she wondered what he really thought about her choices, and how different they were from his own. Did he ever regret what he'd done? Did he think other fat people were stupid, for not having surgery themselves?

Then, when they'd started walking together along the pier, and she'd begun to feel eyes on them, she had another set of questions to concern her. Was it even possible for this version of Mark to desire her now? So far, as a Magic 8 Ball might have said, all signs pointed to yes. Mark was just as kind as she remembered, holding the doors, making funny remarks, sneaking looks at her like he couldn't believe how lucky he was to be with her, delightfully oblivious to the attention they were attracting. Maybe she was imagining it, but as they strolled, Abby thought she could sense guys giving Mark disapproving looks, like he'd let down the team and had an obligation to be with someone hotter. She definitely noticed girls glaring at her, like she'd stolen something to which she wasn't entitled or hadn't earned.

Mark didn't seem to notice any of the looks. Or, if he noticed, he didn't seem bothered. As they walked toward the skating rink he took her hand and held it with just the right amount of pressure, and his eyes never wandered, no matter how many other lovely women passed by.

It was heady. Flattering. After so many bad dates and false starts and so much rejection, being the recipient of that kind of attention had felt so enthralling that Abby could believe that Mark's return was a gift the Universe had given her; a reward for everything she'd endured.

They'd wandered back toward Center City, strolling along the cobbled side streets of Society Hill and Queen Village, enjoying the early spring sunshine, talking nonstop. Occasionally, their hips or their shoulders would brush, and Abby would feel a jolt of excitement, mingled with trepidation. She and Mark had never been naked together. How would she feel about his body? How would he feel about hers?

"If you're free this Thursday, can I take you to dinner?" Mark asked.

"Of course," Abby said. "This is me," she'd said, when they'd reached her door. Mark was still holding her hand, and he'd leaned in to kiss her, the barest brush of his lips against her mouth. Abby barely slept that night. She was completely blissed out, bubbling with excitement, sure that she'd found—or refound—the One. Her person, her soul mate, her *bashert*, as her nana would have said.

On Thursday Mark met Abby on the corner in front of Royal Izakaya, in khakis and another crisply pressed shirt. At a booth in the back of the dimly lit restaurant, with episodes of *Speed Racer* projected over the bar, he'd wielded his chopsticks gracefully as he ate his sashimi, assuring her that the fish was delicious and that he didn't miss the rice, and she'd had hand rolls and pillowy pork buns and split an order of tuna guacamole with him, humming happily at the unctuous, oily richness of avocado chunks and slivers of meltingly tender fatty tuna. She'd felt his eyes on her face—on her mouth, specifically—as she licked her lips. But that night, when he'd walked her home, all he'd done was kiss her. Much more extensively than the first night.

"Do you want to come up?" Abby asked, a little breathlessly. Her back was up against the warm brick next to her building's front door, and she could feel that he was interested.

He'd paused. Abby had held her breath. "Next time," he finally said. "I don't want to rush you."

"I think we know each other well enough," Abby said.

"True. But I still think we should take our time. There's no rush, is there?" He leaned close, murmuring, "We get to enjoy this part."

Abby nodded. She still couldn't quite believe that this was happening, that of all the cities in the country, Mark had picked Philadelphia; that of all the places he could have volunteered, he'd picked Kensington.

"Are you busy Saturday?" he asked.

She'd felt her heart sink. "I'm busy all weekend. Remember Kara Taft from Golden Hills? She was in my bunk. She's getting married, and her bachelorette party is in New York, on Saturday night."

"How about I make reservations somewhere for a week from Saturday, then?"

Abby had happily agreed. Then she'd gone to New York, and had her interlude with Sebastian, which had felt like a delicious dream, or maybe even the Universe giving her a palate cleanser, one last lovely treat before she settled down with the man she was meant to be with forever. Sebastian was just a fling; nothing that could ever turn into something real. Mark was real.

On the Saturday night after she returned from New York, Abby put on her prettiest dress, an ivory-colored maxi dress with puffy sleeves and a fitted bodice and a neckline cut low enough to give Mark a preview of coming attractions. He'd picked her up in an Uber and taken her to dinner at Morimoto (raw fish without rice, Abby realized, was one of the foods Mark could eat without worrying). After dinner, they'd stepped into the warm night and, without discussion, began walking toward Abby's apartment. They didn't talk about what would happen next. They didn't need to. Mark held her hand, and Abby felt like his grasp was the only thing keeping her tethered to Earth. She was that happy.

Her bliss ended as soon as she'd unlocked the door. Even though she'd spent the afternoon cleaning (at least, the parts of the afternoon when she wasn't removing hair from various parts of her body), she knew her place looked untidy and undone, especially compared to Mark's apartment, which was completely furnished and decorated in a manner suggesting good taste and competence. Mark's place looked like a grown-up's home, while Abby's apartment looked like a room in a youth hostel, a way station for someone young who didn't have much money or many things and wasn't planning on staying for long.

"It's kind of a mess," Abby said, cringing, wishing she'd moved the pieces of the IKEA television stand she'd been trying to assemble for longer than she cared to remember into a closet. Mark looked around, inspecting her jumble of furniture and possessions. There was the dark blue velvet couch, her pride and joy, with an unframed poster of a Monet watercolor thumbtacked above it. A glass coffee table she'd inherited after Eileen and Gary the Businessman had redecorated stood in front of the sofa; a soft, fringed, pumpkin-colored throw, one of the few things she'd bought for herself as an adult, hung (unevenly, she saw) over its back. There were a pair of metal barstools standing in the kitchen, in front of the breakfast bar, but there was an empty space under the window where a table should have gone. On the windowsill, an orchid Lizzie had given her was clinging valiantly to life, despite Abby's haphazard attentions. Waist-high stacks of books teetered against the walls, next to the recycling she'd meant to take out and the canned goods she'd been meaning to drop off at the mutual aid food pantry. Everything looked temporary, tenuous, thrown together, and barely thought through. It was not the home of a person who knew who she was, or how she wanted her living space to look.

Abby moved quickly to take Mark's hand and convey him to the bedroom. She lit the candles she'd had at the ready, casting the room in a romantic glow (and, she hoped, disguising the piles of laundry on the floor, as well as the truly embarrassing number of self-help books on her nightstand). She pulled him down to the bed, and he'd kissed her, her forehead, her cheeks, her neck, her shoulders, whispering that he didn't know how he'd gotten so lucky.

It wasn't the electric, immediate connection she'd felt with Sebastian. It wasn't fast or frantic. It was slow and measured and thoughtful; good, but in a different way: the fulfillment of a promise their bodies had made long ago.

In bed, Mark was as gentle and considerate as he was everywhere else. "Are you ready?" he'd whispered, when both of them were naked, and he was hovering on top of her, his absurdly toned torso held aloft on his newly muscled arms, and Abby, laughing a little, said, "I've been ready since I was sixteen."

Mark told her she was beautiful. He'd touched her gently, with something that felt like reverence. Abby tried to relax, to be in the moment, and not compare, for example, the way that Mark's formerly soft, yielding body, the body that had made her feel so safe, was now taut and muscled, that every part that had once felt gentle and welcoming now bulged or rippled, stiff and firm. In the flickering candlelight, when he sat back on his heels to roll on a condom, he looked like a Greek sculpture, like Narcissus kneeling in front of the pond. When he was finally inside of her, he'd paid close attention, taking frequent looks at her face, asking if it was all right, if she wanted more or less pressure, if he was still in the right spot, until she pulled him down and kissed him, rocking her hips, setting the pace, until he was moving with her, and all he could do was gasp her name.

Abby woke up with sunshine streaming through her window, illuminating the reddish highlights in Mark's dark hair, a wedge of golden skin on his cheek (and a gigantic dust bunny that Abby quickly kicked under the bed). Lying beside him, she'd felt blanketed in an unfamiliar contentment, an unassailable sense of rightness.

Abby had gone to the same college as her brother. When she graduated, she'd moved into her sister's former apartment. In each case it had felt like stepping onto a treadmill that was already in motion, where the journey was preordained. Meeting Mark again; falling in love with him, felt like a variation on that theme, the natural next step. Here were the answers to the questions about what she'd do with her life, and who she'd do it with. Here was an approved path forward, with clearly delineated stops along the way. Easy and comfortable. Meant to be.

It hadn't taken long—especially not with a pandemic-accelerated timetable—before Abby began spending two, then three, then four nights at Mark's place, which was bigger than her apartment, not to mention fully furnished, with a large, flat-screen TV that got all the premium streaming services (Abby was still using her parents' passwords when she wanted to watch Netflix or HBO). She'd brought a toothbrush over one night, then a few pairs of underwear. Mark had given her a drawer in his dresser and, more importantly, a shelf in the refrigerator for things she wanted to eat that he couldn't, insisting, bravely, if not entirely convincingly, that she was welcome to keep any food she liked in the house. Abby knew that he meant it . . . but, after seeing him carefully relocating her ice cream to the very back of the freezer one too many times, or noticing the way his lips would thin when she ordered pasta at a restaurant, she'd decided it was better to keep her treats back at her own apartment.

Abby's father had invited them for Thanksgiving the first year they dated. He'd hosted a big, casual buffet for his children and their spouses and significant others, plus all the strays and orphans from his synagogue. Abby had reintroduced Mark to her siblings, whom he'd met, years ago, at her bat mitzvah, along with Simon's wife and Marni's husband and Abby's new stepmother, Shira. Abby had found them seats at the table. She'd fixed Mark a plate of skinless turkey breast and plain unbuttered sweet potato, and tried not to feel sad when she saw him taking a double portion of green bean casserole, then carefully extracting each bean from the mushroom béchamel sauce and fried onion topping.

Abby's mother had hosted them for Chanukah that December. "You remember Mark," Abby had said sweetly, knowing there was absolutely no chance her mother would recognize her formerly larger boyfriend.

"Mark! Of course!" Eileen had said warmly. Then she'd cut her eyes at Abby, as if to say, *He got skinny. Why can't you?* Abby had been forced to put an extra dollop of sour cream onto her latkes as revenge.

Then Mark's parents had wanted to meet Abby, which meant a late-December trip to Long Island and a night of very quiet, surprisingly hot sex in Mark's boyhood bedroom, on a squeaky twin-size bed, underneath a poster of the Islanders. They'd kissed on New Year's Eve at midnight, as 2021 became 2022. In the spring, they'd gone away for a long weekend to Jamaica, and that summer they'd rented a place with one of Mark's doctor friends and his wife for two weeks at the Jersey Shore.

"Do you think you and Mark will get married?" Izzie asked. Izzie and Howard were both doctors, who'd been married for two years.

"I'm not sure," Abby had said. By then, she was almost positive that Mark wanted to spend the rest of his life with her. Abby could certainly imagine it happening. She was happy with Mark. But, somehow, she wasn't in a hurry to bring that day closer.

Their second year together had unfolded in much the same manner. Abby spent three or four nights a week at Mark's place, and she liked being there, but was always happy to come home, where she could keep whatever she wanted in the refrigerator, and nobody chided her when she left the toothpaste uncapped. She and Mark would go for walks together, but he ran by himself, and she rode her bike without him. They discovered a mutual passion for putting puzzles together, for taking long walks to different neighborhoods, and they binge-watched all six seasons of *The Americans* and all seven seasons of *Mad Men*.

Abby had worked hard to improve her self-esteem, to arrive at a place where, if she couldn't love her body, she could at least feel neutral toward it, and exist peacefully within it. But she wasn't blind, or ignorant of the way the world perceived her. Mark was one in a million; the kind of man with whom any woman, big or small, beautiful or ugly, would be happy to spend her life. He was handsome and hardworking, he was steadfast and kind, and being his wife would mean that Abby would never want for anything, or have to feel aimless or adrift. She was lucky to have him; lucky that, of all the girls in the world, Mark had picked her. And maybe she should have been in a hurry to lock it down, to demand that Mark put a ring on it, which she knew he'd be happy to do. But things were already so good. Why change them?

That's what she'd told herself. That's what she'd thought right until she'd left for the Amtrak station and New York. Right until she'd seen Sebastian again.

After lunch, Abby helped Jasper pack up the leftovers and load the coolers back in the van, then reminded everyone to reapply their sunscreen and refill their water bottles. She rode sweep, mostly keeping Lily Mackenzie company, and having a not-entirely-unpleasant conversation with her mother about a scandal involving a movie star's yoga-instructor-slash-Instagram-influencer wife, who'd claimed to be Spanish and had faked an accent for years before the Internet sleuths discovered she was from Medford, Massachusetts.

"I don't understand why someone would do something like that," Eileen said, and Abby agreed that she didn't get it, either.

"But you have to respect her commitment. I mean, all those years of"—Abby did her best to replicate the way the woman spoke—"how you say, coo-cumbray?"

Eileen laughed, shaking her head. "Maybe it was just role-playing that got out of hand."

Abby wasn't sure what was more shocking—that Eileen knew what role-playing was, or that she'd let her daughter know that she knew. She decided not to dwell on it. If Eileen was happy, and not driving Abby crazy, she'd do her best to enjoy it.

As Abby had predicted, Sebastian and Lincoln were way out front . . . although, to their credit, they'd been eating actual food at lunch, not just lab-engineered food-like substances. At three thirty, she had just finished checking the mileage to the hotel and was congratulating herself on having successfully avoided

Sebastian for the entire day when she saw him standing by the side of the trail, holding his handlebars and frowning at his front wheel.

Abby waved her mom on ahead and let her bike coast to a stop. "Flat tire?" she asked.

He gave a curt nod.

Payback! was Abby's first gleeful thought. She scolded herself for being petty, and reminded herself that, as the trip's leader, she needed to display calm and expertise.

Abby unclipped her feet from her pedals, climbed off her bike, and leaned it against a tree. She saw that Sebastian, who was still stubbornly refusing to wear his reflective pinny, had managed to figure out his quick release and get the front wheel off the bike. He had his two tire irons seated underneath the rim, but that was as far as he'd managed to proceed.

"Need a hand?" Abby asked. Clearly, he did, but she'd be damned if she was going to jump in before he explicitly requested her help.

"No," Sebastian said.

"Okay, then." Abby watched him, sipping from her water bottle.

"I've got this. You can go," said Sebastian, as one of the tire irons slipped free and fell to the ground. He muttered a curse, then said, "This isn't a spectator sport."

"I'm not spectating," said Abby, who decided that she would have given large amounts of money to be able to climb on her bike and pedal away. Even when he was sweaty and grumpy; even though she knew he'd slept with hundreds of other women—maybe thousands!—she still found Sebastian annoyingly attractive. "We're not supposed to abandon our riders if they're having mechanical difficulties." She kept her tone casual, watching as his lips compressed, wondering if he'd read any of the small print on the Breakaway literature. Her guess was that he hadn't even read the large print.

"Fine," he said shortly, and continued to wrench, fruitlessly, at his tire.

"I wouldn't want to ditch you in your hour of need," she said.

"This is not my hour of need."

"That's fine. No worries. I'll just keep you company until you're back on the road." Abby sat at the base of a tree, unfastened her helmet, and pulled her hair free of its scrunchie, shaking it loose, then smoothing it back into a ponytail, watching Sebastian struggle and curse. When he'd finally gotten his tire free from the wheel's rim and pulled out the deflated tube, Abby extended her hand.

"Give me your tire. I'll check it for glass." She thought she would relish every second of Sebastian's struggle, but what she'd realized was that she just felt sorry for him. And, still, attracted to him. He was wearing a white bicycle jersey that had gotten sheer with sweat in the vicinity of his shoulders, and in his Lycra shorts, his legs looked like the Platonic ideal of male legs.

His face was stony as he handed Abby the tire, more or less shoving it at her with a muttered word that might—if Abby was feeling generous—have been "thanks." He wasn't looking at her. Abby wondered if that was on purpose as she ran her fingers carefully along the inside of the tire, eventually finding a tiny shard of glass.

"Here's your culprit," she said, after she'd carefully worked it free.

Sebastian grunted. Abby pulled a dollar bill out of her jersey's back pocket, folded it in half horizontally, then placed it inside the tire, against the spot where the glass had poked through. Sebastian rummaged in the bag fastened to his seat post. He'd just extracted a fresh tube when Lincoln, who'd gone off to use what Jasper called the facili-trees, came strolling out of the woods.

"You haven't gotten that changed yet?" he asked, wiping his forehead.

Sebastian didn't reply.

"He's not in a very good mood," Abby stage-whispered.

"That's an exciting change of pace," Lincoln stage-whispered back.

"Both of you be quiet," Sebastian grumbled after he'd attached the nozzle to his pump, put air into the tube, then threaded the valve stem through the wheel. "And for God's sake, stop staring."

Abby ostentatiously turned away. "I have averted my eyes," she announced, and sat down again, face tilted toward the sky. Lincoln sat beside her and offered her a strip of fruit leather. She gnawed at it while Sebastian kept up a steady stream of curses and imprecations. Finally, he got the tube inflated and in place and worked the tire back onto the wheel.

"Well done!" Abby said, giving him a cheesy grin with a thumbs-up on top. Sebastian glared at her. Then Lincoln frowned at him pointedly, and Sebastian's expression became contrite.

"I'm sorry," he said, his voice a low rasp that Abby felt in the pit of her belly.

She swallowed hard. "It's fine. Just let me know if there's anything I can do to make this a better experience." The words were barely out of her mouth before her mind served up a scene from that night in his bedroom. They'd been lying on their sides, facing each other, kissing. He'd had his hands on her hips and one of his legs between her legs, the top of his thigh angled so that she could grind against it. *Get on top*, he'd said. *I want to see you.* She'd done as he'd urged her, and he'd reached up, cupping her breasts, holding them in his hands, groaning, *God, you're beautiful.*

"Want to ride with us? Keep us company?" Sebastian asked, his voice still that low, intimate rumble. Abby could feel herself blushing.

"I should go check on everyone," she said and picked up

her pace, counting the days in her head. Twelve more days, she thought. Less than two weeks, to avoid him, and not murder her mother. She'd get the riders to Buffalo, alive and in one piece. She'd make a decision about Mark, and the rest of her life. She'd figure it out, somehow.

Morgan

Day Four: Hudson to Amsterdam
Seventy-one miles

Did you find someone to help you?" Olivia asked.

"Not yet." Morgan's mom was in the shower, and Morgan had taken her phone to the far edge of the hotel parking lot, so that she wouldn't be overheard. She was already dressed, in bike shorts and a tee shirt, and, underneath it, a sports bra that was squeezing her painfully. Her breasts usually felt tender the day or two before she got her period. Part of her wanted to hope that's what this was, that she wasn't really pregnant, and that all she had to do was wait.

But part of her knew better.

"Like, I'm not even sure they'll give you the pills if they don't think you've got someone to take you home, or to your hotel, or whatever, and take care of you," Olivia said.

Morgan felt her insides clench, and her breath catch in her throat. They would give her the pills. They'd have to.

"How many days until you're in Syracuse?" Olivia asked.

"Three."

"I really think you should talk to your mom," Olivia said.

Again. Morgan closed her eyes. "Just give her a chance," Olivia said, before Morgan could explain to her—again—why the idea of telling Lily was a nonstarter. "And if she tells you no, you can just get to the appointment by yourself."

"There's no way." Morgan's voice was muted. She knew what her mother would do, if she learned about Morgan's intentions. Lily would stick to Morgan, every minute of the day, not leaving her alone for a second, not giving her a chance to slip away and take care of things. Then they'd be home, and she'd tell Morgan's dad, and Brody, and that would be the end of it. They'd probably lock her in her bedroom until it was time for her to give birth.

"I'll find someone," she told Olivia.

"Okay," Olivia said. "And I'm here if you need me."

Morgan ended the call and went back to the room, thinking that she had no idea how to make good on her promise; no idea who, in this group of strangers, she could trust with her secret.

The hotel room wasn't fancy, but it was clean. It had two beds, a flat-screen TV, a bathroom with a toilet and a tub. The sink, with a coffeemaker, and their empty water bottles beside it, was outside the bathroom door. Her mother was standing in front of the sink, wrapped in a towel, blow-drying her hair. She smiled at Morgan in the mirror. "Ready for another day of riding?" she asked, and Morgan felt so wretched, so dishonest and deceitful and low that, for a minute, she wasn't sure her legs would hold her up. She felt herself wobbling and put one hand on the desk to steady herself.

"Yeah," she said, and made herself smile. "Can't wait."

Be her friend Lincoln had told him. Sebastian was going to do his best . . . but it wasn't easy.

"How can I get her to be my friend when she thinks I slept with every woman in Brooklyn?" he'd asked Lincoln that morning. Lincoln had put down his coffee cup, given Sebastian a long, level look, and said, "Maybe you should have thought about that before you slept with every woman in Brooklyn."

"Not helping," Sebastian had muttered.

"Okay," Lincoln had said. "Ask her about herself. Get to know her. Find out what she likes to do." He squeezed sunscreen out of a tube and rubbed it onto his cheeks and his forehead. "Lana and I were friends before we started dating. Sometimes, it's nice to genuinely like someone, and spend time getting to know them before you sleep with them."

"Point taken," said Sebastian.

"And stop looking at the Internet," Lincoln said. "You're making yourself crazy."

Sebastian knew his friend was right, that he was just torturing himself. He knew, too, that the story would die down, especially if he didn't do anything that would add fuel to the fire. But he couldn't stop poking at the wound, or pressing on the bruise, or pushing his tongue into the place where a tooth had once been. Choose your metaphor. He was no longer trending on Twitter, which was good, but the story had jumped to more of the big gossip websites, which was bad. And also meant that the story might have traveled to a place his sister or his parents could conceivably see it. *Ignore it,* he told himself. Sure, there were people out there laughing at him, but they weren't people he'd ever meet, so what did he care? *Other people's opinion of you are none of your business.* One of the Scoop's freelancers had told him that, explaining how she never, ever looked at comments on her stories. His sister was a social-media Luddite, who used Facebook to keep up with her high school friends and never ventured onto other platforms. And as for his parents, they were usually too wrapped up in their own drama to pay attention to his.

That morning, Sebastian rode slowly, letting the rest of the riders pass him, until he spotted Abby's white helmet, with her ponytail threaded through the back. She wore a pale-blue jersey that left the tops of her arms and her freckled shoulders bare. He felt his pulse speed up, and gave his body a stern scolding, reminding himself of the mission: *be her friend.*

"Hi, Abby."

She didn't meet his eyes as she asked, "Is everything all right?"

"Everything is fine. I just thought I'd ride with you for a little while. If that's okay."

"Sure." Her tone was not, in Sebastian's opinion, especially inviting. He decided to behave like he'd been invited anyhow.

"So. Have you lived in Philadelphia all your life?" he asked.

"Yes."

Again, Sebastian reminded himself not to ask questions that could be answered in a single word.

"What are the best things about it?"

"There are lots of good things."

"Such as?"

"Good restaurants. Lots of places to ride your bike."

"What's your favorite restaurant?"

"Oh, I can't pick just one favorite. Like, there's the place with the best sushi, and the place with the best Turkish food, and the best fried chicken, and the best Szechuan and the best Cantonese and the best Vietnamese and the best Thai."

"Okay. Yum. Point taken." He took a swig from his water bottle and asked, "Is Doctor Mark a big foodie?"

"He . . ." Abby appeared to be considering her answer. "He's more of a 'food is fuel' guy."

"Ah." *Okay,* Sebastian thought. A thing she liked that Doctor Mark didn't. "Is he a big cyclist? Do you guys do trips together?"

Abby paused, then said, her voice tight, "He doesn't ride a bike."

"At all?" Sebastian asked.

"He never learned as a kid. There were extenuating circumstances."

"Was he born without legs?"

Abby didn't laugh at that, or even smile. "We've known each other a long time. We do lots of things together. It's fine if he doesn't ride with me."

Leave it alone, Sebastian told himself. *Be her friend.* And so, even though he wanted to stay on the topic of Mark, who didn't like food and didn't ride a bike, he asked, "Are you a big Eagles fan?"

"Not really. But when you live in Philadelphia, you kind of can't help being caught up in it, when they're having a good year. I remember, when they won the Super Bowl in 2018, it felt like the whole city was out in the streets, cheering." Finally, she smiled a little. "And when they finally called the election for Biden, in 2020, everyone in my neighborhood came outside, and we were all dancing in the streets."

Sebastian nodded and described the exultation in his own neighborhood . . . and realized, gratefully, that he hadn't thought about the whole TikTok mess in at least five minutes.

"How was COVID for you?" he asked. "Did people leave Philadelphia the way they left New York?"

"Some did," Abby said. "But almost everyone in my neighborhood stuck it out." She told him about a photographer friend who'd started a project of photographing families from a distance, as they sat on their stoops or waved at her from their front windows, and how she'd worked with a mutual aid organization to deliver lunches to food-insecure families. "It was awful for the kids who'd been getting breakfast and lunch at school. The schools in Philadelphia stayed closed much longer than they did in other cities. And online learning did not go well for a lot of kids." He heard the *click-click-click* of Abby's derailleur as she shifted gears.

"There's a family on my block with three little girls. I taught them all how to ride their bikes in the spring of 2020, just so they'd have something to do outside of the house."

"That was nice of you," Sebastian said. *Stellar observation*, he thought. Really top-notch.

"How about you? Did you run for the hills?"

"I did go home for a little while. You know. Portable job, and all of that." He didn't like thinking about the weeks he'd spent back in New Jersey. His mother's drinking had picked up, because of the stress, or because of the uncertainty, or because it was a day that ended in *Y*, and his dad had been even more distracted than usual, because he was trying to manage his job and his wife and also take care of his own mother. Grandma Piersall was in an assisted living facility, and the staff had been decimated by the virus. Nurses and aides had gotten sick, or they'd quit before they could get sick. The place hadn't allowed visitors. Sebastian's dad had resorted to sitting outside of his mother's window on a folding chair, talking to her on the phone, so she could see him as well as hear his voice and know that she wasn't alone. Between his own mother "napping" on the couch most afternoons from two or three o'clock on, and his father spending hours on the phone, trying to get someone at his mom's facility to talk to him, or someone at the state ombudsman's office to deal with his complaints, it had been pretty miserable. Sebastian had been happy to get back to Williamsburg, even if the neighborhood felt, he imagined, like London after the blitz—bombed out and empty, eerily quiet.

"Did you ever get it? COVID?" he asked.

"I feel like everyone's gotten it at this point," she said. "I was lucky. I had a very mild case, last October. No real symptoms, except fatigue. How about you?"

He told her that he'd gotten it the previous summer; how

it had almost been a relief. Lincoln had brought him Gatorade and Theraflu, and Lana had left chicken soup outside of his door every night.

"You're lucky to have friends like that," she told him.

Look at me, Sebastian thought to himself as the trail sloped downhill, along the canal, and Abby's ponytail fluttered in the breeze. Having a conversation with a woman! Being her friend!

She told him about the guy in her bicycle club who never stopped talking on rides, unless he was singing, and how sometimes she could handle it but sometimes she found him so annoying that she fantasized about buying him a muzzle. He told her about how, during the pandemic, he'd ordered hair clippers from Amazon and had tried to give himself a haircut and had ended up using the wrong attachment and shaving a bald furrow down the center of his skull.

They pedaled along, and the grass was very green, and the sky was very blue, and it had been twenty entire minutes, and 4.3 miles, according to Sebastian's Strava, since he'd thought about TikTok.

"You're very easy to talk to," he said.

"Thank you for ending that sentence with 'to talk to,'" Abby said. Sebastian thought for a few seconds, then snorted. Abby paused, then said, "You know, I'd hardly ever done anything like that before, the night we met. I'm really not a one-night-stand person."

Sebastian wasn't sure what to do with that information. If he'd been going on instinct—specifically, if he'd been going on the instinct telling him to do whatever it took to get together with Abby again—he'd have said *It didn't have to be a one-night stand. We can pick up right where we left off.* Instead, he said, "Yeah. Same here."

Abby turned her head to meet his gaze. Then she started

laughing. Then he started laughing, too, and said, "Actually, I was a virgin when you met me. You took my maidenhead."

"Do you want it back?" she asked. "And also, that can't be true."

"Why can't it?"

"Well." He thought that, if he could see her face, she'd be blushing; that delicious pink flush he remembered. "If I'd actually taken your maidenhead, wouldn't we have had to do other things?"

"Other things?"

"You know," Abby said. "Other things." She lowered her voice to a stage whisper. "Butt stuff."

"Butt stuff!" Sebastian repeated, laughing. "Oh my God."

"Why is butt stuff funny?"

"Butt stuff," said Sebastian, "is always funny."

"Not the way I do it," she said, in a pretend-sexy voice that sounded actually sexy to Sebastian, and because he was a guy, a guy who'd slept with her, he found himself picturing sexy things. And then, because he was a guy who was also trying to be friends with Abby, and not sleep with her again, he made himself stop picturing them, and forced himself, instead, to picture Abby with Mark.

Except he had no idea what Mark looked like. "Do you have a picture of Mark?" he asked as casually as he could.

Abby's smile disappeared. "I can show you one when we stop," she said. "He's got dark hair and brown eyes, and he's terrifyingly fit."

"Terrifyingly fit?" Sebastian filed that away for future consideration.

"He runs six miles every single day." Abby related this information calmly, but he thought he could hear something—was it envy? frustration?—underneath the factual tone.

"Six miles every day is a lot," said Sebastian. "Is he training for a marathon?"

"Only if the marathon is his life. He's done them before, though. And he's a very clean eater. Lots of salmon and chicken breasts."

This felt like a possible minefield, a place where it would be easy to say the wrong thing. So Sebastian said, "You guys met at summer camp?"

"It was actually a weight-loss camp. Fat camp."

Another minefield, Sebastian thought. Avoid, avoid, avoid.

"Is he the same person he was when you were teenagers?" he asked.

Abby's voice was very dry. "He's about half the size he was back then. But yes, I'd say he's very similar. Obviously he's got more education now, and he's lived more places, and done more things, but . . ." She pedaled and seemed to be thinking. "He's always been kind. Bighearted. And he's funny, in a kind of quiet way. That hasn't changed. How about you?" she asked. "When was your last serious relationship?"

Sebastian didn't want to tell her that there'd never been one; that, just as she was not a one-night-stand person, he'd never had more than a handful of hookups with the same woman. "It's been a little while," he said.

"Like, how long?"

He thought about saying *college,* or *I can't really remember.* He thought of offering up COVID as an excuse. Instead, he told her, "I've never really had a serious girlfriend."

"Wow," said Abby. "What's up with that? Like, who broke you?"

"No one broke me," he said, a little indignantly.

"Are you sure?"

"I think I'd remember."

"Not always," Abby said. "Maybe you've repressed it."

"Maybe no one hurt me, and I've just never met the right person."

"Yeah," Abby said. "But you're how old? Because at our age, most people have had a few serious relationships."

"I guess I'm the exception," he said lightly.

"Are your parents married?" Abby asked.

Sebastian felt his shoulder blades draw together, and his hands tighten on the handlebars. Avoid, avoid, avoid. "They are."

"Happily?"

Sebastian found himself remembering his college graduation. His parents and Lincoln's family, out to dinner at a restaurant in Middletown with a view of the Connecticut River. They could see the men's and women's crew team, rowing up and down, through the windows. He remembered his mother ordering a bottle of champagne—"To celebrate our sons!"—then drinking most of it, plus a number of glasses of white wine. Lincoln had been looking at Sebastian, and Dr. and Mr. DeVries had been looking at each other, their faces increasingly concerned as his mother's voice got louder, her gestures more emphatic. His father, eventually, had excused himself and helped his mom to her feet, guiding her out of the restaurant and back to the car.

"They love each other" was what he said to Abby. His voice sounded hollow. He thought that what his mother really loved was white wine, and what his father really loved was having a problem to solve. That, and being the hero, riding to his wife's rescue, saving the day. "It's . . ." He paused. "I don't know. Maybe it's not the healthiest relationship."

He waited for Abby to press him about it, or connect the dysfunction of his parents' marriage to his own failure on the relationship front. Instead, she said, "I'm sorry." Sebastian felt an unexpected lump in his throat. He'd never talked to anyone but

Lincoln about what was going on with his parents, or what it had been like when he'd gone home in 2020.

"What about your parents?" he asked.

When she answered, he could picture her rolling her eyes. "Oh, Lord. That's a saga. Honestly? I don't think the two of them should have ever been married at all. My dad's basically a hippie, and my mom . . . well. You've seen my mom."

"She doesn't seem that bad." She was sober, Sebastian thought, and actively taking an interest in her child, both of which made her a significant improvement on his own mom.

"She's a fancy lady. She has her charities, and her exercise classes, and her friends, that's all she ever wanted. I really do not know what she was doing with my dad in the first place. But they're both remarried, and now, I think, they're both with the people they should have been with all along."

"Everyone's living happily ever after, huh?"

"Well, isn't that what everyone wants? To be with someone who loves them and understands them, and isn't trying to change them?" Again, Sebastian heard, or thought he heard, that note of envy, or sorrow, or something other than straightforward happiness, in her voice. Was Mark trying to change her? Did Mark not understand her? If he was trying to be her friend, Sebastian should know these things. A friend would be interested. A friend would want details.

"That sounds right," he said cautiously.

"You should keep that in mind," Abby said. "You know, just in case you ever meet someone you decide you want to be in a relationship with."

Glumly, Sebastian realized that he probably wouldn't be meeting anyone anytime soon. How much time would have to pass before the stink of Internet humiliation would fade? Before he wasn't instantly recognizable as a cautionary tale, a walking red flag? He'd have to give up the apps, he realized. Maybe he'd move as far away as possible, to somewhere like Alaska.

He must have made some amused noise out loud, because Abby asked, "What's so funny?"

"Just that I'm probably going to have to move someplace far away, if I ever want to . . ." He considered saying *have sex* and decided, instead, to say, "date, again."

Abby looked at him, eyebrows scrunched, nose adorably wrinkled. "You think so?"

"Well, yes. Insofar as I'm currently an Internet scandal. Hashtag fuckboy." Which was, actually, one of the milder hashtags he'd seen applied to his situation.

"Yeah, but you're also . . ." She gestured at him with one small hand. Her cycling glove covered her wrist and palm but left her fingertips bare, and he wanted, very badly, to feel her hand in his own hand, or against his cheek, or his chest.

"Yes?" He was half-teasing, but also truly wanting to hear what she thought.

She shook her head. "You know . . ." she said. He wondered what she was feeling, and if she felt connected to him, drawn to him, the same way he felt connected and drawn to her.

"Tell me," he said. His bike had gotten so close to hers that their feet were almost brushing as they pedaled.

"I will not." Abby started riding faster. "I should go check on some of the other riders."

Sebastian kept up.

"Tell me!" he said again, in a comic-book monster voice.

"I have to go!" she called over her shoulder. And then she was gone, cresting a hill, leaving the faintest smell of flowers behind.

Sebastian looked to his left and saw that Ted, Ed, and Sue, the Spoke'n Four's three riders that day, had come up alongside him.

"What are you waiting for?" Ted called.

He stared at them blankly.

"You've been riding together for an hour and a half," Ed told him.

"And you looked happy," said Sue, taking her hands off her handlebars to clasp them at her heart, then to make shooing motions at Sebastian. "Go after her!"

"She's got a boyfriend," Sebastian felt obligated to say. The older riders were quiet for a moment.

"A boyfriend isn't a husband!" said Ted, and Sue rode up behind him, close enough to thump him on the back of his helmet.

"We're rooting for you!" Ed called as the three of them rode off, leaving Sebastian behind them, shaking his head, wondering if his intentions were really so obvious to strangers when they were still, for the most part, a mystery to himself.

Sebastian

Day Five: Amsterdam to Utica
Sixty-one miles

The Breakaway cyclists pulled into their hotel in Utica at just after four o'clock on a postcard-perfect summer afternoon. The skies had been clear, the weather, mild, with a gentle tailwind to push them along, as the path wound through parks and forests, over bridges and past locks. Dozens of locks. All of which the Spoke'n Four seemed determined to photograph. All day long, the two women plus Ed had been getting off their bikes to marvel at the ingenuity of previous generations, to inspect the mechanisms and pose by the historical markers. Sebastian had barely noticed any of it. He let Lincoln collect their hotel keys and their luggage and take a shower while Sebastian fidgeted and tried not to look at his phone.

Dinner that night was at a Middle Eastern restaurant, where the riders were greeted by the scents of garlic and oregano and fresh pita, and a hostess, who exclaimed over them like they were long-lost family members who'd come back from the Crusades.

"Breakaway riders come here every year," Sebastian heard Abby tell Lincoln, as the owner threw her arms around Jasper and kissed him on each cheek.

"Come, come!" she said. "Your room is all ready!" She led them to a room in the back of the restaurant, with windows on all three sides, where a table was already set with platters of dips and falafel, baskets of warm pita, and pitchers full of water that the waitress couldn't refill fast enough. Sebastian sat down between the two mother-daughter duos, intent on continuing his efforts to make Abby see him as a person, a friend, not just a former one-night stand.

It would have been easier if Abby wasn't avoiding him. Ever since their ride together the previous day, she'd been keeping her distance, and it felt like whatever progress he'd made toward earning her trust had evaporated. Every time he opened his mouth, she leaned away from him. Every time he asked a question, she answered him in as few words as possible, addressing the space just above his left shoulder, never once looking in his eyes.

He watched as she completed her trip around the table, checking in with each rider, asking Lily how her legs and back were feeling, asking Dale if his derailleur had stopped making that weird noise. When she was finally sitting down, he came and sat beside her.

"How are your legs?" he asked.

She just stared at him.

"Is your derailleur still making that noise?"

She looked puzzled.

"You're taking care of everyone. I just think someone should take care of you."

He saw the way her eyes got a little wider when he said it. This close to her, he could see a handful of freckles across the bridge of her nose, the single curl that had escaped her bun to brush at the nape of her neck.

"That's very nice of you," she said. "But I'm fine. Really. I'm just doing my job."

Before he could stop her, or say anything else again, she gave him a tight smile and left to huddle with Jasper.

At one end of the table, the Spoke'n Four were talking quietly. At the other, Andy Presser and Morgan Mackenzie sat, their heads bent together, so close they were almost touching. Carol Landon was talking to Morgan; Richard Landon was talking to Dale Presser, and Kayla was telling Ezra that even though they were on vacation, he had to eat something green, and no, olives didn't count.

Abby was laughing at something Jasper had said. She looked so unselfconscious, so happy and relaxed. He felt a tug in his chest and rubbed it. Annoyed, he realized that Abby was smiling at someone who wasn't him. Was it just that he'd never cared about being rejected? A lack of other women, upon whom he could turn his focus, and maybe make Abby jealous?

"Heartburn?" Eileen asked him, taking the seat opposite her daughter.

"Maybe." *Your daughter is going to be the death of me,* Sebastian thought.

Eileen gave him her thin-lipped smile. Most of the riders, per Breakaway's instructions, had packed just a few off-the-bike outfits: a pair of pants or shorts and a few tee shirts. Eileen, though, had debuted a brand-new outfit every night, including shoes and accessories. That evening, she wore a sleeveless orange dress, with matching sandals and a straw handbag.

Abby, on the other hand, had stuck to the rules, and had come to dinner every night in cropped cargo pants and a tee shirt, with Keens on her feet and her curly hair in a loose bun. No accessories but the small, sparkly earrings she'd worn every day; no nail polish or makeup . . . but she must have packed perfume, Sebastian thought, taking a discreet but appreciative sniff when Abby took a seat on the opposite side of the table.

Sebastian leaned over to refill her water glass. Abby murmured her thanks.

"So you and Lincoln are roommates?" Eileen asked. She was on Sebastian's left side, Lincoln was on his right.

"Housemates," Sebastian said. "We were roommates freshman year of college, and we've lived together ever since."

Eileen looked puzzled. "Lincoln, I thought you were married?"

"That's right," Lincoln said.

"So you're . . ." Eileen frowned.

Abby was grinning. "Just say it, Mom," she urged Eileen. "Spit it out."

"Polyamorous?" Eileen said. "Or do people just say poly?"

For a moment, Sebastian had no idea what she was talking about. Lincoln figured it out first. "Oh, no, no. We're not romantically involved. Just roommates."

"I rent the garden apartment on the first floor of the house Lincoln and Lana own," said Sebastian.

"Oh, well. That makes much more sense," Eileen said.

"But it's a lot less interesting," Abby said. "I've never met a throuple."

"Who's a throuple?" Ted boomed. Sue stood on her tiptoes and spoke into his ear. Ted shook his head, looking disappointed.

"Well," said Eileen. "It's wonderful that you've stayed connected, all those years." She nibbled at a shred of carrot from her salad.

Sebastian turned to Abby. "Have you tried the falafel?"

"Not yet," Abby said. Sebastian passed her the platter. Abby speared a ball of fried chickpeas and popped it in her mouth. It crunched as she chewed. She glanced at her mother, who picked up the salad, brandishing the bowl at Abby with a tight-lipped smile. Abby shook her head. Eileen set the bowl down.

"How many miles did we ride today?" Eileen asked.

Abby swallowed and patted her lips. "Sixty-one," she said, and held up a hand preemptively. "Do not ask me how many calories that burned. I have no idea."

Eileen looked hurt. "I wasn't going to ask that," she said.

"You were thinking it," Abby said. She was, Sebastian thought, trying to sound teasing, but he heard an edge in her voice. "I know your how-many-calories-did-it-burn face."

"Oh, Abby!" Eileen said. "You're such a comedian!"

"Bet," Abby said flatly. "I'm hilarious." She scooped hummus up with a wedge of pita. Eileen sat for a moment, before quietly excusing herself and finding an empty seat near Lily at the other end of the table.

Sebastian saw Abby's shoulders slump.

"Hey," said Sebastian, a little more sharply than he'd meant to. Abby looked up. "You should take it easy on her."

Abby's look became a glare.

"She's doing this trip with you, right?" Sebastian asked.

Abby rolled her eyes. "Believe me, I'd have been fine if she'd just gone to a spa like usual."

"But she wants to be with you," Sebastian said.

"I doubt that she's doing it just to be nice," Abby said. "Either she wants something, or she's trying to make a point. I haven't figured out which yet."

"At least she's here," said Sebastian, thinking that Abby had no idea how lucky she was, to have a mother who was present and interested. And sober. "At least she shows up for you. You should be grateful."

"Oh, should I?" Abby raised her eyebrows. A pink flush darkened the tops of her cheeks. She gave him a smile that bared her teeth. "If you're impressed with her parenting, let her know. Maybe she'll adopt you. Take you under her wing for the rest of the trip." She sipped from her glass demurely as Lincoln's gaze moved from Sebastian to Abby.

"Everything okay here?" he asked, giving Abby a pleasant smile and Sebastian a harder look.

"Fine," said Abby. "Everything is fine."

Morgan

Day Six: Utica to Syracuse
Sixty-two miles

"Can you keep a secret?" Morgan asked Andy Presser, after she'd gotten him alone, away from her mother and his parents, when they'd stopped for lunch, thirty miles out of Utica.

"Uh-huh." He nodded, bobbing his head up and down. "Why? What's going on?"

Morgan's hair swished as she turned around, looking over her shoulder, checking to make sure her mother wasn't close enough to listen. Lily had looked a little disappointed when Morgan had said, "Is it okay if I sit with Andy?" but all her mom had said was, "Drink lots of water." It had been fiercely hot that day, and humid, the sun beating down, the air sticky and thick. Morgan had already reapplied her sunscreen twice, and she could feel that she'd already sweated it away.

"I'm great with secrets," said Andy.

Morgan swallowed hard. Andy was such a nice guy. Like a Great Dane puppy, all gangly arms and legs. He'd probably jump up and start licking her face if she let him. He had bright blue eyes, and freckles, and a friendly, welcoming kind of face. He'd offered to fill her water bottles that morning, and pumped up her tires the day before, and his eyes followed her wherever she went. She could tell he had a crush on her, and she was getting ready to take advantage of that, and she felt horrible about it, but she was going to do it anyhow.

Andy reached across his plate, piled with sandwiches and orzo salad, like he was going to pat her arm or take her hand, then seemed to think better of it and let his hand drop. "What's going on?"

Morgan licked her lips. "It's . . ." Without meetings his eyes, she said, "I have an appointment in Syracuse, tomorrow morning."

"An appointment?" Andy repeated.

"At Planned Parenthood."

"Oh," said Andy. Then, after a beat of silence: "*Oh*." She didn't miss the way his gaze dropped toward her belly, then quickly flickered up and away.

Yeah, Morgan thought. *Oh*. She felt shame burning through her, along with anger at Brody, her boyfriend, who was walking around an army base with no idea what was going on, while she was all alone, trying to find a way out of this trap.

"I know where it is, and it's not that far from the B and B where we're staying." Morgan had checked and rechecked the map to make sure of it. The Planned Parenthood office was less than two miles from their lodgings for the night, and less than one mile from the trail. "I'm going to ride there. I just need to figure out how to do it so that my mom doesn't find out." She paused. "And I need someone to come with me."

"Your mom doesn't know?" Andy asked, his voice cracking.

"No," Morgan said. She looked around and lowered her voice. "No," she repeated. "She doesn't know and she can't find out. I'd be in so much trouble."

"Okay." Andy nodded. "Okay." He drained his water bottle,

then tapped his fingers on his knee, thinking. "Okay. So maybe, in the morning, we can tell Abby that you and I are riding together, and that we'll catch up with everyone at lunchtime? We can hang back from the rest of the group, and I'll go with you to your appointment."

Morgan nodded. That's what she'd been thinking.

"Only . . . are you going to be able to ride when it's over?" His Adam's apple jerked as he swallowed. "And do you know how long it's going to take?"

Morgan shook her head. "The appointment's at ten o'clock tomorrow morning. I don't know how long I'll have to stay, or how I'll feel when it's over. I don't even know if they'll, you know." She swallowed hard and made herself say the words. "If they'll do it—the procedure—at the appointment, or if they'll give me pills to take later." At least she knew that those were the choices.

"Okay," Andy said.

Morgan looked at him. *What do you think of me now?* she wanted to ask. *Do you look down on me? Do you think I'm dirty, or dumb? Are you hoping I'll sleep with you because I slept with some other guy?* But Andy didn't seem to be thinking any of those things. Maybe she'd underestimated him. Maybe he was better than that.

That, somehow, made Morgan feel even worse.

"You'll help me?" she made herself ask him. Andy swallowed hard, then nodded.

"Sure," he told her. "Whatever you need."

Abby

She'd tried her hardest to avoid Sebastian, but it felt like everywhere she turned, every time she looked over her shoulder, there he was, pedaling along, smiling at her. When they'd stopped at Utica Bread that morning, before they'd gotten on the trail, he'd ordered her a chocolate croissant. That afternoon, at lunch, he'd offered her a packet of electrolyte powder to dump into her water bottle. That night at dinner in Syracuse, at Dinosaur Barbecue, he'd asked the waitress for an extra pitcher of water and kept her glass full. "So tell me," he said, nudging a plate of corn bread toward her, then making a show of pulling out his skinny reporter's notebook, "how you got started riding your bike?"

Abby pushed her plate away, and sat her hands flat on the table, thinking about how to begin. If she was going to be honest, she'd say, *Biking saved my life*. Only that sounded horrifically cheesy; not the kind of thing she could say to Sebastian. She'd never even said it to Mark.

And a guy like Sebastian had never needed his life saved, had he? The world was an endless series of red carpets for a guy like that; unrolling, one after the other, so that his feet never had to make contact with the dirt. Every door (and many pairs of legs) would open at a touch. The Sebastian Piersalls of the world glided.

The Abby Sterns of the world, on the other hand? They thumped along, gracelessly. They had to hustle and grind. Or shrink.

Abby shook her hair out of its bun, then smoothed it over her shoulder, thinking about how to begin.

"My parents split up when I was thirteen. My dad moved out, to a house five miles away." Four point seven miles, actually. Abby knew the precise distance. She'd ridden it hundreds of times as a teenager. Even after she'd gotten her license, there wasn't always a car available for her to drive. And she'd still preferred to travel under her own power. "My parents shared custody. I spent three nights a week at my mom's house and three nights a week at my dad's, and I'd switch off every Saturday."

"That must have been rough," Sebastian said. Abby nodded, still trying not to look at him, not wanting to be so vulnerable in his presence. She still barely knew him. It was possible he was the kind of guy who would weaponize a confession to serve his own ends.

"So both of your parents got remarried?" Lincoln asked.

Abby nodded. "Right. Parents split up, dad moved out." Abby remembered how they'd broken the news, calling her and her brother and sister into the infrequently used living room, where they both sat, her mother in an armchair, face perfectly composed, legs neatly crossed, her father on a love seat, his jeans rumpled, shirt untucked, hands dangling, looking like he'd been crying.

"Your father and I have decided to separate," Eileen had said . . . and, for all the fighting they'd done, for all the times they couldn't agree on anything, Abby had found herself dry-mouthed with shock. Eileen's voice had been uncharacteristically gentle as she'd explained how it would work, how Abby's dad would have an apartment nearby, until he found a house. How the kids would spend Saturday nights and Wednesday afternoons with him. How he'd call the house every night, how he'd be available to them. Abby's father's voice had been muted and hoarse when he'd told them, "I'll always love you, and I'll always be your dad."

"You watch," Marni had said after Abby and Simon had gathered in Marni's bedroom. Abby's big sister had been summoned home from college for the announcement. She'd been gone only a few months, but, in her college sweatshirt, with a blue streak of dye in her hair, she already looked like she'd outgrown their house and her brother and sister. "Either she's got a boyfriend or he's got a girlfriend, or both of them have someone else. And this whole 'Dad's got an apartment and you'll see him twice a week'? All of that 'I'm always going to be your father'?" She'd made a dismissive flicking gesture with one hand as Abby had stared at her, numbly, and her brother, red-faced and visibly miserable, had looked at his feet. "That won't last six months."

Marni had been only half-right. Eileen did have someone else. Either Gary Fenske had been waiting in the wings or Eileen had found him with impressive rapidity after her separation. But Marni was wrong about Bernie Stern, who had never given up on being a father. He'd found a house nearby, where Abby had her own bedroom. He'd gone back to school, to become ordained as a rabbi. He'd learned to cook.

Abby told Sebastian and Lincoln how her dad would make all of her favorite meals on the nights she spent at his place—chicken Parmesan, grilled sirloin, his famous Meat Loaf Surprise. "The surprise was bacon," Abby stage-whispered. She didn't mention how, at least once a month, her father completely forgot when it was his night and would be surprised (and try to hide it) when he got home from the synagogue and found Abby doing her homework in his kitchen. Nor did she tell him how wonderful it was when her father cooked because of what she ate at her mother's house. Grilled boneless, skinless chicken breasts, SnackWell cookies, and Lean Cuisine were the staples of Eileen's table. When she did cook from scratch, it felt like her goal was to remove as much fat, salt, and, subsequently, flavor from any dish she prepared.

"My dad taught me to ride my bike when I was little. Once my parents were divorced, that was how I got back and forth between their places." She told them how, in eighth grade, she'd started taking bass lessons at the School of Rock in Philadelphia. "I had to bring Shirley with me when I changed houses on Wednesdays. I'd ride through town with a bass guitar on my back."

"Shirley?" asked Sebastian. "Oh, wait. I get it. Shirley Bassey."

"Exactly," said Abby, secretly pleased that he'd gotten the reference so quickly. Mark hadn't understood the joke, not even after Abby had explained.

She tried to tell them how her bike had given her freedom from her mother's high standards and restrictions and her dad's occasional cluelessness and carelessness; how being able to go to the places she chose, under her own power, had made her feel like she could take care of herself, at a time when she didn't entirely trust either of her parents to do it. Biking was her refuge. She could escape from Eileen's cool silences or judgmental glares, her mother's meals of barely dressed salads and unbuttered sweet potatoes. She could get away from her father's hurt looks and heavy sighs, the chagrined look on his face when she was forced to tell him that there was no food in the refrigerator or no gas in the car or that he'd forgotten about her recital or performance or dentist appointment.

Whatever was happening at whichever house she was at, Abby's bike could save her. She could say, "I'm going on a bike ride," and go off by herself: to a friend's house, or the Willow Grove Mall, or to the path that ran from Center City all the way to Valley Forge. She could pedal, feeling the wind against her face, until she was calm again, until she'd gotten some perspective, until whatever had happened no longer felt as dire, and she didn't feel so sad.

"Biking made me who I am," Abby concluded. She removed a wet wipe from its package and rubbed barbecue sauce from her fingertips. "It saved me." Those dorky, ridiculously sincere words seemed to echo in the restaurant, audible even through the noise of other diners and music from the jukebox, and Abby wished, immediately, that she could unsay them. She glanced at Sebastian as a waitress came to clear the table; bracing for scorn, or boredom, but seeing neither one. He looked interested, and thoughtful. She wondered if biking had been like that for him. Except what did Sebastian need to be saved from?

"And how about you two?" she asked, looking at Lincoln first. "Lifelong cyclist?"

"I'm a city kid. I learned to ride in Central Park, and on the Hudson Greenway," Lincoln said.

Abby finally let herself turn toward Sebastian. "How about you?"

"I grew up in the suburbs, so I'd ride to my friends' houses." It sounded idyllic. Which figured. Of course this handsome, confident man had enjoyed a perfect childhood, with two married parents and just one house. "I didn't really get into it until I moved to New York, after college."

"I made him ride with me," Lincoln said.

"That is true," Sebastian said. "And I'm grateful every day."

"You should be," Lincoln said. "If it hadn't been for me, the only exercise you'd get would be . . ." Lincoln's voice trailed off. Abby felt her neck get hot and she tried not to squirm as she refilled her water glass.

"What about Mark?" Sebastian asked. His tone was calm, almost indifferent. His eyes were on his notebook, but the set of his jaw looked pugnacious. "Does he want to learn to ride someday?"

Abby blinked. "Biking is my thing. Just like running is his thing. It's fine. I think it's fine when women have their own interests." She did believe this. She just hoped she sounded convincing.

Sebastian looked skeptical. "So how often do you ride? Like, two or three times a week?"

"Something like that." It was actually more like three or four times, and that wasn't counting the riding she did to run errands, or to visit Lizzie's house, or to get from her apartment to Mark's, or from Mark's place back to hers, or to work in the morning. Most Saturdays she did a group ride with her bicycle club, and almost every Sunday she did her own thirty-mile loop first thing in the morning, as a way to center herself and prepare for the week ahead.

"And how far do you go? Twenty-five, thirty miles?"

"Depends on the day," Abby said.

"On average."

She thought. "Twenty-five or thirty for the weekday rides. Longer on the weekends."

"So two or three times a week, for three or four hours at a time, you're literally riding away from this guy." Sebastian's voice was neutral. Abby's head was churning with fury and guilt. It felt like Sebastian had peeked into her brain and effortlessly plucked out one of the only things about Mark that she wished were different, like he was now holding up that thought, pointing at it, making it impossible for her not to see it.

"I once dated a woman who didn't ride a bike," Ed was saying, from his spot at the middle of the table. "Didn't last."

His wife patted the side of his arm. "It didn't last because she emptied out your retirement account and used the money for her essential oil business."

Ed's expression was mournful. "Well," he said, "there was that."

Abby forced herself to look directly at Sebastian. "Have all of your girlfriends been stage-five clingers?" she asked. "Were you joined at the hip, every minute of the day? Oh, but wait—you don't have girlfriends, do you?"

Lincoln murmured, "Yikes." Sebastian's expression was no longer neutral, or thoughtful, or anything close to pleasant. He was, instead, unabashedly glaring at her, eyes narrowed, jaw clenched. If looks could have killed, Abby would have been bleeding out into the shawarma.

"When actual grown-ups love each other, they're okay with spending time apart," she said, and hoped she'd delivered the line coolly.

His expression and his posture didn't change—at least, not overtly—but she could tell that he was angry. "It just doesn't seem to me like you've got a lot in common with this guy."

Abby's knees were trembling. She felt breathless with fury. "Mark and I have a lot of things in common."

"You just got through telling us how much you love riding your bike, how it's your favorite thing, how it made you who you are, how it 'saved your life.'" He'd actually hooked his fingers into air quotes to deliver the last line. Abby felt her skin go icy. It was her own fault, for being honest like that, for being so vulnerable in front of a guy she barely knew.

Sebastian appeared not to notice her distress. He said, "It's important to you. And he hasn't learned how to do it."

"You don't get it," Abby said. Her voice was calm as her pulse thundered in her throat. Her fists were clenched. "You don't have any idea about what it takes to be part of a couple."

He gave another shrug. "If there was something I really loved to do, something that was important to me, I'd want my girlfriend to do it with me."

"Well, you'd need an actual girlfriend to find out."

Sebastian's face went stony, and Abby felt concurrently

ashamed and relieved. Ashamed of herself for being mean, which, as someone who'd absorbed a fair share of the world's unkindness, she tried never, ever to be. Ashamed that she'd hurt him; ashamed that she'd felt that impulse in the first place, that she'd wanted to hurt him. And, also, she was relieved. This connection she'd felt between them, the bond of memory and intimacy—how easy he was to talk to and how it had felt to be naked, skin to skin with him—now she knew, for sure, that it had all been in her head. Or, if it had been real, it was over. If there had been a thread stretching between them, she'd snipped it. Now she could stop her stupid, pointless yearning. She could stop hoping that Sebastian was actually attracted to her, to Abby Stern, the person, and not as a novelty, or a body to warm his bed. Men like Sebastian did not fall for girls like her. Maybe in romance novels or rom-coms they did. But not in the real world.

Besides, she had Mark.

"All set here?" asked the waitress, with the check in a leather envelope in one hand. "You need anything else?"

"We're all set," Abby said. "Everything was delicious." She held out her hand for the check and made herself smile.

Kayla

Day Seven: Syracuse to Seneca Falls
Sixty-one miles

It was a secret, something she'd never told her husband, something she'd barely admitted to herself, but when Kayla had gotten pregnant for the second time, she'd secretly, quietly, hoped that the baby would be a girl.

They had had Andy by then, and she and Dale had decided that the second child would be their last. Buying a nice house in a good school district, taking the occasional, reasonable vacation, and eventually sending their children off to college, from which they'd graduate with no more than the average amount of debt, would be tough but feasible on their combined salaries. Three kids would tip the scales from *possible* to *impossible*. She'd cried, quietly, in private, when she'd learned that she was having another boy, and she'd ignored her friends and her own sister when they'd tried to soothe her, telling her what a challenge daughters could be.

When Ezra had arrived, most of Kayla's regret evaporated. Unlike his brother, who'd had colic and had barely slept for the first weeks of his life, Ezra had been a calm, sweet-natured baby, who slept through the night at eight weeks and was happy in his car seat, happy in his stroller, happy just about anywhere. As the years went on, Kayla had seen for herself what had happened when her nieces and her friends' daughters became teenagers, when the moms were dealing with cutting and depression and disordered eating, friend drama and boy drama, birth control discussions and pregnancy scares.

With every year that had passed, she'd gotten happier about being a boy mom, and proud of the relationships she had with Andy and Ezra. *Thank God I have sons and not daughters,* she'd think, smugly—arrogantly—when she'd hear one of her friends' horror stories. She'd taken care to establish open lines of communication with her sons early on, mindful of her own parents' failings. When she'd asked her mother where babies came from, her mom had said, "From mommies' tummies" and then hurried out of the room. The next day, Kayla had found a book on her bed, one that had explained the basics in clinical language that had, somehow, left her with more questions than answers. When she'd gotten her period, her mother had told her that there were supplies in the bathroom, underneath the sink, without a word on how to use them, or any questions about how she was feeling. Kayla had been left to glean the rest of her sex education from friends and her biology classes.

Kayla didn't want her sons growing up ignorant or ashamed. She'd used the correct terms for their body parts, even when they were hard for her to say, and she'd bought them better books when they were ready. As her boys got older, Kayla talked to them, not just about pregnancy and disease but also about consent and pleasure. Andy and Ezra knew, Kayla hoped, how to treat women with respect, to be mindful of their boundaries and, eventually, solicitous of their enjoyment. Best of all, her boys knew they could come to her with anything. She had promised them that she'd listen and not judge, no matter what, and she'd never had cause to regret that promise . . . until that morning, when Andy knocked on her door.

It was just before seven o'clock in the morning, in the bed-and-breakfast they'd arrived at the night before, and she could hear rain drumming on the roof. Dale was still sleeping, lying on his back on the left side of the bed, the same side he occupied at home. When she opened the bedroom door she saw Andy in his pajama bottoms and a hoodie. His feet were bare, his hair was rumpled, and he looked very young.

"Mom?" he said. She still hadn't gotten used to how deep his voice was these days; how he no longer sounded like a kid. "Can I talk to you?"

"Of course." Kayla reached up with her thumb to smooth his eyebrow. Andy had grown six inches in the last eighteen months. His face had gotten more angular, his jaw more defined as he'd lost that little-boy softness, but Kayla could still catch glimpses of the toddler whose thighs had once been as soft and squishy as loaves of Wonder Bread, the little boy who'd worn yellow rain boots and a Batman cape to preschool for three weeks in October, in advance of Halloween. The sweet, good-hearted boy who'd once asked her to put extra cookies in his lunch because his friend's mom never packed dessert and who, in elementary school, had invited his whole class to his birthday parties so that no one would feel left out.

Kayla pulled on her own sweatshirt and a pair of socks and led Andy downstairs. The house where they'd stayed was a redbrick Georgian house in a quiet, residential neighborhood, with a wraparound porch and eight bedrooms, half of them with fireplaces. She could hear someone—Jasper, she assumed—in the kitchen. There were already carafes of coffee on the dining room table, with a platter of mugs beside them.

Kayla poured herself coffee and sat down at the table. Andy took a seat opposite her and asked, quietly, "Can this be just between us?"

"Sure," said Kayla. She wondered if that girl Morgan had already broken his heart. When the first girl Andy had gotten a crush on, two years ago, when he'd been in ninth grade, had told him she just wanted to be friends, Kayla had been sad, but not surprised. When she'd been a teenager, she wouldn't have given a boy like Andy a second look. *Just wait,* she'd told him. You're going to find someone who thinks you're the best thing since sliced bread. He'd looked at her, red-eyed and miserable, asking, *Is sliced bread really that great?*

Kayla sipped her coffee, waiting until Andy got his long arms and legs settled. "What's going on?"

Andy knit his fingers together and looked down at them as he spoke. "If I knew a secret . . . if someone told me something, and made me promise not to tell, but I thought the person maybe wasn't going to be safe . . ." His voice trailed off. He unlaced his fingers and started drumming gently at the table.

"Okay." Kayla's pulse sped up. "The person with the secret. Is it someone I know?"

"Yes. But I can't tell you who."

Kayla thought. "How about this? Tell me what's going on but don't use any names. We'll just say it's theoretical."

Andy nodded. "Okay." More drumming. "What if, theoretically, I knew that someone was pregnant and didn't want to be? And she can't, um, do anything about it where she lives, so she made an appointment at the Planned Parenthood in Syracuse, and, theoretically, she wanted me to come to the appointment with her, and she made me promise not to tell her mom?"

Kayla swallowed hard. "This wouldn't be a pregnancy you had anything to do with? Theoretically?"

Andy looked shocked. Then he shook his head. "Theoretically, no."

"So this girl wants an abortion, and she doesn't think her mother would let her get one?"

"I said I'd help her. Theoretically." Andy sounded wretched. "I want to help. She needs someone to go with her, and make sure she's safe. Only . . ." His shoulders slumped. "I don't want her to get in trouble, and I don't want to get in trouble myself." In a low voice, he said, "I wish she could tell her mom. But she says she can't."

"Is there another adult she could talk to? Is her dad a possibility?"

Andy shook his head. "Her dad's, like, a pastor. And I'm worried that, if her mom finds out she did this, she's going to be mad at me. Like, she'll think that I encouraged her or helped her set it up or something."

Kayla could certainly imagine things unfolding in just that fashion. Her throat was tight, her belly felt knotted. "When is this theoretically happening?"

"This morning. Her appointment's at ten o'clock. She wanted me to ride with her, to the place. Only . . ." Andy gestured toward the windows. "I don't even know if we're riding today."

"Okay." Kayla took another sip of coffee. "It's good that you told me."

Andy's eyes were wide. "Please don't say anything to Morgan or her mom. Please. I promised her I wouldn't tell anyone."

"Don't worry. I won't." But even as she was promising, Kayla felt troubled. How would she feel if she learned that Andy or Ezra had gotten a medical procedure without her knowledge, and that some other adult had known? Even if it was something as insignificant as a piercing or a tattoo, she wouldn't like it. She could only imagine how someone with the beliefs she assumed

Lily held might feel about learning that another parent had aided and abetted in her daughter's abortion.

Thank God, she thought, feeling relief, then guilt and shame, as she thought of her sister, her friends, and their daughters. *Thank God I don't have girls.*

"I just—I want to help her. I want to make sure she's safe. And I don't know what the right thing is," Andy said. Kayla felt her eyes sting as she thought, *I have raised a good and decent child.*

She sat, running through the possibilities in her mind. "How about this? Tell Morgan that, if she wants, she can talk to me—"

"No!" Andy said. "She doesn't want anyone else to know! She made me promise I wouldn't tell anyone." Andy looked, if it were possible, even more miserable.

Kayla held up her hand. "Tell her," she continued, "that you promise your mother won't freak out or get mad or tell anyone else. Tell her that your mother will go to the appointment with her, if she wants an adult to be there with her."

Andy's eyes were wide. "You'd do that? You'll help her?"

Kayla nodded, realizing, as she did it, that her mind was made up. What would she have wanted, if she'd been in Morgan's situation? Or if Ezra had been the girl she'd longed for, and had gotten in trouble? "Yes," she said. "I will." She put down her mug and got to her feet. "Go get dressed," she said. She waited until she heard Andy's door close, before she pulled out her phone and tapped out a text. It takes a village to raise a child, the saying went. So, now, it would take a village to help one.

"Okay," said Abby, pulling her scrunchie out of her hair and wrapping it around her wrist. She'd poured herself a cup of coffee but hadn't touched it since Kayla had started to talk. "Tell me one more time."

Kayla kept her voice low. "Andy told me that Morgan has an appointment at the Planned Parenthood in Syracuse at ten o'clock this morning. She asked him to go with her. She told him that her mother doesn't know, and that her mom can't find out." Abby nodded. "I guess her family's very religious, and she thinks they'd be angry if they found out," Kayla continued. "I know that Andy just wants to be a good friend to Morgan. But I'm worried that her parents are going to find out and be angry at the people who knew." She swallowed hard. "And maybe get the authorities involved. I don't want Andy getting in that kind of trouble." She swallowed again, dropping her voice. "And, if I'm being completely honest, I don't want to get in trouble, either."

"Oof," Abby said. "Okay. Let me think." She rocked back and forth in her chair at the dining room table, turning her scrunchie around and around her wrist. Kayla wondered how old Abby was, and if she'd ever been through this kind of situation before. "Morgan's fifteen, right?"

"Fifteen. And from Ohio. She needs a parent or guardian's consent to get it done there. The law's been challenged, but right now . . ." She shrugged. "I'm worried that her parents could go after Andy. Or me. Or you, now, I guess." She smiled weakly. "Sorry."

"Or Breakaway," Abby said, half to herself.

"I'm— I don't know what to do," Kayla said. She lifted her hands, then let them fall. "The last thing I want is to force a fifteen-year-old to have a baby." She bit her lip. "The only thing I want less than that is for my son to end up in trouble because he tried to help."

"Okay," said Abby, squaring her shoulders as she nodded.

Kayla wondered, briefly, whether telling Abby had been a good idea, if maybe she should have just figured it out herself. "Thank you for telling me." Abby thought for a minute. "Would it be better if I took her? If it comes out, you and Andy can just say you had no idea."

It was tempting . . . but Kayla made herself shake her head. "No offense, but I think Morgan probably wants someone who's closer to her mom's age." *She probably wants her actual mom,* Kayla thought, but didn't say.

Abby's lips were pressed together tightly. "If Lily and her husband find out, if they're angry enough to sue someone—and I'm not sure they would be, because that might expose Morgan— but if it happens, they'd probably be more likely to go after a company and not a person."

Kayla nodded. "I—I still think I should take her. No matter what ends up happening. No matter what her mother thinks. If she's going to go there, she shouldn't go alone."

Abby still looked troubled, but she nodded, and said, "I don't think today's going to be a riding day. Jasper will drive everyone to Seneca Falls. So maybe let's get Mrs. Mackenzie on the first trip. Then, if you're okay with it, you and Andy can take an Uber to the clinic and stay with Morgan during her appointment."

"Do you think her mom will let Morgan stay with us?" But even as she asked, Kayla had a thought. "Maybe I could tell Lily we're looking at Syracuse University—that because we can't ride today we're going to take a tour of the campus."

Abby nodded. "And then Jasper can come back and get you guys."

Kayla nodded. She was thinking that it would then be on Morgan to keep her secret and not let her mother know where she'd been or what she'd done. She wondered if Morgan would be able to pull it off. She didn't think she would have been able to do it, to keep a secret of that magnitude at Morgan's age.

"I think we've got a plan," Abby was saying. "Let me know if anything changes, or if there's anything I can do."

"I will."

Abby left the dining room and went trotting briskly up the stairs. Kayla watched her go before following, slow-footed, heavy-hearted, wondering what the right thing was, what the moral thing was, and how she was supposed to know.

Morgan

7:00 a.m.

When she woke up, it was raining. Not a gentle shower, either, from the sound of it, but a genuine storm.

Morgan lay in bed, listening to the thunder rumbling above her head, and the hiss and crack of lightning. Wind slapped at her window, and when she pulled back the curtains, she saw the tree branches bent almost horizontal by the storm.

We can't ride in this, she thought, followed by, *I won't be able to get to my appointment.* Her stomach clenched, and bile surged up her chest. She swallowed hard, looking over her shoulder to make sure her mother was still asleep. Every day for the past five days, she'd felt on the verge of throwing up from the moment she woke up until around lunchtime. Her breasts ached. Her heart hurt even worse.

In the bed, her mother murmured something, smacking her lips as she rolled from her back to her side. Morgan closed her eyes. She wanted to crawl into bed with her mother, the way she had when she was little. To pull the blanket over her head until she was all in the dark, surrounded by her mother's smell of powder and shampoo. To pretend that none of this was happening.

She shook her head sharply. She wasn't a little girl anymore, and she couldn't pretend. She got out of bed and started to gather the clothes she'd laid out the night before. She would get dressed, find Andy, figure out what to do next. She wasn't giving up or giving in. She was going to get to that appointment and end the pregnancy. She was going to take her life back.

Morgan unplugged her phone, tapped out a text to Andy, and crept into the bathroom with her arms full of clothes, telling herself that, by this time tomorrow, it would be over and done.

Kayla

7:15 a.m.

Kayla Presser slipped back into her bedroom and got herself dressed in the dark. She could hear noise from the kitchen; the sound of voices and the radio. She could smell eggs and bacon and coffee. Breakfast smells. They made her stomach lurch as she went back downstairs, pulled up a chair at the dining table, and sat down to wait.

Morgan and I are going to meet in the dining room at seven thirty, to go over the plan, Andy had texted.

Let me talk to her first, Kayla had written back. She'd checked the forecast, which predicted thunderstorms all morning, and rain and gusting wind all day long. *No one could ride in this,* she thought as Morgan appeared, dressed in an oversize tee shirt and sweatpants that hung from her hip bones. Her body went stiff when she saw Kayla instead of Andy.

"Hi, honey," Kayla said.

Morgan murmured a greeting, leaning forward so her hair covered her face. Kayla approached her the same way she'd sidled up to a spindly-legged fawn she'd once seen in her backyard; trying not to spook it, hoping it wouldn't run. Morgan had the same big, liquid eyes, the same long limbs; the same look of wobbly uncertainty, like she was poised on her tiptoes, ready to flee. *She's just a kid*, Kayla thought miserably. Just a baby herself.

"Morgan," Kayla began. "Andy told me about your appointment today." She saw the girl's dark eyes widen as she turned her head, her gaze darting toward the staircase. Kayla reached out and touched Morgan's shoulder lightly. "Come sit with me, okay? You're not in trouble, I promise. I want to help." Morgan looked terrified, but she let herself be led to the table. Kayla continued speaking in a quiet, lulling voice. "I'm not going to tell anyone. I know you're probably angry at Andy for breaking his promise, but he wanted you to have an adult with you at your appointment. To make sure you got there safely. To ask questions. To take care of you, after."

Morgan was trembling, breathing fast, looking ready to run. But she didn't. Instead, she gave the tiniest nod, and mouthed the words, *Thank you.*

"Are you sure you can't talk to your mom about this?" Kayla asked, putting the slightest emphasis on *your*.

Immediately, Morgan shook her head. "No. She . . ." Morgan looked down, dark lashes fanned against her cheeks. A tear slid down her face and plopped down on the table. "She thinks it's murder. She'd never let me. Please don't tell her. *Please.*"

"Okay," Kayla said. Her heart felt like a lump of clay in her chest. "I understand. Andy and I will get you there, and we'll stay with you for your appointment, and take you . . ." *Take her where?* Kayla wondered. *Back here? On to Seneca Falls?* "Take care of you after."

Morgan once again murmured, "Thank you." She sniffled, then wiped her cheek and lifted her head. "Only we're not going to ride today, are we? What if they make us all get in the van and go to the next place?"

"Andy's going to be looking at colleges next year. We can tell Abby and Jasper that we made plans to take a look at Syracuse University after we realized we couldn't ride. Then Jasper can pick us up this afternoon. And being in a car might be better for you than getting on a bike, if you end up . . ." She let her voice trail off. "Do you know if you're having a procedure today?"

Morgan blinked, then shook her head. "I don't know. I hope they're going to give me pills—it's still early enough. But they said they have to examine me first."

Kayla nodded. "So I'll go with you and Andy. We'll call an Uber."

Morgan bent her head, smoothing her fingers along the table-cloth. "Okay. That—that's good. Thank you." Her head wobbled like a blossom on the slender stalk of her neck, and Kayla was struck by the sheen of her hair and her dark, clear eyes. *She's going to be so beautiful when she's done growing up,* Kayla thought, and found herself suddenly furious, burning with rage at punitive laws and the clueless men who made them, without ever having to see, firsthand, the consequences; at conservative parents and disappearing boyfriends. At the world, and everyone in it who would hurt a girl like Morgan. "We'll take care of you," she said, and she felt, more than heard it, when Morgan whispered another, "Thank you."

Sebastian

8:28 a.m.

Sebastian woke up before his alarm went off and came downstairs, dressed for riding. He'd said good morning to Abby as he'd passed her on his way to the porch, where they'd locked up the bikes the night before. She'd barely glanced at him, keeping her head down, her lips pressed together tightly as she'd hurried away. Sebastian tried not to stare after her. He'd pushed too hard, the night before, at dinner, goading her about Mark. He'd probably undone whatever minimal progress he'd made toward getting Abby not to think he was scum. Her, and the rest of the Internet. He'd given in and googled himself that morning, and he was sure that some of the most trenchant and cruel bits of criticism had permanently engraved themselves on his brain. Thousands of comments, tweets, Instagram posts, subreddits, and listicles and even a few think pieces, including one in the *New York Times* titled "The End of the Big Man on Campus," which held up his mockery as a sign of feminist progress. Sebastian was all for it . . . except when he was the impetus.

He was angry, and confused, and he knew the best thing for it was to move, to get on his bike and pedal far enough and fast enough for his brain to quiet down.

He'd almost made it to the front door when Abby grabbed his arm. "We're not riding today," she told him.

"Maybe you're not," said Sebastian. "I am."

For a moment, Abby glared at him, as thunder boomed overhead. Sebastian wondered if he should have apologized for going at her so hard the night before. Then he remembered how hard she'd gone at him, and he felt angry and frustrated, itchy and desperate to move, all over again.

"I'll be fine," Sebastian said impatiently. "Bikes have rubber tires. The rubber's grounding."

"Actually, that isn't true," said Abby. "A bicycle's tires don't have enough surface area to diffuse a lightning strike. Even if it is just heavy rain, that's going to reduce your visibility and traction," she said. "And fifteen miles of the route today would be going on roads. With cars."

"I really need to get some exercise." Sebastian's shoulders were stiff, his voice toneless. "And I'm allowed to go, right? It's not against the rules."

"You're allowed to ride if you want to." Abby started to say more, then shut her mouth. Sebastian wondered if she was going to apologize to him, or if her plan was to keep trying to talk him out of it. "Come back inside," she finally said. "Eat breakfast."

"I'm not hungry."

"Then drink some coffee."

"I'm not—"

"Then stand in a corner and count sheep," Abby said, her voice turning sharp. "I've got something else to figure out. Then we'll go."

Sebastian stared at her. "Who's this 'we'?"

"You and me. If you insist on doing this."

Sebastian shook his head. "I don't need an escort."

"Company rules," said Abby. "No riders go without a leader on the road."

"I don't need help," he snapped.

"Unless you get another flat," Abby said.

Sebastian's legs were twitching with a desire to move, to go, to be anywhere but here. Even though he knew Abby was right. He could barely change a flat on his own in optimal conditions. If he got one on a rainy day, he'd be screwed. "Look," he said, "I really would prefer to be alone."

"Yeah, I'm getting that," said Abby. Her voice was clipped. "I'll ride ten bike lengths behind you. I won't talk to you. I won't make any eye contact. But I can't let you go by yourself."

For a moment, neither of them spoke. They just stood on the porch, Abby in her pajama bottoms (pink flannel, with a pattern of red and white hearts), Sebastian holding his bike as the rain poured down outside.

"Okay," he finally said. "Fine." He wheeled his bike back against the wall, then poured himself a cup of coffee and stood in the dining room corner. Abby didn't even bother to look at him as she walked out of the room and up the stairs.

Abby

Abby trotted back up to her room to pull biking clothes out of her bag, thinking that she shouldn't have been surprised. *There's always one,* Lizzie had told her, when she'd briefed Abby about what she could expect. There was always one troublemaker, someone who'd insist on riding, no matter what, and it was almost always a man.

Lizzie had told her about the last trip she'd led, a ride from New York City to Washington, DC. One of the riders was signed up for a Strava challenge where he had to ride a certain number of days consecutively. This guy had refused to get on the sag wagon even when there was a severe thunderstorm warning. He'd ended up with a broken arm after a bolt of lightning sent a tree toppling into the road and he hadn't been able to stop fast enough to avoid it. That wasn't even the worst case of Tough Guy–itis that Lizzie had seen. In Ireland, she'd told Abby, there'd been one bozo who'd insisted on pedaling through a hailstorm. "I didn't come here to sit in a van, I came here to ride my bike!" he'd yelled at the leaders. (Lizzie had told her how the guy had also asked for a refund because he'd failed to hit his personal four-hundred-mile-a-week goal or his target heart rate on two days of the weeklong ride.)

Abby had stuffed her pajamas and toiletries into her bag and was pulling on her socks, muttering to herself about stupid, selfish assholes who just had to get their miles in, when Kayla Presser knocked on her door. Her eyes widened when she saw Abby's attire.

"You're riding today?" Kayla's expression was gratifyingly stunned.

"Sebastian wants to ride. I'm going with him."

Kayla's expression was eloquent on the topic of men who insisted on riding in the rain. "Okay. I talked to Morgan about the plan, and she's in." Abby saw how Kayla's forehead was furrowed, her characteristic sunny smile replaced by something close to a grimace. "At breakfast, I'll tell everyone that I'm going to take Andy on a tour of Syracuse University, and that we've invited Morgan along."

"Sounds perfect. And making an announcement in front of the whole group is smart," she said.

"Right?" Kayla tried to smile but only managed a grimace. "Nobody wants to fight with their kid in public. And maybe there's something else Lily can do in Seneca Falls?"

Abby considered. A plan was beginning to form. Unfortunately, it involved the last person to whom Abby wanted to appeal. But she couldn't think of anything else to do. If home was the place where they had to take you in, then surely parents were the people who had to help you when you needed help.

She sighed, rubbed her eyes, and uttered words she rarely had occasion to say. "Let me go talk to my mother."

Ten minutes later, she knocked on Eileen's door.

"Mom?"

"Just a minute," Abby heard Eileen say. The bedroom door swung open, and Eileen was standing on the threshold.

Abby hadn't seen her mother in bedclothes in the past several decades. Her imagination had filled in the blank with silk peignoirs, or crisp cotton pants-and-top pajama combinations, styled like menswear, just oversized enough to make Eileen's petite frame look even more dainty. But instead her mother was wrapped in a ratty bathrobe that was the opposite of chic. There was a stain on the collar, and one of the sleeves was coming unraveled. Abby was pretty sure the garment dated back to her mother's first marriage, and, while it might have once been a pretty pale pink, at this point in its life it was a washed-out absence of color, a dingy grayish-white. Abby saw her mother's bare feet underneath it, small and pale and fragile. She saw her mother's hands, clutching the lapels, the nails perfectly manicured, without so much as a ragged cuticle or a chip in the gel polish, even though she'd been riding her bike outdoors for eight hours a day . . . but the hands were age-spotted and thin-skinned, with bulging veins. It occurred to Abby that not all the dieting in the world could stave off death. No amount of exercise could keep Eileen young forever. Someday, her mother would die. *And leave a beautiful, skinny corpse,* Abby thought.

"What is it?" asked Eileen. Without the usual three coats of mascara, her eyelashes were wispy, and her lips, without liner and lipstick, were the same color as her skin.

"Can I come in?"

Eileen looked puzzled, but she opened the door, then stood aside, sweeping her arm to indicate the neatly made bed. Abby perched on its edge and said, "Morgan has an appointment at Planned Parenthood this morning. We're trying to find a way to get her there without her mother finding out."

"Oh." Abby watched Eileen absorb this news. She walked across the room slowly to the wooden desk, settling herself into its spindly chair, a piece of furniture Abby wouldn't have attempted herself. Eileen crossed her legs, pulled the lapels of her robe to overlap more tightly, and looked at her daughter, head tilted, eyes narrowed.

"Is she going to Planned Parenthood to get birth control, or is she going because she should have gotten birth control a few months ago?"

"The second thing," Abby said.

Eileen nodded, looking thoughtful, not judgmental. "Who else knows?" she asked.

"Morgan told Andy. Andy told his mother. Kayla told me. Morgan and Andy were going to hang toward the back when we started riding, then go to the clinic, and catch up at the end of the day. Except . . ." Abby gestured toward the window just as an especially vigorous gust of wind sent a sheet of rain slapping at the windowpane. "We aren't riding today. So now the plan is for everyone to get in the sag wagon, or catch a ride in the RV, and head to Seneca Falls." She rolled her eyes. "Except that dipshit Sebastian is insisting that he wants to ride, so I've got to ride with him."

"You're riding in this?" Abby heard the pulse of alarm in her mother's voice. She found herself unexpectedly touched. "Is that safe?"

"I didn't know you cared," she said dryly.

"Well, that's being a mother," Eileen said, matching Abby's tone. "You never stop caring." She turned back to the window, looking out at the rain. "Do you really have to ride?"

"It's my job. And I need to get Morgan squared away before I go."

Abby watched as her mother smoothed her robe, tapping her tongue against the roof of her mouth. A familiar gesture, accompanied by familiar sounds that sent Abby right back to her childhood: sitting at the kitchen table, watching her mother poach eggs, or smear the thinnest layer of apple butter on her single slice of whole-grain toast.

"Can Morgan reschedule her appointment?" Eileen asked.

"I think," Abby said carefully, "that time is of the essence."

Eileen smoothed her hands over her legs. "How can I help? What do you need me to do?" she asked. Abby felt a rush of gratitude toward her mother, an upswelling of warmth as sweet as it was unfamiliar. Eileen wasn't asking a bunch of questions, or making Abby repeat herself, or offering suggestions, or digressions, or her own take on the morality of the matter. She'd immediately grasped the problem and had offered to help just as quickly, and, in spite of the dislike that sometimes felt bone-deep and ineradicable, Abby could acknowledge that, sometimes, she and her mother were perfectly in harmony. Sometimes, Eileen got it right.

"If you could make sure Lily gets in the sag wagon for the first run, that would help," Abby said. "Tell her you'll take her shopping, or have a spa day in Seneca Falls. Keep her busy."

Eileen nodded. If she'd heard any judgment in Abby's suggestions about a spa day, any sense that Abby thought her mom was frivolous and vain, her expression didn't change. "I'll do my best," she said. "Only . . ." She plucked at the robe's belt. *Here it comes,* Abby thought.

"What?" she asked.

"Honestly, I don't feel wonderful about helping a child lie to her parent. If it were one of my daughters—or my son—I'd want to know."

Abby swallowed hard, then nodded. "I get it. The thing is, I don't think Lily will give Morgan a choice. And I think Morgan should have one."

Eileen looked at Abby, sparse lashes fluttering as she blinked. "Have you talked to Morgan about telling her mom what's going on? Maybe she's underestimating Lily."

"Kayla said Morgan seemed completely terrified at the idea

of her mother finding out," Abby said. "And, from what I've seen . . ." Abby let her voice trail off.

"Okay." Eileen gave a single nod, and picked up her bulging cosmetic bag the same way Abby imagined a soldier would pick up his gun—spine straight, shoulders back, prepared for battle. Abby felt another stab of guilt, thinking, again, that Eileen wasn't entirely the monster she imagined. At least, not all of the time. "I'll do my best."

"Thank you," Abby said . . . and, impulsively, without thinking, she crossed the room and enfolded her mother in a hug. Abby could feel surprise in the lines of her mother's shoulders, a moment of hesitation, before Eileen hugged her back.

Abby

Downstairs, Jasper had set out the breakfast buffet on a long table in the dining room: yogurt and granola and fresh fruit, blueberry and lemon-poppyseed muffins, oatmeal, bacon, a spinach and feta frittata, still warm from the oven. The Presser boys were making their way through giant helpings of frittata and bacon and muffins. Lincoln was spooning oatmeal into his mouth. Outside, it was still pouring, rain hammering at the road and car windshields. Abby poured herself a cup of orange juice and gulped half of it down as Ted emerged from the Spoke'n Four's RV and jogged through the downpour and into the house.

"Not a riding day," he announced when he'd arrived, with his white hair plastered to his head and water dripping from the tip of his nose and his earlobes. The words were barely out of his mouth when a bolt of lightning tore across the sky. Ted looked up, grimacing, then used a dish towel to dry his face before proceeding to the buffet, scooping himself a bowl of oatmeal, and sprinkling candied pecans and coconut flakes on top. "You know that quote, right? 'Everyone complains about the weather, and nobody does anything about it?'"

Abby nodded. She was wondering if Morgan had told her mother about the make-believe Syracuse campus tour, and what she'd do if Lily tried to insist on staying with her daughter instead of getting in the van.

"Forecast says it's going to be like this all day long," Ted continued. "The four of us are going to get the bikes loaded and meet you at the hotel in Seneca Falls."

"Perfect," Abby said. "I just need to make sure everyone has a plan for the day."

"We're going to do the museums," said Lou, who'd appeared at Abby's elbow. "You and Sebastian are welcome to join us."

Me and Sebastian? Abby stared at her. Lou stared right back, smiling brightly. Abby thought about saying, *We're not together,* or *I have a boyfriend.* She considered asking, *Why would you think we're interested in each other, especially because most of what we've done in front of the group is argue?*

Instead, Abby just gave Lou a noncommittal smile and went back to the dining room table to wait for the rest of the riders. When they'd all gotten breakfast and found a seat, Abby stood, tapping her spoon against the side of her coffee cup.

"So, as you might have noticed, we've got a little weather going on. According to my app, it's going to rain pretty much all day, and we'd be riding toward the storm, not away from it. Therefore, I am recommending that everyone take the sag wagon to Seneca Falls. I know," she said, before anyone could start complaining, "that we'd planned for tomorrow to be a day off, but if the sun comes out and anyone wants to ride, there's a beautiful loop around Cayuga Lake. Does that sound okay to everyone?"

Nods around the table, with an especially enthusiastic nod from Lily, who looked like a death row inmate who'd just gotten good news from the governor. She'd probably been dreading the prospect of riding in the rain. Abby swallowed hard and tried not to imagine how Lily's relief would be replaced by fury and betrayal if she found out what her daughter had planned. Morgan was sitting beside her mother, staring blankly at the wall, both hands wrapped around a mug. Abby clinked her coffee cup again.

"The sag wagon can take five people at a time. I called the hotel in Seneca Falls, and they're going to do their best to have our rooms ready for an early check-in. However, we will need to go in shifts."

"We're going to leave right after breakfast and spend the day at the museums in Seneca Falls," said Sue of the Spoke'n Four. She smiled proudly. "'Men, their rights, and nothing more; women, their rights, and nothing less.' That was the motto of the newspaper she edited, you know."

"Sue used to teach history," Ted announced.

"And those who do not learn history are doomed to repeat it," Lou said.

Abby wondered if Lily was listening to any of this. She gave Kayla a desperate look, feeling weak with relief when the other woman said, "I'm going to take Andy to look at Syracuse University this morning." She looked at Lily. "We'd love to take Morgan along, if it's all right with you."

"Lily, you and I can head to Seneca Falls right after breakfast. There's a wonderful spa there," Eileen said, jumping in before Lily could even open her mouth to object. "I called, and they can fit us in for massages at eleven. We'll let the kids have a day."

"Are you sure?" Lily was looking a little bewildered as she turned from Kayla to Eileen to her daughter. "Morgan, I could come look at the campus with you."

"No," Morgan said. Her voice was quiet, but very firm. "I'll be fine. You should go do the spa thing. I can go with Andy and his mom."

"Okay, so that's Lily and my mom on Jasper's first trip," said Abby, before Lily could argue or object. "Anyone else?"

"I'll join you," said Lincoln, nodding at Eileen and Lily. "Sebastian's decided to ride."

Worried murmurs rose from around the table. Abby felt relieved at how deftly Lincoln had managed to change the subject. "Seriously?" asked Ed. "In this?"

"I'll be fine." Sebastian was standing in the corner, holding a mug of coffee. His voice was wooden, his face expressionless. His toe tapped at the floor, like he could barely hold still.

"Okay. So Sebastian is going to ride, and I'll ride with him," Abby said. "The Spoke'n Four are in their RV, and Jasper will drive Lincoln, Eileen, and Lily, then come back and pick up Kayla, Andy, Morgan, Dale, and Ezra." She turned to the Landons. "What about you two?"

"We've got friends in town. We're going to spend the morning with them, and they'll drive us to Seneca Falls after lunch," Richard Landon said.

"So that's everyone," Abby said. "Jasper and I will load up the bikes, then we'll be on our way." She escaped the dining room as quickly as she could, retreating to the kitchen, where she helped Jasper clean up, pack up the leftovers, and load the Pressers' and Mackenzies' bikes onto the van.

When that was done, she found Kayla, standing on the porch. Together, they watched as her mother and Lily Mackenzie dashed out of the house and climbed into the van. Abby held her breath until she saw Lincoln climb into the passenger's seat and slam the door behind him. Jasper gave two jaunty honks and pulled away.

"All good?" Abby asked.

"So far," Kayla replied. "Dale's going to take Ezra to the science museum. I've got an Uber on the way."

"Text me," Abby said. "Keep in touch. Let me know if there are any problems."

Kayla nodded. "Be safe," she said.

"You, too," said Abby. Sebastian was already outside waiting, helmet on, bike lights flashing, filling his water bottles from a hose attached to the side of the house. *Like he'll need them in this,* she thought. The rain had not abated. In fact, it seemed to be coming down harder than it had been when she'd woken up. She tried to look pleasant and unbothered as she pulled her raincoat's hood up over her helmet and addressed the day's single rider.

"Ready?" she asked.

Sebastian nodded. He pulled his neon green rain jacket over his jersey, but not before Abby noticed how it clung to his chest in an unfairly distracting fashion, and scolded herself for noticing. She'd talked to Mark the night before. They'd had a long, pleasant conversation where she'd told him everything about the bike trip. Everything, except for a single word about Sebastian. "I miss you," Mark had said, at the end of the call.

"Miss you, too," Abby had said, trying hard to mean it. Trying to not think of how there'd been long stretches of riding where she didn't even think about Mark, or her life with him, at all, or how, when she did think about him, she did not find the prospect of going back home appealing. She hadn't told him about the spans of time and stretches of miles when she'd pedaled along and the world felt enormous and full of possibilities, when she imagined being single and didn't feel lonely or afraid . . . just free.

"You really don't have to ride with me," Sebastian told her, raising his voice so she could hear him over the rain. "I'll be fine."

"I'm sure you will be," said Abby, who wasn't sure at all. The day looked like an invitation for accidents and injury. At least they'd be on bike paths for the early parts of the ride. Only there, the issue would be mud, and the way it disguised hazards like loose gravel and roots, rocks and ruts. And the fifteen miles of road riding into Seneca Falls were mostly on two-lane local roads, not especially busy, but drivers wouldn't be expecting to see cyclists on a day like this, so they might not be as attentive as usual. And even considerate drivers would end up sending sheets of water splashing toward the sides of the road, making you feel like you were riding your bike through a car wash, or a tsunami. "But I still have to go with you."

For a moment, Sebastian didn't reply. Abby imagined she could feel the resentment rolling off him, like cartoon squiggles of noxious black. "Look," he finally said. "I'll sign a waiver, or whatever you need. I'll indemnify the company. I promise not to sue if I get hurt."

Abby bet herself that Sebastian had googled *indemnify* at some point during breakfast, and with that thought, it was as if some malevolent spirit got ahead of her tongue. "Don't worry," she said. "I'll ride behind you, and I promise not to make eye contact. No one need ever know about our secret love."

Sebastian stared at her. "Secret love?"

"I'm kidding!" Abby said, rolling her eyes. "It's okay. You just go ahead, whenever you're ready. Pretend I'm not here. I'll see you in Seneca Falls. At the Women's Rights National Historical Park."

"The what?"

"There's a museum dedicated to the passage of the Nineteenth Amendment, and women's rights." Abby gave him her biggest, cheesiest grin. "I know you'll want to check it out. We should all be feminists, right?"

Sebastian just stared at her, shifting his bike from his left hand to his right. "I don't want to make you ride in this if you don't want to," he finally said.

"Lucky for you, I'm part duck. Go on," she said, and nodded toward the street. "Off you go."

He paused for another moment. Then he gave her a stiff nod, climbed onto his bike, clipped his shoes into his pedals, and zoomed away, with his rear wheel sending a plume of water spraying up behind him. Abby noted with satisfaction the way it immediately painted a stripe of muddy brown up the center of his back. She also saw that, as usual, he'd stuffed his pinny into his back pocket, even though, today of all days, he could have used it.

She gave him a head start before turning on her own lights and getting on her bike for what was sure to be a long, wet, slow, miserable slog.

Kayla

The Planned Parenthood was on Genesee Street, a few miles away from where they'd stayed and a few blocks away from the university. Kayla had the Uber take her and Morgan and Andy to the university's admissions building. "We'll walk from there," she said, and realized, ruefully, that she'd already started covering her tracks, that she was already behaving like a criminal.

The rain that had canceled the day's ride also seemed to have kept most of the protestors Kayla had expected at home. There were just a few men holding wet, ragged posters. One had a bull-horn. Kayla made sure Morgan had earbuds in place and her raincoat's hood pulled up before they were close enough to hear what he was yelling. She kept her hands on Morgan's shoulders, guiding her inside.

The waiting room was quiet; warm and well-lit, with rows of padded chairs and the blinds closed over the windows. Kayla collected the kids' raincoats and hung them on a coat tree by the door as Morgan talked to the receptionist. She grabbed a handful of paper towels from the ladies' room and gave them to Morgan, who accepted them with a faint smile, patting her face dry. Then she sat, staring into the distance with her hands fisted inside the sleeves of her sweatshirt.

A half dozen times, Kayla started to speak, to ask Morgan if she wanted to talk, if she had any questions, if she wanted a cup of water, or if there was anyone she wanted to call. A half dozen times, she made herself keep quiet, telling herself to just leave the girl alone; that if Morgan wanted anything, she'd ask. Nobody told you how to behave in a situation like this, she thought, and wished, desperately, for some guidance, or that she'd had a chance to call her sister before the day began.

They hadn't been waiting long when the nurse called Morgan's name. Kayla felt the girl startle, almost jumping up from her chair, before she turned to Kayla. Her dark eyes were wide, her lips were white around the edges.

"Will you come with me?" she asked.

"Of course I will," Kayla said.

"I'll wait," Andy said, his voice cracking as he looked at Morgan. "I'll be right here." Kayla felt her heart swelling as she gave Andy's shoulder a squeeze.

They were led to an exam room. Kayla stayed outside to give Morgan a few minutes to change. When Morgan called, "You can come in now," Kayla opened the door and found Morgan sitting on a paper-draped exam table, wearing a hospital gown. Her long, slender legs and bare feet dangled from the table. She was shivering, her skin goose-bumped, her eyes still wide.

"Everything's fine," Kayla said, and took her hand. "It's all going to be okay. They'll take care of you." Morgan nodded without looking at her.

There was a knock on the door. "Morgan Mackenzie? Good morning. My name is Delia. I'm a physician's assistant. I'm going to be taking care of you today." Delia had long, braided hair, and the rhinestones on her mask twinkled in the light as she stepped into the room. She took Morgan's history—how old she'd been when she'd gotten her first period, when her last cycle had been, if she'd ever been screened for STIs, what birth control she was using.

"We used condoms," Morgan said, her voice tiny. "But maybe we used them wrong? Or something? We only did it twice."

Delia nodded. "Have you ever had a pelvic exam before?"

Morgan shook her head. *Of course not*, Kayla thought, and tried not to let what she was thinking show on her face. Delia's voice was low and soothing as she told Morgan to lie back, showing her the instruments, telling her what would happen and what she'd feel. The instant Morgan's feet were in the stirrups, Morgan reached for Kayla's hand again, grabbing it and holding on hard. She didn't let go as Delia snapped on gloves and talked Morgan through the speculum's insertion, or when she untied her gown and ran an ultrasound wand over the girl's belly. Morgan lay absolutely still, rigid and unmoving, her eyes closed tight, as the room filled with a rapid thumping sound, one that Kayla remembered from her own pregnancies.

"Okay," Delia said. "You're about eight and a half weeks along."

Morgan's voice was very faint as she asked, "What does that mean?"

Delia set the wand back in its stand, and gently wiped the goo from Morgan's belly with a warm wet cloth. "It means that you can have a medical abortion, if that's what you decide."

Morgan sat up and opened her eyes. "That's the pills, right?"

Delia nodded. "If that's what you decide on, you'll get two sets of pills. The first medication is called mifepristone. That's going to stop the pregnancy from proceeding any further. Then, in twenty-four to forty-eight hours, you'll take four misoprostol pills. You'll hold them between your cheeks and gums for thirty minutes, until they dissolve, and you'll want to take your ibuprofen then, too. The bleeding will start within three to four hours after that."

"The bleeding," Morgan repeated, lips thinned. "You mean the abortion."

"Yes," Delia said. "That's right."

"That works," Kayla said, doing the math. "Tomorrow's a day off. We're on a bike trip," she explained to Delia. "But if you take the first pill now, and the second ones tomorrow, and if it . . ." She groped for the words. "If it happens tomorrow afternoon, you should be fine."

Morgan nodded. Delia went on. "Most women pass the pregnancy within four or five hours after taking the misoprostol. The cramping can be strong, and you might see clots the size of lemons." Morgan shuddered, looking revolted. Kayla gave the girl's hand a squeeze.

"But, for some women, it's no different than having a period," Delia said.

Morgan gave a jerky nod. "How long will it—how long will I bleed for?" she asked.

"For most women, the bleeding tapers off after twenty-four hours. You might see some spotting until your next period." Delia's voice was low and soothing as she recited the list of possible complications, and signs indicating that Morgan would need to seek help. "We'll give you a number to call so you'll be able to talk to someone here while it's happening. Do you have someone who can stay with you?" she asked.

Before Kayla could offer, Morgan said, "My mom." Her voice was a little more steady as she looked at Kayla. "If I tell her it's cramps . . . if she thinks it's just my period . . . she'll take care of me."

Delia's gaze moved from Morgan to Kayla. "I'm not her mother," Kayla said. "Just a friend."

"Your mom doesn't know?" asked Delia. Morgan shook her head.

"I can't tell her," Morgan said, her voice quiet, but very firm.

"Morgan has friends who know what's going on," Kayla said. "We'll take care of her. We'll make sure she's okay."

Delia nodded. "Do you understand everything I've told you?" she asked, looking carefully at Morgan. "Do you have any questions? I'm going to give you printouts that go over everything I've told you. I know it sounds scary, but I promise you, this is a very, very common procedure, and the vast majority of women come through it just fine."

Morgan said she didn't have questions. Kayla didn't, either.

"Do you want to talk about birth control?" Delia asked.

"Oh, no." Morgan shook her head. "I don't need that."

Delia and Kayla exchanged a glance over the girl's head. "There are long-term options, for women who don't want to get pregnant in the next months or years," said Delia.

"No," Morgan repeated, her voice firm.

"Okay," said Delia. "If you change your mind, you know where to find us. And if you do have penetrative sex with a man again, make sure your partner is using a condom, and that he's put it on correctly. I can give you some condoms to take with you. Just in case."

Morgan gave another stiff nod, before asking, "Will anyone be able to tell? Like, after I'm home? If something happens, and I have to go to the hospital?"

"When are you going home?" Delia asked.

"In a week," said Kayla.

"Then you'll be fine," Delia said. "And no, nobody will be able to tell that you've had a medical abortion. There's nothing that shows up in a blood test, or an exam." She wheeled her chair over to a keyboard and typed rapidly. "If you end up needing to see your doctor or go to a hospital, you'll tell them you didn't even know you were pregnant," Delia said. "But that's very, very unlikely. The majority of women who take both of these medications—I'm talking ninety-nine percent—they do just fine."

"One pill today, four pills tomorrow. Then it's over," Morgan said, mostly to herself.

"And I need to ask if you're sure about your choice," Delia said. She turned to Kayla. "Can you give us a minute?"

Kayla nodded and stepped out into the hallway. A minute later, Delia opened the door. "She's just going to get dressed. You're all set."

In the waiting room, Andy was sitting where she'd left him. His hair was wet and he was playing a game on his phone. He practically jumped to his feet when he saw Morgan and hurried across the room to meet her.

"I bought you some chocolate," he said, and shoved a bag toward her.

Morgan nodded her thanks and put the bag in her sweatshirt's pouch, which was already bulging with a sheaf of pamphlets and printouts: information about the drugs, about where to get birth control, about websites they could access and numbers they could call. The receptionist had given Morgan three prescription bottles in a white paper bag: mifepristone, misoprostol, and prescription-strength ibuprofen. Morgan stopped at the water cooler, filled a cup, opened the bag, then one of the bottles. Kayla watched her tap the first pill out into her hand.

"You're sure?" Kayla asked one last time.

"I'm sure," Morgan said. She raised her hand to her mouth and swallowed the pill down.

Abby

On a sunny day, the cinder-topped dirt path out of Syracuse would have been as flat and as hard-packed as pavement, a fine surface for riding. On a rainy day, the trail transformed from dirt to mud, which, that morning, seemed to be actively sucking at their tires, making the riding effortful, and keeping the pace extra slow.

Abby ground out the miles along the canal, hearing her tires squelching with each rotation, watching her shoes and her legs and the frame of her bike getting increasingly crusted with mud. She didn't pass any other riders. Probably because they were all sensible enough to stay home.

All morning long, Abby plowed along, shivering, always keeping Sebastian's flashing rear lights in her sights. In his lime-green rain jacket, he was easy enough to see, even with the rain pouring down. She pedaled, and breathed, and mentally cursed him, blinking water out of her eyes, doing her best to ignore her feet, which were turning numb, and the ominous rumble of thunder, which accompanied them for each slow mile they managed that morning. Abby told herself that there were cars and trucks nearby, and that those vehicles would provide bigger targets for the lightning than their bicycles did. She only hoped that, once they started riding on the road, they'd be small enough for the lightning to miss them, but not so small that the drivers and the long-haul truckers wouldn't be able to see them.

After the first hour, she couldn't feel her toes, and her hands were freezing. Abby flexed her fingers, shaking out one hand, then the other, switching her grip on the handlebars, trying to cheer herself up by telling herself that, as hard going as she found it, it was probably even worse for Sebastian, who was pushing through the mud on his skinny, road-bike tires. She thought about Morgan, imagining the teenager sitting in the waiting room with Kayla and Andy beside her, or in a generic exam room, talking to a sympathetic someone in a white coat. She pictured Morgan relieved and happy. She hoped that, unlike every other teenage girl Abby had ever known, Morgan would be able to keep a secret. And she wondered, again, if she'd done the right thing.

They'd been riding for close to two hours when they came to the trailhead at the eighteenth mile. Abby saw a single-story building on the side of the trail, with smoke coming out of its chimney and the scent of a wood-burning fire in the air. Abby wondered what the building was and if Sebastian would want to go in, take a break, and warm up. *Maybe he's come to his senses and he's ready for the sag wagon,* she thought, shivering, as she coasted to a stop. *Maybe he's already called Jasper. Maybe Jasper's already on his way.*

Wishful thinking. "Hey," Sebastian shouted, struggling to make himself heard over the sounds of the storm. "I checked the map, and there's a road we can take for the next five miles." He held out his phone, pinching and enlarging the map so she could see what he'd found, as the wind whipped at their faces. "It's a little longer, but at least it'll get us out of the mud."

Out of the mud sounded excellent. "Let's do it." Abby let him lead, following his blinking taillight off the path and onto a side street. As soon as his tire touched the pavement, Sebastian was off like a shot, pedaling, as Lizzie would have said, like his ass was on fire and his hair was catching. *Like anything could be on fire today,* Abby thought. Her teeth were chattering. She was soaked right down to her bra, and her shoes were so wet she imagined turning them upside down and watching water cascading out. *Macho jerk,* she thought. Selfish idiot. Stupid, stubborn . . .

It was only by chance that she'd looked up, mid-insult, and had her eyes on Sebastian, not on the road or her phone, in its waterproof case, at the exact instant that Sebastian went down. One minute he was pedaling, his feet moving so quickly that they were almost a blur. In the very next instant, his bike went skidding out from under him, and then he was airborne, flying headfirst over the handlebars, his body finally hitting the road with a sickening thud.

Abby swallowed a scream and rode to him as fast as she could. She reached him as he was getting dazedly to his feet. *Shit,* she thought. *Shit shit shit.* In all her years of riding, she'd seen only one bad injury: a woman who'd gotten her tire stuck in the ruts of train tracks, and had gone over her handlebars, just like Sebastian. She'd broken her collarbone. That had been bad. This looked worse.

"Are you okay?" she called. Sebastian had gotten to his feet but didn't seem to have heard her. His bike was lying on the road behind him, the back wheel still spinning. Both of his knees were bleeding. His fancy rain jacket was torn, and he was covered in grit and shivering, with water dripping from his hair and his face.

Abby got off her bike and grabbed Sebastian's shoulders, looking him over, standing on her tiptoes to inspect his helmet, running her fingers over its segments to see if any of them were cracked. "Does anything hurt? Did you hit your head?"

He gave her an annoyed scowl, but she saw his lips were blue and could hear his teeth chatter. "I'm fine. Let me get my bike."

"I'll get your bike. You sit." She led him to the guardrail by the side of the road, quickly checking for poison ivy before she made him sit down, and trotted back onto the pavement, thanking God for an absence of traffic while she collected his handlebar bag and his pump and both water bottles, all scattered on the pavement, then his bike, which appeared undamaged. She wheeled it over to the guardrail, wincing as thunder boomed overhead.

"What happened?" she shouted.

"Don't know. Must've hit something. Branch. Or something."

Sebastian didn't sound good. His teeth were still chattering, his knees were both streaming blood, and his face was alarmingly pale. Abby pulled out her phone and called Jasper.

"Hey there."

"Hey, Jasper. Sebastian's having some mechanical difficulties." She didn't want to alarm anyone else in the van, in case she was on speaker—especially not her mom—and *mechanical difficulties* sounded a lot less dire than *went headfirst over his bike into the road*. "There was a little bit of a wipeout, though, so I'm going to call an ambulance . . ."

"No." Sebastian grabbed her arm. His teeth were still chattering. "No ambulance. I'm fine."

"You have to get checked out." Abby blinked rainwater out of her eyes. "Company policy."

"You. Take me."

She gave him a careful look, examining his pupils, trying to see if they were the same size. "I don't have a car."

"Sag wagon."

She shook her head. "Jasper's all the way in Seneca Falls. That's going to take too long."

"Uber, then."

Abby thought. It was possible that a rideshare made sense. Certainly, it would get them to the hospital faster than waiting for Jasper. Assuming she could even get an Uber here, in the ass end of nowhere. "Okay. Jasper, I'll call you back." She ended the call and looked at Sebastian, trying to figure out what to do first.

"Let me see your helmet." His hands, she saw, were shaking, and it took him a few tries to unclip the straps. "Do you think you passed out when you fell?"

"No."

"No, you don't think so, or no, you didn't?"

"No, I didn't."

"Does your head hurt?"

"No."

"Any dizziness? Nausea?"

"No." He pulled in a breath, looking genuinely contrite. "I just feel stupid."

You should. "Don't worry about it."

"It's my fault." He sounded truly sorry. More than sorry. He sounded wretched. "I'm sorry. I shouldn't have made you ride in the rain."

Facts, thought Abby. She ran to her bike and pulled the first aid kit out of her handlebar bag, removing what she'd need: gauze, rubbing alcohol, Neosporin, Band-Aids. "Let me see your knees."

Sebastian looked down at his legs, then immediately jerked his head up, squeezing his eyes shut. "Eugh," he said, and planted both of his hands on the guardrail like he was trying to keep steady.

"What?" *Shit.* "Are you dizzy? Do you feel like you're going to throw up?" Maybe he'd gotten hurt worse than she'd suspected.

"No. It's blood," Sebastian said, his voice faint. He'd wrapped his arms around himself and had tucked his hands into his armpits. "I get sick if I look at blood."

Awesome, Abby thought. This day just kept getting better. "Okay. Don't look. Just keep your eyes closed." Except she was worried that if he tried to stay perched on the guardrail with his eyes shut, he'd end up falling backward into the culvert, and she'd have to go pull him out, and wouldn't that just be the cherry on top of the day's mud-and-misery sundae? "Can you stand up? Good. Hold my arm. Come with me." She led him, hobbling, down the street, to where a tree in the middle of an empty lot gave some shelter from the wind and rain. It probably made an excellent target for the lightning, too, but Abby couldn't worry about too many things at once. When they arrived, she put her hand on his shoulder, half-coaxing, half-pushing him down onto the wet grass. "Put your head between your legs. Take deep breaths." She could see him shivering, could hear his inhalations, but at least he wasn't arguing. His eyes were squeezed shut, and his lips were pressed together so tightly that they'd all but disappeared.

"Deep breaths," Abby repeated, crouching down to inspect the wounds, which seemed to be lots of long but shallow scratches. "In for a count of four, hold for a count of four, blow out for a count of four. I'm going to clean your knees off, then bandage them. And then I'll see about getting us an Uber. Okay? You just keep breathing, and keep your eyes shut." She squirted off the bulk of the grit with her water bottle, then tore open an alcohol-soaked gauze pad. "Little sting," she murmured, before swiping his knee. She saw him flinch, heard a tiny moan as she worked. She tried to be quick and as gentle as possible as she cleaned the scrapes.

"It's not everyone's blood. Not blood in general. Just my own," Sebastian said. His eyes were still shut, face still pale as skim milk.

Okay, tough guy, Abby thought.

"I'm not a tough guy," Sebastian said, and made a noise that sounded like laughter but contained very little humor. Abby realized she'd been talking out loud. Oops.

"No," she said, mostly to herself, "you're just inconsiderate."

"You're right," he said, through his chattering teeth. "You're right and I'm sorry."

She washed the grit and rainwater off her fingers before opening the packets of Neosporin and starting to dab it onto his scratches.

"It's easier if you just keep moving," he said.

Abby looked up. His eyes were shut, lips pressed tight together, rain streaming down his face. "What's easier?"

"Everything."

She wondered if he was talking only about the day's ride, or if he was referring to something else. The TikTok mess? Their own history?

"You were right about me. I've never had a girlfriend. Not a real one."

"That's okay," Abby said. She finished with his left kneecap and moved on to his right. "Maybe you just haven't met the right person yet."

"No. That's not it. I just"—he extended his arm, palm flat—"kept it moving. Different girls, all the time. Maybe one of them was the right person." He made a rueful noise. "Maybe it was even the girl who made that first video."

Abby considered. She'd seen the first video, and the petite, dark-haired girl who'd made it. The girl had been pretty. She looked like a good fit for Sebastian. No one would stare at the two of them and wonder at the mismatch.

In a voice almost too soft for her to hear, Sebastian said, "Or maybe it was you."

Abby felt herself stiffen, her face suddenly warm in spite of the rain. "Oh, I don't think . . ."

"It's okay," he said. Kindly. "I just want to be your friend."

Which should not have been a disappointing thing to hear,

Abby thought. She should have felt relieved, if she felt anything at all. And yet.

She finished his second leg, considered patting his thigh, or even squeezing it, and decided, instead, to say, in a cheery, chipper tone, "All done!"

"Great." He got to his feet, wobbling slightly, with his eyes still shut. "You go ahead and I'll catch up."

Abby stared at him. "Sebastian," she said, slowly and clearly. "We're not riding anymore. We need to go to a hospital. Remember?"

"I'm fine," he said again. "I want to ride. By myself. Just go."

Abby just stared at him. She took a few deep breaths and then, when she trusted herself to speak calmly, she said, "You have a flat tire."

"I'll change it."

"You can barely change a flat even when it's not pouring rain, and you didn't just fall off your bike."

"I'll be fine."

"Sebastian—"

"I just want to keep moving." He stood up and started walking toward his bike. That was when Abby snapped.

"Jesus Christ, you big, dumb asshole! I'm not letting you ride by yourself in the middle of a thunderstorm, after you just wiped out! Even if I wanted to—and believe me, I very much want to— I'd lose my job if I let you ride alone."

Sebastian turned around and stared at her.

"Look, I get that you want to keep moving. But sometimes you just can't." Abby licked her lips. "You just can't," she repeated.

There was a rising, rippling noise as the wind gusted . . . and then it was as if the sky had ripped open, sending torrents of water down to douse them. The rain poured down, so concentrated that it seemed to fall in sheets instead of drops, blurring the edges of the world, turning everything gray and opaque.

Sebastian reached out and took Abby's hand. His wet fingers closed around hers, and he pulled her back under the tree, until they were right up against the trunk, where the leaves and branches gave them some small measure of shelter. Abby tried to reclaim her hand, but Sebastian kept his hold on her fingers.

"I'm sorry," he said. Abby could still hear the minute tremble of his voice. "I'm sorry I made you come out in this."

"It's okay." Abby did her best to keep her voice low and calm. She was speaking to him, she realized, the way she spoke to the most skittish puppies at Dog Jawn, the tiny, trembly, snarly purse dogs who spent every minute of every day on high alert, with their teeth bared, probably because they were afraid of being torn apart by the bigger dogs. Maybe, in spite of his maleness, his whiteness, and his good looks, Sebastian was like that; big and strong and confident on the outside, tiny and terrified on the inside; a quivering little purse dog in his heart. The thought of a chihuahua's trembling body with Sebastian's face made Abby smile, and Sebastian must have noticed.

"What?" he asked.

"Nothing."

"No. Tell me."

"I guess I was just thinking that you're all bark and no bite," Abby said. "Like the little dogs at the doggie daycare that growl at the big dogs because they're scared."

"You don't scare me," Sebastian said. "I like you. Remember? That's why I want to be your friend."

He's concussed, Abby decided. "Hey, are you sure you aren't feeling dizzy?"

"I'm fine. Sit down with me," he said and, still holding her hand, pulled her down onto a patch of grass against the tree's wide trunk.

"I'm going to see if I can find us an Uber." Again, Abby tried to extricate her fingers. Sebastian didn't seem inclined to let her go.

"Can you . . ." he began, and swallowed hard. "Would you look and see if I'm still bleeding?" he asked.

She looked at his knees. "No. Bleeding's stopped." She opened both of her rideshare apps. Neither of them showed drivers available anywhere in a ten-mile vicinity. Just her luck.

"I need to call Jasper again," she said. "I'm not seeing any drivers around here, so he's going to have to come get us."

Sebastian nodded. She noted, with amusement, that he had closed his eyes again. The apex predator, the alpha dog, brought low by a skinned knee. It would be funny, except he was so obviously freaked out.

She tapped Jasper's number, gave him an update, and sent him a map with a pin dropped to show where they were.

"I'll be there as soon as I can," he said.

"Sounds good," said Abby. She ended the call and sat down again. "Jasper's on his way."

Sebastian didn't seem to have heard her. His eyes were still shut, his face was still pale, and he'd tilted it toward the sky, heedless of the rain that was making its way among the tree's branches to patter against his skin. "I want to talk to you about the TikTok thing," he said. "I want to explain."

Abby shook her head. "You don't owe me an explanation," she said.

"I want to explain," he repeated. "The thing is . . ." He swallowed, and stopped talking, evidently unsure of what the thing was. "Maybe I am scared," he finally admitted, very quietly "My parents . . ."

Abby waited, until he said, "It's kind of dysfunctional. Kind of a mess."

Abby considered, then said, "I think most people's parents are some flavor of mess."

"And if you see a woman only once, she doesn't get a chance

to hurt you," he said, opening his eyes to give her a look from underneath his unfairly long lashes. "Or ghost you."

"I didn't ghost you."

He shook his head. "I woke up and you were gone, Abby. That's pretty much the definition of ghosting." He shook his head, sending water dripping from his nose. "I wasn't even sure you were real."

Abby didn't know what to say to that . . . but she found herself wondering how she would have felt if a guy she'd gone home with had fled from her bedroom before she'd had a chance to say goodbye. She swallowed hard, feeling off-balance. And guilty.

"Stay here a sec. I'm going to grab something." Abby got to her feet, pulled up her hood, and ran to where she'd leaned her bike against a neighboring tree. From her handlebar bag, she removed her microfiber towel and the single long-sleeved shirt she'd packed, thinking she'd need them at some point if the rain kept up. She shoved them into her pockets and ran back to Sebastian.

"Here. Dry off a little." It was still pouring, but at least the tree was giving them some shelter. Sebastian took the towel, gave his face a perfunctory swipe.

"You're shivering," he said.

"I'm fine."

"I'm sorry, Abby." He was very close to her, his thigh pressed against the side of her thigh, with his arm against her arm. "This was dangerous and dumb, and I shouldn't have made you do it."

"It's okay. Really. It's fine." She swallowed hard, steeling herself. "And I shouldn't have ghosted you. You're right. It wasn't very mature." She hesitated, then made herself say it. "Like I told you, I'd never done anything like that before . . ."

He opened his eyes again, just a slit. "Never? I think you said 'hardly ever.'"

"Never," Abby repeated. "It's— I guess it's just not who I am." Also, it wasn't as if she'd had endless opportunities to go home with handsome strangers. But never mind that.

"Hold still." Sebastian reached over—not very far, she realized, they were so close together that there wasn't much distance to cover—unclipped her helmet's chin strap and pulled it off.

"What are you doing?" she asked, a little faintly.

"Come here," he said, beckoning her closer. Abby felt like she'd been hypnotized as she leaned toward him. She wondered if he was going to try to kiss her . . . but what he did was tilt her head forward and gently towel off her hair. He did it just right, his hands firm but not too rough, gently squeezing the strands and rubbing at her scalp. When he stopped, their faces were very close. She could see the blue-gray of his eyes, and the drops of water clinging to his lashes, and she could hear her pulse beating in her ears. For what felt like an endless span of time, they just looked at each other. Then, slowly, Sebastian reached out and put his fingers on Abby's cheek.

She thought, *I have a boyfriend.*

She thought, *He just wants to be my friend. And this is not friendly behavior.*

She thought, *He is going to kiss me. I should stop him.* She pictured her arm, lifting, her hand, pressing on his shoulder, pushing him away. But, even though she could imagine every step, her body did not seem interested in stopping Sebastian's mouth's inexorable progress toward her own.

Abby let her eyes slide shut, and her lips part as Sebastian got closer, and she could feel his breath on her skin.

That was when Abby's phone rang.

"Hey there!" Jasper said, sounding cheerful and chipper. "Just dropped off the first crew, and I'm on my way back to you. Google says thirty-seven minutes. And I'm bringing hot coffee."

"You're an angel from heaven," Abby said.

"Sit tight. Stay safe. I'll see you soon."

Abby ended the call. Sebastian was still very close to her, still looking at her with something close to wonder on his face. She took the towel out of his hands and handed him her shirt. "Put this on."

He looked down at it. "It's yours. You take it."

"You're wet."

"We're both wet."

"Yeah, but you fell off your bike and hit your head. And you're hurt. And your jacket got ripped."

He looked down, noticing the damage to the garment for the first time.

"And I'm still worried that you've got a concussion. I think you might be in shock." She more or less shoved the shirt into his hands.

Sebastian took it. Then he looked at Abby, smiling slightly. "Are you trying to get me to take my clothes off?"

She rolled her eyes. "I'm trying to get you to put clothes on. I'm trying to make sure you don't die of hypothermia."

He considered the shirt, then looked at her again. "If I put it on, will you have dinner with me tomorrow?"

Speaking slowly, increasingly convinced he'd suffered a brain injury, Abby said, "I have dinner with you every night."

"Yeah, but we're going to a nice place tomorrow night."

She stared at him. It was true that the group had a reservation at Sackett's Table, which *Food & Wine* had named one of the best restaurants in upstate New York. Abby was surprised that Sebastian was paying enough attention to the itinerary to know about it.

"So will you sit with me at dinner?"

"Why?"

He looked a little indignant. "I like you," he said. "I would like to be your friend."

"Friend," Abby repeated. Sebastian just looked at her. Then, very slowly and deliberately, he brushed his fingertips against her cheek. Abby's sharp inhalation was audible, even over the rain.

Get a hold of yourself, she thought, and shook her wet hair back over her shoulders. "Look. You just had a near-death experience . . ."

Sebastian snorted. "I fell off my bike. I didn't survive a ten-car pileup. There was no white light that I felt like I needed to go toward."

"You had a traumatic experience," Abby amended. "And you might have hit your head. And it's cold. And—again—I have a boyfriend. I can't go on a date with you!"

"Who said date?" Sebastian asked reasonably. "It's just dinner. We can go as friends."

Abby tried not to think about how badly she wanted to just give in, say yes, throw her arms around him, and kiss him until neither one of them noticed the rain or the cold. "You don't know anything about me," she said.

Sebastian, smiling a little, shook his head and reached for her hand again. "I know you pack scented candles when you go on bike trips."

Abby stared at him. She'd mentioned her candle during a lunchtime conversation that she'd had with the Spoke'n Four, about useless luxury items that people brought with them, and the ridiculous things other riders did to cut weight, like snapping their toothbrushes in half or shaving bars of soap down to tiny slivers, but she didn't remember Sebastian listening, or even being at the table when they talked.

"I know you ride thirty miles by yourself every Sunday morning. I know your best friend is Lizzie, and you met her when you were eight and she was forty-two, and she's the one who got you into leading bike rides. I know you used to think your bike was a magic carpet, and it could take you away when your parents were fighting."

Abby continued to stare at him. She was pretty sure her mouth was hanging open, too.

"I know you know how to change a flat tire."

"Yeah," Abby muttered. "When we've got some free time, I'll teach you." Sebastian reached for her hand.

"I know you," he said.

Above their heads, the rain seemed to be slowing from a biblical torrent to a more standard downpour, and Sebastian's words were echoing. *I know you.*

Abby's throat felt tight, and her heart was knocking strangely in her chest. "I should go take a look at your bike."

She tried to stand. Sebastian moved his grip from her hand to her forearm, keeping her in place, keeping his eyes on her face. His wet hair curled around his cheeks and forehead, and the pallor of his skin only served to emphasis the slate-gray of his eyes, the elegant curves of his mouth.

"Have dinner with me," he said again.

Abby gave up. "Okay. How about this. If you put my shirt on, and if you don't give me a hard time about going to the hospital and getting checked out—"

"I'm fine—"

"And," Abby continued, talking over him, "if you promise to stop being a jerk and wear your pinny without complaining every single day instead of just sticking it in your pocket—"

Sebastian muttered something about how everything always came back to the pinny.

"Then," Abby concluded, "I will have dinner with you. As a friend. If you still want to have dinner with me." *It isn't going to happen,* Abby told herself. Either he'll come to his senses, or he'll be in the hospital, being treated for a concussion, which he has, and which is the only reason he's being nice to me.

"Deal," said Sebastian. He stood up and pulled off the green rain jacket he'd torn in the fall and the short-sleeved white cycling jersey underneath it. Abby tried not to look but ended up looking, and immediately regretted her lack of willpower. In the rain and the dimness, he looked just as good as he'd felt in the dark, with a chest and upper arms that a sculptor might have molded, and just the right amount of chest hair. Mark had his chest waxed regularly, which Abby thought might have had less to do with the hair and more to do with a distaste for anything unruly or out of his control, anything that signaled that his body, not his brain, was running the show.

She didn't want to think about Mark.

Sebastian wriggled into her shirt, which didn't look as ridiculous on him as she'd thought it might. A little short in the arms, a little loose in the chest, but it did not look like he'd pulled on a pup tent, which had been her fear.

"I like this," he said. "It smells like you."

Concussed! Abby thought, as loudly as she could, as Sebastian sat back down with his back against the tree. He spread his legs and patted the soggy ground between them. "Come sit."

Abby pictured herself sitting between his legs, leaning back against his chest, his arms wrapped around her, and felt her entire body flush with longing. "Yeah. No."

"We have to keep warm," he pointed out.

"I'm okay," Abby said, even though she wasn't. Her teeth had started chattering, and her toes and her fingers were both numb. *Fuck it,* she thought, and carefully lowered herself onto the wet ground, not between his legs, but close beside him.

Sebastian made an amused, huffing noise. He slung his arm

over her shoulder and pulled her against him, so every inch of her side was pressed up against the warmth of his torso, and her own dry shirt.

"There you go, my little lemon drop," Sebastian murmured.

Lemon drop? Abby thought. Sebastian had turned himself toward her. He slid his left hand up her neck, cupping the base of her head, rubbing gently. With his right hand he reached over, pulled one of her curls out straight and let it boing back into place.

CONCUSSED, thought Abby. And, *Mark.* She thought about her boyfriend, back at home; her mother, just a few dozen miles away. And, finally, she thought, *Oh, I am in so much trouble.* She let herself lean into him, feeling his warmth, inhaling his scent. With her eyes closed, she could almost pretend she was dreaming as his left hand slid down around her shoulder, as he tilted her face up and brought his mouth down to meet hers. His face was wet, his cheeks were cold, but his lips, when they pressed against hers, were the warmest thing in the world.

"Abby," he murmured. She could feel his thumb, stroking her cheek, then, featherlight, rubbing over her eyebrow as his other hand changed the angle of her head, letting him deepen the kiss. For a moment she felt his tongue slip against hers, then he pulled back to nibble at her lower lip. *Oh, God, he's so good at this,* she thought, and let herself be greedy for a minute, letting her hand drift over his shoulder, then up and down the broad, strong planes of his back.

Sebastian made a low, pleased noise and settled one arm around her shoulders, the other around her waist, lifting her until she was practically in his lap.

"You're cold," he said, and started kissing her neck. Abby felt gentle suction, flickers of his teeth, the warm brush of his tongue, and, oh, she was melting, melting like sugar in the rain, like the Wicked Witch of the West. Sebastian tilted her head back, exposing more of her neck to his ministration. "Gotta warm you up." He wrapped his arms around her, pulling her tight against the relative dryness of her own shirt.

"Abby," he whispered, and brought his mouth down against hers again. Abby felt herself softening, her body warming, like candle wax, as her arms wrapped themselves around his neck, pulling him close.

They were kissing when a horn honked. Abby jerked her head backward, jumping to her feet as she saw Jasper behind the wheel of the van. He pulled up close and rolled down his window. "Well, don't you two look cozy!" he called.

Abby, who'd secretly been hoping that Jasper would get lost, or that the sag wagon would break down, bolted away from Sebastian, hurrying over to the sag wagon and leaning into Jasper's open window.

"We need to go to the hospital," she said in a low voice. "I'm pretty sure he's got a concussion."

"Is that what you were doing?" Jasper sounded amused. "Checking him for a concussion?"

"I'm serious," Abby said, feeling herself blushing.

"Why?" Jasper asked. "Is he dizzy? Did he puke? Or pass out?"

"No, and he says he doesn't have a headache, but he's acting very weird."

"I don't have a concussion." Sebastian had gotten to his feet and was walking over to them.

"But you agreed that you would go to the hospital," said Abby, and led him around the van, opening the passenger-side door. "You sit," she said. "Jasper and I will get the bikes."

Sebastian had climbed into the van's backseat. Abby and Jasper trotted off through the rain.

"Can you forget that you saw anything?" Abby asked in a low voice.

"Forget what?" he replied, his expression innocent.

Abby smiled at him, weak-kneed with relief, even though her cheeks were still hot. She felt dizzy and unsettled and more than a little ashamed. There weren't explicit rules against leaders fraternizing with the paying riders, and Lizzie had told Abby that it happened. And then there was Mark, the unresolved situation hanging over her head, like a boulder dangling from an increasingly frayed length of rope. And her mother, along for the ride, watching everything with her gimlet gaze. And Morgan. Abby took a moment to hope that Morgan had gotten to her appointment safely, that her situation had been resolved and her mind was at ease.

Once the bikes were stowed, Abby buckled herself into the front passenger's seat, and Jasper climbed behind the wheel. In the rearview mirror, she saw Sebastian giving her a puzzled look. Abby did her best to ignore it, wiping her phone's screen dry and starting to google.

"Okay, there's an urgent care and an actual emergency room in Seneca Falls. What do you think?" she asked Jasper. "The hospital, right?" She started the directions to the hospital, then looked up *signs of concussion*, wondering if *sudden attraction to unsuitable person* would be one of them. "Do you want me to call Lincoln?" she asked Sebastian, without turning around to look at him.

"I'll do it. Hang on." He didn't put the phone on speaker, but the van wasn't that large, and Abby could hear every word.

"What happened?" Lincoln asked. "Are you okay?"

"Yeah. I hit something and went flying off the bike. I'm fine. Abby and Jasper are driving me to the hospital so I can get checked out because that's the company policy."

Silence. Abby could imagine Lincoln, who'd watched Sebastian fighting with Abby over wearing a reflective pinny, trying to absorb the news that his friend was now willing to go to the hospital with her, without even putting up a fight. "Do you have your insurance card?" Lincoln finally asked.

"Yup."

"Okay. Text me when you get there. I'll come meet you."

"Fine. But there's nothing wrong with me. My knees got scraped, but Abby bandaged them."

"Were you bleeding?" Lincoln asked. "Did you pass out?"

"I was, but I didn't. Abby took care of me."

Lincoln's voice turned wary. "I hope you thanked her."

"Oh, I did." In the rearview mirror, Abby saw Sebastian wink. She looked away, feeling her cheeks get hot again.

Sebastian ended the call and smiled pleasantly at Abby in the rearview mirror. Abby shook her head. She was starting to wonder if maybe *she* was concussed, if she'd bonked her head at some point, if she was going to wake up, still in bed in Syracuse, and discover that the whole morning had been a dream. Then, with a stab of guilt, she thought about Morgan, and Andy, and bent over her phone to text Kayla and check in. But even as she typed, part of her was still feeling Sebastian's warm lips against hers, Sebastian gripping her fingers, Sebastian pulling her into his lap and calling her his little lemon drop.

Lily

2:00 p.m.

The morning in Seneca Falls turned out to be one of the nicest times Lily could remember. Jasper had driven them right to their hotel. She and Eileen had checked in, dropped off their luggage, then borrowed umbrellas and walked out into the rain, past the Wesleyan Chapel, where, a plaque informed them, the first women's rights convention had been held in 1848. A long span of gray stone, covered in trickling water, ran parallel to the sidewalk, inscribed with the words of the Declaration of Sentiments. The rain tapered off just enough to let Lily and Eileen slow down and read them.

"'When, in the course of human events, it becomes necessary for one portion of the family of man to assume among the people of the earth a position different from that which they have hitherto occupied, but one to which the laws of nature and of nature's God entitle them, a decent respect to the opinions of mankind requires that they should declare the causes that impel them to such a course,'" Lily read. She walked on, to the section that outlined what the convention's attendees saw as men's abuses toward women, and read them in her head:

He has monopolized nearly all the profitable employments, and from those she is permitted to follow, she receives but a scanty remuneration.

He closes against her all the avenues to wealth and distinction, which he considers most honorable to himself. As a teacher of theology, medicine, or law, she is not known.

He has denied her the facilities for obtaining a thorough education—all colleges being closed against her.

He allows her in Church as well as State, but a subordinate position.

"Amazing how far we've come," Lily murmured.

"Amazing how far we still have to go," Eileen replied.

The spa was just around the corner from the sculpture, decorated in shades of taupe and beige, where the piped-in sound of water trickling over rocks competed with the sound of the actual rain outside. The air smelled like lavender and sage, and the attendants and aestheticians all wore white tunics and soft-soled shoes, and spoke in low, hushed voices, like they were nurses at some very posh hospital. Lily had been assigned a female masseuse, which spared her the awkwardness of having to request one, and if the woman thought it was strange that Lily kept her underwear and brassiere on, she didn't say so.

Lily had never had a massage before. She thought she'd be uncomfortable and self-conscious, and she had been, at first, feeling a stranger touching her body, but when she was finally able to relax, she couldn't believe how wonderful it felt, to have the woman's warm, strong hands working at the stiff muscles of her neck and shoulders. "Lots of tension," the woman murmured.

"Teenage daughter," Lily replied, and the woman made a humming noise of understanding.

When the massage was over, Lily and Eileen were led down

a candlelit corridor and seated in high, padded chairs, with basins of bubbling water for their feet. Lily felt like a queen as she sat, sipping cucumber-infused water while a young dark-haired woman bent over her, clipping her nails, smoothing her calluses. There were six people getting pedicures, and their matching white robes functioned as something like a uniform, erasing the differences that would have been conferred by shoes and handbags and clothing. Eileen wore a glittering bracelet that Lily assumed was made of real diamonds, along with diamond stud earrings that glittered in the lights, and her cheeks were faintly freckled, the same as Abby's.

Thinking of Eileen's daughter made her think of her own, and the pleasant sensations of lightness and bonelessness that had suffused her disappeared, replaced by a familiar weight that settled over her shoulders, the worry that her child was becoming a stranger.

"You have two daughters?" she asked Eileen.

"That's right. Abby's sister, Marni, is my oldest. Thirty-eight already!" Eileen shook her head. "I can't understand how I got so old."

Lily wanted to ask a million things: Did your daughters hate you when they were Morgan's age? Did they talk to you about their lives? Were they moody, hard to know, aggravating? Did you ever feel like they hated you? Did you ever feel like you hated them; or like they were strangers who'd just shown up in your house one morning?

"And Morgan's your only one, right?" Eileen asked. "She seems like a sweetheart."

Lily knitted her fingers together in her lap. At home, if one of her friends had paid her this compliment, Lily would have been happy to take it. *Yes, Morgan's a good girl.* But she was far from home, in the company of a woman who didn't know her, who she'd probably never see again. Maybe this was a chance for her to get some answers. "She's hard," Lily finally said, her words rushed, her voice small. "She's . . . confusing. Hot and cold. Like, this trip. The plan was for her to bike with her father, and for me to ride in the sag wagon, but when her dad couldn't make it, she seemed okay about doing it with me. Not just okay, but insistent." Lily could still remember Morgan telling her that it would be fine, even without her dad, that she didn't want to reschedule or postpone, that she wanted to do the trip they'd planned on the days they'd planned it. *You and I will have fun,* she'd told Lily. "I thought she really wanted to spend time with me. And then, as soon as we got here . . ." Lily made a chopping gesture with her hand, one that, she hoped, communicated how thoroughly Morgan had ignored her.

"Well," said Eileen. "That sounds pretty normal for teenagers. Sometimes, they don't even know what they want or it changes from minute to minute. I'd love to tell you that it gets easier, but I'm not sure it's true." There was silence for a moment as the women bent over them and began painting their toenails in careful, precise strokes: pale pink for Lily, dark red for Eileen. "I don't know if you know this, but I didn't tell Abby I was coming. I just showed up."

Lily hadn't known. She looked at the other woman, who was staring down at her own feet.

"If I'd asked, I think she would have turned me down. I think she feels like I'm trespassing on her turf." Eileen sipped from her own glass of cucumber water. "I'm telling myself, she may not want me here right now. But, someday, she'll remember that I showed up for her. She'll know that I tried." Eileen took another sip. "I think that's half of parenting, especially when they're older. You just keep showing up."

Was that true? Lily had shown up, after Morgan had begged

her not to postpone the trip, after Morgan had promised she wanted them to spend time together. She'd shown up, she'd been present for her daughter, and now Morgan was ignoring her.

Lily did her best to inject good cheer into her voice, which came out sounding falsely hearty. "I should remember I'm lucky. Morgan's a good girl," she said, half to Eileen, half to herself.

Eileen just gave a quiet, "Hmm." The aestheticians indicated that they were to prop their legs on foam blocks. Lily thought the warm rocks they were rubbing against her calves felt ticklish and too hot.

"Just make sure she knows you love her. No matter what," Eileen said. Her expression was oddly intense, and she'd turned herself sideways in the pedicure chair so that she was looking right at Lily. Something was nagging at Lily, tugging at the edges of her consciousness—something Morgan had said? Something about the way she'd looked; some gesture she'd made? Lily tried but couldn't bring it to the front of her mind. She smiled weakly and nodded, resolving to speak to her daughter as soon as she arrived, to ask what was going on and not give up until she'd gotten an answer.

Sebastian

*B*e *her friend,* Lincoln had told him. And, Lord, he was trying. But he couldn't deny how badly he wanted to be more than a friend to Abby Stern.

This one is different, Sebastian imagined saying to his friend. *I know it. She's the one.*

Those words should have scared him. But his heart felt like a single piece of confetti, held aloft by a sweet spring breeze. He was enamored, he realized, shaking his head in wonder. Infatuated. How long had it been since he'd let himself have feelings for a girl that were emotional, not just physical? Not for years. Maybe not ever.

"You're all set," the doctor told him, already on his way out the door. Sebastian got off the exam table, where his wet shorts had left a butt print on the paper drape. He wasn't lying to Lincoln. He did want to be Abby's friend, and more. He wanted to know everything about her; to hear her entire life story, to find out where she'd been and where she wanted to go next. He wanted to bring her bowls of pasta in bed, and tease her, and call her his lemon drop, and ride his bike with her, all over the world. Now that he'd found her, he never wanted to let her go.

He turned the corner, excited to see her . . . except, it turned out, only Lincoln was waiting, showered and dry and dressed in his off-the-bike clothes. "Abby was freezing. She went to the hotel to take a shower and check in on everyone," he said, tapping at his phone, presumably to summon a car for the two of them. That task completed, he put his phone in his breast pocket and gave Sebastian a disapproving look. "Why did you want to ride in this weather?"

Sebastian shrugged. "I—I just felt like moving."

Lincoln was still looking at him. "Are you sure you're okay?"

Sebastian nodded. "I asked Abby to have dinner with me."

"What do you mean?" he asked, speaking slowly, like he still thought Sebastian might have hit his head. "You have dinner with Abby every night."

"Right. But we're going to sit together."

Lincoln exhaled noisily. He shook his head, giving Sebastian a look that said, as clearly as words, *Back on your bullshit.* Sebastian followed him down the hospital hallway, his bike shoes click-clacking with each step. "This isn't anything nefarious. I just want to get to know her."

Lincoln didn't say a word.

"As a *friend*," Sebastian added. Lincoln didn't reply.

The silence became uncomfortable until Sebastian felt like he had to say something else.

"I'm not going to hurt her."

Lincoln gave him a long, hard, assessing look. "Okay," he said. "But what if she hurts you?"

For a minute, Sebastian didn't know what to say. "What do you mean?"

Lincoln pressed his lips together. "Do you remember when Lana and I broke up?"

Sebastian did. Lincoln and his girlfriend had gotten together the September of their sophomore year, and were together and

happy for the next almost two years. Then, the summer before senior year, Lana had gotten a summer internship in Mexico City,
and had told Lincoln she wanted to see other people; that it made
sense for them to have some freedom before committing to a serious relationship. Lincoln hadn't been happy, but agreed. They'd
had the most cerebral and civilized breakup Sebastian had ever
seen. Then Lana had gone off to Mexico, and Lincoln had gone
home, to New York, where he'd been fine, until the day in July
when Lana had posted a picture of herself, smiling in the arms of
a handsome colleague named Jorge. That afternoon, Lincoln had
shown up at the *Jersey Journal,* where Sebastian was interning.
His eyes were red-rimmed, and he'd smelled like marijuana and
beer, which was completely unprecedented. He'd gone online,
found the cheapest flight to Mexico that had two seats available,
and was leaving the next day.

"Come with me," he'd told Sebastian. "I have to get her back."

Instead of accompanying him to Mexico, Sebastian had
brought him home, to Lincoln's parents' place on the Upper West
Side, where Lincoln was staying for the summer. They'd sat in the
kitchen, and, clumsily, Sebastian had tried to console his friend,
and explain why flying down to Mexico was a bad idea. *You and
Lana agreed on this,* he'd said. Give her a chance to look around.
Once she realizes how much better you are for her, she'll come
back. If you love something, set it free!

Lincoln had glared at him. "If you start quoting memes at me,
I will end your life."

Sebastian had stayed with him, sleeping on the floor of Lincoln's childhood bedroom. Lincoln hadn't cried—at least, not in
front of Sebastian. He hadn't broken plates, or burned clothes, or
even deleted all of Lana's pictures from his phone or blocked her
on social media. He'd just been quietly, thoroughly, abjectly miserable for the rest of the summer. Sebastian remembered lots of

sighing and long silences. Lincoln had lost weight, and he'd barely smiled. It was as if all the world had lost its savor; like there was no pleasure left for him anywhere. Sebastian had done his best to help. He'd gotten Lincoln set up on the apps, and Lincoln had gone on a few dates with girls he met on them, and a daughter of his parents' friends, but nothing had taken. Lana was the only one he wanted.

In the hospital corridor, Sebastian groped for the right words. "I remember. It was hard for you."

"Hard for me," said Lincoln, and shook his head. "It felt like chewing on glass, every day. I wanted to die. I mean, I wasn't actually going to kill myself, but that's how much it hurt. I didn't want to be in a world where I wasn't with her, where she didn't want me. It hurt. And it kept on hurting until we were back together." Which had taken months, Sebastian remembered.

"Do you understand?" Lincoln asked him. "If you're in a relationship with someone, if you let yourself be vulnerable, you can get hurt."

"I know."

Lincoln's expression was dubious. But Sebastian did understand. He got it. If he was with Abby, if he let himself love her, and if, somehow, she loved him, she would have his heart in her hands, every day. He would be giving her power to wound him, to hurt him, to make him not want to live. To leach all the color from the world; to steal all the savor from food; to turn minutes to hours and hours to days and the rest of his life into a painfully slow slog to its inevitable end. He shook his head in confusion . . . and admiration. How had Lincoln done it? How did anyone?

"It's scary," he finally said.

"But worth it," said Lincoln. "If it works, if you find your person, everything you suffer is worth it."

Abby

Abby had her Uber stop at a drugstore on the way back from the hospital, and she ran across the sidewalk through the rain, hurrying up and down the aisles, gathering what she needed. After she'd made her purchases, her phone buzzed with a text from Kayla. *All good. Just got in the sag wagon. Morgan seems fine. We're on our way.* Abby texted her mother next, who wrote back *Still at the spa. Here until 4. Everything okay on your end?*

Second group on its way, Abby wrote . . . and then, swallowing hard, *Thanks for your help.* The bubbles indicating typing appeared, then vanished, until, finally, the thumbs-up emoji floated over Abby's last text.

All good, Abby told herself. Now it was just a matter of keeping an eye on Morgan and hoping that the girl was able to keep her secret.

At the hotel, Abby collected her room keys and went to her room, where she finally peeled off her cold, wet clothes, groaning as she stepped into the bliss of a hot shower. When she'd gotten all the dirt and blood and grease off her, when her toes and fingers were no longer numb and she was finally warm again, she dried off, got dressed, put her wet hair in a bun, and knocked on the door of the room that Lily and Morgan were sharing.

"Just a minute!" Morgan called faintly. When she opened the door, she was wearing an oversize tee shirt, enormous sweatpants, and a pair of fluffy white chenille socks. Her face looked wan; her eyes were red-rimmed.

"Hi," she said, her voice just above a whisper, as her gaze darted left, then right.

"It's just me," Abby said. "My mom is keeping your mom busy for the rest of the afternoon, so you've got a few hours to yourself. I wanted to see how you were doing."

Morgan's shoulders slumped. "You know?"

"I know you had an appointment," Abby said carefully. "I just want to make sure you're okay."

Morgan bowed her head. Her shoulders twitched in a tiny, almost invisible shrug, before she said, "Thank you."

"I brought you a heating pad, and some snacks." Abby raised the bag, and Morgan opened the door wide enough for Abby to step inside. "How are you feeling?"

"Okay," Morgan said. "For now. I have to take two different medications. One today and one tomorrow. I already took the today stuff. I guess tomorrow is when it'll . . . you know." She took another breath. "Happen."

"You've got Tylenol, right?" Abby asked. She nodded at the bag. "The heating pad should help. When my friend Marissa had an abortion, she said it helped her a lot."

Morgan's head jerked up, her gaze moving from the floor to Abby's face. "Your friend had an abortion?"

Abby nodded. "Lots of women have abortions," she said, thinking that Morgan might not know this, that, in her bubble, in her red state, she might never have met, or even heard about, a real-life woman who'd ended a pregnancy. At least, not one who'd be willing to talk about it.

"How was it for her?" Morgan's fingers were tugging at the hem of her shirt and she was once again addressing the carpet. "Was she okay? After?"

"She said the cramps were pretty bad," Abby said, not wanting to mislead Morgan about what she could expect. "But they only lasted a few hours. Then it was over. And she was fine. She said junk food and rom-coms helped." Abby started pulling out the snacks she'd bought. "I've got sweet, I've got salty, I've got sour, and I've got chocolate. The four food groups!"

"I'm not very hungry." Morgan licked her lips and swallowed again. "I just wish I was home. In my own bedroom. My own bed."

Abby made a sympathetic sound, thinking about how she always felt safest in her own bed, barricaded behind a row of pillows. "Do you want me to stay with you for a while?"

"No thank you," Morgan said. "I think I'm going to try to take a nap." She gave Abby a quavering attempt at a smile. "I didn't sleep much last night."

"I understand," Abby said. "How about tonight? My room has two beds, and you're welcome to come hang out. We can watch movies."

Morgan appeared to think it over before shaking her head. "Thank you. But I think I'll be okay."

Abby nodded, even as she thought that Morgan looked a long way from okay. "And I'm sure Andy would be happy to keep you company if you wanted."

Morgan nodded, smiling faintly. "I think I need to stay away from boys for a little while."

"You've got my phone number. I'll be in my room, if you need me. And we'll check tomorrow, and the next day. You probably won't feel up to riding, so I'll let Jasper know to expect you." Abby paused. "What are you going to tell your mom?"

Morgan set the drugstore bag down on the bed and raked her fingers through her hair. "Just that it's my period," she said. "Which—maybe that's kind of true."

"That's a good way to think about it," said Abby. "You must be relieved."

Another faint smile flitted across Morgan's face as she said, "I'll be relieved when it's over."

Abby touched Morgan's arm. "Get some rest," she said. "And text me if you need anything—more snacks, or something to drink. Or if you want someone with you. I'm here," she said. "And Kayla's here. We're all here to help. Whatever you need. We've got you."

Morgan thanked her and closed the door. Abby went to her room. She ordered some Chinese food and lay in her bed, eyes closed. After the riding, and the rain, the accident, after the interlude with Sebastian and the stress of keeping Morgan's activities a secret, she should have been exhausted. But she didn't feel even slightly sleepy. She felt like she could run a marathon, or go dancing, all night long. Her mind was full of Sebastian: how he'd looked at her, what he'd said, how his mouth had felt against hers when he'd kissed her in the rain. It gave her the same feeling she'd had when she'd learned how to ride a bike—that she was weightless, that she was flying, that she was powerful and beautiful, and nothing could ever hurt her.

Abby

Day Eight: Seneca Falls

The day after the storm dawned bright and sunny—a perfect morning to ride a loop around Cayuga Lake. Abby had told the group to be ready to ride at nine in the morning. At seven o'clock, she woke up to find her phone vibrating with texts. She glanced at the screen, swallowing hard as she read the first few messages. Quickly, she tapped out a text to Morgan—*What happened? Are you okay?*

No reply came. Abby dressed quickly, brushed her teeth, and hurried down to the hotel lobby, where the Breakaway riders were gathered by the coffee urn. Eileen was perfectly dressed, in white linen pants and a hot-pink sweater set. Kayla Presser wore denim shorts and a tee shirt. Her hair was in a ponytail, her eyes were puffy, and her skin was still creased from her pillows. Lily Mackenzie was even more disheveled, with slippers and pajama bottoms visible beneath the hem of her bathrobe. Her voice was high and frightened. Her hands swooped through the air as she spoke.

"Morgan and I went to sleep at eleven o'clock last night, and when I woke up this morning, she was gone." Lily's voice was trembling as she pulled an iPhone out of her robe's pocket. "I thought maybe she'd gone to get coffee or something, but then I found her phone. She left it in the room, so I can't use it to track her."

"Okay. Let's not panic," Abby said.

"She never goes anywhere without her phone. Not anywhere." Lily sounded accusatory, as she looked from Eileen to Kayla to Abby. "I called her father, and her best friend at home. Nobody's heard from her."

"Okay," said Abby, turning back to Kayla. "And Andy's gone, too, right?"

Kayla nodded. "He was gone when we woke up this morning. I think he's got his phone, though. At least, I didn't see it in the room."

"So they're probably together." Abby poured Lily a cup of coffee and ushered her over to a quartet of armchairs around a coffee table near the front doors. Kayla and Eileen sat down, and Abby said, "Start from the beginning. Start from last night."

Lily wrapped her hands around the mug, took a sip, and began. "Morgan didn't want to go out to dinner. She said she had cramps, and that she wasn't hungry, so I let her rest. I ordered in food from a diner, and I think she had a little soup, and we watched a movie, and we were both in bed at eleven. Then, this morning, I woke up and she was gone." Lily sipped more coffee, then licked her lips, the same anxious gesture Abby had seen Morgan make, before she turned to Kayla. "Did Andy say anything to you last night? Did something happen yesterday when Morgan was with you?"

Abby exchanged a quick look with her mother. Lily saw it, and her expression shifted from bewildered to suspicious. "Did something happen?" she asked. When no one answered, she said in a loud, jagged voice, "Will someone please tell me what's going on?"

Eileen pressed her lips together. Kayla looked at her feet. "Is Morgan's bike still here?" Abby asked.

"I don't know." Lily looked slightly less furious. Maybe she was just relieved to have a task on which she could focus. "I'll check."

Abby nodded. "Once we know whether she's got her bike or not, we can make a list of everywhere she might have gone, and then we'll start looking."

"Should we call the police?" Lily asked. "What if she's been kidnapped? What if there's . . . I don't know, child traffickers—"

Abby held up her hand. "It's been less than twenty-four hours, and at least we're pretty sure she's with Andy. I don't think the police are going to take it seriously yet. We can call them, but I think we should also look ourselves."

"I want to call the police," Lily said, her hands balled on her hips.

"Okay," said Abby. "Do you have a recent picture of Morgan? They might ask for one."

"Oh, God," Lily said. Her body seemed to crumple. She wrapped her arms around her shoulders and started to cry. Eileen put her hand on the other woman's back.

"Come on," Eileen said. "Let's go see if her bike is here or not." Abby felt grateful . . . along with the unsettling sensation that came with feeling something other than frustration and anger toward her mom.

The elevator doors slid open, and Sebastian, looking adorably rumpled in a tee shirt and shorts, scanned the lobby until he saw her.

"What's going on?" he asked.

"Morgan and Andy are missing," Abby said.

He gave a businesslike nod. "How can I help?"

Ten minutes later, Sebastian was on his bike, riding into

downtown Seneca Falls to look in the coffee shops, and Kayla and Lily were working their phones in opposite corners of the lobby. When Lily was occupied, Abby gave her mother an interrogative glance—*Do you know anything?* Eileen pressed her lips together and shook her head. Abby's shoulders slumped. *Where are you, Morgan?* she wondered as she looked up the phone number for the hospital. *Where are you, and are you all right?*

Morgan

All night long, Morgan had lain awake, staring up at the hotel room ceiling, with her mother sleeping in the bed beside her and the prescription bottle containing the second round of pills clutched tight in her hand. *I have cramps,* she'd told Lily. Her mother had given her a puzzled look, a look that had burned like grabbing a hot pan's handle and felt like it lasted a month. Morgan had made herself meet Lily's gaze until, finally, her mother had said, "I'll get you some Advil," and had left her alone.

Morgan pretended to be asleep when her mom ordered dinner. She'd pretended to wake up long enough to eat a few mouthfuls of soup, which was all her knotted belly could tolerate. She'd watched the movie her mother found, or at least she'd kept her eyes on the screen, and she'd faked sleep again after Lily turned off the lights and came over to kiss Morgan's cheek. She had come so close in that moment, so close to telling Lily the truth, to opening her mouth and blurting out everything. But Morgan had pressed her lips together and she'd made herself keep quiet, and finally, her mom had gone to the bathroom to brush her teeth and had climbed into her own bed. The shades were drawn, and the room was dark, quiet except for her mother's gentle exhalations, and Morgan's heart, loud as thunder in her ears.

I can't do this, Morgan had thought to herself. Not with Lily in the room. Not with Lily around. She was convinced that, once it began, her mother would look at her and know exactly what was happening; exactly what Morgan had done.

At six in the morning, she'd texted Andy. *Can u talk?* She'd been prepared to wait for a response, but he'd written back right away. *What's wrong?*

She couldn't begin to tell him, couldn't type those words and watch them appear on the screen (and what if someone got her carrier to turn over her messages, like they'd done to that poor girl in Nebraska, the one Olivia had told her about?). Instead she wrote, *Is there somewhere we can go?*

Meet me by the elevators in 10, Andy had written. Morgan pulled back the covers and slipped on her shoes. She'd worn her sweatpants and a tee shirt to bed, so she didn't even have to get dressed. She'd set her phone on her bed before she eased the door open and padded down the hall with the room key and the medications in her pocket and the heating pad Abby had given her tucked under her arm.

Andy was waiting in the hallway, yawning and rumpled, smelling of sleep. He was carrying a blanket and a pillow.

"Are you okay?" he asked her. "Did you take the rest of the pills?"

"Not yet," Morgan said. It hadn't been twenty-four hours yet. Her body felt exactly the same as it had the day before, and the day before that—her breasts achy and tender, her nose suddenly a hundred times more attuned to smells. Just then, she could catch a whiff of cleanser and the ghost of the previous day's sunscreen on Andy's skin. "They said to wait twenty-four hours. That's at eleven. I just couldn't be in the room when I did it." She lowered her voice. "With my mom."

Andy nodded. "There's a gym on the ground floor," he said.

"There's a treadmill and yoga mats and stuff like that. No one's in there. I checked. I know it's not—not great," he said, stammering, "but it's quiet, and there's a TV, and I can bring you more blankets, and . . ."

"That's a good idea," Morgan said. "Will you stay with me?"

Andy swallowed audibly. "Yeah. Sure. Of course."

Morgan followed him down the stairs. She was thinking about her mother, and how Lily would feel when she woke up and saw Morgan's bed empty, and Morgan's phone on the bed. She knew she should have left a note or sent a text. Too late for that now, though.

"Follow me." Andy led her down a hallway on the hotel's first floor and used his room key to open the door marked FITNESS CENTER, which turned out to be a small room with a mirrored wall and a padded, wipeable rubber floor. Lined up in front of the mirrors were a single treadmill, an elliptical machine, a pyramid of hand weights, and a stack of yoga mats. A television hung on the wall in the corner, and below it, there was a table with a miniature refrigerator full of pint-size bottles of water, a stack of hand towels, and a bowl of oranges and waxy-looking apples.

Andy piled the yoga mats against the wall, arranging the pillow and the blanket on top. Morgan sat down, cross-legged, and after a minute, Andy sat beside her.

"Do you want some water?" he asked. "Or—or tea, maybe? They put out tea and coffee in the lobby."

She nodded. "Tea, please," she said. Andy went to get it, and Morgan watched him go, wondering why she couldn't have dated a nice guy like Andy. His attention made her feel soft inside, sweet and gooey, like when she and her mom used to make candy, and the hot sugar would change from individual grains to a soft ball of caramel on the stove.

Morgan didn't want to think about her mother. She did not

want to remember the way her mom had showed her how to use the back of a spoon to stretch the caramel, or how they'd watched together as its color went from amber to glossy dark brown. She didn't want to think about how the smell of sugar mixed with the scent of the pine needles from the Christmas tree in the living room, or sitting next to her mom on the couch, using needle and thread to make popcorn and cranberry garlands, while her dad sang carols and built a fire in the living-room fireplace. There would be no more Christmases like that if her mother knew what she'd done. Morgan probably wouldn't even be allowed to come home.

She groaned and collapsed on her side, her head on the pillow, the blanket pulled up to her chin. When Andy came back, she pretended to be asleep, listening as he set the cup down on the floor, then sat at the foot of her makeshift bed. At some point, feigned sleep became real, because, when she opened her eyes again, an hour had passed, and Andy was looking down at her, biting his lip.

"My mom keeps texting," he said, holding his phone. Morgan saw that it was after eight o'clock. "Your mom—I think she's really worried. She doesn't know where you are, and she wants to call the police."

Morgan gulped. "Did you tell your mom where you are?" she asked, her voice very small.

Andy shook his head. "I didn't answer any of her texts."

"Okay."

"But I think you need to talk to her. Or one of us does. She needs to know that you're okay."

Morgan stared up at him. "I can't."

Andy's throat jerked, and he rubbed his hands on his shorts. "You can't avoid her for the rest of the trip. You were going to say you had cramps, right?" His face got a little red.

Morgan nodded. She reached into her pocket, pulled out the bottle, read the directions she'd already committed to memory: *Place 4 misoprostol pills (200 mcg each) between your cheeks and gums and hold them there for 30 minutes as they dissolve. You should not speak or eat for these 30 minutes, so it is good to be someplace quiet where you will not be disturbed. After 30 minutes, drink some water and swallow everything that is left of the pills. This is also a good time to take a painkiller like ibuprofen, as the cramping should start within three hours.*

"Wait," she said. Before Andy could say anything, before she could second-guess herself, she opened the bottle, shook the pills into her hand, and tucked them between her cheeks and gums, two on each side, wincing at the bitter taste as the medication began to dissolve, watching the clock until thirty minutes had passed. *It's done,* she thought. Her heart was pounding with elation and terror, shame and regret, and relief. More than anything else, relief that she'd done it and that, soon, it would all be over.

Lily

You went to the gym and fell asleep there?" Lily repeated. Morgan looked awful. Her hair was tangled, her lips were chapped, and there were circles under her eyes. Lily had taken one look when Morgan had come shuffling into the lobby at ten thirty in the morning, with Andy trailing shamefacedly in her wake, and, immediately, Lily had known that something had happened, that something was wrong. "Upstairs," she'd said, her voice sharp. Morgan had followed her onto the elevator and back to their room. Lily hung the DO NOT DISTURB sign on the door handle, closed the door and locked it, then turned to face her daughter.

"Andy wanted to show me some yoga," Morgan said, with her eyes on the floor. In between frantic calls—to the police, to Don, in Arizona, to Morgan's friend, Olivia, who she'd tracked down at summer camp—Lily had gone back to the room and straightened up, to keep her hands busy. Both beds were made, and she'd set Morgan's duffel bag on top of the luggage stand, after going through each item and telling herself that her daughter wouldn't go far without her phone, her retainer, or her beloved flat iron.

"You were in the gym with Andy?" Lily could hear her voice,

a loud and undignified squawk. She was remembering that Andy had been carrying a blanket and pillow when he and Morgan had come traipsing into the lobby . . . but surely Morgan wouldn't have been brazen enough to carry those items into the lobby if she and Andy had been doing something illicit. Andy seemed nice, well-mannered, and his parents seemed like decent, upstanding people . . . but Lily knew that young men who seemed pleasant were, sometimes, the ones that could cause the most harm.

"I have cramps," Morgan said. "I—my legs were sore. Everything hurt. He was trying to help me." She sniffled, one hand rubbing at her eyes. "I'm still not feeling good. I think I just want to stay in bed today."

Lily looked at her daughter, examining her face, her clothes, her puffy, red-rimmed eyes. They had planned to spend the day going to the museums—there was one for women's rights, and another one dedicated to the movie *It's a Wonderful Life*, which was one of Lily's favorites. Bedford Falls, the movie's setting, was based on Seneca Falls. Lily suspected that those visits would not be happening.

Morgan didn't look like herself. She was clearly exhausted, visibly miserable. But why? What had happened? Had Andy Presser done something to her? Hurt her, somehow?

"I'm sorry," Morgan said. She went to her bed and lay down, curled on her side, her back toward Lily and her face toward the wall. Lily stared at her for a moment. Then she sat on the edge of her daughter's bed and stroked Morgan's hair, rubbing her back. "Honey," she said.

"I just want to be alone," Morgan said, in a tiny, tearful voice. "Please, just let me be by myself for a little while."

"I want to make sure you're all right. You scared me." Lily touched Morgan's hair again and then asked, quietly, "Did Andy do something?"

"No!" Morgan bolted upright, and her voice was loud. She

shook her head, then lay down again. She curled in around herself more tightly. "Andy's a nice guy."

"Did someone else hurt you?"

Morgan shook her head, but Lily felt her daughter's body stiffen, very slightly, under her hand.

"Did something happen?"

Another headshake.

"Honey, you can tell me. Whatever it is." Lily felt like she was groping in a dark room, feet bumping into furniture, hips banging into tables, everything just vague shapes lurking in the blackness.

"You'll be mad at me," Morgan said.

"I promise I won't be angry. But I need to know what happened." She took a deep breath and made herself ask, "Does this have something to do with Brody?"

If she hadn't been watching and listening so carefully, she'd have missed Morgan's minute nod, the sound of her daughter's hair moving against the pillowcase. *Maybe he broke up with her,* Lily thought . . . but her mother's heart, or intuition, or even just her own experience, was suggesting something else that seemed more likely. "Did Brody make you do something you didn't want to do?"

Morgan pressed her hands together. "Not—not exactly."

"You can tell me," Lily said, stroking Morgan's silky hair, moving gently, speaking softly. "You can tell me anything."

"You'll be mad." Morgan's voice was choked with tears. "You'll be so mad, and you won't . . ."

Lily waited.

"You won't love me anymore," Morgan finally whispered.

"Oh, honey." Lily kept her voice steady, even as terror grabbed at her with icy fingers. She bent closer, squeezing Morgan's shoulders. "There's nothing you could do to make me not love you. You're my baby."

At that declaration, Morgan started sobbing, crying so hard that her body shook.

"Whatever it is, it's going to be okay," Lily said calmly, even as a red film descended over her eyes. Had Brody done something? Had he hurt her daughter? Oh, she would kill him if he'd hurt Morgan. She would end him. She'd tear him apart with her bare hands. "I promise. I won't be mad, and I won't ever not love you."

Morgan cried harder. Then she sat up, sniffling as she wiped her streaming eyes. "Brody . . ." she began.

Lily waited, making herself keep quiet, willing her body into stillness.

"He—he didn't force me or anything. He didn't hurt me, or, or . . ." Morgan grabbed a handful of her hair and started twisting, wrapping the strands around and around her hand as she stared down at the bedspread. Her voice was toneless and soft. "We only did it twice, and I didn't even like it. And we used condoms. We were careful. Only . . ."

No, Lily thought. Oh, no.

"I got pregnant," Morgan cried. Her body swayed toward Lily's, like she wanted to rest her head on her mother's shoulder, like she wanted Lily to hold her, but Lily couldn't move, couldn't speak. She sat, stunned and frozen, her body turned to a pillar of salt, like Lot's wife, listening as Morgan sobbed and told the rest of it. The pregnancy test. Telling Olivia. The plan they'd made. The appointment at the clinic in Syracuse. What she'd done there, with Kayla and Andy's connivance, the day before.

"Are you mad at me?" Morgan cried, the words barely intelligible. "Do you hate me?"

"Oh, honey. No. No. Of course I don't."

"And you can't be mad at Andy or Mrs. Presser." She'd raised her head and looked at Lily intently from her streaming eyes. "You can't be. It's not their fault."

"I'm not," said Lily. "I'm not angry at anyone. I just—" She breathed in slowly, her mind a whirling tangle. "I just wish you'd told me. I wish I'd been with you."

"But it isn't—but you don't . . ." Morgan wiped at her eyes, then swiped at her nose with her sleeve and finally turned to look at her mother. "You think it's murder," she said, her voice very low.

Lily got up from the bed and went to the bathroom. She turned on the taps at the sink and ran the water until it got hot. She soaked a washcloth, collected a hand towel and a box of tissues, and sat next to her daughter on the bed. Gently, she used the warm, damp cloth to wipe Morgan's face, the way she'd done when Morgan was little, sticky with chocolate or her favorite marmalade. Other kids liked grape jelly or strawberry jam on their toast or with their peanut butter sandwiches, but Morgan had always liked marmalade. *You have a sophisticated palate,* Don had told her, and Morgan had spent days repeating the phrase in her piping, little-girl voice: *I have a sophisticating palate!* Morgan's narrow shoulders shook with sobs. Her eyes were squeezed shut, like she couldn't even bring herself to look at Lily, and Lily felt shame snaking up her throat, as undeniable as the tide, as memory.

"I have something I need to tell you," Lily said, and waited until Morgan opened her eyes and looked at her, before she drew a deep breath and began.

"When I was eighteen," she began, "I had a boyfriend."

Once upon a time, Lily Mackenzie had been Lily Lawrence. She had grown up in a small, rural town in central Pennsylvania, a town where the school district gave kids vacation on the first day of hunting season, where there were six churches and a Christian day school that sent three buses of students to Washington for the March for Life every January. Lily and her parents and her two older brothers had lived in a small Cape Cod–style house with three bedrooms and two bathrooms and a crabapple tree in the backyard.

During her last year of high school, Lily had grown three inches and two cup sizes, and convinced her mother to let her put golden highlights in her brown hair. Lily dabbed Calvin Klein's Obsession behind her ears every morning and wore push-up bras to school, and the boys she'd known since kindergarten, the boys who'd ignored her in favor of her prettier, bolder friends, had started taking notice. So had her best friend Sharon's older brother, Benjamin.

They'd met at a party at Sharon's house, on a Saturday night in June after she and her friends had finished high school. There'd been a bonfire in the backyard, a cooler full of ice and bottles of soda (and another cooler, in the back of a classmate's trunk, full of beer). Lily remembered the dress she'd worn that night, pink eyelet cotton, with a flounced, tiered skirt, and thin straps that set off the tan of her bare arms and shoulders. She had never felt so pretty, so desirable, and when Ben had walked over to her, two beers held by their necks dangling from one hand, appreciation on his face, she'd felt lucky. Special. Chosen. Ben and Lily had spent the whole night talking, first by the bonfire, then on a couch in Sharon's living room. He'd asked for her number and brushed the lightest kiss on her lips at the end of the night, one finger tucked under her chin to tilt her face toward his, and he was nothing like the high school boys who'd shove their tongues inside your mouth like they were trying to inspect your molars, when they weren't knocking their teeth into yours. Ben's mouth had been gentle, and he'd tasted like whiskey, and he'd smelled like aftershave. Lily had been instantly besotted.

Her parents hadn't approved. Ben was twenty-three, and Lily was three weeks away from her eighteenth birthday. He was a man, and she was a girl. They'd told her she couldn't see him, which, of course, had only made her want to see him even more. So they'd met in secret. It had been easy enough. Lily hadn't even had to lie. "I'm going over to Sharon's house," she'd tell them. She wouldn't bother adding that Sharon was at her summer job as a lifeguard; that Sharon's parents were both at work, that no one was at Sharon's house except Ben. All summer long, she invented sleepovers, movies and parties, bonfires at the lake, and last-minute babysitting jobs.

Lily had grown up going to church every Sunday. She'd promised to stay a virgin until she got married, but her promise had felt misty and far away when Ben had his mouth pressed against her neck and his hands up her shirt or down her pants; like words spoken by a stranger. They'd had sex half a dozen times, and they'd always used condoms, but then, when the week before her college orientation had arrived, Lily's period didn't.

Ben had panicked. "I can't get married," he'd said. "I can't have a kid. I don't even have a job!" By then, Lily had noticed that he hadn't been trying very hard to find one. She didn't blame him. If she had a nice place to stay, parents to pay the bills, and a mother to cook her dinner every night, she might not have put much effort into a job search, either.

Lily had taken a home pregnancy test and, when it had given her the news that wasn't news at all, she had called up her pediatrician, Dr. Rosen, who'd been taking care of her since she'd been a baby. He'd told her to come in at the end of the day, when the office was empty except for the receptionist and the nurse. She'd sat on the exam table, in the little room with the poster of the food pyramid on the wall, where she'd been weighed and measured and checked for ear infections and poison ivy. With her eyes on her lap, she'd asked about confidentiality.

"You're an adult now," he'd told her. "So the standard rules apply. Anything you tell me stays between us."

She'd told him what had happened. He'd asked her questions, his voice calm and nonjudgmental, and then a nurse had come to take a urine sample, just to be sure.

When the test had come back positive, Dr. Rosen had written out three prescriptions, tearing each sheet from his prescription pad and slipping them into an envelope before handing them to her. One had been for birth control pills. The other two had been for the medications that would end the pregnancy. "There's a pharmacy in Harrisburg that keeps this in stock," he'd said.

Lily had left the office, almost dizzy with relief that there was a pill she could swallow that could solve her problem, that she wouldn't need a surgical procedure, or the money to pay for it; that, best of all, her parents wouldn't ever need to know. She'd driven the forty-five minutes to Harrisburg. There, she bought the medication and swallowed the pills. The bleeding had been heavy, the cramps worse than any she'd previously experienced. She'd swallowed Tylenol and stayed in her bedroom with the shades pulled down, getting up every hour to change her pad.

And then it had been over. She'd gone off to college, with her birth control pills in their plastic clamshell zipped into the front pocket of her backpack. Four years later, she'd graduated with her teaching certificate. She'd gotten a job teaching third grade at a school in Pittsburgh and had rented a studio apartment in Squirrel Hill. Most of the other teachers were nice, but they were middle-aged or older, already married and settled. Lily had joined a hiking club and signed up for a wine-tasting class. She attended different churches every Sunday in the same spirit. She liked hiking, she liked wine, and church gave her similar structure and community. It was true that the beliefs she'd grown up with were important to her, but, if she was being honest, she was looking for friends more than Jesus at that point.

Donald Mackenzie had been the youth pastor at the third

church she'd tried. He'd had a round, open face that made him look younger than twenty-nine, and wore his red hair in a brush cut. He'd started to talk to her at the Newcomers' Cake and Coffee, asking her where she was from, where she'd gone to college, and how she liked Squirrel Hill. His voice had been confident, the same full, booming tones he used to preach, but Lily had seen the flush creeping up his neck as he'd said, "Maybe, if you're free on Saturday night, we could go somewhere?" They'd played a round of mini-golf, and had dinner at Ruby Tuesday, where Don had ordered iced tea and the second least-expensive entrée. When the food arrived, he had bowed his head in prayer, murmuring a blessing over his grilled chicken before taking a bite. "I know it's not fancy," Don had apologized, and Lily had told him it was fine, that she didn't need fancy and that she was having a very nice time. She hadn't been lying: Don was kind and respectful, a good listener, kind to his parents and close to his brother and sisters. He was ambitious, too, outlining for her his plan to eventually have his own pulpit. "I'll never be rich, but I should be able to support a family," he'd said. Nine months after they'd met, Don had proposed, with what he called the world's smallest diamond. Lily had cried when she'd said, "Yes."

She'd cried again when she'd told him that she wasn't a virgin, whispering, "I wish I'd waited for you." Tenderly, Don had wiped her cheeks and said, "It's all in the past. Whatever's done is done." On their wedding night, he'd been gentle with her, undressing her with shaking hands, joking about how she'd have to show him what went where. He'd been so endearing, clumsy at first, trying so hard not to rush her, not to go too fast, even though she could feel him trembling with desire, struggling to restrain himself, to hold back so it would be good for both of them.

She'd told him she wasn't a virgin, but she'd never told him about the abortion . . . even though she was almost certain that

Don would have forgiven her. Except he would have asked if she'd repented of her sin. He would have wanted to know if she was truly sorry for what she'd done. And Lily would have had to lie to him. She hadn't repented, and she wasn't sorry.

So she'd kept quiet. When she'd gotten pregnant with Morgan and her gynecologist had asked, with Don in the room, whether Lily had had any previous pregnancies, she'd answered, "No," almost without thinking. The truth was that she barely remembered those terrible five days between the positive pregnancy test and her trip to Harrisburg with Dr. Rosen's prescription in her purse.

And then they'd had Morgan, their perfect, lovely girl. Morgan, who could paint and draw so beautifully from the time she'd gotten her first watercolor kit, who'd earned extra money doing calligraphy for wedding invitations and menus; Morgan, who was modest and sweet and radiantly pretty. By Morgan's tenth birthday, Don was the head pastor. If the teachings about chastity and piety and living a godly life were more stringent than what Lily had grown up believing, if the purity balls and the promise rings felt a little cult-y and creepy, Lily had deferred to her husband, and had kept her secrets.

In the hotel room, Lily finished her story and folded her hands in her lap. Morgan was looking at her with fascination; like her mother's face had been a mask, and Lily had pulled it off to reveal a different face beneath it.

"Did you feel guilty?" Morgan asked.

Lily knew she had to be honest. "I didn't feel guilty then. Now? The truth is that I hardly think about it at all." But that wasn't completely honest. Lily swallowed. "I told the baby I was sorry I wasn't ready for it yet. And I asked it to wait for me. I told myself that its soul would go back to heaven and wait until

I was ready. I believe that's what happened. And that the baby—my baby—was you." She smiled at Morgan and wiped at her eyes. Morgan looked at her solemnly, then handed over the box of tissues, watching as Lily dried her eyes.

"Will you ever tell Daddy?"

Lily considered. "I don't know." In all her years of marriage, she'd never once seriously considered the idea of telling Don what she'd done when she'd been eighteen, only a few years older than her daughter was now. Maybe it would be better if she had. Maybe it wouldn't change anything about the way he thought, what he believed and what he preached. But maybe it would.

"Will you tell him about me?" Morgan whispered . . . and that answer, at least, Lily knew.

"It's up to you, whether you tell him or not. It's your story to tell."

Morgan nodded, biting her lip. Lily hugged her again and stroked her hair.

"I want you to have everything. I want you to go anywhere you want to go. I want you to be whoever you want to be. I want . . ." She'd gestured with her hands, which were exactly like Morgan's, long, fine-boned fingers, oval nails, slender wrists. "I want you to have everything. Everything you want." Lily steadied her voice, making it clear and certain. "Everything in the world."

Abby

At eleven o'clock in the morning, after Morgan and Andy had been reunited with their families, a group of the Breakaway cyclists had gathered in the parking lot so that Abby could lead them on a ride through the green and brown patchwork quilt of farmland, toward the distant sparkle of Cayuga Lake. The sky was still the blue of a Tiffany box, the air felt clear and sharp as cut crystal. The route took them along a two-lane highway, a ribbon of pavement that passed through unspoiled pastures, old forests, and new construction. They stayed on the shoulder (except for Ted, who had a tendency to drift toward the center of the road), and the cars and trucks that passed them gave them plenty of room. Sebastian had started off at the front of the pack with Lincoln. Abby had ended up riding with Eileen. She coasted down a hill, watching her mother's face as they passed a gas-station-cum-weed shop.

"It's legal," Abby said, when she saw Eileen's lips purse. "Have you ever tried it?"

"Marijuana?" Eileen rolled her eyes. "Sure, in college. Everyone at least tried it back then."

Abby had a hard time imagining her mother as a college girl, sitting on a dorm-room floor, holding a joint to her lips. Her mind wanted to put present-day Eileen into the scene, imagining her mom in a cashmere twinset and a fresh blowout, frowning censoriously at the assembled pot smokers while they stuffed their faces and telling them how long they'd need to spend on the treadmill to burn off all of that candy and all of those chips.

"Left turn!" Abby called as they came to a stop sign. The riders turned off the highway and onto a two-lane road, passing a development of newly constructed houses, a warehouse, another farm. Sheep stood in the meadow, peering at them curiously as they rode past. One of them looked up and offered a laconic "baaaa," before going back to his mouthful of grass.

Abby wiped sweat off her face with her shoulder and told herself to just get it over with. "Thank you for helping yesterday," she said. Her voice sounded a little stiff, but at least the words and the sentiment were right.

"You're welcome," Eileen said, sounding just as stiff.

Abby clicked into a higher gear. "Do you think Morgan's going to tell her mother what happened?"

Eileen considered. "If I had to guess, I'd say yes."

Abby swallowed hard. "And on a scale of one to ten, how furious do you think Lily's going to be?" *And what are the chances that she's going to sue all of us?*

"Zero," Eileen said immediately.

Abby stared at her mother. "Even though her daughter just went against everything she's been taught, and everything her parents believe?"

"I think all of those beliefs and values go right out the window when it's your own child," Eileen replied. "I think, in the end, every mother wants what's best for her kids. And forcing a teenager to have a baby . . ." Eileen shook her head. "Lily has to know that wouldn't have been good for Morgan. That it wasn't what Morgan wanted."

Yes, Abby thought bitterly. *It's wonderful when a mother respects their teenage daughter's wishes.* She didn't say anything. Neither did Eileen. They pedaled along the edge of the lake, a vast expanse of dark blue that glittered in the sun. There was a park near the waterfront, where Abby called a halt.

"Lunchtime!" she said. The riders parked their bikes and pulled the lunches they'd packed out of panniers and handlebar bags (during the hunt for Andy and Morgan, Abby had texted the riders to apprise them of the situation and to tell them to go find food for the Cayuga Lake ride, along with a list of nearby shops and delis).

"Come sit with me," Eileen said. She led Abby to a table slightly removed from the rest of the group. Abby watched as her mother pulled out her lunch—a salad with a side of carrot sticks. Abby had bought a turkey, bacon, and avocado sandwich, a cookie, and a bag of chips at a coffee shop. Neither of them spoke as Abby unfolded a paper napkin and Eileen dipped her fork into her container of dressing, coating each tine with the smallest amount possible.

"Hey, Abby." Sebastian swung one long leg over the picnic table's bench. There was at least twelve inches of space between them, but Abby could still feel, or imagined that she could feel, the heat from his body; the warmth of his regard. She could also feel her mother's attention sharpening.

"We still on for tonight?" he asked, unwrapping an enormous hoagie.

"Mm-hmm."

"What's happening tonight?" Eileen asked.

"Oh, nothing," said Abby. As Sebastian said, "We're having dinner together."

The line between Eileen's brows deepened. "Don't you always have dinner together?" Eileen asked.

"That's what Abby said!" Sebastian had the nerve to look pleased with himself.

"We're just going to sit together and Sebastian is going to interview me," Abby said hastily, hoping to forestall her mother's interrogation. Wondering if there was any way Eileen had figured out what had transpired the day before. There was no way she could have known, Abby told herself, and hoped that she was right; that it wasn't written all over her face. As she hoped, she also remembered how Mark had helped to get Eileen on the bike trip. Did that mean they were still talking? Was Mark casually calling her mom for updates—*Hey, Mrs. F., just want to hear how it's going out there?* Was her mother casually calling Mark, unprompted—*Hello, Mark, just wondering if you were aware that there's a very handsome young man on this trip and he and Abby seem to be spending a lot of time together?*

"So you two are friends now?" Eileen was asking. Her tone was innocent, and her expression gave nothing away, but Abby knew when she was being judged. After a lifetime's worth of experience, of course she knew when she'd done something wrong or disappointing; when Eileen had weighed her in the balance and found her wanting.

"It's just dinner," Abby muttered. Eileen's chipmunk-bright eyes stayed fixed on her daughter.

"Oh!" said Sue, taking a seat next to Sebastian. "You two are having dinner together?"

"We are," said Sebastian. Sue and Lou both looked delighted to hear it. Lou actually clapped her hands together, beaming. Eileen said nothing as the rest of the Spoke'n Four sat down. Today, their jerseys were kelly green with white lettering.

"Where's Andy?" Lou asked Abby quietly.

"In the doghouse," Ted boomed, not quietly. "You know he ran off with Morgan this morning."

"Shh!" Sue hissed as Ezra's head popped up.

"Andy's taking a day off," said Abby.

"And Morgan's with her mom. I think they're going shopping," said Eileen. Abby gave her mother a grateful look.

"Andy's with his mom, and Morgan's with hers, and both of them are in trouble," Ted said, oblivious to the other three's attempt to shush him. Sebastian smiled at her. Abby ducked her head, but she couldn't keep herself from smiling back. In spite of Eileen's scrutiny and judgment, in spite of her fear, or maybe paranoia, that her mother and her boyfriend were both onto her, she felt happy. She had zero hopes of things with Sebastian going anywhere, the same way she'd had no expectations the night they'd hooked up in Brooklyn. At least, she was doing her best to keep from hoping for things that would never happen. And, just like she'd been on that night, she couldn't wait to be with him, to be close enough to feel the warmth of his body, to bask in his attention, even if it was only for the length of a meal.

At home, in her apartment in Philadelphia, Abby had a closet full of clothes and a drawer full of lingerie; a vanity full of makeup, and a hairdresser around the corner. Here, in her hotel room, she had a tinted ChapStick and a travel-size bottle of lotion. Her only jewelry were the tiny studs in her ears. Her only footwear were a pair of slip-on sneakers and her cycling shoes, and her only grooming products were deodorant, and the hotel-provided shampoo and conditioner.

Abby shook her head, and started twisting her curls with her fingers, murmuring "My kingdom for a diffuser," when she heard a knock on her door. She opened it to find Lou and Sue, standing in the hallway.

"We heard there was a fashion emergency," said Sue.

"And we've come to the rescue," said Lou. "Come with us!"

Abby found her shoes and let Lou and Sue lead her out of her room and out the door, across the puddle-dotted parking lot, and into the Spoke'n Four's RV. Abby was amused to see an IF THE TRAILER'S ROCKIN', DON'T COME KNOCKIN' bumper sticker affixed to one of the windows.

"Lemonade?" asked Ted.

"Ooh, yes, please."

Ted smiled and handed her a glass as Abby looked around. There was a small living room up front, with built-in couches on each side, a table between them, and a wide-screen TV on one wall that looked like it folded up into the ceiling. Beyond that was a tiny kitchen, with a sink, an oven, a microwave, and a two-burner stove. A closed door beyond that must have led to the bedroom. Bedrooms? Maybe there were bunk beds, Abby decided.

"Come!" said Lou. "Sit!" She ushered Abby to the couch. A folding light-up makeup mirror, already plugged in, was centered on the table, along with a hair dryer, a curling iron, a large acrylic box full of brushes and lipsticks and eye shadow palettes, and four pairs of earrings, and half a dozen bracelets and necklaces.

Abby shook her head, staring at the jewelry. "This is so nice!"

"Oh, please," said Ted. "You're doing them a favor. This is the most fun they've had all week."

"We think you and Sebastian are lovely together," said Sue.

Abby blinked. *Lovely together?* Did they know what had happened yesterday, in the rain? And if they knew, who else did?

Abby sat back on the couch as Lou handed her a pot of moisturizer, a brand that Abby recognized from her own mother's vanity. "Dab," Lou instructed. Her blue eyes were bright, her fingers warm as she took Abby's chin in her hand, turning her face from one side to the other before she began opening drawers in the makeup kit, rummaging through an assortment of pots and sticks and palettes and brushes.

"Lou used to work at the Chanel counter at Bloomingdale's," Sue said.

"Many moons ago." Lou's hands were quick and gentle as she patted various creams onto Abby's skin and used a pencil to darken her brows. Abby closed her eyes and figured this was as good a focus group as any.

"You guys like Sebastian?" she asked.

"Well," said Sue, bustling out of the bedroom with more accessories. "He's employed. He's intelligent. You both love cycling."

"And he's very good-looking," Lou said dreamily.

"Ouch," said Ted, slapping his hand to his chest.

"And he likes you," said Sue. "And you like him. You two fit together. And when you find someone like that, it is a rare and wonderful thing."

Abby considered. *You two fit together.* Did that mean she didn't fit with Mark? Or that they did fit, but less well? "Eyes closed, please," Lou murmured. Abby complied. The warmth of the trailer, the way her muscles were loose and relaxed from the day's ride, plus the excitement of her early morning were all making her drowsy, in spite of her anxiety, her worries about her mother, and what Eileen knew, and what, if anything, she was telling Mark.

"What about the TikTok thing?" she made herself ask, even though she was far from certain she wanted to hear the answer. "I'm not sure Sebastian's cut out to be a boyfriend."

"Or," said Ed's voice from somewhere behind her, "maybe his rambling days are over and he's ready to settle down."

"It's not about where he's been, it's about where he's going," Ted boomed.

"Do you like him?" asked Lou, as she gently worked a brush

along Abby's brow bones. "Because that's what matters." The other woman cupped Abby's chin, turning her head left, then right, and Abby said, low-voiced, "I don't want to get hurt. And I think he could really hurt me."

"Sometimes," said Sue, "you've got to take that risk. If you don't open yourself up to possibilities—even bad ones . . ."

"Then nothing ever happens," said Lou. "Good, bad, or indifferent. Now! Let's decide what you're wearing, and then we'll finish your eyes and give you a lip."

"Oh." Abby hadn't even considered the option of new clothes. "I'll just wear this. It's all I've got with me."

Sue looked disappointed. "Don't you want to try a dress?"

"Okay, but what if I'm in a dress and Sebastian's just got on his shorts and tee shirt? I don't want to be overdressed, do I?"

"Don't worry about Sebastian," Lou said with a merry, I've-got-a-secret smile. "The boys are going to take care of him."

Abby didn't voice her other concern, which was that, of the quartet that was the Spoke'n Four, only Ted's clothes would fit her. She was pleasantly surprised when it turned out that Sue had a number of skirts and dresses made of jersey fabric that had elastic waistbands, or enough give to fit her. They were a little long but definitely better than her regular clothes.

She tried on three dresses and ended up choosing a pale-blue sundress of silky cotton jersey. It was sleeveless, with a square neck, fitted over her chest, flaring at her knees. She was twirling a little, enjoying the swishy feeling of the fabric against her legs when Sue handed her a pair of flat, strappy white sandals with silver buckles, and Lou showed her two necklaces, one made of silver and turquoise, the other a strand of dark-blue glass beads. "Sue, what do you think?"

Sue put her finger against her lips. "The silver one."

"I agree." Lou used a pale-pink lip stain, with a little bit of sparkle, and lined Abby's eyes in silver, and used subtle shades of sky blue and silver on her lids before asking, "How do you feel about false lashes?"

"I'm in your hands," said Abby, and sat very still as Lou used tweezers to apply individual lashes.

"There. Perfect!" Lou stood up and clasped her hands against her heart.

They ushered Abby back, through the kitchen, past closed doors that she assumed led to the bathroom and maybe a pantry or a closet, and into a room with a queen-size bed, a dresser, and a full-length mirror in the corner. "Voilà!" said Lou, spinning her around.

"Like a young Nicole Kidman!" Sue said.

"No, no," said Lou. "Like Steven Spielberg's first wife!"

"Kate Capshaw?"

"No," said Lou patiently, "Kate Capshaw was his second wife. His first one was the gal with all the curly brown hair. Amy something. She was in that movie with the pickle guy!"

"Amy Irving! *Crossing Delancey!*" said Sue. "Oh, I loved that movie."

Abby listened, smiling, and tried to keep her gaze unfocused, taking peeks at parts of herself that might look good, or at least acceptable. It was a skill she'd honed after years of confronting herself in mirrors, beneath the pitiless light of dressing rooms, dorm rooms, restrooms . . . pretty much any room with a mirror, she thought ruefully. Except, as her gaze traveled from her hair to her face to her dress to her new shoes, she was surprised to see that she looked about as good as she could remember looking. Her hair, freed from its cycling ponytail, fell down her back in a tumble of shiny, frizz-free curls. Her eyes looked bigger and wider; her lips shone beneath a layer of pink gloss, and the dress clung to her curves in a way that made her hope that Sebastian, who'd seen her in skintight bicycling shorts and neon jerseys that hid nothing and flattered even less, would be impressed.

Again, Abby remembered the feeling of his fingers on her cheek, his hand cupping her head, his tongue, warm and agile, in her mouth, and felt her entire body flush. She felt like a cherry cordial, her insides gone liquid and sweet.

"Here," said Sue, and led Abby to the dresser. "Pick out some perfume."

Abby spritzed three different bottles in the air before settling on a light floral scent, spraying it on her throat and her wrists. *Sebastian will like this,* she thought. She wondered if Mark would like it, too, and shut her eyes, telling herself to just, for once, stop thinking; just live in the moment and enjoy the night ahead.

She floated out of the RV and across the parking lot, back up to her hotel room to await Sebastian's knock, which came at six thirty on the dot.

She opened the door, still only half-believing that any of this was actually happening. And there he was, so handsome she could barely stand to look at him, in khakis and a light blue button-down shirt, with a bouquet of daisies tied in a yellow ribbon in his hand.

"Wow," he said, looking at her in a way that made every inch of her skin feel warmer. "You clean up nice."

"Thank you." He, too, seemed to have gotten the Spoke'n Four makeover treatment. Abby saw that his khakis were slightly too big, the shirt just a little short in the sleeves, and that they'd given him a red-and-gold tie.

Sebastian touched the knot of his tie as he endured Abby's inspection. "I feel like I'm in eighth grade and my dad helped me get dressed for the school dance."

You would have never gone to a school dance with me, Abby thought. Then she scolded herself, because what did she know?

Maybe she would have been exactly Sebastian's type. Maybe the thirteen-year-old boy he'd been would not have called her Flabby Abby. Maybe, instead, he would have asked her out, shown up at her house, met her parents and her stepparents, and looked at her the same way.

"Just so we're clear," she made herself say, "this isn't a date."

Sebastian didn't seem upset. "It's whatever you want it to be."

Not helping, Abby thought, as she picked up the purse that Lou had lent her.

Sebastian offered her his arm. "Ready?"

Abby smiled up at him. "All set."

Jasper had the sag wagon pulled up in front of the hotel, with the Spoke'n Four's RV behind it, but Sebastian led her past both of them, over to a waiting Prius.

"Wait, what's happening?" asked Abby, as Sebastian asked the driver his name, held the door open, and waited for Abby to get in.

"I got us an Uber."

"Oh. That's completely unnecessary." *But nice,* she thought.

"I know," he said, "but I want this to feel special."

Abby watched out the window for the five minutes it took to drive to Sackett's Table. The restaurant had been written up in both *Food & Wine* and the *New York Times,* and Lizzie had told her that Marj had made the reservation months ago, even before people had signed up for the trip.

"Piersall, party of two," Sebastian said.

"Right this way," said the hostess, giving Sebastian a dimpled smile and leading them to the very far end of the group's table, past Eileen and Lincoln, the Landons and the Pressers, Lily and Morgan, and the Spoke'n Four, who gave Abby not-too-discreet thumbs-ups as she walked by.

"I tried to get us our own table, but . . ." Sebastian said.

"No, it's fine." Abby saw Lincoln watching as Sebastian held out her chair for her. She felt her mother's eyes, too, as she smoothed her dress and adjusted her seat. Then Sebastian sat down, diagonal from Abby, close enough that she could feel his knees bump against hers.

"Hi," he said, his voice low.

"Hi," Abby replied.

Abby thought it would be awkward, the way things could be after the first time you'd been intimate with a new person. All she'd done so far with Sebastian—at least, all she'd done with him over the last week—was kiss him and bandage his knees, but she was still prepared for it to feel weird, the two of them struggling to find things to talk about and discovering how much they didn't have in common, and how they really didn't know each other at all. But, as the night progressed, Abby realized that they had gotten to know each other, on their bikes or over previous meals. Even better, it turned out that when Sebastian wasn't grumpy or preoccupied, he was good company. He told her the story of how he'd met Lincoln in college, how they'd had nothing in common, yet eventually became best friends. He told her about his dad, who taught economics—"I was the only kid in the neighborhood whose allowance came with a lecture about scarcity, supply and demand, and costs and benefits."

"What's your favorite story that you've written?"

"Tell her about the X Games," said Lincoln.

Sebastian rolled his eyes a little and said, "Let me tell you about the X Games." It turned out he and Lincoln had attended the games together, and had written about them for the school's newspaper when they were undergraduates.

"Lincoln was fascinated by the skateboarding," Sebastian confided. And Lincoln, indignant, said, "It takes real skill to do what they do!"

When the server came, Abby and Sebastian each ordered a cocktail, deviled eggs, and homemade potato chips to start with. They split a pasta entrée as a second course, and then Abby ordered stuffed chicken and Sebastian picked a pork chop from the butcher's case. It turned out neither one of them knew much about wine.

"Tell me more about Scoop.com," she said. Sebastian smiled. And that took them through the rest of a bottle of wine that they'd struggled to order (they'd finally just told the sommelier to pick something nice and not too expensive), and dessert and coffee.

"You have the prettiest smile," Sebastian murmured. Abby blushed. And smiled. "You seem like a happy person."

"I'm not happy all the time," said Abby. Having all this charm and attention focused on her felt like diving into deep water without an oxygen tank, equally exhilarating and terrifying. She could get hurt. She could end up permanently damaged; scarred for life. Sebastian was still looking at her, intently, his eyes on her face. On her mouth. Abby wanted to be alone with him somewhere. She wanted to close her eyes and lean into him, feeling his mouth against her neck, hearing his voice in her ear.

"Want to walk for a while?" he asked. She nodded. She couldn't remember leaving the restaurant. It felt like one moment they were inside, with cappuccinos and tiramisu, and the next moment they were on the sidewalk, halfway back to the hotel, beneath a sky that was clear and full of stars.

They strolled until they reached a sculpture depicting two women shaking hands as a third woman stood off to the side. Abby pointed at the monument. "Name those suffragettes!" she said. "No googling."

Sebastian looked at her, smirking very slightly. "Susan B.

Anthony and Elizabeth Cady Stanton, being introduced by Amelia Bloomer," he said. "Obviously."

Abby stared at him, so surprised it took her a few seconds to muster a "Whoa."

"You're assuming I only know about men?" Sebastian inquired, a little indignantly.

"Well . . ."

"It just so happens," he said, "that I believe that both men and women have made major contributions to our country." He paused for a beat of silence. "Also, there's a plaque," he said, pointing it out.

Abby started laughing. One of her earrings had gotten stuck in her hair. Sebastian reached out and gently untangled it. *That*, Abby told herself, *was absolutely not something a friend would do.*

She took a step back, asking, "Do you know the Susan B. Anthony quote about women and bicycles?"

Sebastian shook his head.

"Oh, it's my favorite." Abby straightened up, pulling her shoulders back, reciting from memory. "She said, 'I think the bicycle has done more to emancipate women than any one thing in the world. I rejoice every time I see a woman ride by on a bike. It gives her a feeling of self-reliance and independence the moment she takes her seat; and away she goes, the picture of untrammeled womanhood.'" Abby felt her cheeks flush, and hoped she didn't sound too dorky. All she could see on Sebastian's face, though, was interest. He sounded almost wistful when he said, "Maybe I should send my mom on a bike trip."

Abby's tongue felt slightly thickened from the alcohol. "Is your mother's womanhood trammeled?"

Sebastian could have laughed it off. She'd left him the option. Instead, he looked thoughtful. "She drinks," he finally said.

"Oh." Abby licked her lips and swallowed hard, trying to

think of an appropriate response. How much? Is she getting help? Is this a recent development, or has she been drinking your whole life? She said, tentatively, "Was it the pandemic? I know a lot of people were struggling . . ."

"The pandemic didn't help." Sebastian sounded gruff. "But I think things were bad before that. I didn't notice for a long time. And then, when not noticing wasn't an option, I didn't want to think about it." He made a visible effort to look cheerful again. "A bike ride would do her good."

"I think every woman should go on a bike trip. Every girl, too." Abby thought about Morgan. "Every girl should know how to ride a bike. Because it means she knows that she can get somewhere, all on her own. And if she's in a bad place, she knows that she can leave." She could hear an admonitory voice in her head, sounding a lot like Eileen as it told her to shut up, to say less, that men didn't like too much talking, that they definitely didn't appreciate lectures and they extra-especially did not like lectures about feminism. Abby snuck another look at Sebastian, bracing for boredom or scorn. She saw no evidence of either one.

"Do you ever lead trips just for girls?" he asked.

Abby shook her head. "I barely lead trips at all. I was a last-minute replacement here. That first day, I was terrified." She gave him a smile. "I'm sure you could tell."

"I couldn't. You were great."

Abby tapped her fingers against her side, thinking. "I know there's an organization in Philadelphia that teaches kids how to build their own bikes. People donate their old bikes, and mechanics volunteer their time. The kids learn all about bike assembly and repair, and when the course is over, they get to keep the bikes they built. And my club runs beginner rides, so new riders can learn about safety, and riding in traffic, and how to climb hills. But there's nothing just for girls." *Maybe there should be,* she thought, and filed that idea away.

Sebastian put his hand on the small of her back and guided her along the sidewalk, toward the hotel. Abby's borrowed sandals slapped against the pavement. Her hips and shoulder brushed companionably against Sebastian's. It was nice, she thought. Cozy. Every time they touched, she caught a whiff of his cologne. Or, more likely, a whiff of Ted's or Ed's cologne. It didn't matter. In the cool of the evening, his hand felt pleasantly warm. It reminded her of how it had felt to kiss him in the rain. It had probably been the single best kiss of her life, she thought. And then she thought of Mark, and felt guilt wrenching at her, twisting in her guts.

"Are you thinking about Doctor Wonderful?" Sebastian asked.

Abby looked at him sharply. Sebastian's voice was teasing, but his expression was warm and unguarded and hopeful. She shook her head. "Do we have to?"

"I'd like to know," Sebastian said. "Just as your friend."

Abby didn't know what to say. With all her heart, she wanted to tell Sebastian she was single. But was she really prepared to end things with Mark, who was, in fact, wonderful? To dump a sweet, caring, handsome, gainfully employed guy so she could have a no-strings-attached vacation fling, with a guy who probably didn't want anything more?

Abby turned her hot cheeks up to the cool night air . . . and the voice she heard in her head, the voice that gave her the answer was, surprisingly, her mother's. *You're a beautiful young woman. You deserve to have choices.* Staying with Mark because she thought he was her best, and possibly only, option, marrying him with the doubts she had, because she'd been hurt before, was wrong. Wrong for her. Wrong for Mark, too.

"I don't know," she muttered. And then, deciding that she

owed him some kind of explanation, she said slowly, "It's compli-cated. Mark loved me when I was a teenager. He loved me when I felt like my own mother didn't even like me very much."

"How could anyone not like you?" Sebastian asked. As they stepped into the elevator, he let his hand drift up, stroking along her back to rest at the nape of her neck. Abby felt her body prick-ling with goose bumps, her inhalations getting shallow. She knew she should make him stop. She didn't. Couldn't.

"All mothers love their kids, right? But she always acted like I was broken. Like there was something wrong with me. Like I was broken, and it was her job to fix me."

"There's nothing wrong with you," he said, his voice low. "And I don't think you're broken."

The elevator doors slid open, and they stepped into the hall. Sebastian's hand had come to rest on the small of her back.

"I like you," he whispered. He pressed his lips against her forehead, then her cheek, then reached out to take one of Abby's curls between his fingertips, pulling it straight, then letting it boing back into place. "I think this one's my favorite."

Abby let her eyes flutter shut.

His lips were warm and confident when he kissed her. His hand cradled the back of her neck as his tongue urged her mouth open.

I should not be doing this, Abby thought. And gripped his shoulder with one hand, grabbing his upper arm with the other.

"Can I come to your room?" he asked, his voice a low murmur that she could feel right between her legs. She nodded, and took his hand, letting him lead her down the hall, into the room, onto the bed.

"Wait here," he said. "Close your eyes." She obeyed without thinking. "Give me your key," he said. Abby handed it over. She heard him leave, then heard him return. "Open your eyes," he said. When Abby did, she found the room lit by the glow of half a dozen candles in glass jars, flickering on the desk, on the dresser, on the windowsill; clothing the walls and the bed in shadows, softening the hard edges, turning the bare-bones hotel room into something romantic and dreamy. Abby felt tears pricking at her eyes. She was remembering Chris, back in college, who'd hustle her into his dorm room in the dark, only after checking to make sure that there was no one around to see them together. Chris would have never lit candles for her. Chris hadn't even bothered to make his bed.

Sebastian pulled her against him, fitting her against the warm, solid length of his body. He touched her cheek, the way he had that afternoon, only this time his hands were warm and dry as he stroked his thumb tenderly against her lower lip.

She didn't even think of trying to stop him when Sebastian eased her down onto her back. She let him kiss her neck, her throat, her cheeks, then her lips again. With his body pressed against hers, she could feel that he was just as into this as she was, and it was the most wonderful feeling in the world.

Abby thought about Mark, back in Philadelphia. She thought of her mother, who was probably back in her room, a few doors down; her mother, with her gimlet gaze, who didn't miss a thing. "Is it okay if we don't do everything tonight?" she whispered.

Sebastian nodded, then looked down at her. "But can we do some things?"

"We can do lots of things." She sat up and pulled off Sebastian's tie, then unbuttoned his shirt. He reached for the hem of her dress, looking at her, waiting for her nod before he pulled it off over her head. Abby had a flicker of regret that she hadn't packed a single cute undergarment—not the black lace bra and matching panties she'd purchased to wear on Valentine's Day.

"Okay?" he asked as he reached behind her and unfastened her bra with impressive dexterity.

"Yes." Abby nodded. They kissed, undressing each other until

Sebastian was in his boxer-briefs and Abby wore nothing but her underwear and a pillow she kept trying to clutch against her midsection, the pillow that Sebastian kept moving away.

"Abby," he whispered as she tipped up her face to kiss him, thinking that it had never felt like this, not ever.

Sebastian

When he woke up, it was the middle of the night. Abby's scent was all around him, the skin he couldn't stop touching, the curves of cheek and chin and shoulder. He remembered her careful fingers, wiping the blood off his scrapes, smoothing on ointment and bandages. Abby calling him out on his bullshit, until he'd told her what was really going on. Abby giving him her dry shirt, insisting that he wear it. Abby, with her curls and her freckled nose and her hazel eyes. Abby, who made him laugh.

The candles were still flickering. He got up, blew them out, then got back under the covers. He touched her gently, then more firmly, cupping her shoulder with his hand until she blinked, then looked at him, wide-eyed in the dark.

"I looked for you after you left," he said.

She squinted at his face, still looking, and sounding, half asleep. "What?"

"That morning, at my apartment. I looked for you."

"You did?"

"Except I didn't know your last name. Or anything about you, except that you were a bridesmaid. I went back to the bar . . ."

Abby's eyes widened.

"You were . . ." He breathed in, touched her shoulder. Tried again. "That was the best night of my life."

"Really?" Before he could answer, she said, "Mine, too. But I didn't think you'd want to see me again."

"You could've left your number and found out." He swatted her gently on her bottom, pretending it was punishment, but, really, it was just an excuse to touch her.

She sat up, tucking her knees against her chest, wrapping her arms around them, making herself small as she looked up at him gravely. "I didn't want to be disappointed. Or have you be disappointed in me."

He looked at her and shook his head. "Abby . . ."

"It was so nice. I just wanted to remember it like that. And not ruin it, waiting for a call that wouldn't come. Or an actual date that didn't go well."

He stared for a moment, looking puzzled. "Of course it would have gone well," he said. "We got along. We had great chemistry. We had fun!" he said, then looked at her. "We did, right?"

Abby smiled at him. "We did," she confirmed.

Sebastian, stretched himself out on the bed, gently easing her hands away from her knees, coaxing her body down against his. "We wasted two years," he growled in her ear, smiling as he felt her shiver.

"I was playing hard to get," she whispered back, and turned her head until their lips met, and she could kiss him in a manner suggesting she wouldn't make him wait for her, or be without her, ever again.

Abby

Day Eleven: Medina to Buffalo
Fifty-four miles

They left Seneca Falls the next morning and rode to Rochester, where Abby and Sebastian spent another night together in a hotel. Abby rode with Sebastian for part of the day. She studiously ignored him at dinner, then tiptoed down the hall at eleven o'clock, when, she hoped, her mother was asleep and unlikely to wander down to the vending machines. The day after that, they rode forty-one miles, from Rochester to Medina. Abby spent most of that day with the Landons. He was an investment banker, and she worked in finance, and they'd originally planned on a tour through Tuscany, combining cycling with wine tasting, but had decided to stay close to home. Carol's mother, it emerged, was failing. "We didn't want to be overseas in case . . ." Her voice trailed off.

"In case we were needed," Richard said. Carol smiled at him gratefully.

"Richard's a big wine buff," she told Abby.

"We'll get there someday," he said. Abby didn't miss the look that passed between them, Carol's face grateful, Richard's expression proud and content. They weren't the horrible snobs that she'd imagined. They were partners, Abby saw. They would sacrifice for each other; help each other through the hard times. She wanted that for herself. But when did sacrifice become self-abnegation? When were you giving up too much? Would she end up resenting Mark if she stayed with him and none of their vacations involved bikes, even though cycling was what she loved best? Sebastian could ride with her. But was he prepared for a relationship? Would he even be capable of fidelity?

She wished Lizzie were there. She wished she had the kind of relationship with her mother that would allow her to ask Eileen her questions. Abby pedaled onward, with her head down, keeping her thoughts to herself. She rode all day and spent most of each night talking with Sebastian, when their mouths weren't otherwise engaged. He told her more about his mother's drinking. She told him more about her parents' divorce. He told her his parents hadn't dropped him off when he started college. She told him how she'd been banished to Camp Golden Hills.

They talked about everything except Mark and what would happen when the trip was over. It was like swimming underwater in the ocean; visiting a world that was strange and beautiful, knowing you couldn't stay too long; that you couldn't hold your breath forever. At some point, Abby knew, she'd have to come up for air.

On the eleventh day of the trip, the last day of real riding, they followed the trail from Medina to Buffalo. Sebastian pedaled beside Abby. The weather was still summer-warm, but, as they'd gotten farther north, the signs of encroaching autumn had become harder to miss: the leaves changing colors; the absence of riders under eighteen on the trail.

Lily and Morgan were back on their bikes, riding side by side. Morgan had spent two days in the sag wagon, and Lily had ridden with her, out of sympathy and solidarity, and because she still wasn't an enthusiastic or seasoned cyclist, and the mileage had been killing her. She'd been happy for the break, and Morgan, from what Abby could tell, was happy for the company.

On their way into Buffalo, Abby told Sebastian about the bike trip she'd taken in college through the Finger Lakes, with a couple who'd brought their eighteen-month-old toddler along in a Burley trailer, and how the child had cried, nonstop, every minute and mile of every day.

"She was teething, I guess." Abby smiled a little at the memory. "And she'd just learned how to walk, so she didn't want to be strapped into the trailer all day long. The only words she knew besides Mama and Dada were 'no' and 'down,' but oh my God, she screamed them. All. Day. Long." Abby shook her head, remembering. "Everyone on the trip would take turns riding behind whichever parent was towing her and singing lullabies or making faces. Whatever we could do to keep her calm. It was a nightmare. Three people actually asked for refunds." She shook her head, thinking that it was funny now, but it had been extremely unfunny at the time. "And there were newlyweds on the trip—this couple that had gotten married the month before. They were doing the trip as part of their honeymoon. When we started, the woman was saying that she couldn't wait to get pregnant, that she loved babies, that she was so excited to start a family. I swear to God, when the trip was over, her husband had scheduled a vasectomy."

"Sounds awful," Sebastian said. And it had been. Only Abby could picture it differently. A baby in a trailer, hitched to the back of Sebastian's bike. Abby riding with Sebastian, telling him stories, making him laugh. The three of them, at the end of the day's ride, sitting around a campfire, underneath a starry sky; together in the tent, all night long (with the baby conveniently disappearing for that part of the fantasy).

"Do you think you'll stay in Brooklyn for the rest of your life?" Abby asked.

"I like being there now. But I can also imagine settling down someplace a little quieter. And a lot less expensive."

"I was thinking," Abby said, a little hesitantly, "about what we were talking about last night."

Sebastian grinned. In Medina, they'd gone out for pizza for dinner, and the group had stayed in a boutique hotel in an old stone building, where the rooms were small and quirky, oddly shaped, decorated with cycling posters and paraphernalia. Abby's room had an antique Schwinn hanging on the wall. And a queen-size bed underneath it.

"Remind me what we talked about?" Sebastian said.

"My job," Abby said, with a touch of asperity. "We talked about what I'm going to do with my life."

"Ah," said Sebastian. Abby cringed a little, remembering the speech she'd given about how she loved dogs but didn't want to walk them for the rest of her life. She'd been curled against him, her cheek resting on his chest, his hand stroking her hair, and she wasn't sure how closely he'd been listening.

"So what's the thing you like best?" he asked.

"Leading bike trips," she said. "Except it's not really the kind of thing you can do year-round if you want to live in one place."

"Facts," Sebastian acknowledged.

"It's fine to follow the seasons when you're in your twenties, but if you want"—Abby hesitated—"kids, or a family, or a house, or any of that, it doesn't work."

Sebastian asked if it would be possible to earn enough money during the summer months to support herself during the year. Abby said that it was not. He asked if she'd be willing to take less-fulfilling work—dog-walking or office temping—to support herself in the nonsummer months.

"That's fine for now. But, again, if I decide I want kids, it won't work."

Sebastian pedaled in silence for a moment. "What about doing something with cycling and girls?" he asked. "Like, a program just for girls. You could teach them to ride if they didn't know how, and lead rides, and take them on trips."

"I'd have to see what kind of programs are out there. Make sure there's not something like this already." It was a good idea. But the thought of building something from the ground up, figuring out what kind of permits and insurance she'd need, and if she'd have to work with a bike shop or an existing organization, and where she'd find other adults to help, and how she'd recruit the riders all left her feeling overwhelmed, crushed, and exhausted before she'd even begun.

"But you'd be great!" he said when Abby told him that. "And it could work. You could stay in one place, in Philly, or wherever." Abby wondered if wherever meant Brooklyn, but didn't ask. "It'd be everything you love. Biking, and . . ." He waved his hand. "Girl stuff. All of the feminist whatever."

Abby raised her eyebrows. "'The feminist whatever'?"

"You could lead trips when it's warm enough and have classes when it's not. You could ask bike shops to volunteer or donate stuff."

"I could." Abby's mind was turning as she wondered how it would work and whom she could ask. "Maybe. Maybe there's a niche." After a minute, she said, "Thank you."

"I didn't do anything."

"You took me seriously," Abby said. "That's important."

"Any time," Sebastian had said.

Abby leaned over her handlebars.

"How about you?" she asked. She made her voice mock-serious and asked, "Where do you see yourself in ten years?"

"I don't know. I like my job. But I think I'd like . . . I don't know. Kids. A house. A family. Not this minute, but maybe some-day," he said as Lincoln put on a burst of speed to join them.

"I think you'd be a good father," Abby was saying.

Abby was 90 percent positive that she'd heard Lincoln cough the word *bullshit* under his breath. Sebastian, meanwhile, was looking flattered. "Oh, yeah?"

"Absolutely," she said. "You can teach your kids all about being prepared, and asking for help when they need it."

"Hey, I got that flat changed. Eventually."

"Mister I-don't-need-your-tire-irons."

"I wasn't that bad!" Sebastian protested.

"You were," said Ted, coasting past.

"Sorry, but it's true," said Sue, trailing behind Ted.

"Oh, and you can also model good behavior about listening to your leaders, and following directions and staying safe," said Abby.

Sebastian smoothed out his vest. He'd kept his promise and had put it on for the past two mornings, without complaint. Without too much complaint, at least. The things we do for love, he'd said, as he'd pulled it on that morning. But he'd only been teasing. Of course.

"If I start a group, maybe I'll invite you to come and teach kids how to handle it if they almost crash into a truck. We'll call it Seething Hotly 101."

"Seething hotly?" Sebastian repeated.

"Oh, come on. Don't tell me you don't know that's what you were doing." She switched into a lower gear as the path rose in a gentle hill, and felt her spine stiffen as she spotted Eileen, who'd been riding with Carol Landon.

"Hello, ladies!" Abby called, her voice hearty and cheerful-sounding. "Everything okay?"

"Lovely," said Eileen with a tight-lipped smile. Abby's skin prickled, and she felt a drop of sweat slide from the back of her neck to the small of her back. Did her mother know what was going on with Sebastian? Had she seen something? Figured it out somehow?

She heard Sebastian and Lincoln coming up behind her. "Hello, Mrs. Fenske!" Sebastian called.

"Eileen," said her mother with that same taut smile. "Please."

Abby moved her hands from the brake hoods to the handlebar drops, a position that left her hunched over the top of her bike with her gaze toward the ground. The trail, which had been cinders and dirt, was paved now, winding along the canal, through a park. On a gentle grassy slope, a father was helping a little kid fly a kite. A woman walked a fancy-looking dog with pink ribbons braided in its ear fur and a put-upon expression on its face. Buffalo was approaching. Instead of the long expanses of emptiness, they were riding through an actual neighborhood now, and she could hear the sounds of traffic nearby. Buffalo, then Niagara Falls. The end of the trip. The end of whatever this was with Sebastian.

Abby clicked into a higher gear and picked up her pace. "I'm going to check in with Lily and Morgan," she said to Sebastian. "I'll see you both at lunch." She pedaled hard, legs pumping, lungs burning, getting away from her mother, wishing she could escape her thoughts, her guilt, as easily.

Sebastian

Tell me everything," said Lincoln as soon as they'd passed Eileen and Carol Landon. Lincoln had, of course, noticed Sebastian's absence from their hotel rooms for the past three nights, but, so far, had kept quiet.

"I'm not telling you everything," Sebastian said.

"Tell me something, then," Lincoln wheedled. When Sebastian didn't, Lincoln said, "I'm suspecting the whole be-her-friend experiment is over?"

He sounded a little snippy. Sebastian nodded, then said, "It isn't what you think."

"I guess not, if you actually spent three nights in a row with her."

Sebastian didn't answer. "Tell me what's going on," Lincoln said. "Come on. Give me something. I'm married. I'm never going to kiss a woman again for the first time. I have to live vicariously."

"There is nothing to tell," said Sebastian, feeling suddenly chivalrous.

"Oh, there's plenty to tell," said Lincoln. "Do you like her?"

"I do."

"Are you planning on seeing her again?"

And there was the crux of it. Sebastian did want to see Abby again. But if Abby wanted babies soon, if she was looking for another man to slot into the serious boyfriend/possible husband position for the wedding he bet her mother had already started to plan, Sebastian didn't think that was him. At least, not yet. "She lives in Philadelphia," he said.

"There's this marvelous new invention called the train," said Lincoln. "Perhaps you've heard of it?"

"We haven't made any plans yet."

Lincoln wasn't letting it go. "What do you want?"

Sebastian didn't answer. He didn't know if he wanted to be her boyfriend. He didn't know if he wanted to be her husband, or anyone's husband; the father of her children, or of any children at all. But he absolutely wanted to see Abby Stern, on bikes and in bed and all the places in between. "I want to see her when the trip is over."

"So?" asked Lincoln. "What am I missing? What's the issue?"

The handlebar tape was coming unraveled from the right side of the handlebar. Sebastian rewrapped the loose end as best he could, one-handed.

"You need to figure it out," Lincoln told him.

"I will."

"Because this is the last day of riding . . ."

"I know."

". . . and tomorrow we're going to Niagara Falls . . ."

"I am aware."

". . . and the day after that we're going back to New York City."

"Yes. Got it. I have the same itinerary that you do."

"So if you're going to say something, you better say it soon," Lincoln concluded.

"I know!" Sebastian practically shouted. He thought about telling Lincoln that it was complicated; that Abby had a boyfriend. But Lincoln already knew that. And, he realized, emphasizing that particular tidbit made him look even more caddish than the Internet currently believed. If that was even possible.

Lincoln pulled his water bottle out of its cage, took a swig, and replaced it. "Abby makes you laugh," he said. "I like her. And I think Lana would like her, which is more important." He paused, long enough for them to round a bend as they followed the trail through a park. They were riding past houses now, which had views of the greens and the canal and the swing bridges over the water from their backyards. Old guys on folding chairs sat on the banks with fishing rods; little kids kicked a soccer ball. In the distance, Sebastian could make out the silhouette of skyscrapers. Buffalo was getting closer with every rotation of his wheels. His heart gave an uneasy twist.

"Back to civilization," Lincoln said, echoing Sebastian's thoughts. Sebastian found himself wishing that the trip would keep going; that they could ride into Canada, past Niagara Falls and Lake Ontario, and onward from there. Bike trips—any trips—were a liminal space, a kind of between place, apart from the routines of work and job and waking up in the same place every morning. Sebastian wasn't ready for it to end. Especially not when he thought about the pretty pink Abby's skin flushed when he'd kissed her, how she'd slipped both her small hands into his hair and tugged it, gently, then hard enough to make him shiver.

He found himself staring into the distance with what he suspected was an extremely moony smile on his face. He sniffed the air. "Do you smell that?"

"Honey Nut Cheerios," said Lou, who'd come up on their left. "There's a General Mills factory in Buffalo, so whatever cereal they're making, that's what you're smelling. Last time Ted and I came through, everything smelled like Lucky Charms."

She waved and rode off. Sebastian looked at his friend. "Isn't Sue married to Ted?"

"I think so? And don't change the subject. If you want to be with this woman, you'd better say something."

Sebastian nodded, thinking that Abby knew everything that was important about him; everything that mattered. She'd seen him at his weakest and his worst, as the butt of a thousand Twitter and TikTok jokes. She'd seen him naked. And he'd seen her. He knew the way she'd fuss with her ponytail when she was nervous or thinking; the way she would arrange the pillows to make her burrow every night, and how, sometimes, she'd pull a pillow over her stomach when they were in bed, and how he'd have to kiss her and touch her until she forgot about how she looked and he could gently pull the pillow away and toss it on the floor.

He wanted to spend more time with her. He wanted to learn everything she liked, her favorite songs and movies and restaurants. He wanted to go with her on another bike trip, just the two of them. Maybe it wasn't love. Maybe it was too soon for him to be sure. But he wanted more time with her. Of that, he was positive.

The Empire State Trail ended (or began, depending on which direction you were going) on the shores of Lake Erie in Buffalo. The Breakaway riders arrived at just after four o'clock in the afternoon. They took turns posing at the blue-and-gold metal plaque that marked the trail's terminus. Morgan, who'd been riding in the sag wagon, still looked a little pale and drawn, but she smiled when she posed with Lily, and the Pressers arranged their boys and bikes and bodies in front of the sign, laughing as Abby took their picture. Sebastian took a picture of Abby with her mother. Abby took a picture of Lincoln and Sebastian ("Want to make a TikTok?" she'd asked them, her face innocent, and they'd both shouted, "No!" at the same time). Then Lincoln had taken pictures of Sebastian with Abby. He'd put his arm around her, pulling her close, and she'd looked up at him, smiling, a little flushed.

He'd wanted to kiss her, but Eileen was still around. They'd have the night together, and all day tomorrow, for deciding what came next. Instead of pleasant anticipation, Sebastian felt anxiety nibbling at the edges of his happiness. Three more nights. Two more days. Then all of this would be over.

They got back on their bikes, and Abby led the group through downtown Buffalo, onto a quiet, tree-lined street, to the night's B and B. He'd been riding beside her, and they'd been laughing, coasting along, talking about where to go for dinner, and how many Buffalo wings they'd eat, when Sebastian saw Abby go very still.

He followed her gaze and saw a dark-haired man who was standing in the driveway of the house where they'd be staying. He was medium-sized, trim and fit in khakis and a button-down shirt. His hair was short, and he had the sharp jawline of a superhero, and he was looking at Abby, expressionless.

"Oh, shit," Abby said softly, and let her bike coast to a stop.

"Abby," said the man. He pulled out his phone, consulted its screen, and looked up again, eyes narrowed. He wasn't looking at Abby, Sebastian realized. He was looking at him. His skin prickled as he squeezed his brakes, pulling over by the side of the road and unclipping his shoes from the pedals.

"Mark?" Abby's voice was a little squeaky. "What are you doing here?"

Instead of answering, Mark waited until Abby was close enough, then brandished his phone's screen at her. Abby looked down, at whatever he was showing her. When she raised her head, he could see a flush creeping up her neck.

"It's not—it isn't . . ." She swallowed. "Mark. Let's go inside and talk."

Mark didn't answer. Instead, he marched up to Sebastian. "Is this you?" he asked, and showed Sebastian his phone.

Sebastian felt a swooping sensation, a kind of preemptive motion sickness, the way you'd feel after you'd been buckled into a roller coaster but before the ride began. He made himself look. BROOKLYN F-BOI STRIKES AGAIN! The headline looked like it was on someone's Tumblr and not, thank God, Page Six again. Underneath the headline was a picture of him, at a table in a restaurant, bent toward a woman who was unquestionably Abby. He realized that photograph had been taken back at Sackett's Table in Seneca Falls, and it had been cropped to remove the rest of the Breakaway crew, making it look like it was just the two of them, having a romantic dinner by candlelight.

"You're that guy from TikTok," said Mark. It wasn't a question.

Sebastian lifted his hands. "Hey, man," he said. "I can explain."

"No need," Mark said tightly. "I think Abby can speak for herself."

In rapid succession, Sebastian had a number of realizations. The first was that he'd fallen in love with Abby. Not just a crush, not just infatuation, but love, for the first time in his life. What would happen if she didn't choose to end things with Mark and be with him? And could he blame her, if that was her decision? He was, he acknowledged, not exactly the best bet. Not precisely a sure thing. Not compared to someone like Mark.

The other riders were arriving, one by one, pulling up on the sidewalk or into the driveway to watch the show. "What's going on?" Ted asked, craning his wattled neck toward Mark, face screwed up in an effort to hear.

"I think that's her boyfriend," said Sue.

"Isn't Sebastian her boyfriend?" asked Ed.

Then the three of them turned toward Sebastian. He gave them a wordless shrug, his eyes on Abby.

"Just give me a minute," she was saying to Mark. "Let me

make sure the group's okay, and we can go talk." She turned toward the assembled audience, which now included every person on the trip except Lou, who was driving the Spoke'n Four's Winnebago. Abby's mother, Sebastian saw, was standing over her bike, hands folded on her handlebars, eyes hidden behind her sunglasses. He couldn't do anything but watch as Abby rolled her bike up the driveway and left it there, leading Mark toward the house without even a look in his direction.

Abby

Abby tried to stay calm, breathing deeply as she consulted her phone for instructions on how to unlock the door. Mark was right behind her, and she could feel how angry he was. She punched the code on the door's lock, pushed it open, and led Mark into the bed-and-breakfast's living room. It had high ceilings and uncomfortable-looking reproductions of antique furniture: a couch upholstered in red-and-gold-striped silk, two wing chairs, a demilune table against the wall. There was a bowl of potpourri on the coffee table, and a cutesy chalkboard sign propped on top of a minifridge, advising guests that bottled water, Gatorade, and PowerBars could be purchased for three dollars apiece. Abby sat down on the couch. Mark stood.

"So?" he said, his tone unpleasantly accusatory. "What's going on?"

Just do it, she told herself. She felt sick with guilt and shame, furious at herself, and at whoever had taken and posted that picture, and at whoever had given Mark the news in a way that cast her in the worst possible light. She knew how much it was going to hurt, but she knew what she had to do. Rip off the Band-Aid. Get through it. And then at least it will be over.

"You never even told me this guy was on your trip." He

glared at her, eyebrows raised high. "I guess there was a reason for that."

"For most of the trip I didn't even see him. He was so far ahead of the group, it was like he was on his own trip." Which was true. Or, at least, it had been true at the start.

"Clearly you saw him at meals. At the hotels, too, right?"

Abby gulped.

"Tell me nothing happened," Mark said.

She bent her head. "Mark . . ."

"Tell me," he repeated, his voice hoarse. And Abby knew she couldn't lie.

Very softly, she said, "I'm sorry."

"Oh, God," he said, and sounded disgusted, like Abby was something nasty on the sole of his shoe. Which, she supposed, was what she deserved. Her behavior had not exactly been honorable. Not even close. "That guy, Abby? Really? You cheated on me with that guy? The guy who's a fucking Internet punch line?"

She gave a tiny nod. In all the time she'd known Mark, she'd rarely heard him curse, and she'd never seen him looking so hurt or angry. His voice was venomous as he raked both hands through his hair.

"Abby," he said, "what the fuck?"

She didn't have a good answer. She didn't have any answer. She tried to keep her voice steady as she repeated, "I'm sorry."

Mark dragged his hands through his hair again. She heard him breathing in and out. "Okay," he finally said. "So what do you want? Are we breaking up?" Before she could reply, he gave her a look that was both flat and incredulous. "Before you answer, let me just say how absolutely fucking ridiculous and insulting I find it that you'd pick that . . ." He spluttered as he tried to come up with a word, and finally just gestured derisively in the direction of the driveway. "*That* . . . over me."

"You're right," she said quietly. "I know."

"I mean, what the fuck?" He raised his voice. "This guy's a sex addict! He goes through women like they're M&Ms!"

Which, of course, made Abby remember the bag of that candy Mark had left under her pillow, one night at Camp Golden Hills. Mark was so sweet, so dear, so kind. So why didn't she want him? Why couldn't she picture a future with him without getting weak-kneed and nauseated and wanting to get on her bike and ride far away?

"All your talk about how women are people and you don't want to be objectified, and then you go and hook up with a guy like that." His voice was bitter.

Sebastian's not a guy like that, Abby thought. Except maybe he was. At least, he had been, very recently. And he told her he wanted to change, but could she believe him? How well did she know him? How much did she trust him? Was it even possible for him to be any better?

"I don't get it," Mark was saying. "I don't understand. Is that all you think of yourself? Is that what you think you're worth?"

"Maybe," she said, in a tiny voice. *Maybe that is all I think of myself.* She didn't have a career. She lived in a place her parents had found, and still used her parents' passwords to watch TV. She'd never finished her master's degree, she didn't own a car, and she had less than a thousand dollars in her checking account. The only thing she'd figured out how to do in her years on the planet was live relatively happily in a larger body, and she couldn't even manage that all the time. Maybe, deep down, she didn't believe that she deserved any better than someone like Sebastian, any more than a few hours of fun with a guy who'd probably forget about her the minute he got back to Williamsburg, like he'd forgotten about dozens, maybe hundreds, of women before her.

Mark was wiping furiously at his eyes. "I love you."

"I know," Abby whispered. "I'm sorry, Mark. I'm so sorry."

"We had a life together. Which you just tossed in the trash." He grabbed at his hair again, took a shuddering breath, and sat down on the couch beside her. Abby let him take her hand.

"I could forgive you," he said, staring straight ahead. "We could try to get through this. If that's what you want." He turned toward her, giving her a hard look. "Is that what you want?"

Abby felt her eyes getting hot and her throat get tight. She knew what the truth was and made herself say it. "You deserve someone better than me."

Mark dropped her hand and shook his head. "So that's it, then?"

"I'm sorry," she whispered, wishing the ground would open up and let her fall through it; wishing she'd never met Sebastian; wishing she was anywhere but here. "You're a wonderful man, and a wonderful boyfriend, and I know . . ." She swallowed hard, wishing that life had a fast-forward button, so that it could be an hour or a day or a week or even a year from now, and this would be over.

"Why?" Mark asked. When she didn't answer, he said, "Hey, you don't get to give me the silent treatment. I deserve an answer. What's he got that I don't have? Besides lots and lots and lots of experience?"

He knows how to ride a bike, Abby thought, but did not say. A wiser woman doing a side-by-side comparison of Mark and Sebastian would have chosen Mark in a heartbeat. He was the safer bet, the sure thing. Even if Mark couldn't ride a bike, even if he sometimes accidentally threw out her leftovers or let her ice cream get freezer burn, even if the sex, even at the beginning, had been good instead of great, Mark was the better choice. Mark would love her forever; he'd be steadfast and unfailingly kind and a wonderful father. Sebastian might not even remember her name next week. He might not want to be a father at all.

And yet, Abby thought. And yet.

"He doesn't have anything you don't have," she said, her voice muted. "You didn't do anything wrong. It's nothing you did. It's me."

Mark's voice was bleak. "So this is it?"

Abby nodded without meeting his eyes.

Mark made an unpleasant noise and got to his feet. "I guess we'll always have Camp Golden Hills."

And feet, Abby thought. She'd be on her own for finding pictures of disgusting feet.

"I'll text you when I'm back home with a good time to come pick up your stuff," he said. Then he turned and walked stiffly out of the room, out of the house, and out of her life, for good.

Abby sat on the sofa. She wasn't sure she could move, and she knew she'd be crying soon, but, so far, the tears hadn't come. She imagined a woman ripping up a winning lottery ticket and throwing its snippets down a sewer. Was that what she'd done? Had she just tossed away her only chance at happiness? Would life with Mark have made her happy? Or would it have ultimately felt like a too-tight pair of jeans, something that looked good from the outside but made her feel constrained, confined, like she'd never take another comfortable breath again?

She rested her head in her hands and thought about how Mark had felt like her destiny; how running into him in Kensington had felt like Karma nudging her toward the natural next step. But maybe she'd been on the wrong staircase. Maybe it was time to stop doing things because they were expected, or conventional, or easy. She'd be home soon, and she'd be at the bottom again, starting over from nothing, but at least she'd be the one deciding where to go.

Abby heard footsteps approaching, someone coming down the hall, and her pulse sped up. But the person who entered the living room wasn't Sebastian. It was Eileen.

"What happened?" she asked.

Oh, God, thought Abby. "Can you not be here?" she asked. It came out sounding nastier than she'd intended.

Eileen looked startled. Then hurt. She folded her arms over her chest and pressed her thin lips together.

"I wanted to make sure you're okay."

"I am fine," she snapped, somehow managing to make the words sound closer to *Like you care.*

"Did something happen with Mark?" Her mother's brow was furrowed. Her voice was full of what sounded like genuine concern. *Too little too late,* Abby thought.

Her head was crackling with static. Her fury built and built, and crested, and she said, in a voice that hissed like a whipcrack, "Just leave me alone. I don't want you here, I never wanted you here in the first place, so just go. Okay? Just go." Her face was burning. "Maybe if you hurry you can catch Mark before he takes off. You guys can go be thin and happy together. Eat hummus with a spoon and brush your teeth for dessert."

Eileen's eyes got very wide. She opened her mouth, starting to say something, before she changed her mind and turned around, hurrying back down the hall. Abby stood for a minute, breathing hard, hands shaking, wondering what she'd done, and what else was left in her life for her to blow up or burn down. She'd lost her boyfriend (*Lost?* a mocking voice inquired. More like *threw away*) and pissed off her mother, and where was Sebastian? Why hadn't he come to find her, to comfort her, to tell her that he wasn't what Mark said he was, what the whole world thought he was, and that he'd take care of her and always be true?

Abby balled up her fists and squeezed her eyes shut. *Sebastian is not the answer,* she told herself again. But oh, God, she hated the thought of being single or, worse, dating again. She had already spent so many years alone, had endured so much humiliation. Guys in the world whose eyes skipped right over her as if she were invisible. Men on the apps with weak chins and receding hairlines, beer guts and bald spots who felt absolutely no compunctions about inboxing her to tell her how much prettier she'd be if she went to the gym, went on a diet, ate less, exercised more. She loathed the idea of more of that.

She could hear the other cyclists moving through the house, clomping up and down the hallways, talking. She let her gaze move toward the stairs again. Sebastian was so appealing, and everything they'd done had felt so good. Abby could still feel her cheeks, her chest, the insides of her thighs tingling where his stubble had abraded them. Part of her wanted to climb the stairs, take off her clothes, take a hot shower, and go to him, letting him hold her, letting him make it all go away.

But she couldn't. She couldn't just fall into bed with another guy. Or, even if she could, it would not be the right thing to do. She'd let her relationship with Mark fill in too many of the blank spaces in her life, and it was more than Mark, or any man, should have been responsible for doing. It was her job to fill in those blanks; her job and no one else's.

And so, instead of walking up the stairs to Sebastian's room, she went out of the living room, managing to nod pleasantly at Lily Mackenzie, then back outside, to where she'd left her bike.

She pulled out her phone and used Strava to find a popular thirty-mile loop around the city. She went outside and filled her water bottles at a hose on the side of the house. She reapplied her sunscreen, squeezing the dregs out of the bottle in her handlebar bag. She shook out her hair, then smoothed it back into a pony-tail, which she threaded through the gap in her helmet. Then she set her phone in its handlebar-mounted holder and swung her leg over the top tube. She allowed herself one last look over her shoulder at the house. Then she started to ride.

Sebastian

Sebastian couldn't remember the last time he'd felt as wretched and miserable and powerless as he'd felt watching Abby lead Mark into the house.

He'd started to go after her. Lincoln had stopped him, with a hand on Sebastian's forearm and a warning look on his face. "Give her some space."

And so he'd gone past the living room and up the stairs, to the room he'd been assigned. It had its own tiny bathroom, hardwood floors, two big windows that looked down over the street, and a high four-poster bed.

Sebastian took a quick shower, listening for the sounds of slammed doors or raised voices, for Abby's feet on the stairs or Abby's voice or her knock. He imagined opening the door and seeing Abby there, telling him she'd sent Mark away. Reassuring him that she'd believed him when he'd told her that he'd changed, that he genuinely cared for her, and that she was not the final square on some fictitious bingo board.

After ten minutes of waiting in a towel, he was starting to get cold, and he'd noticed that his wet hair was dripping on the floor. He got dressed, combed his hair, put on his shoes, and sat on the edge of his bed, scrolling through the pictures he'd taken on the trip, lingering on the one of himself and Abby, in front of the blue-and-gold metal plaque that marked the end of the trail. He had his arm around her waist, and she was looking up at him, smiling. *Where are you?* he texted. *Is everything okay?*

Abby didn't reply. When a knock finally did come, Sebastian jumped off the bed.

"Just me," said Lincoln.

"Have you seen Abby?" Sebastian asked. Lincoln shook his head.

Sebastian went downstairs, asking Jasper, then Lily, then each member of the Spoke'n Four, if they'd seen her. Nobody had. He'd gone outside, to the garage where they'd stowed their bikes. Abby's bike was missing . . . so at least he knew what she was doing, even if he didn't know where.

He thought about getting on his own bike and trying to find her, but by then night was falling, and he realized that, unless she'd lost her phone, or her phone had died, she knew he wanted to talk to her, and was choosing not to respond.

He texted her again—*Where are you?*—then allowed Lincoln to drag him into the van, and out to dinner. He ate Buffalo wings and waited. He drank beer and waited. He listened to the other riders talking about their favorite days of riding, the best things they'd eaten, where they'd be going on their next adventures, and waited. Back at the bed-and-breakfast, he called Abby's phone and got no answer, and he texted, and heard nothing, and he finally fell asleep, with the light next to his bed still turned on and his phone in his hands.

Abby wasn't at breakfast the next morning. Sebastian was eating a frittata, not tasting it, when Jasper approached the table. "If I could have everyone's attention?" When the group quieted down, he said, "Abby asked me to tell you all that she's taken the train back to Philadelphia. She had some things she had to take care of. She wanted me to tell you that she enjoyed riding with all of you."

"But we didn't get to say goodbye!" said Sue. Morgan looked disappointed, and Lou was straight-up glaring at Sebastian, like Abby's absence was his fault. He cornered Jasper in the kitchen, pestering him for information Jasper did not have.

"I don't know anything besides what I said," Jasper told him. When he went to Eileen to ask if she knew anything more, all Abby's mother did was repeat Jasper's line. "She has some things to deal with. That's all I know."

That morning, Sebastian rode the twenty-three miles to Niagara Falls and spent the day following Lincoln around like a despondent six-year-old who'd been dragged on a family road trip, riding the *Maid of the Mist*, feeling the water from the falls beading on his face and in his hair, trying not to think of that day in the rain with Abby, the day when he'd kissed her.

She's thinking, he told himself. *She's making up her mind.* He only hoped that she wasn't dwelling on the TikTok mess; that she wasn't reconsidering him or rejecting him completely; ghosting him again.

"Give her some space," Lincoln told him, over dinner at a bar that night. "If you love something, set it free. If it comes back to you, it's yours. If it doesn't, it never was." He tilted his head. "A wise man told me that."

"I hate you right now," Sebastian said, glaring at the table and his barely touched burger.

"Hate yourself," Lincoln said. "That's what you told me when Lana and I broke up. And that worked out!" He clapped Sebastian's shoulder. "Just be patient. What will be, will be."

"You like seeing me suffer," Sebastian said.

Lincoln shook his head. "No," he said. "But it's possible that it's your turn. You know?"

Sebastian considered this. He thought about how lucky he'd been, right up until Alyssa had posted that TikTok, how his life was an unending stream of Frisbee games and bike rides, drinking with friends and sleeping with an endless variety of girls. He had work he loved, a nicer apartment than he should have been able to afford, the guaranteed advantages that being a white guy would give him, even as some of his fellow white guys complained that those advantages weren't real, or that, at least, they weren't as meaningful as they'd once been.

He wasn't used to losing, he realized. He picked up his burger, feeling the ketchup on his fingers, and set it down without a bite.

"Can I make a suggestion?" Lincoln asked.

"Can I stop you?" Sebastian replied.

Lincoln visibly steeled himself. "If you really want to be in a relationship with Abby, or with anyone, maybe you need to think about what's been going on. Why you felt compelled to sleep with so many different women."

"I didn't feel compelled," Sebastian said. "It was more like feeling, Why not?"

Lincoln tore open a wet wipe and didn't respond.

"Are you going to tell me that I'm compensating for some hole in my heart? Some void in my life? My mother didn't love me, my dad was never home?" Sebastian was trying for sarcasm, but Lincoln was still looking at him, without his usual expression of tolerant forbearance. Instead, his friend was looking at him pityingly. Which, of course, made Sebastian remember the many occasions when his mother had been unavailable and his father had been busy tending to her; how neither of them had ended up with a lot of time or energy for him.

Sebastian couldn't stand it. "Not all of us have perfect nuclear families. Not everyone gets lucky the way you were lucky," he said.

"You're right," said Lincoln.

"I don't need therapy," Sebastian said, feeling his lips twist as he almost snarled the last word. He was remembering the family sessions at his mother's rehabs; how frustrating and pointless they'd felt. What was the point of blaming your parents, when you couldn't go back in time and make them do it differently? Why dwell on the past when it couldn't be changed? Just keep moving ahead. That was Sebastian's motto.

Lincoln held up his hands. "I didn't say anything about therapy. Maybe you don't need it, although I kind of think everyone could benefit from having someone to talk to. And look, I don't know what's going on with you. Why you are the way you are. Whether it's your family, or whatever. But Lana and I have discussed it—"

"Oh," Sebastian interrupted. "Oh, great. I'm glad I'm giving you two something to talk about."

"—because we're worried about you," Lincoln concluded. His voice was quiet, firm, and steady as he held Sebastian's gaze with his own. "We want you to be happy."

And Sebastian found he had nothing to say about that.

Abby

Philadelphia

On Sunday morning, Abby slept in.

It had been a long three weeks since the trip had ended and she'd gone scurrying back home. But she'd gotten through those awful first hours and days after a breakup, and had come home resolving to do better, to make a start toward turning her house into a home and building a life that she wanted.

She got out of bed and opened the blinds. Sunlight striped the hardwood floor and the bright pink-and-gold-patterned carpet that had come from Etsy the day before. The bookshelf that she'd finally assembled was full of her books, arranged by color. She'd gotten three posters framed, and had hung them, along with a giant antique mirror she and Lizzie had found at a vintage store on South Street (they'd needed to hire a U-Haul to get it home, and to recruit four members of the bicycle club to wrestle it up the stairs). There was an actual table in the kitchen, and a dedicated work-from-home space with a desk by the window. A row of potted plants stood on the windowsill, and the bags of clothes had finally made it to the donation bin. It didn't look like Lizzie's place, with its layers of belongings, collected over a lifetime of adventures. But it no longer looked like a dorm room, or a featureless, anonymous place to sleep.

Abby had told Marj, at Breakaway, how much she'd enjoyed leading the group, and Marj told Abby that Abby had gotten excellent feedback from her riders, and promised she'd keep her in mind for future adventures. Abby had gone back to work at Pup Jawn, so she'd be able to cover her rent. And then, she'd started to figure out the next piece and whether there was a way to get paid for doing the thing she loved. A bike club to empower young women. She would start by talking to Lizzie, and Gabriella, her librarian friend, who'd set up the camp in Kensington. They'd probably know who else could help.

She'd done her best to keep busy, but she hadn't been able to stop thinking about Sebastian. At least, so far, she had managed to keep herself from calling or texting him. Nor had she googled him, or tried to find him on social media.

The day that Mark had confronted her in Buffalo, and for a few days after, Sebastian had barraged her with texts. *Abby, please call me* and *Are you okay* and *Can we talk?* She hadn't responded, and the texts had stopped. Since then, there'd been nothing. Abby told herself that it was for the best and turned toward the task of telling friends and family that she and Mark were no more.

She'd started with Lizzie, biking to her friend's apartment and giving her the whole saga as she sat on Lizzie's couch with Grover snoozing on her lap.

Lizzie was enthralled, sympathetic, and outraged in turns as Abby told her about Morgan Mackenzie's detour, her nights with Sebastian, and about how the Breakaway ride had concluded.

"Do you know how awful it is to tell a guy that it isn't him, it's you? No matter how much you mean it, it always sounds like a lie," Abby said. She could still picture how devastated Mark had looked, that blank, shocked expression on his face. She could also still hear the bitterness in his voice as he'd asked, *That guy, Abby? Really?* "I hate myself for wasting so much of his time."

"You couldn't have wasted his time if he wasn't willing to let his time be wasted," Lizzie said. "Look at it this way—he got to spend, what? Almost two years with you? He was lucky," Lizzie said, as Abby groaned.

"I feel like I ruined his life."

"I think," Lizzie said carefully, "that maybe you're giving yourself a little too much power here." She leaned forward. "And Eileen? Did she see it go down?"

Abby shook her head, grimacing like she'd swallowed something bitter. "She saw him there, and she knows we talked, but I didn't see her after that. And I think she knew there was something going on with Sebastian."

"Oof," Lizzie said softly. "So what's your plan?" When Abby didn't answer, she said, "I take it you haven't seen Eileen since you've been home."

"I kind of snapped at her at the end of the trip," Abby said.

"So you'll apologize."

"And she doesn't know that I broke up with Mark."

"So you'll tell her."

Abby nodded. She was dreading telling Eileen that she and Mark were through, almost as much as she'd dreaded telling Mark himself, but she knew it had to be done.

"Let's put a pin in Eileen," Lizzie said. "Can we talk about the TikTok guy now? The Romeo of Red Hook? The Gowanus Don Juan?"

Abby closed her eyes. "Can we not?"

Lizzie leaned close to shake Abby's shoulders. "You skimped on the details. I want the whole story. Every twist, every turn. Leave nothing out."

"Okay," Abby said. She found that she was smiling, a little, in spite of everything. Even if she never saw Sebastian again—and she was pretty sure that she would never see Sebastian again—she would remember how it felt to be desired by a guy like that. She could carry it with her like a keepsake or a jewel; a treasure to pull out and consider when she needed to remember that she was worthy; that a guy like him had found her desirable and beautiful.

In the end, it didn't take long to tell the story. Lizzie clasped her hands, sighing happily when Abby told about their first kiss, in the deluge between Syracuse and Seneca Falls. She'd squeezed Abby's hand when she recounted how she had sent Mark away, then gotten on her bike without talking to Sebastian; riding loops around Buffalo until the sun went down.

"He was texting me nonstop that day, and right after, but nothing since then." Abby sounded glum. She felt glum, and foolish, swinging between regret at breaking up with Mark and yearning for Sebastian.

"Do you want to see him?" Lizzie asked.

"Of course I want to see him." Abby wanted to do everything with Sebastian, everything he'd let her do. Everything they'd already done, and everything they hadn't tried yet. "Except . . ." Except Sebastian probably didn't want anything like a real relationship . . . and Abby was almost thirty-four. Even if she froze her eggs, she didn't have time to waste on unserious men.

Which brought her back to Mark, who was serious.

"Was I an idiot?" Abby asked quietly. "Tell me if I was an idiot."

"Oh, I'm not going to tell you anything," Lizzie said. "You know the answer."

"Do I, though?"

Lizzie waited.

"Mark is kind," Abby said. "He's patient. He hardly ever loses his temper. He doesn't yell. He's smart. He's successful." She swallowed. "And he loved me." She thought about the way Mark had looked at her, the first night she'd brought him to her apartment; with adoration and amazement, even awe. *How'd I get so lucky,* he'd whispered, kissing her neck.

"And he told me that he thought he could forgive me. That we could get through it, if I wanted to."

"And?" asked Lizzie.

"And he loved me," Abby repeated. It sounded like she was trying to convince Lizzie. Or maybe herself. "He was good to me." Abby bowed her head and concentrated on scratching Grover behind the ears.

"And?"

Abby swallowed hard. "And he's boring," she admitted very quietly. "No. That's not fair. It wasn't him. I was bored. Sometimes." She rubbed her hands on her thighs. "But he doesn't eat sugar. He doesn't ride a bike. He doesn't . . . you know." *Make me feel like I'll die if I can't touch him,* she thought, but did not say.

"Okay, he doesn't set your soul on fire." Lizzie looked at Abby, her expression patient and nonjudgmental, even though Abby was pretty sure that Lizzie had an opinion on the matter. "And Sebastian?" Lizzie prompted.

"He's very . . ." Abby remembered a hotel room, lit by candlelight. She let her eyes close. "He's really good-looking. He smells amazing. He has a good relationship with his best friend. Cares about his job. And he rides a bike." Out loud, it didn't sound like much.

"You could text him. Ask him to come down here. See where things go. If it doesn't work out, there are other fish in the sea," Lizzie said.

"Okay, but how many of them are going to like me?" Abby asked.

"Can we not do the fat-girl self-deprecating shtick?" Lizzie said. Grover, who'd caught the shift in her tone, raised his head to glare at Abby, an effect only slightly diminished by the doughnut squeaky toy in his mouth. "It's so early-aughts."

"I'm not being self-deprecating. I'm being realistic," Abby muttered. If Eileen had been a force for evil in her life—or at least a force for denial and self-loathing—Lizzie had been a force for good, a living example that it was possible to move through the world in a larger body without hating yourself.

Abby didn't think her friend was lonely . . . but Abby did wonder if maybe Lizzie might have wanted a traveling companion, or even just someone waiting for her when she came home; someone who'd want to hear her stories and look at her pictures. Someone who would tell her to wear her sunscreen before she went to the beaches in Cuba, or reminded her to pack long underwear before she went skiing in Banff; someone who'd track her plane online as it crossed the Atlantic and listen to her stories when she got home. What was the point of a life like Lizzie's if there wasn't someone paying attention? What did it matter if you had great stories if there wasn't anyone to hear them?

"Do you ever get lonely?" Abby asked her friend.

"Sure," said Lizzie. "Sometimes. Everyone's lonely sometimes." She scooped Grover into her lap. "But you know what? I think occasionally lonely is better than being stuck with the wrong person forever." Grover looked up at her adoringly. Lizzie scratched him underneath his chin.

"Tell me the rest of it," Lizzie said. "You said there was something else you wanted to talk about."

Abby took a deep breath. "I had an idea. It's just an idea. I don't know if it's possible, or how I'd even go about doing it."

"What's the idea?"

Abby pinched the bridge of her nose. She was worried that

if she told Lizzie what she'd decided, if she spoke it out loud, it would sound impractical or impossible; like something Abby could never hope to accomplish . . . or like something that someone else was already doing. Abby wasn't sure which one of those things would be worse.

"I was talking to Sebastian and his friend about cycling, and why I loved it so much. I talked about being a kid, and how my bike gave me some independence. How I could get myself between my parents' houses, and go to the mall or the bookstore, and it let me feel more . . ." Abby tried to find a word that wouldn't make Lizzie roll her eyes, or snort, or both. Stable? Centered? Calm?

"Happy," she finally said. "And I told you about what happened with Morgan. So my idea was starting a cycling club for girls. I could take them on rides and teach them about bike maintenance and repairs and safety. And maybe we'd build up to a weeklong bike trip in the summer." She paused, then added, "In a blue state. With a possible side trip to Planned Parenthood."

Abby braced for skepticism, but Lizzie just looked thoughtful. "You know, it sounds a little bit like Girls on the Run. Except for the Planned Parenthood part."

"Obviously," Abby said.

"My niece did that in elementary school. There's running, but they also talk about body image and peer pressure and self-esteem. Stuff like that."

"Yes!" Abby said. "Exactly!" She pulled her knees up to her chest. "Except I'm not qualified to do any of that, except the biking. I can lead rides. But I thought maybe—I mean, I've got friends who are teachers, or therapists. I could find people—professionals, people with training—who work with girls. And I know it sounds ridiculous, about Planned Parenthood, but maybe there'd be some way to, you know, quietly spread the word, so that girls who needed to go there . . ." Abby closed her eyes. "It's stupid."

"No," said Lizzie. "It's not stupid at all. It's actually sadly necessary. And kind of great." Lizzie set Grover on the floor and got to her feet. She held her arms out, and Abby stood, and let her friend hug her. "My little girl is all grown up," Lizzie said, and started humming "Sunrise, Sunset" as Abby giggled.

"Will you help me?" she asked.

Lizzie nodded. "You should talk to Neighborhood Bike Works." Abby knew the group taught kids in low-income neighborhoods how to build bikes from donated parts and let them keep the bikes they'd built. She raked her hands through her hair, still thinking. "And as for the other part, the detour to Planned Parenthood part . . . if women in the 1950s and 1960s figured out how to spread the word about who to call and where to go, I don't think your idea is crazy at all."

"So you think it could work?"

"You'll never know unless you try."

And I'm going to hate myself if I don't, Abby realized. She thought about Morgan, about how scared Morgan must have been, how alone she must have felt, even in the group, and the courage it must have taken her to tell Andy her secret. The Breakaway women had helped Morgan when Morgan needed help, and Lizzie had saved Abby, when Abby had been a girl in need of saving. There were other Morgans and other Abbys out there; a world full of girls and young women who needed friendship or support or skills or reliable contraception, and not enough people who'd risk their own comfort to help them. Someone had to take the risk. Why not Abby? Being a single lady could work to her advantage. If she ended up in jail, she wouldn't be leaving a husband and children behind.

"You look like you've come to a conclusion," Lizzie had said.

"I think I have," Abby said. "I still have to talk to Eileen."

"Into the lion's den!" Lizzie cheered. "Do you have a will?"

"No," Abby said. "If she kills me, you can have everything. Just get rid of anything embarrassing before Eileen goes to clean out my apartment."

"Done and done," Lizzie said, and gave her a hug, for good luck.

Abby spent Rosh Hashanah with her father, listening to him chant the prayers and deliver a sermon on tolerance and loving one's neighbor in a practical, not merely theoretical, way.

The morning of Yom Kippur Abby went to Eileen's synagogue. "You look wonderful," Eileen said when Abby met her outside the sanctuary. Other congregants were streaming into the building. Some wore white, to resemble the angels, with canvas sneakers on their feet, obeying the edict about not wearing leather or animal products on the holiest day of the year. Eileen wore a chic black suit and red-soled black stilettos. She held Abby's shoulders lightly and looked her up and down. Abby had always hated when her mother inspected her. It was like being appraised by a scale with a face, a machine-human hybrid that could tell her down to the ounce what she weighed, and whether it was more or less than what she'd weighed the last time she'd come home. Eileen had pursed her lips. "You look . . ."

Don't say it don't say it don't say it, Abby thought.

". . . healthy," Eileen finally concluded. Which was, of course, code for *thinner,* but at least indicated that she was trying not to actively offend. They'd gone inside together, just the two of them. Marni was with her in-laws in New Jersey, and Simon had told her he was going to shul in New York City, although Abby had her doubts.

Abby stood with the rest of the congregants when the young

female rabbi chanted the *vidui*, the collective confession, an al-phabetical list of sins, all acknowledged in the first-person plural, because, according to Jewish tradition, every single person has fallen short of Divine perfection. The congregation chanted to-gether.

> *We have trespassed*
> *We have betrayed*
> *We have stolen*
> *We have slandered*
> *We have caused others to sin*

Abby found herself thinking of Morgan, how she and Ei-leen had helped Morgan lie to her mother. That, thank God, had worked out in the end. A week after the trip had ended, Lily had sent Abby an email, expressing regret that she hadn't gotten to say goodbye in person, thanking her for keeping Morgan safe, for making sure Morgan hadn't been alone.

> I wish I could have been there myself, but I understand
> why she felt she couldn't tell me (and I know that part of
> growing up means finding other adults in whom you can
> confide). I am thankful that Morgan had friends and other
> adults around her. She is healthy and well and enjoying
> her junior year of high school.

> *We have turned away*
> *We have ignored our responsibilities*
> *We have been perverse*
> *We have acted wantonly*

Abby looked at her mother. Eileen's eyes were tightly closed. She was thumping one fist gently on her chest with each line of the prayer. Abby wondered what her mother was thinking, if any of this had any meaning to her, or if the High Holidays were just an excuse to show off a new outfit while surrounding herself with people who were also not eating. Then she scolded herself for not even making it to sundown without being judgmental and unkind. *Do better*, Abby told herself. *Try harder.* Even if Eileen doesn't make it easy.

> *We have caused suffering*
> *We have been stubborn*
> *We have refused to see Hashem's hand*
> *We have rebelled*
> *We have incited*
> *We have sinned*
> *We have strayed*

On Yom Kippur, observant Jews confessed in public. They were also charged with personally asking forgiveness of people they had hurt. Abby knew what she needed to do. *Just get it over with*, Abby thought. When services were over, she went back home with her mother and said, "How can I help?"

"Come with me," Eileen said, and Abby followed her into the kitchen, where every appliance and countertop gleamed. A white box with "apple cake" written on top stood on the cake stand. A paper bag full of bagels waited on the counter, breathing their warm, yeasty scent into the air.

Eileen began pulling vegetables and packets of smoked fish out of the refrigerator. Abby got a serrated knife, a cutting board, and the white porcelain platter her mother always used. The bagels were still warm, springy on the outside, pillowy in the middle. How many years had Abby laid out platters of bagels and watched her mother take a single half and eviscerate it, pulling out the soft white guts, filling it with vegetables and the tiniest dab of cream cheese?

Abby climbed onto a stool at the breakfast bar and got to work. Eileen went to the counter to select a knife, then walked the long way around the island before pulling a chopping board out of the drawer. *Never sit when you can stand, never stand when you can walk, never hold still when you can be moving* was one of Eileen's mantras. She'd walk from the laundry room to her bedroom a dozen times, carrying a single piece of clothing with each trip, and at the mall or the supermarket, she would park as far as she could from the entrance, the better to sneak in a few extra steps.

Stop judging, Abby told herself as Eileen started slicing a cucumber into thin rounds. Her mom had changed into a simple linen shift. Abby saw, with a little amusement, the tan lines that her cycling shorts had left beneath the hem of her dress. *And stop putting it off.*

"The last day of the trip was interesting," Eileen said, before Abby could begin. She finished up the cucumbers, arranged them neatly on the platter, and started in on the red onion. "Everyone asked where you'd gone. And Sebastian looked miserable." Eileen paused, looking at Abby carefully. Abby stayed quiet, working hard to keep her face expressionless.

"And," Eileen continued, "it turns out that Ted is married to Lou, and Ed is married to Sue."

Abby felt her eyes get wide. "Wait, what?"

"They swap," Eileen said, with a smug-looking smile. "On the bike trips. They told us all at brunch, before we went back. They say it keeps things fresh and exciting."

"Oh my God," said Abby. "So they're swingers? A foursome?"

"A polycule," said Eileen, pronouncing a word she most likely hadn't known before the trip. "They have an arrangement. They're all friends, and they've been doing . . ." She waved her free hand. ". . . that . . . for thirty years. They say nobody gets jealous, and that nobody gets hurt. And, as far as I can tell, they seem happy."

"Happy," Abby said, her voice muted. "That's good."

"Andy told me all about it," Eileen was saying. "Evidently, the lifestyle is very big on TikTok. That's what they call it, you know. The lifestyle."

"You don't say." Abby tried to sound cheerful. "Lily wrote to me. It sounds like she and Morgan are fine."

"I'm glad to hear it. That's what all mothers want, you know." Eileen's voice had a touch of asperity, but she sounded a little mournful. "They want to be included. They want their daughters to let them in."

Not going near that one, Abby decided. She set her hands on the white marble countertop, which matched the white tiled backsplash and the white painted cabinets. "Mom, I want to apologize. I shouldn't have snapped at you the way I did the last day of the trip." Abby clenched her abdominal muscles and curled her toes against the soles of her shoes. "I also want to tell you that Mark and I broke up." Which wasn't completely honest— completely honest would have been *I broke up with Mark*—but it was the best she could do. She suspected that Eileen might have figured it out already. Still, she braced herself, in case Eileen decided to hurl the onion at her. Or the knife. She got ready for shrieking, for weeping, for the rending of garments and the pulling of hair. Maybe Eileen would disown her. *I have no daughter,* her mother would wail. She imagined her mother sitting shiva. Eileen would probably welcome the excuse to buy a few new little black dresses.

But, instead of screaming or crying or asking Abby what she'd been thinking, or declaring that Abby was dead to her, instead of any of that, Eileen simply nodded. She went to the sink, washed off her knife, and calmly began rinsing a colander full of heirloom tomatoes. "Are you okay?"

Abby stared at her mother, momentarily speechless. "Yes. I mean, I'm sad. I hate that I hurt him. And I'm a little lonely these days." As much as she knew that she and Mark were not right for each other, it had still been a comfort to have someone in her life, in her bed; someone who knew her. Someone who was familiar with her history and would listen to her stories.

Eileen sniffed, before picking up a tomato and slicing it in half. She stared down at the cutting board, then looked up.

"I owe you an apology, too."

"For what?"

"I need to show you something." When her mother reached for her phone, Abby wondered if it was going to be something about Sebastian—something new, something even worse than everything she'd already seen. A way to warn Abby off; a way to make her feel more terrible about breaking up with Mark.

Eileen scrolled for a moment, then passed her phone across the counter. Abby looked at the screen. It was a photograph. Abby thought, at first, that she was looking at a picture of herself: a little girl with curly hair standing in front of a swimming pool, squinting in the glaring light of a summer afternoon. The girl wore a sleeveless sundress, and Abby could see familiar contours: solid arms and thighs, a softly rounded belly. Thick wrists and ankles, big hands and chubby fingers, the proportions that had so dismayed her mother for as long as Abby could remember. The expression, too, was familiar. The little girl was smiling, but her expression was tense and guarded, and her shoulders were hunched. Abby recognized the body, and the expression . . . but Abby didn't recognize the sundress or the setting, and the girl's hair was a few shades darker than she remembered hers being at that age.

"Where is this?" Abby asked. "When was it taken?"

"Wrong questions," said Eileen. "Look again."

Abby looked again. And, when she did, she could also see subtle differences in the shape of the girl's face and features. The lips were a little too thin, the brows a little too dark. The question, she realized, wasn't *when*, but *who*.

"Is that . . ." Abby's heart was beating very hard.

"Me," said Eileen. "When I was six years old."

Abby stared at the photograph, shocked into speechlessness. Eileen could have confessed to being an alien, sent to live among the humans, or told Abby that she had a secret life and another family, or that she was considering running for president, and Abby would have been less stunned. Each of those scenarios felt more plausible than imagining her mother as a former fat girl, a girl who'd looked like Abby's almost-identical twin. "I don't understand." She looked up. "I didn't know."

"I didn't tell you." Eileen sat her hands flat on the counter. "I was ashamed, I guess. And I was trying to help you." She looked down, staring at the tomato, which was spilling seeds and juice into the cutting board's gutter. "I remember how hard things were for me. How my mother would criticize. How awful the other kids were. The names they called me . . ." Eileen paused. "I was lonely," she said quietly, looking off into the distance, not meeting her daughter's eyes. "I was very lonely for a very long time. And I thought that losing weight would fix it."

Abby's tongue felt thick and heavy. Her brain felt waterlogged and slow; her emotions a tangle. She wasn't sure whether she was angry, or sad, or disappointed, or something else entirely. "How long were you . . ." *Don't say fat*, she reminded herself. Abby might have gotten comfortable with the word, but Eileen still thought it was a horrible insult, a borderline slur.

"For a long, long time. Until after I was married and became a mother." Abby felt her mouth fall open. Eileen shrugged. "I'd show you pictures from when I was a teenager and a young woman, but there weren't many of those to begin with, and I think I burned the ones that were left." She pursed her lips. "I always wondered if you'd ask to see the wedding album, from when your father and I got married. Or pictures from when you were a baby."

"You're overestimating my interest in weddings and babies," Abby said.

Eileen pressed her hands together. Abby saw her mother's wedding band and diamond engagement ring—a significant upgrade from the one she'd worn while married to Abby's dad—hanging loosely on one finger. There were a few age spots on her mother's hands; a few veins, prominent under the skin. Her mother's fingers and wrists were precisely the same shape as her own. Why hadn't she noticed that before?

"When I was a girl, I was lonely," Eileen said. "And then, when other girls started dating, I didn't have as many options as they did. I think there were boys who didn't mind the way I looked. They just didn't like the way their friends would treat them if they asked me out."

Abby, who'd experienced this phenomenon herself, found that she was nodding. It took an effort to make herself stop.

Eileen picked up her knife and began cutting her tomatoes again. "There were places like Camp Golden Hills when I was growing up. They advertised in the back of *Seventeen* magazine. These tiny little ads, like they were secrets. I begged my parents to send me. I thought, if I could just lose weight, it would fix everything." She made a face, shaking her head. "And they told me if I wanted it badly enough, I'd do it myself. That all I needed was some discipline. 'Eat less, exercise more,'" she recited. "Like that ever works."

"But that's what . . ." *That's what you told me.* Except had Eileen ever said those words? Or had she simply sent Abby to a summer camp where the management believed them to be true?

Abby thought of every tasteless, joyless meal her mother had ever served; the years of every plate being half filled with vegetables, the grilled chicken breasts and sweet potatoes with the merest gloss of butter. She thought of how there were never cookies that weren't SnackWells in her mother's pantry, how there was only ice milk, never ice cream in her freezer, and how any cake—apple cake for break-the-fast at Yom Kippur, yellow sheet cake with chocolate frosting for Abby's birthday—would disappear the day after it had been served, even when there should have been plenty left over. "Gone," Eileen would say when Abby would work up the nerve to ask about it, and Abby knew better than to make further inquiry. She just understood that the cake had been disappeared, and that she was wrong, and weak, for asking, for wanting more.

"It worked for you, didn't it?" Abby asked.

Eileen rubbed her fingertips against her forehead, then lower, to smooth her eyebrows. "No," she said. "It didn't."

Abby stared at her mother's sinewy arms, her short, highlighted hair and flat chest. The last tomato, split in two, dripping on the cutting board. The knife beside it. "What do you mean?"

"I mean, I had gastric bypass surgery, after the three of you were born." And if Abby had been surprised to learn that, once upon a time, Eileen had been fat, she was now shocked, almost to the point of speechlessness.

"When?" she asked, her voice rusty.

"When you were three, and Simon was five, and Marni was seven." She picked up the knife, then set it down. "Your father was dead set against it. Back then, it was much newer, and a lot riskier. 'There are side effects,' he told me. 'You could die.' But I'd gained weight with each baby, and I hadn't been able to lose it, and my doctors were starting to say all the things doctors say, about being prediabetic, about how the weight wasn't good for my joints and heart. They'd lecture me about my weight, even if I was there for an ear infection." Her face had changed again; her expression now rueful and angry. "I remember once I had a stomach bug. I couldn't eat for a week. I was throwing up constantly. And when I finally got sick enough to go see a doctor—which I hated doing, because, no matter what I was there for, I always got the same lecture . . ."

". . . they congratulated you." Abby's face felt numb. Eileen nodded.

"My doctor told me to keep doing whatever I was doing. Which was puking nonstop."

"I hope you got another doctor," Abby said.

Her mother smiled sadly. "I got the surgery. I told your father that I wanted to be healthy, so I could be around for you, and him, a long, long time."

"Not healthy. Smaller," said Abby, her voice sharp. "You wanted to be smaller."

"Smaller. Okay. Fine." Eileen raised her hands in surrender. "You're right."

"Did it ever occur to you that maybe you weren't the one with the problem?" Abby asked. She could hear how loud her voice was, how angry she sounded. "That maybe it was the world's problem, not yours?"

Eileen's head drooped. "I wasn't going to change the world," she said. "Maybe I should have tried. Probably that would have been the better thing to do. The braver thing." She sniffled, and Abby tried to harden her heart, to hang on to her rage, lest she end up feeling sorry for Eileen. "But I've never been very brave."

Eileen looked up. Her eyes were teary as she met her daughter's gaze. "I'm not like you."

Abby swallowed hard. She knew how to handle a disappointed Eileen, a judgmental Eileen, an Eileen who was angry or frustrated or bitter or resigned. She did not, she realized, have the first idea what to do with an Eileen who was sorry, an Eileen who was actually apologizing, admitting to her mistakes and telling Abby that Abby was the brave one. A formerly fat Eileen. An Eileen who'd once been like her.

Abby licked her lips. "Did Dad end up being okay with you getting the surgery?"

"Oh, he was terrified." Eileen's lips curved in a small, private smile. "I wore him down. I told him there were side effects to being overweight." She shook her head. "I told him it was my body and my choice. And, eventually, he gave in."

Abby put her hands on the counter, trying to ground herself. She could smell the warm bagels and her mother's perfume; could feel the cool air of the kitchen, could hear, faintly, her stepfather, upstairs on the phone. Gary the Businessman didn't take even the High Holidays off.

Speaking slowly, Abby said, "So my whole life, you've let me think that you're a naturally thin person, and that if I just ate like you, I'd be thin like you. And, meanwhile, your stomach's the size of a tennis ball." That bubble of anger was swelling, supplanting her sympathy and sadness. "Why didn't you tell me? Do you have any idea how it felt, growing up fat with a mother who looked like you?"

Eileen addressed the counter, not meeting Abby's eyes. "I didn't tell you because I thought if I was careful when you were little, if I made sure you never gained weight in the first place, then you wouldn't end up . . ."

"Fat," Abby snapped.

"Lonely," said Eileen. "Unhappy. I didn't want you to be left out. I didn't want other kids being mean to you, the way they were to me. And I didn't understand how much of it was genetic. I don't think anyone knew back then." She drummed her fingers lightly on the countertop. "I promise, I really did want things to be easier for you than they were for me. When you started dating, I wanted you to have options. And, when you were grown up and going out into the world, going to college, applying for jobs, I didn't want people to judge you. To look at you and think that you were lazy, or weak. And I know the world has changed, and people see things differently now. I know you can be healthy without being skinny. I know that there are doctors who won't bully you, or assume you aren't taking care of yourself when you're bigger, or blame every health problem on your weight." She paused for a breath. "I understand that I didn't always make the right choices, or explain myself very well. I know you're angry at me. But I thought—"

Abby's mind replayed what her mother had told her, seizing on the words *dating* and *options*. "What about you?" she said. "Did you marry dad because you didn't have choices? Because no one else wanted you?"

"Oh, Abby," her mother said sadly. "I don't have a crystal ball. I don't know who else might have wanted me. I don't know how it might have turned out." She gathered up the sliced tomatoes and arranged them on the platter, then started scooping cream cheese out of its plastic tub, into a glass dish. "If I hadn't married Bernie, I wouldn't have had you. Or your brother and sister. So I can't regret it. Not at all. And I know I've made mistakes. I know I haven't always done the right things." She looked Abby in the eye. "But everything I did, right or wrong, I did because I love you. I only ever wanted things to be easy for you."

"And for me to look good in your wedding pictures," Abby said, her voice tart.

"Well, yes," Eileen said. "That was part of it. A silly, superficial part. I'm ashamed about it. And I apologize if I ever made you feel . . ." She swallowed hard. "Not beautiful. Because you are. And you always have been. You're beautiful, inside and out."

Now she's going to hug me, Abby thought. Then I'm going to stand up and find out that I'm wearing ice skates, because hell has frozen over. Or I'm going to wake up in the hospital in Seneca Falls with a concussion.

"I know I didn't go about it the right way. I know that now. But I just wanted what every mother wants. I wanted you to be happy. I wanted you to have choices." She looked into Abby's eyes, her expression beseeching. "I wanted you to have all the choices in the world."

Abby knew this was the moment where she should have said, *I understand.* Or even, *I forgive you.* But she could still feel the sting of being exiled to Camp Golden Hills, the pain of feeling like her body was wrong and shameful, piled on top of the fresh grief of being alone. "And look how well that worked out," she said.

"Oh, Abby." Eileen walked around the counter and perched on the barstool next to Abby, close enough that Abby could smell perfume, and the retinoid cream Eileen dabbed under her eyes at night. Eileen touched Abby's hair. "Mark was a nice guy. But being a nice guy doesn't make him the right guy for you."

Abby stared at her mother, shocked beyond words. Eileen's hand was very gentle as it smoothed her curls. "Come on. This can't be such a surprise. Your father was a nice guy. *Is* a nice guy. But we weren't a good fit. And you and Mark weren't a good fit, either."

"You . . ." Abby shook her head, wondering how many more surprises Eileen had for her. "I thought you loved Mark! I thought you wanted me to marry him!"

Eileen looked genuinely puzzled. "Why would you think that?"

Abby shook her head again, still feeling like the world had gone sideways, like nothing was what she'd thought and everything had changed. Like, if she reached for her water glass she'd find herself grasping a goldfish, or a hammer. Had she been completely wrong about her mother? Had Eileen been enthralled with the idea of Abby marrying a nice Jewish doctor because she was convinced Mark was the best (and possibly only) man who'd love her second daughter? Or had Abby herself internalized those ideas about who, and what, she was supposed to want, about what she deserved and what was possible for someone like her? Had she swallowed them all down, all those rigid notions and demeaning expectations and hashtag life goals, then, somehow, projected them onto the size-two screen that was her mother? Her mother, who, it turned out, had been a victim of diet culture, too?

Abby closed her eyes. She was remembering how her mother would comb her hair when she was little, using a wide-toothed plastic comb, gently teasing out each knot, telling Abby how pretty her hair was. Had she made herself forget the times when Eileen had been kind to her? Had she erased those memories on purpose, unwilling to see Eileen as anything other than cold and critical, judgmental and withholding? Unwilling to believe, no matter how many times she said it, that Eileen really did want her to be happy?

"Abby," her mother was saying. "Mark never ate dessert and he doesn't ride a bike. And he wasn't willing to change."

"He . . . but I thought . . ." Abby sniffled. "He's a doctor!" she blurted.

"He is," Eileen confirmed.

"And he loved me!" Abby sniffled.

"He did," Eileen agreed. "But sometimes that isn't enough."

Abby shook her head. She folded her arms on the table, rested her head on her forearms, and cried a little, in the dark space she'd created, as her mother stroked her hair.

"When you were my age, you had two kids and a house," Abby said in a muffled voice.

"And when I was ten years older than you, I was divorced," Eileen said. "If I learned anything, it's that you don't need to rush. You can take your time and find the right person. Someone who's going to love you, just as you are. Or even when you can't love yourself." She gave Abby's hair a final fond pat, then gathered the rest of the vegetables, arranged them on the tray, and began opening the packages of smoked fish. The air filled with the scents of lox and smoked sable. Abby's mouth watered.

"So what's going on with Sebastian?" Eileen asked. "It seemed like the two of you enjoyed each other's company."

Deep breath, Abby thought. *Buck up.* "Sebastian is a lot of fun," she said. "But I don't think he was looking for anything serious."

"Well." Eileen began arranging slices of lox on another platter. "Maybe you don't need serious right now."

"I'm almost thirty-four," said Abby.

Eileen waved that information away with the knife's blade. "Please. Friedelle Gould's daughter froze her eggs and had a baby last year, and she was forty-two. You girls have options."

Abby shook her head. She and Sebastian had only had four nights together, and one of them had been two years ago. She barely knew him, and most of what she knew wasn't promising. Sebastian wasn't a relationship kind of guy.

And yet. And yet, she still wanted him. And her mother was still looking at her; her gaze unwavering, steady, and full of love.

"Call him," said Eileen. "Invite him to Philadelphia. See what happens."

"And what if he doesn't want to come?" Abby swallowed

down something that felt sharp-edged and tasted bitter. "What if it was all about the chase, and he's not interested, now that I'm available?"

Eileen's tone was matter-of-fact. "Then you'll know. And you'll move on." Her mother carried the platter of fish into the dining room. Abby sat, thinking.

It made sense. It was unassailably logical. It was the rare occasion where both Lizzie and her mother were telling her to do the same thing. Except the thought of actually doing it, of running the risk that Sebastian would send her a politely worded *thanks but no thanks* text, made Abby feel dizzy and sick. It made her want to do what she'd done back in Buffalo: climb on her bike and ride away, as fast and as far as she could go.

But that wasn't an option. At least not now. Soon, the doorbell would be ringing, the house filling up with friends and relatives, Gary the Businessman's kids, and Abby's siblings and niece and nephew.

Abby greeted the guests as the sun set. She stood beside her mother as Eileen lit the candles and said the blessings. She ate an everything bagel with whitefish salad and red onions, and half of an egg bagel with cream cheese and lox. She didn't pass judgment on her mother's plate, and hoped that Eileen wasn't passing judgment on hers. At the end of the night, Eileen packed a bag with apple cake and rugelach, bagels and spreads, and helped Abby pack up her panniers.

"Do you forgive me?" Abby asked her mother.

"Of course." Eileen slipped a container of whitefish salad into the bag, then clipped the pannier closed. "And I know it'll take time before you can forgive me. But I'm glad I told you. I've been meaning to do it for a long time." She pulled Abby into a hug and, for once, Abby let her mother embrace her, without thinking about her own body, or Eileen's, or how soft and squishy and possibly revolting she probably felt in her mother's small, sinewy arms.

"I want you to be happy," Eileen whispered. Abby nodded, and tried her hardest not to think about her mother as a body and tried, instead, to think of her as a soul—wounded and defensive; vulnerable and loving. A mother who only wanted the best for her child; who was trying her hardest; who regretted her mistakes.

"Thank you," Abby said, and Eileen kissed her cheek in farewell.

One Year Later

Abby

August 2024

In the months that followed the Breakaway trip, Abby stuck to her schedule. She ate breakfast and exercised every morning. She'd walk, or do walking/jogging intervals, or a bike ride; or she'd take a yoga class or do core work in her living room. She continued her efforts at home improvement, hanging half a dozen plates over the refrigerator in the kitchen, installing hooks in her coat closet, tending to pots of basil and thyme, tomatoes and cucumbers on her tiny balcony. She went to her father's house for Shabbat dinners, and to Sunday brunches with her mother, meals that gradually began featuring more carbs.

At first, a dozen times an hour, a hundred times a day, she'd think about Sebastian. There would be things she'd want to tell him, or show him, or ask him. Abby was forced to admit, unhappily, that she'd let herself imagine things with him that she'd never imagined with Mark, not just this restaurant or that museum but a whole life. Days spent together. Long walks and picnics, movie dates and concerts, and drinks at her favorite bars and dinners at her favorite restaurants. Nights in bed, at her place or his.

She couldn't stop herself from thinking about him, but she didn't let herself call or text. For the first month, she crossed each day off her calendar, getting through them hour by hour, sometimes minute to minute. She started a gratitude journal and a skin-care routine, and was reminded that trying not to think about someone meant that, inevitably, you ended up thinking about him, even when you were making your absolute best effort to forget about the time he'd held your hand with rain-chilled fingers, or kissed you in front of a statue of Susan B. Anthony, or told you you were beautiful.

Fall became winter. Abby had written up a proposal for a bike club and submitted it, along with a résumé and references, to a friend of Lizzie's who worked as a guidance counselor at one of the private Quaker schools in the city. After a background check, the school's headmaster had agreed to give Abby a tryout, and, on a cold Monday in January, the first day after winter break, she'd met with the four kids who'd shown up at the fountain behind the Art Museum. Two of them had hybrid bikes, one had a road bike, and the fourth had a three-speed so small that her knees almost bumped her chin when she pedaled. Abby walked them all to the nearest bikeshare kiosk, so the girl could rent something more size-appropriate, and then she'd had them all pedal in circles around the fountain, making sure they could ride safely before leading them in an eight-mile loop, out Kelly Drive, over the Falls Bridge, and along the freshly paved trail on the other side of the river.

She went to other schools with her bike club proposal, and eventually she was running a different club each day Monday through Friday, working with two private schools and three public ones. The public schools paid her a pittance. The private schools paid a slightly more generous pittance. Abby didn't mind. She had work that satisfied her and utilized her skills, and that felt more important than making a fortune. As long as she could pay her rent and her health insurance, she'd be fine.

On weekends, she volunteered with Neighborhood Bike Works in West Philadelphia. She taught kids how to fix bikes and how to ride them, and led them on adventures through Fairmount Park, into Manayunk, on out-and-backs along Forbidden Drive. Once she'd done that for six months, she'd launched the club she called Girls Ride Philly: a free club that would teach any girl who wanted to learn how to ride a bike (and help her find one if she didn't have one already), and offer workshops from local experts on nutrition, study habits, conflict resolution, and self-esteem. *We'll end our season in August with a thirty-mile bikepacking trip*, Abby had written. *Join us, and see how far you can go!*

On the first ride for Girls Ride Philly, on the first Saturday in May, five girls showed up: shy Connie, with her long, dark ponytail, who looked a lot younger than twelve, and thirteen-year-old Sally, were classmates in West Philadelphia. Madisyn, twelve, and Ryleigh, fourteen, were sisters. Ryleigh had an ancient ten-speed, and Madisyn had borrowed a cousin's BMX bike. Hannah, the fifth girl, lived in Queen Village, and reminded Abby of herself. She had shoulder-length curls, a sarcastic sense of humor, and, she quickly made clear, zero interest in exercise. "My parents made me do this," Abby overheard her saying.

"Hello, ladies. My name is Abby, and I'm going to be riding with you." The girls were sitting on benches beneath an arbor in the Azalea Gardens. Abby was standing in front of them, holding her bike with one hand, dry-mouthed, sweaty-palmed, feeling the worst imposter syndrome she'd experienced since she'd gotten up in front of the Breakaway riders for the first time and said she'd be their leader. "Let's take a look at these bikes."

Ryleigh's chain was rusty. Sally's rear tire was flat. Madisyn's derailleur made an ominous clunking sound whenever she switched gears. And, when Abby asked, "Has everyone ridden a bike before?" Hannah's nod did not look especially confident.

Abby squirted lubrication on Ryleigh's rusty chain, used her multitool to raise Madisyn's seat, pumped up Sally's tire, crossed her fingers about the funky derailleur, and made sure everyone's helmet was on correctly.

"I don't want to be here," whispered Hannah.

"I know," Abby whispered back.

"People are going to laugh at me," Hannah said. Unlike the other girls, who'd worn shorts and tee shirts, Hannah wore baggy sweatpants and a loose sweatshirt. It was a warm day, and Hannah looked sweaty and miserable as she stared at her feet.

"I'm not going to laugh at you," Abby said.

"Everyone's going to be faster than me," she said.

"Good thing this isn't a race," said Abby. Hannah didn't smile. "I will ride with you," Abby promised. "We'll take it slow. Just give it a try, okay? Maybe you'll have fun."

The first ride was the eight-mile loop down Kelly Drive, then back up Martin Luther King Drive. Abby told the girls to ride single file, to pay attention, to call out "On your left!" when passing walkers or runners. It took them almost an hour. After the first mile, Hannah complained that her legs hurt. After the second mile, she announced that her butt hurt. By the third mile, she said that everything hurt. "Just keep pedaling," Abby said. She rode beside Hannah and, eventually, they were back where they'd started: Sally wiping off her sweaty face, Madisyn and Ryleigh arguing about who'd gone faster. Connie was beaming, and Hannah, in spite of her aching legs and sore bottom, was quietly glowing with pride.

Every Saturday, Abby led her riders on different loops through the park, past the Please Touch Museum and the Japanese Tea House and the Belmont Plateau. Once a month, when the ride was over, they'd go to a coffee shop and listen to a guest speaker, typically one of Abby's friends, or a friend of a friend: a psychologist who talked about self-esteem, a nutritionist who talked about eating to be healthy and strong, a teacher who discussed note-taking strategies and good study habits. Abby thought about what she wished she'd known, or been told, when she was their age, and tried to find people who could fill in those blanks. Even though she knew some of the girls were facing challenges she couldn't imagine, she knew, or at least hoped, that riding a bike would give them some respite, and the speakers would give them some knowledge, and those things, combined, would give them some strength.

Eileen had sent her, without comment, Sebastian's article about the Empire State Trail ride when it had been published, three weeks after the trip had ended. Abby had held her breath, imagining the worst, but the story was a straightforward travelogue about the trail, the riding conditions, the different trips you could take and the different outfitters that led them. The photographs were all shots of Lincoln or Sebastian on the trail, and what looked like handout art from the New York State tourism board. There was a single mention of Breakaway, and no mention at all of Abby. She'd thought about writing to him, to tell him she'd enjoyed the story, but decided not to. He had her number. If he wanted to get in touch, he could. But, as the months went on, he didn't. Abby did her best to forget him and move on.

Then, one Sunday morning in August, almost a year after the last time she'd seen him, a story landed in her inbox. Lincoln had sent it. *Thought you'd want to see this,* he'd written. *Hope you're well.* Abby had swallowed hard and clicked the link. The headline read THE BREAKAWAY, and the byline was Sebastian Piersall.

Abby sank down in her office chair and began to read.

The best trips can change you. You start off in one place, as one version of yourself, and you end up, days or weeks or months or even years later, not just having been somewhere else, but, maybe, having become someone else. Hopefully someone better. You've been new places, you've seen new things, you've faced challenges and overcome them. All of that, ideally, leaves you new and improved . . . or, if not completely new, at least somewhat improved.

That's how it went for me.

Last August, at the end of the summer, I rode my bike from Midtown Manhattan to the Canadian border. I wrote about the route, the scenery, the history of the Empire State Trail, the various outfitters that run trips and the small towns and big cities you'll see along the way.

What I didn't mention in that story was that I started off the ride in disgrace; in the midst of a public shaming that commenced the second day of my ride.

All through my twenties, and into my thirties, I'd been active on the dating apps, meeting different women every weekend. I didn't see the harm in it—I was having a good time. Then one of my dates got together with her friends, and seven out of eight of them realized they'd spent time with me (you can insert your own air quotes around "meeting" and "spent time with me"). Cue the social media mob. For a few days back then, I was the Internet's main character. I trended on Twitter; I made a few late-night-comedians' monologues. I was a cautionary tale; a target; a punch line in padded shorts.

You can google it. I'll wait.

If there's one thing biking is good for, it's giving you time to be alone with your thoughts . . . especially if you're riding through the woods of upstate New York, where the scenery's pretty but not especially exciting, and you're undisturbed by cars, or people, with nothing to focus on but whatever's going on in your brain. As the miles unspooled, I went through all the stages of grief: denial (this can't be happening!), anger (I didn't do anything wrong!), bargaining (maybe if I post an apology this will all go away), depression (my love life is over), worse depression (my entire life is over), and, finally, acceptance—as in, maybe I did do something wrong. Maybe I need to think about why I felt the need to behave like a kid who'd just stepped into Baskin-Robbins and was determined to sample all thirty-one flavors before he left. Maybe I need to, as the saying goes, do some work on myself. Maybe there's a problem here.

That mess was compounded by the fact that the ride leader was a woman I'd met, years before. We had met the old-fashioned way: in a bar, at the tail end of a bachelorette party. We didn't spend much time together, but I felt an immediate connection with her, a sense of I want to know this person, and I want her to know me. I'd never felt like that before. But I didn't get her number. I didn't expect to ever see her again. When it turned out that she was the one leading this bike trip, I felt incredibly lucky, that the Universe was giving me another chance. When the scandal began, I felt incredibly un-lucky, that this woman was seeing me in the worst light possible. I thought she would never trust me . . . and, worse, that she'd be right not to trust me.

I knew that it was time to make changes. And, as it turned out, the two weeks on my bike were just the start of my journey. Without going into the goopy, woo-woo therapy-speak details, I spent the next weeks and months working on myself, trying to figure out why I'd had bountiful sex but very *little intimacy. Some of it had to do with my family, and some of it had to do with toxic masculinity, living in a culture that rewards men for conquests when what we're really doing is hiding, avoiding, refusing to be vulnerable—which is, of course, a thing you need real strength to do.*

I started my trip with all of my armor on. I rode for miles, along roads and beside rivers, through tunnels of green, beneath canopies of trees, as summer slid into fall, with my armor cracked. When the trip was over, I had to make a decision. Did I want to patch up my old suit, put it on again— gorget, gauntlet, breastplate, vambrace, greaves—and keep on the way I'd been going? Or was it time to find a different way of being in the world?

I went for the second option. The road less traveled; the harder path. And it was terrifying. I felt naked in the worst way; soft and defenseless, vulnerable to every faint breeze and passing slight. Which, I have come to believe, is how most people feel most of the time. Life hurts. It's full of heartache, loss, and disappointment, and even the best things come salted with sorrow. But you can't leave yourself open to the good things— happiness, true love, real connection—if you aren't willing to risk being hurt.

So that's my happy ending. Seven-hundred-plus miles later, I am newly vulnerable and still alone. And if you're wondering whether I got the girl in the end, if I've found true love, the answer is no. Or maybe it's not yet.

But I know I've gotten better. I know I'm not who I was when the journey began. And maybe there's hope for me yet.

There was a single illustration, a photograph of Sebastian, standing over his bike, with his helmet tucked under his arm and the trail unwinding behind him. His chin was lifted, and he was smiling, just a little, looking right at the camera. Right at Abby. His face was so familiar, and so dear. She wanted to reach through the screen and touch him. She wanted to email Lincoln and ask why he'd sent her the story, and if Sebastian still thought about her, and if there was still a chance for the two of them. She wanted to call Sebastian and ask him those things himself.

But her riders were waiting, and she couldn't let them down.

She sprayed sunscreen on her arms and smeared it on her face. She pumped air in her bike's tires, locked her apartment's door behind her, then lifted her bike onto her shoulder and carried it down the stairs. She road north on Eleventh Street, then west on Spruce, her heart beating fast, telling herself that if Sebastian had changed, she had, too. She'd figured out what she wanted to do with her life. She'd filled in some of the blanks. She'd gotten braver. Maybe she was worthy now. Maybe she was ready.

She bent over her handlebars and picked up her pace, inching past fifteen miles an hour, quads burning, breathing hard, racing to meet her riders. For once, there wasn't a train blocking access from the street to the Schuylkill Banks. Abby coasted through the gates, bounced over the train tracks, dinged her bell, called out "On your left" to a trio of oblivious runners occupying seven-eighths of the path, following the trail as it curved along the river, under the Walnut Street Bridge, up a gentle rise, past the skate park, then down a hill behind the Art Museum and onto Kelly Drive.

Mark had found someone new. Abby knew that he would, and honestly hoped he was happy. The last picture he'd posted on Instagram showed him and his new girlfriend, grinning and brandishing their finishers' medals at the end of the Broad Street Run. Abby was glad he'd found a woman who could run with him, someone who wouldn't think Mark's food preferences felt like torture. She wished him well.

She rode on, trying to think about the day ahead—a twenty-mile loop down Forbidden Drive, onto the towpath in Manayunk, out toward Valley Forge, then back again. Their season-ending camping trip was coming up, and the girls had gotten so much better. Hannah could make it the entire way around Kelly Drive and West River Drive without stopping, or complaining, and Connie could ride in the city, in the bike lanes, without turning into a trembling, teary wreck, and Sally could climb hills without getting off to push her bike.

They'd come so far. She was so proud.

She rode past the Falls Bridge, down the sidewalk, past the SEPTA depot and through the intersection of Ridge Avenue and Main Street. The trail narrowed and rose steeply before falling again and meandering along the Wissahickon Creek, beneath a green canopy overhanging trees. Abby was pedaling uphill when she saw the sign. It was a piece of poster board, taped to a wooden stake, stuck into the grass on the side of the trail, with a single word written on it.

ABBY

Puzzled, she braked to a stop and looked both ways before executing a U-turn. She coasted downhill until she reached the sign, and confirmed that it did, indeed, say her name.

Well. There were lots of girls named Abby in the world. Maybe one of them was having a brunch or a baby shower at the restaurant in the park. She started pedaling again, riding past the sign that said ABBY until she reached one that said STERN.

"The heck?" she murmured, and kept going, riding faster, looking to see if there were more signs.

There were. The third sign read I. The fourth one said MISS. The fifth one said YOU. The sixth sign had no words. It was just a heart, a red heart on white poster board.

Abby's own heart was in her throat as she crested the gentle slope that ended with a parking lot on the right-hand side, and the Valley Green restaurant on the left. Down by the creek, parents were helping kids toss chunks of bread to the ducks. In front of the parking lot, Abby saw her riders, in the new tee shirts they'd gotten the week before, sherbet orange with electric-blue lettering that said PHILLY GIRLS RIDE. And there, in the center of the group, was Sebastian, at the end of the path, standing in front of a bench, holding his bike in one hand.

Seeing him again made her feel like an arrow had lodged in her heart. He looked so good, his face tanned, his long-sleeved jersey tight against his chest, staring right at her; like she was the only thing he'd ever wanted. Like Abby Stern was his heart's desire.

Abby let her bike coast to a stop, leaving plenty of space between them. She rested her hands on the handlebars and kept one foot on the pedal, poised for a quick getaway if it turned out one was required.

"Sebastian. What brings you to Philadelphia?" she asked, and was glad that her voice sounded steady.

Sebastian gestured in the direction of the signs. "I missed you. I wanted to see you." The girls were watching this unfold, their eyes moving from his face to hers, intent on every word. Sebastian was just as handsome as she remembered, but he looked . . . not older, exactly. More mature? Less slick? His hair was styled differently, or maybe disarranged from his helmet, and his expression looked open and undefended, as the riders gathered around him, giggling.

"Your friends helped me with the signs," he said. "I saw you guys on Instagram."

Abby felt like her heart was a balloon, getting lighter and bigger with every breath she took. She forced herself to try to be prudent and mature, not to do the thing she most desired, which was tossing aside her bike and throwing herself into his arms.

"Lincoln sent me your story," she said.

"What'd you think?"

"It was . . ." She licked her lips, and looked at the girls, who were watching, wide-eyed, like this was the best movie they'd ever seen. "It was very provocative."

"Provocative," he repeated, and smiled. "Can I ride with you?" he asked.

Abby felt weak in her knees. Weak everywhere. "Well. We are a girls' riding club," she said.

"Miss Abby, you shouldn't assume gender," Ryleigh teased.

"Yeah, we don't even know Sebastian's pronouns!" said Sally.

"He brought us doughnuts," Hannah said. "He can come."

"Can you give us a minute?" said Abby.

The girls indicated that they could. Abby could feel them watching as she led Sebastian toward the water and, she hoped, out of hearing range. He wheeled his bike along, holding its handlebars, looking at her pleasantly, his expression open and expectant.

"What are you doing here?" Abby asked. "How'd you find me?"

"I got in touch with your mother and found out where you'd be today. But I've been following the group on Instagram. It's really impressive. And I've been thinking about you ever since the trip ended." He wheeled his bike a few inches forward, then back again.

Abby looked at him. *Why do you like me?* she wanted to ask. *Why did you pick me?* If she and Mark didn't match, there was even more of a disparity between her and Sebastian. He could have any woman in the world. Why her?

"You don't know me," she said, instead of any of that. "Not really."

"So I'll get to know you."

"You don't live here," she said.

"So I'll visit," said Sebastian. "And you can come see me. We can see each other on the weekends. I'll buy you tickets for the bus."

"Jeez." Abby said, shaking her head. "Not even the train?"

He rolled his eyes and said, "If you want the train, I'll get you tickets for that." He gestured toward the path, and the girls, who were clearly trying to eavesdrop. "We shouldn't keep them waiting."

He reached for her hand, and Abby let him take it, feeling that electric thrill running right through her, that sense of rightness and completion.

"I want to get to know you," he said. "I want to see your places. I want to see where you went when you were a kid." He gestured toward the bag suspended behind his seat post, hanging over his rear wheel. "I brought other clothes. We can go out to dinner tonight, if you want."

"Stop," Abby said, her voice muted, thick with tears. She couldn't let herself look at him, couldn't let him get within touching distance. If he touched her—if he kissed her—it would be over. She would be lost. "Stop being so nice to me."

"Why?" he asked.

"Because . . ." Abby said. Her voice was a choked-off squeak and she made herself say, "Girls like me do not belong with guys like you."

"Abby." He looked shocked, almost angry, and she felt him touching her hand, then her chin, then her cheek. "There aren't girls like you. There aren't guys like me. There's just you, and just me, and I missed you, and I want you to meet my parents . . ."

Abby was shaking her head, trembling a little, her throat tight and her eyes stinging, and there was a huge smile on her face. "Okay," she whispered.

"Okay?"

She nodded.

"Abby," he whispered, and pulled her against him with his free arm. He stroked her hair, then her back, his hands warm. He rubbed her neck, then that spot at the base of her skull that made her feel like she was melting. He bent down, solemnly raised her chin, and pressed a grave, gentle kiss against her lips. Then he reached for his bike and handed Abby hers.

Maybe she and Sebastian would never get married, Abby thought as she walked back toward the waiting girls. Maybe she would never marry at all. Maybe she'd choose a life like Lizzie's, an adventuring life, where she traveled the world and taught girls what she knew. All she knew for sure was that, for today, for now, she could have Sebastian. And, for today, it was exactly what she wanted.

She put on her own helmet, swung her leg over her bike, and coasted in a half-circle until she was facing her riders. "This is my friend Sebastian—"

"We know," Hannah said, rolling her eyes. "We know everything."

"And he's going to ride with us today. Is everyone ready?" Nods all around. "Helmets on, then," she said as Sebastian looked at her, his expression full of pride. It made her feel warm and shivery at the same time; happy and lucky, like everything she wanted could be hers.

"Okay, then," she said. "Let's ride."

Acknowledgments

I love riding my bike, and I loved writing this story about cycling, traveling, and girls and women finding their way in what feels like an increasingly hostile world.

At Atria, I am grateful to Natalie Hallak, who gave this book such smart and thoughtful attention. Thanks to Lindsay Sagnette, Jade Hui, Esther Paradelo, Elizabeth Hitti, Shelby Pumphrey, Lacee Burr, Paige Lytle, Zakiya Jamal, Katie Rizzo, Alison Hinchcliffe and Rebecca Justiniano, and to Libby McGuire and Jonathan Karp.

Lauren Rubino was a crucial fresh set of eyes as we closed in on the finish line. Shelly Perron did a wonderful job copyediting the manuscript. Any mistakes are my own. As always, James Iacobelli makes the covers look delightful and inviting.

On the audio front, Sarah Lieberman and Elisa Shokoff are thoughtful and creative about finding just the right people to lend their voices to my words.

I am so grateful to Dacia Gawitt and family for sharing Marjorie Gawitt's story with me and allowing me a glimpse of their beloved Marj—a devoted reader, talented cook, and friend to all. I was honored to use her name in this story.

In Hollywood, I am grateful for the help of Michelle Weiner (no relation) and my brothers, Jake and Joe Weiner (relations). Shout-out to my sister, Molly, who always makes me laugh.

Jasmine Barta keeps my website looking right and my newsletter running smoothly (and if you haven't seen my website or signed up for my newsletter, you can go to JenniferWeiner.com and fix that right now!).

I am grateful to Celeste Fine, my agent, and to John Maas, Park & Fine's editorial director and my first reader, whose help in shaping this story and these characters was invaluable. Thanks also to Andrea Mai, Emily Sweet, Elizabeth Pratt, Mahogany Francis, and Theresa Park.

My assistant, Meghan Burnett, is one of my trusted first readers. Not only is she smart and funny and insightful, she's a tremendous help on the home front, whether we're figuring out a thorny plot twist or the tree in front of my house that the city's making us remove.

As always, I am grateful to my daughters, Lucy and Phoebe, who let me spend time in the neighborhood of make-believe—and on my bike. Special thanks to my husband, Bill Syken, who lets me go and is happy to welcome me home.

Speaking of my bike, I am grateful to all the members of the Bicycle Club of Philadelphia, especially club founder Tim Carey, who is a lifelong cyclist and is himself a vivid chronicler of two-wheeled adventures. Tim's ridden across the country, led trips from Florida to Philadelphia, and knows every inch of Philadelphia and the story (or, at least, a story) of every street and bridge and building (he likes to say that two-thirds of what he tells the riders is true, and one-third's made up, and it's our job to figure out which is which). His Facebook ride reports are replete with descriptions of mileage and meals and scenery, along with varied creative spellings of his beloved ramen noodles.

When the pandemic closed down the world in 2020, I started riding again, and was delighted to find that Tim was leading bike rides every day of the week. Riding my bike kept me healthy and sane, and getting back on my bike helped me navigate not only a global pandemic but my own season of losses, both personal and political.

I am grateful to Tim and to the people I met on the BCP rides: Johanna Blackmore, Ginnie Zipf, and especially Dani Ascarelli, her sister, Silvia Ascarelli, and Silvia's partner, Clive Jenner, with whom I rode from Buffalo to Albany in the summer of 2022.

The Empire State Trail is real, as is Neighborhood Bike Works, here in Philadelphia (NeighborhoodBikeWorks.org) . . . and, while Abby imagines a version of Girls on the Run for bikes, it turns out, there's a real organization called Girls in Gear, which, per its website, "helps riders learn about themselves, their bikes, and their community" and has riding clubs in New Jersey, Pennsylvania, and Ohio. You can learn more at GirlsinGear.org.

The trails and organizations in *The Breakaway* are real. So are the challenges Morgan faces. Since *Roe v. Wade* was overturned, the barriers women face when they want to end a pregnancy are mounting. Some states have instituted so-called heartbeat laws, banning all abortions after six weeks, well before many women know that they are pregnant. Other states have banned abortion medication, with the possibility of a nationwide ban looming on the horizon. And you don't have to have a novelist's imagination to see the impact of these laws. All you have to do is read the news.

My mother marched and protested for abortion rights, and I marched and protested for abortion rights. *We won't go back,* we chanted . . . except we have. I've passed along my pins and signs to my daughters, with the hope that, someday, abortion will be safe, legal, and rare, and that every girl and woman will be able to make choices about her reproductive life for herself. Meanwhile, the work goes on.

Susan B. Anthony said it best. Cycling is freedom. And, just like she did, I wish for freedom—every freedom—for girls and women.

The Breakaway: Topics and Questions for Discussion

1. Many of the characters in this book struggle with the concept of choice: Abby is choosing between settling down as a podiatrist's wife or choosing a man she is inexplicably drawn to; Morgan is grappling with a choice that complicates her relationship with her faith and family; Eileen tells Abby that the reason she sent her to Camp Golden Hills was to make sure she had options—the freedom to choose a life and a partner she wanted. Discuss what guides these characters' choices. How are they impacted by their own beliefs and experiences versus those of broader society? How does the novel contribute to the larger conversation of women's choice and freedom in the United States today?

2. A "breakaway" is a cycling term for the moment during a race when one rider separates from the pack and attempts to build a lead toward victory—a strategy with risks but also potential rewards. What is Abby "breaking away" from during the events of this book? How are other characters also "breaking away"?

3. With Mark, Abby has found a relationship that makes her feel comfortable and accepted, with a man she's known for most of her life. By contrast, a relationship with Sebastian would push her out of her comfort zone. Is being comfortable in a relationship the same thing as settling in a relationship? Is it bad?

4. Sebastian insists he didn't do anything wrong to the women online because he never misrepresented himself to them. How do dating apps change how we think about relationships? Do they encourage authenticity, or do they reward people who perform what they think would-be partners desire? Who's at fault—Alyssa, who assumes men will realize that no one just wants hookups forever, or Sebastian, who takes her at her word?

5. Abby's friend Lizzie (not to mention the Spoke'n Four) represents an alternate path to a life well lived compared to the one Abby saw modeled by her own mother as well as other adults in her life. What appeals to Abby about Lizzie's path, and what scares her? How do Abby's values change throughout the course of the book?

6. Abby is in her midthirties, an age when most of her friends are settling down. She has resisted putting down the traditional roots of a desk job, a marriage, and a house in the suburbs. To what extent is Abby's struggle timeless versus a unique situation faced by women in their midthirties today? Did this conflict resonate with you or remind you of anyone in your life? Why or why not?

7. Morgan seeks help from Kayla, an adult outside her own family, because she fears her mother's judgment. It is so important for teenagers to find adults they can trust, but when should adults keep the secrets of somebody else's child, and when are they obligated to involve the child's parents? Do you think Kayla, Abby, and Eileen did the right thing? What would you have done in that situation?

8. The bike trip brings together a group of strangers. While everyone on the trip knows somebody else, they all spend time getting to know new people, and we see the group come together in surprising ways by the trip's end. Discuss the theme of building community in the novel. Are we our truest selves among strangers? How are the main characters influenced in powerful ways by conversations with people they've just met?

9. Several characters spend their journeys reflecting on their relationships with their mothers, and many of them have things they wish they could have told their mothers, or wish their mothers knew. In what ways are the different characters' mother-child relationships unique and in what ways are they universal? How have you seen this play out in your own life? What do you wish your mother knew, or had known, about you? If you could tell your mother anything, what would it be?

10. What will you remember most about *The Breakaway*?